Song of Atlantis

By Brian Power

For Kathy and the patience she showed
during the past six years.

INTRODUCTION

Why did I write *Song of Atlantis*? I began it in 2008, and finished the first version in 2014. *Song of Atlantis* is an accumulation of knowledge gained from a range of sources: diverse personal life experiences going back to my childhood; non-mainstream books speculating on ancient phenomena; and a desire to paint a hopeful future for the planet.

I wanted to articulate themes that guided my life: good versus evil; the power of strong human values and ethics; the strength of characters unhindered by doubt as they served a higher purpose and unflinchingly confronted evil; the power of spirituality; and the sustainment of the earth.

Where to begin?

When I was a child back in the 1950s, our television entertainment was top-heavy with western dramas. Cheyenne, Maverick, The Lawman, Sugarfoot, Wanted Dead of Alive, Gunsmoke, and Palladin, and a slew of other western offerings dominated our weekly staple of TV viewing experiences. The whole country was fascinated by cowboy lore. When we kids played cowboys and Indians, I always liked being an Indian. I saw myself on a painted pony riding through a mountainside forest and stopping on a ridgeline at the vista of a great river valley.

Another form of entertainment for us at that time was comic books. While my parents forbade me from buying the more lurid tales of murder and mayhem, I was allowed to purchase comics about real and fictional western personae (e.g., *Ben Bowie, Mountain Man*). Most of those comic books had a certain format. The first half of the comic carried the main story, usually ending up with the hero facing some crisis that would not be resolved until the next month's edition of the comic was published. That went on and on until we got bored with the character and moved on to buy the adventures of another character.

The middle section of the comic book was often devoted to advertisements for all kinds of gadgets that would appeal to the mind of a pre-adolescent boy. Items such as jackknives, slingshots, air rifles, BB guns, compasses and camping gear come to mind.

Just after the advertising section occasionally there would be a two- or three-page short story, maybe about a man escaping from Indian captivity, or a Pony Express rider thwarting highway robbers. One such story, for some unexplained reason, stuck in my memory. It was about a Wild West show that was performing in England, probably around the late 1800s or at the turn of the century.

Our European neighbors, at that time, were fascinated with the United States and had heard and read many adventures, both true and fabricated, regarding the settlement of the American West. To them it was romance and adventure. To our Native Americans it was less so. In these Wild West shows, the reenactments of battles, using real American Indians who always lost the battle, gave the Europeans great amusement. These Europeans were, of course, a people whose economies and affluence depended largely on extracting natural resources (coal, diamonds, minerals, etc.) through the sweat and blood of subjugated people who lived all across the globe in their far-flung colonies.

So it was Jolly good fun to see how the Yanks got control of their continent from the primitives.

But I digress. Back to this this comic book short story, on one of its days off, the Wild West show troupe had been invited by a bunch of young English nobles to witness a polo match. The American Indians with the show, all from the legendary tribes of the Great Plains (Lakota, Cheyenne, Commanche), were fascinated and amazed by the spectacle of a polo match. At one point, one of the more arrogant English polo players taunted the Indians and challenged them to come out on the pitch where they would surely see the superior horsemanship of their English betters.

The Indians knew they were being insulted, and one of the elders of the group nodded to one of the younger members indicating that he was to represent them in the polo match. The Indian swung onto his smaller mustang pony, and of course mopped the field with the Englishmen.

For some reason, that story stuck with me as I got on with the pains of growing up and becoming an adult. Growing pains of all kinds stuck with me, as I am sure they did with many of you. In my childhood I met and hung around with a wide assortment of characters, and we had our share of laughs and adventures. We swam, we played, we mowed lawns, and we had fun. But some of the other stuff about growing up had its own particular brand of ugliness. All of this ended up in my memory bank waiting to be dumped out in my novel.

My adolescence, with all its pain, ended up, later in life, being a gold mine. It would require serious and painful digging, but some of those memories informed the shape of some of my characters.

Memories and experiences of relatives, friends, religion, the Marine Corps, music, literature, philosophy, and more, kept accumulating. In the mid-1990s I read some books that discoursed on alternative theories about the origins and purposes of ancient constructions like the Great Pyramid at Giza, the Sphinx, Stonehenge, Machu Pichu, Nazca Lines in Peru, Aztec cities and more. I was hooked.

I thought, "Why not pull all this together and tell a story about the Great Pyramid that will be a lot more than something that nerds or conspiracy theorists might like?" I wanted to reach a broader audience. I had made several attempts over the years at writing a novel and always hit a dead end. Not this time.

One night in the early spring of 2008, around 11:00 after my wife had gone to bed, the house was quiet, and there were no distractions. I began typing. I did this every night for weeks, typing and revising, usually from 11:00 until 2:00 in the morning or so. By the way, I'm retired, I'm a night owl anyway, and it was fun. The comic book story about the Indian humiliating the arrogant British snobs on the polo field immediately jumped into my mind. When I began to write, I knew that I needed to do a version of that story as one of my chapters. In order to do that, one of my main characters (later to be THE main character) had to be an American Indian.

One of the most interesting things about writing this book was the nearly out-of-body experience I had as the story developed. It was like some force took over my body as I typed. I found myself on more than one occasion saying, "Wow, I didn't know (the character) was going to do that!"

I highly recommend the experience.

After a number of drafts, I engaged the services of an editor who guided me to think and write more descriptively. That's not easy. It involves moving from the "tell-them-the- story" mode to the "show-them-the-story mode." Once I got practicing that, the book began to flesh itself out.

My other major breakthrough came when I asked a friend (and fellow writer) to read my latest draft. He did, and then proceeded to show me a copy of some writing wisdom he once received. It was all about the concept that less is more. I was having a tendency to exposit on minutiae. I realized that I could take about 50 pages out of the book and it would read better.

An early critic of this masterpiece was my youngest son. He pointed out several flaws I was using in portraying some of my characters.

My oldest son, who works in the film industry, gave me great advice on creating story arcs.

My wife is the inspiration for my main female hero. The similarities between thems are endless.

So my advice to you, dear reader, and maybe fledgling writer, is to take a bunch of words, pile them up and dump them onto some paper. Then listen to your friends and relatives, and proceed to take away from that paper anything that doesn't look like a good novel.

Your success is assured.

BP// late 2018

PROLOGUE

...(N)ine thousand was the sum of years which had elapsed since the war. Of the combatants on the one side, the city of Athens was reported to have been the leader and to have fought out the war; the combatants on the other side were commanded by the kings of Atlantis, which . . . was an island greater in extent than Libya and Asia . . .

Plato,

Dialogues, 250 BC

Atlantis, 12,500 years ago

Amon Goro, Master Architect of Atlantis, twice read the summons "... to answer for treachery and sedition against the good order ..." and sank into his chair. He was expected to report immediately to a hearing before the Elders. The palace guard who delivered the summons said, "We must go now, sir. Delay will not be tolerated."

Rivulets of icy sweat trickled down Goro's spine. Rarely these days did people so summoned ever return. He knew the cause of the summons. What had started as an intellectual exercise with friends two years before might now be a death sentence. His legs felt liquid as he tried to stand. He wilted back into his chair for the second time. The guard grabbed him by the tunic and pulled him to his feet. "Time to show courage, sir. There's nothing to do but face it, whatever it is."

Goro allowed himself to be led to the front entrance. There, from his hillside home, the ocean's salty breeze refreshed him. He paused, leaning against an alabaster pillar to look, perhaps for the last time, at the harbor a half-mile away lined with wharves where fishermen and merchants worked their trades. Holding up a hand to stay the guard, he shifted his gaze to the colorful marketplace thriving with merchants, and finally to the palace high on the cliff where his fate was to be determined. He noted the irony that it was he who had designed that palace. Goro made up his mind. Whatever the outcome, he was determined to walk there with his head high. He knew he was innocent of the charges, yet all the time knowing that his innocence might serve for nothing. So be it. No need to appear to be yet another disgraced official headed to his doom. Removing the guard's hand he said, "Best if I walk on my own."

"Good for you, sir." And then in an aside, "Make us all proud."

Goro looked at the guard and saw nothing but reassurance in his eyes.

On his fifteen-minute walk to the palace, he read the fear in the faces of vendors, merchants, and pedestrians -- a look that wasn't there several years ago. People glanced at him and turned away quickly, like he was already dead. He dared not compromise any of his merchant friends – the seafood vendors, carpenters, and tradesmen that he had always treated courteously and knew them and their families by name -- by acknowledging them in the presence of an elite palace guard. Most Atlanteans still had not adjusted to armed soldiers on every corner, even though that was the state of affairs for the past ten years.

The current Council of Elders had engineered an unprecedented growth of government control over individual lives. The new regime had stepped into a power void created by the "accidental" deaths of several former key leaders who perished when their airship crashed on a fact-finding mission to Newland, the continental landmass to the north. The five new leaders on the Council of Elders consolidated their power by creating pervasive angst and fear among the population. They achieved their objectives by publishing edicts that highlighted the problems Atlantis faced, and then pointing the blame at targeted groups. First the problems were all caused by the poor. Then it was the fault of the intellectuals.

Always the final message was the same: We, the Elders of Atlantis, will solve all your problems.

The wealthy elite, however, liked this new sense of order. They saw individual expression, no matter how harmless, as a threat. The message was soon made clear to the population: If you can't carry your weight, and you can't support your government, there is no place for you in Atlantis.

2

Goro remembered how it used to be. Some were rich, some were poor, and some fell somewhere in the middle. But all of the citizens loved Atlantis –- Atlantis the land given by the Creator, and Atlantis
the empire. Life was a challenge, as it was everywhere, but neighbors and communities supported each other. The abrupt change in leadership was soon followed by the disappearances. First to go were the outspoken, next the disabled, and finally the poor. No one knew where they went. Some said to labor camps in distant lands. Others claimed they were brought out to sea and dumped.

The well-educated knew that it was only a matter of time before the long hand of the Elders was clamped on their shoulders.

Our world has changed, thought Goro, and not for the good.

The laws. The laws we had so carefully crafted over thousands of years, now corrupted and worthless. Those now in power made new laws, and the powerless could do no more than comply with this new concept of "justice." Those in power had chosen a course of action; the weak were left with no choice but to call it justice.

•   •   •

Goro couldn't help but ruminate about the history of his people.

More than 11,000 years ago, he thought, two eras in the way we measure time, Atlantis emerged as a culture and rapidly advanced to possess exceptional mathematical knowledge, and, ultimately, advanced technology. They called themselves The First People of the World.

He reflected how at the beginning of the second era, the ice sheets hundreds of miles thick that covered much of the northern and southern hemispheres, but not Atlantis, began a sudden, rapid melting cycle. Over the past 5000 years, the trillions of tons of ice covering much of the northern hemisphere and the higher elevations of the southern hemisphere had melted. Following a thousand year era marked by rising sea levels and massive continental drifts, sea levels finally stabilized and new population centers had formed along the coasts of the world. For all the rising of the waters, Atlantis seemed to rise with it.

Across the ocean North of Atlantis, along the coastal lands of the large east-west continental mass called Newland, the people of the outside world were beginning to change. They were establishing communities and struggling with the cycles of the sun and moon, learning the art of agriculture -- when to plant and when to harvest, how to create new strains of edible wheat, corn and oats. Atlantis established basic trade routes with many of these new communities.

Set in the semi-tropical southern ocean several thousand miles below Newland, the island nation of Atlantis had largely been spared the ravages of the ice cover except in its highest mountain regions. The majority of its five and a-half million square miles consisted of fertile farmlands, tropical rain forests, rivers abundant with fish, and busy coastal urban centers and ports. Its population at one time had been more than five million. Although the island nation recently had become increasingly subject to frequent mild earthquakes, it was a beautiful place to live.

Once in power, the new leaders began plans to dominate the world. After ten years, they had re-written the whole concept of governance so that power was concentrated at the highest levels. Local government had largely become ceremonial while the military, which had largely been ornamental, expanded greatly. The army had power over every aspect of daily life. Conscripted units deployed across the globe to enslave local populations. These slaves were to extract vital minerals and raw materials from previously ice-covered areas to provide Atlantis with the necessary ore and mineral resources to build advanced technologies with the ultimate goal of exploring the heavens.

Goro remembered the hard years of survival following the failure of this experiment. The targeted populations in Newland rose up in rebellion, often led by Atlanteans who had exiled themselves rather than submit to the new leaders. In the resulting wars, Atlantean armies, using new forms of weaponry, created massive fires all over the globe that turned the skies black and caused torrential rainfall and flooding worldwide.

Newly emerging population centers all across the globe were decimated. Half the Atlantis population starved to death when crops could no longer survive the deluge. Only thanks to the foresight of some enlightened scientists and engineers, habitable caves had been hollowed out of the mountainous areas and much of the remainder of the population was able to survive the devastation. Those who could not get to the mountain sanctuaries eked out a life of subsistence, mainly along the coasts where there was still an abundance of life sustaining seafood.

The crisis lasted for centuries, and after it passed, those outside survivors represented a reservoir of resentment and fuel for rebellion against government control.

The new leadership did not give up on their quest for global dominance. Instead they planned the next phase more carefully using an aggressive plan for colonization as the centerpiece of their strategy. The end result would be the same, with colonized areas dominated and led by Atlantis émigrés, and the local populations providing the heavy labor. But with the loss of half its population during the years of flood and famine, Atlantis would have to devise an efficient way to provide the vast technical support required by mining engineers, administrators, and deployed armies.

The global colonization plan was no secret to Goro, or to anyone else in Atlantis, for that matter. Like the government or not, simple mathematics had proven that, even with the losses suffered in recent years, the population of Atlantis would grow exponentially over the next two millennia. The island paradise, despite its vast size and natural resources, would, at some point, no longer be able to sustain a growing population. But the resources of the rest of the planet would. The tools and industries needed to support the Atlantis émigrés would require extensively deployed power sources. That is where Amon Goro believed he would have a chance for distinction and immortality.

As Goro and his military escort walked the few miles to the palace, he remembered the conversation that had started what was now becoming a personal catastrophe. Two years earlier he was having dinner one evening, as he regularly did, with some old friends from the university – an engineer, a physicist, a musician, a chemist, and a philosopher - and the discussion turned to the topic of colonization. This was a polarizing issue with many of the people of Atlantis. While the majority opposed the concept, the elders strongly pushed for it and simply crushed any opposition to it and any other of their policies. However, implementation of the plan seemed to be the big stumbling block.

After dinner, and a couple of servings of wine, the conversation came around to the problem of supplying the energy needs for well-educated colonizers who would bring industry and technological advancement to the far reaches of the planet. On the island continent energy was abundant. Atlanteans had mastered the science of tapping into geothermal, solar, wind, and ocean based hydrogen and tidal energy sources, and all of those could be implemented locally. But what about the other realms of the earth where such technologies might not be sufficient or too challenging and costly to build in the immediate aftermath of colonization?

Goro, as an architect, felt that one centralized power plant could answer these needs. If one centralized energy source could be developed, energy could be beamed to collectors in space and re-transmitted to earth. There would be no need to build an infinite number of power plants all over the earth's surface, or to waste precious labor in the effort. But what kind of energy could be produced on that big a scale?

His academic friends agreed to take this on as an intellectual exercise and pledged to meet periodically to see if they could come up with a plausible solution.

Much to the surprise of his colleagues, it was the musician who provided the critical element of the solution. At one of the monthly meetings shortly after this exercise began, Dari Monto presented an idea that caught everyone's imagination. Dari was considered one of the most innovative composers in all of Atlantis. His concerts always drew huge crowds seeking the solace of music to help them forget the repressive times in which they lived. Stifled by the tyranny of rigid conformity to government edicts, the people sought outlets in music and dramas that carried subtexts of subversion. The government had not yet caught on to this. Otherwise it would have demanded full censorship. That would come eventually, but for now the musicians and playwrights were in demand and concert performances were sold out.

Dari had also been in the forefront of pioneering technologies that had music as their foundation. particularly the hand-held communications/cutting/lifting device.

He posited, "The earth constantly resonates in a musical key well below what we can hear or feel. Have you considered tapping into this natural resonance to provide the energy required for such an endeavor?"

The others looked at each other in bewilderment. "What do you mean when you say, 'in a key well below what we can hear or feel?'"

"We know that whales and dolphins communicate in tones that are below our hearing. So do other creatures of both the sea and land," he responded. "And some beasts can hear in frequencies well above the human range of hearing.

"It would be an obvious solution," he said. "The earth itself never stops vibrating. If this could be amplified and channeled, surely a chemical could be introduced that would respond to this resonance and the earth itself would be a catalyst to transfer the chemical into a reaction that would produce energy."

The chemist, Torba Gelnar, enthusiastically agreed. "We are already familiar with using hydrogen energy which we compress into pressurized containers to operate both industrial and farming equipment. And hydrogen converts to pure microwave energy when stimulated at .438 cycles per second."

Dari responded, "That is excellent! That is precisely the resonance of a musical key, though a different one from the earth's resonance. The earth's resonance is 369.99 cycles per second. If the earth's vibrations could provide the initial stimulation, all we would need is a machine to filter and convert the resonance to the new key at 438 cycles per second, and we would have the electromagnetic sound wave we need.

Torba responded, "Yes, that probably could easily be done on a small scale, but then what?"

Goro was awestruck by this idea. He stood up and began pacing back and forth. "If we could produce it on a massive scale, if you'll pardon the pun, and project it to an orbiting reflector in space, it could be transmitted around the globe and beamed down to ground collectors. But we would need a machine of massive size to do this. I am scrapping every theory I have been working on and focusing on this new concept."

Over the next two years, the group met almost monthly and brainstormed ideas. They all agreed to challenge every idea in order to scrutinize it from all possible angles to see if it would work. Many concepts were abandoned at these meetings, but the ones that remained joined the nucleus of the solution.

They all looked forward to the monthly meetings but were wary of how these gatherings could be perceived. Dari once even commented, "The powers that be might think we are plotting something." They all laughed that idea away and agreed to go forward as it was purely an academic exercise. They surmised, 'who could possibly think that an academic exercise was subversive?'

Recently they had agreed on certain fundamental principles of design involving highly resonant granite. The scientists and musician had been working on an experimental theory about energy conversion. Once he heard their ideas, Goro went to his offices to modify his design for the power plant. He was not heard from for months, and he directed that his subordinates handle all other architectural activities.

And now this summons shocked him into reality. He realized that he should have made a proposal to the Elders back when the idea was still in its infancy. All the secrecy that he and his friends had been hiding behind was looking more and more like a conspiracy to overthrow the Elders of Atlantis.

.   .   .

Goro's stomach was churning, but he remained adamant about presenting an outward appearance of confidence. The palace was not far away, but today it felt like he was walking up a long, difficult slope with a huge weight on his back.

Upon arriving at the palace, the guard escorted him to the inner chambers where a senior functionary with an unpleasant demeanor sat behind a large desk. Dressed in the crimson trimmed robes of a senior bureaucrat, the man was completely bald with an unlined face and no eyebrows or eyelashes, so his age seemed indeterminate. His red-rimmed eyes were narrow-set and his tight mouth gave the appearance that he had no lips. He was much shorter and of slighter build than the average Atlantean. His long, slender fingers were busy moving documents around his desk. After a few minutes, the man finally looked coldly at Goro. The Master Architect of Atlantis mustered up his courage and introduced himself, saying that he had been summoned to a hearing of the Elders. The man looked back at Goro, his mouth slightly curled in what might pass for a smile, and said, "Ah, yes, Amon Goro. The elders are expecting you. Go right through that entrance."

Goro felt a strange calmness pass through his body. I have done nothing wrong, he thought. I will simply present them with the outline of our idea. If that be treason, well, so be it.

The guard escorted him to the entrance of the Hall of Elders. Just as he placed a gentle hand on Goro's back encouraging him forward into the chamber, he whispered, "Show them courage, sir. They'll respect you for it."

Across the far side of the cavernous room, the five Elders of Atlantis sat behind a long polished granite desk set on a marble platform about three feet high. Seated centrally between the five was the senior elder, Tezcar Tilcopan. To say he was a formidable and foreboding presence doesn't come remotely close to revealing his impact on others. He had raven hair and a full black beard. His dark eyes were cold – two dead ebony caverns beneath coal-black, bushy eyebrows.

Goro forced his focus on the other four elders, avoiding the black iced dagger glare of Tilcopan.

"Amon Goro," began the elder to the right of Tilcopan, "it has come to our attention that for the past several months you have been neglecting your work as master architect of Atlantis. It has also come to our attention that you have been meeting secretly with several other men who hold responsible positions at the university and in government. What do you have to say about this?"

Goro's mouth felt as dry as a ball of cotton, but he forced himself to speak. Remembering the words of his guard, he began, "Esteemed Elders of Atlantis, I have been working for the last two years on a project that I wanted to remain secret until it was ready to present to you. Your plans for the people of Atlantis to colonize the far reaches of the earth and to exploit the resources of the planet for the enrichment of our own society are well known. It is toward that end that my colleagues and I began what was initially a purely intellectual exercise but which has evolved to a nearly fully formed practical plan to help you reach this goal. If you will grant me just a few days I will put together a presentation that will demonstrate for you how your vision can be achieved."

Tilcopan held up his hand motioning the others to silence. He glared intently. "Look at me, Amon Goro." And as Goro complied, an icy chill began permeating his body. "You had better be speaking the truth, Master Architect of Atlantis. For if you are not, you will die a gruesome death as a traitor to your people. The law forbids our intellectuals to meet in private about anything."

Goro's blood ran cold. An incredible chill gripped his insides and he experienced the feeling that his bones had been removed and that he would collapse on the floor. It was all he could do to remain standing.

With his head bowed to the floor, Goro responded, "Esteemed Elder, I swear by all that I own and all that I have become that I am telling you the truth. In three days time at this very hour I will return to you and give you the reassurances that you seek. If I do not return as promised, do with me what you will."

"Have no doubt we will. Go now," said the dark leader, "and make no mistake about our resolve."

For the next three days, Goro ate and slept little. He drove his staff relentlessly to build the bare-bones model of what he knew would be his architectural masterpiece. On the appointed day and at the designated hour, with Goro in the lead, four of his assistants carried a pallet on which sat his architectural model, draped in a white sheet, and entered the chamber of the Elders. Off to the side he saw his academic colleagues standing against the wall under guard and looking terrified. He tried to give them a reassuring look, and turned to face the Elders.

Over the next three hours, Amon Goro methodically presented the background and development of his group's plan. He unflinchingly answered each of their concerns. At the end of his presentation he unveiled the model for the power plant and explained its functions. He had designed his model so that parts of it could be removed to show the interior functions. He was confident in answering their questions..

Tezcar Tilcopan, unmoving and impenetrable, remained silent through the presentation. His stare was beyond intimidating. Amon Goro tried to avoid looking at him directly.

Goro's idea was so comprehensive in scope and massive in scale that Tilcopan simply nodded to the others. Dismissing Goro and his associates to await their summons, the leaders debated the plan for several days.

Three days later, Goro and his colleagues were again called to the palace.

After they were assembled, Tilcopan rose to his feet and spoke. "Amon Goro, the Council of Elders has reached a decision on your proposal. We find that it has much merit, and fits well with our plans for global dominance. You have our approval to utilize all the resources you need to make this happen. We want you to begin immediately."

Goro, lightheaded, at first nearly fainted. Gathering his strength, he felt himself shaking with emotion, but remained stoic, standing rigid, his face a whirlwind of elation and resolve. He looked over at his colleagues, sharing with them the common relief of escaping punishment. He could hardly believe that his proposal had been accepted.

"It will be done as you have commanded," he said.

——— ——— ———

Knowing her fate, Atlantis sent out ships to all corners of the Earth.
On board were the Twelve:
The poet, the physician, the farmer, the scientist,
The magician and the other so-called Gods of our legends.

Donovan, *Atlantis*

Not all those who wander are lost.

J.R.R.

Tolkien, *The Lord of the Rings*

North America, 8,000 Years Ago

Kulen Golendar resigned himself to his task. For many years, he had been responsible for sending out twelve person teams each year to Newland, north across the ocean, and to Hourglass, the north-south continents far to the west of Atlantis across another great ocean. As Exploration Master of Atlantis, he had inherited the job from his father, who had inherited it from his father, and so on going back generations long since passed. But now all that was ending.

Atlantis sent twelve-person exploration teams to study emerging cultures all over the world. These teams evaluated their developmental stages, and made recommendations regarding the level of intervention Atlantis should interject to nudge the culture forward. Primitive, cannibalistic cultures were taught how to live as civilized communities and set up mutually supporting agricultural programs for their development. These teams had a great deal of success because they appeared, with their flying vehicles and technology, to be gods to these primitives. Nomadic cultures that relied on hunting received little intervention while agricultural communities were given stone circles to teach them how to read the cycles of the sun and stars and improve planting cycles. As those cultures progressed, teams would provide lessons in astronomy and basic mathematics.

After each team had been out seven years, it would return to give a comprehensives report of its progress. In this

13

way, the leaders of Atlantis would know every year what was working and where it was working, as well as what was not and where it was not, all over the globe.

Not all of the teams came back intact.

Unfortunately, about 4500 years earlier, new leaders in Atlantis, impatient men intent on dominating the world, had taken control. After attempting unsuccessfully to colonize the planet and force the emerging cultures to work as slave labor, they precipitated a calamitous war. Still intent on exploiting the planet's resources, they built the great power plant to serve the energy needs of Atlantean-led mining communities across the globe.

Fearful of another disaster, the far-sighted leaders who were out of political power spent years secretly organizing an army mainly made up of Atlanteans who had been forced to live outside the survival caves during the great rain and darkness. These people rose up against their cruel leaders, removed them from power, and held public executions. All the leaders were killed, save one who fled to the sparsely populated continents, referred to as Hourglass, far to the northwest across the second biggest ocean.

After overthrowing their leaders, the first people formed a new society that forever banned warfare. They quickly evolved a philosophy that had persisted and become ingrained in the consciousness of every citizen of Atlantis. The people of Atlantis knew that they were extremely advanced compared to all other people of the world. They dedicated themselves to gradually introducing astronomy, mathematics and limited technology to the emerging cultures.

The reborn Atlantis continued sending exploratory parties across the globe every year to find out the levels of development of the new civilizations. It had been evident after the end of the great ice-melt
that the first promising signs were seen in Persia, Giza, India, and China, and four thousand years after that in what is now Central and South America, and eastern and southeastern North America.

The people of Atlantis were very patient. And they knew from their vast history and enormous mistakes of past colonization attempts, that the evolution of cultures must be nourished, not pushed. They wanted a better planet than the one they inherited after the last cataclysm. As a culture, they had adopted the mission of seeding the world with information that would eventually lead to the advancement of civilization.

The Atlanteans knew that to force technology, astronomy, and mathematics too soon on newly developing cultures would meet with failure. But those who called themselves Egyptians had shown early promise. From the Atlanteans, who had created aircraft capable of flying to the highest levels of the atmosphere, and from which were launched satellites that soared up to stationary orbit, the Egyptians learned that Giza, the land at the head of the great river delta, was the geographic center of the land masses of the earth.

The giant pyramid complex that Atlantis had built was a source of marvel to the Egyptians, though at that time they had not a clue as to its purpose. Gradually the educational teams from Atlantis taught the Egyptians just what they would need to begin forming a sophisticated society. It would take thousands of years, but Giza became the test site for the new approach to developing the world.

But natural disaster faced the people of Atlantis. During the third five thousand year era, a time characterized by earthquakes of increasing numbers and intensity, their continent had begun to drift on its tectonic plate. The Council of Elders convened to discuss options. They debated the merits of complete migration to Newland, to the north, and Hourglass, to the northwest . They debated staying on Atlantis at all costs. And they debated a combination of the two.

What they finally agreed on was that while the majority of Atlanteans would be allowed to flee to the other continents, a selected group were to stay on Atlantis, for it was on this ancestral home that the ancient archives were housed. The vast wealth of Atlantean knowledge reposed in deep caverns that held constant temperatures. They had been carved out in the time of the great wars as a refuge. Now they had been expanded and refined to house Atlantis' greatest treasure – its knowledge.

And it would be here that the last people of Atlantis would deal with their fate and preserve these treasures.

The drifting of Atlantis had become a critical issue. Ninety-five percent of the land mass was now well below the frigid zone of the southern hemisphere.

The Council of Elders issued a directive for Kulen Golendar to recall all the exploration teams.

While not unexpected – it was certainly inevitable – Kulen was heartbroken at seeing the work of countless generations come to an end. So much had been done, and there was so much more to do, particularly on Hourglass, a fertile territory that held incredible promise.

Kulen looked at his communications device, pressed a button and sent out the automatic recall message on the network frequency. He contacted his wife and daughter and told them that now was the time. They were to meet him at the prearranged location for transportation to the caverns. On his private channel, he also sent a secret communication to his son, Palen, who was leading one of the exploration teams in northern Hourglass.

Once again the population of Atlantis was directed to resume life in the underground caverns. This time it was a permanent move.

•   •   •

Four years earlier Palen Golendar and his 12-man team had flown across the wide gulf to land at the mouth of the great river on the northern continent of Hourglass. Concealing their aircraft, they began their northward march. For every hundred-fifty miles of northward march, they explored the western and eastern sides of this enormous river to a range of fifty to four hundred miles. About 700 miles north of the gulf, another major river joined it from the west.

Their mission was primarily reconnaissance and research. Other teams would follow later to guide the natives in building stone calendars in order to introduce agriculture. The tribes to the east of the great river showed great promise. They had formed agricultural centers, and under Atlantean influence were learning the art of breeding stronger strains for each of their primary crops.

The tribes west of the great river, however, seemed to be mostly nomads who hunted their food and gathered only free growing fruit and ground tubers. They had been extremely resistant to change and had rejected the idea of relying on agriculture for their sustenance.

About a month before the northern hemisphere spring equinox, far to the north of the great gulf, Palen's team stood at the junction of two great rivers. Palen, as team leader, decided to split up the team and explore further to the north and west. With the detailed image maps produced from the survey satellite above the earth, they knew what kind of terrain they would be going through, but they didn't know enough about the indigenous peoples who lived in the area. Their mission was to find out more than had been discovered in previous expeditions, and they were under strict orders to minimize their involvement with these peoples.

With their hand-held devices, they would be able to communicate with each other on the command channel daily at noon, and more often if needed.

From earlier explorations, they also had knowledge of the languages of some of these people, and their translating monitors were programmed so that they could communicate easily with most of the natives they had encountered.

One team had gone north with the caveat that they not explore beyond the great lake. A second team headed south and west. The team Palen attached himself to was heading northwest to explore the new great river. They would follow its north bank. All of the teams were to return to the headwaters position within the past week.

The team from the west showed up at the rendezvous point minus one man who had fallen mortally wounded, trampled by a rogue beast from a great herd of buffalo.

The team that had gone north had returned intact.

But three weeks earlier, following the torrential rains of spring brought on by an early thaw, Palen's team had been caught on a rocky peninsula far up the river. Though they were well protected in a shelter of rocks, the river had flooded, spewing all manner of tree trunks and branches in its muddy wake. The team left the shelter of their rocks trying to get to higher ground, but one man lost his footing, slipped and crashed into the two below him. They were all swept away in the river.

After the storm, Palen sat and thought about his predicament. He sent a communication to the other teams telling what happened saying he would rejoin them at the appointed time.

When the waters receded, he began his return to the rendezvous point. Retracing his way along the river, after about three miles he found the remains of his friends. He pulled them up on the bank of the river, and using his hand-held device, dug a deep grave for them. Singing the ritualistic prayers for the dead, he buried them deep and securely, covering them with enough rocks so that no predators would defile them.

As he was standing over their graves, something hit him on the head, and all went black.

History has many cunning passages.

.S. Eliot

T

Chapter 1

Makoshika State Park, Montana, Present day

Gordon Tallbear, PhD, Director of Anthropological Research for the Denver Center, stared at the computer console in his mobile office. Stunned by what he saw, he quickly threw on his bush jacket and headed for the main lab.

Tallbear and his hand-picked team of forensic anthropologists were in the Badlands in eastern Montana at Makoshika State Park. Named for the Lakota Indian word meaning "land of bad spirits,"
Makoshika was mysterious and primal. But mystery and beauty are not mutually exclusive. A superficial look revealed a barren land - arid, boney, bleak, practically a moonscape - with grey ridges jutting up like dragons' teeth. The chilly wind sweeping down the slopes, creating a moaning sound, seemed to be saying, "Don't stay here long." Yet closer scrutiny revealed stunning shadows and subtle shades of stark beauty. Now, in early October, it was past the time for the colorful scattered summer wildflowers that struggled for a brief existence.

Though similar in many ways to the Badlands of nearby South Dakota, this Montana site exposed much older rock formations. Over the millennia, the Yellowstone River and its tributaries, draining down from the mountains to the west, cut deep into the layers of earth to provide a glimpse into the enigma and anomaly of a realm once subtropical, much like the southeastern Unites States. The layers and layers of sediments left by these rivers compressed over the eons to form mudstone, sandstone, shale and clay. The brownish-gray sediments traced back 65 million years to the period when the Rocky Mountains were being pushed into the sky by the unstoppable movement of tectonic plates. Scientists and explorers in this region methodically peeled back layers of clay to trace a transition from the age of dinosaurs to the age of mammals. Preserved in the clay of this once swampy region are dinosaur and other reptilian

19

skeletons, as well as abundant evidence of tropical vegetation. And now the land produced one more mystery.

When people first migrated to the northern plains, perhaps 11,000 years ago, or even earlier, they found the Badlands a place either to avoid, or to hide in. The nomad warriors of this north central region found the Badlands to be a temporary refuge to shield them from their enemies, and a natural barrier that diverted the teeming buffalo herds migrating from the north into the range of their arrows and spears on the northern Great Plains.

．　　　．　　　．

The ten-hour road trip from the Denver Center headquarters in Colorado was uneventful. The only thing passing motorists would have noticed was a caravan of seven large recreational vehicles, unmarked and unremarkable from the outside. Inside was another story. All were powered by advanced hybrid technology

Four were used as living quarters and office space. The other three were super-equipped rolling laboratories outfitted for wide range of sophisticated lab analyses. Rooftop solar panels provided any extra power required.

The anthropological team had arrived a week before, having been alerted by the discovery of a mummified human believed to have lived in the area 8,000 years ago. A Smithsonian grant-funded archaeological expedition looking for dinosaur fossils inadvertently uncovered the well-preserved human remains in the clay-rich soil of this remote and desolate region. The age estimate was based on the strata layers in which it was discovered as well as a preliminary field carbon dating test.

At Makoshika, Tallbear's team made camp. The dig was a two-mile hike over rough shale terrain. While the team expected the remains to be an early ancestor of Native Americans, they also held out hopes that this would be another of the "unique" finds.

Over the past three years, Gordon Tallbear had travelled all over the world with Denver Center anthropological teams to examine twenty-seven sets of unusual human remains that challenged scientific expertise. Mostly intact skeletons of nineteen males and eight females, that had died anywhere between 12,000 and 8,000 years ago, had been discovered in southern Japan, central China, Siberia, Norway, Peru, Australia, India, Guatemala, Mexico, Arizona, South Carolina, Southern California, and Washington. Despite intensive forensic testing, none of these remains resembled any people of the known cultures in the world. But DNA analysis showed that they did resemble each other genetically and morphologically.

The men were all six-foot to six-foot two inches tall – exceptional for the age in which they lived – and would have weighed around 200 pounds. They had very high bone density, and apparently subsisted primarily on fish and fruit. The women were all five foot seven to five foot nine, and proportionately had the same genetic make-up as the men.

At Makoshika, treating the discovery site much as a modern police force would treat a crime scene, the team conducted a detailed documentation of the levels of strata, clay density, and other physical features around the discovery site and carefully wrapped and sealed the remains for transport back over the two miles of rugged terrain.

At their mobile laboratories, before they had even begun the examination, Gordon placed a call to the Denver Center asking that an electrical engineering team be dispatched to the site. Along with the body there had been another remarkable discovery. Buried with this man was a thick leather pouch about the size of a backpack. It contained what was apparently a sophisticated tool unlike anything discovered anywhere in the world before.

While awaiting the arrival of the engineering team, and under strict security conditions that allowed no unauthorized communications outside the lab site, they began the forensic examination.

The mummified remains, that they nicknamed Badlands Bill, produced a wealth of information.

Bill was not of the same origins as Native Americans. In a case involving the discovery of a human skeleton – dubbed Kenniwick Man -- in the state of Washington, courts ruled that Native American tribes could not claim remains not genetically connected to their tribe. This, as well as other similar rulings elsewhere, allowed the Denver Center team to submit such discoveries to forensic examination normally forbidden by the American Indian culture.

The other discoveries around the world were mostly skeletons, with two sets being partially mummified. Badlands Bill was completely preserved. Though the remains had been dehydrated, the team scanned its image into a computer and projected how he would have looked like in real life. Similar to the other the other twenty-seven, the body did not fit into the genetic stream of any known culture on earth.

Badlands Bill was probably around thirty years of age when he died.

He was about six feet two inches tall – an extraordinary height for a man of that time.

He probably weighed about 200 pounds.

He subsisted primarily on fish and wild fruit.

He had remarkably strong bones.

A flint arrowhead was embedded in his shoulder. The team speculated that perhaps he was fleeing from some of the locals when he was wounded, and then he stumbled into this clay pit and was
buried by a cave-in. A CPT scan of the body revealed that the arrowhead, leaf-shaped and carefully crafted with broad serrated

edges, was formed of a silica-based stone. This fit the definition of a Cascade point, referring to the Cascade Phase, which was roughly 7,500 to 11,000 years ago. Radio-carbon dating of his bone marrow confirmed that he lived 8,000 years ago.

Hector Moineau, Gordon's chief assistant, initiated the computer scanning program that morphed the mummified body into a realistic image of what Bill would have looked like alive. He stood in the mobile laboratory switching his gaze in disbelief from the mummified corpse to the computer-enhanced image. The rest of the forensic team stood silently off to the side, shocked by the image on the screen.

"Better get Gordon over here," said Hector.

As soon as Gordon arrived, he looked at the body and then at the enhanced image on the computer. His heart began beating a little faster and he almost felt dizzy.

He was looking into a mirror.

A day after the anthropological team arrived and had begun the examination of the mummy, the five person engineering team arrived by helicopter and began examining the contents of the leather bag.

The apparatus appeared to be a hand-held device, more or less paint-brush shaped with a curved handle, and its sides looked like pineapple skin with 12 indentations. It weighed 1.5 pounds and was made of an extremely lightweight metal. No one could figure it out. The technicians carefully cleaned and preserved it in a vacuum container.

While the anthropology team was examining Badlands Bill, a young electronics engineer scanned the device into his computer. After scrutinizing its size, weight, and dimensions, he carefully examined its external properties. He speculated that the device was not made of any metal that was available 8,000 years ago. Its technological purpose at first eluded him.

Letting his imagination go a little further, he hypothesized that the indentations on the side of the device might be power controls of some kind. He took the device out of its container and pressed one of the indentations, promptly blowing a hole the size of a quarter in the lab wall. Everyone came running to see what happened and there was a buzz of excited conversation.

The engineers began theorizing. One of them observed that it looked similar to the strange object seen in the hands of people in Mayan carvings. Another talked about the Central American pre-Columbian legends that said strange men had come to those cultures and helped them build their massive pyramid cities. They wondered if this could be the "smoking gun" that might explain how ancient cultures cut and moved massive rocks and formed such ancient wonders as the Great Pyramid at Giza, Stonehenge, and possibly other sites. Those cultures, having no wheel or cutting tools, apparently had the assistance of outsiders who carried "magic" in their hands.

Speculation that an advanced culture was responsible for the Great Pyramid, Stonehenge, and any number of other phenomena, was not new. In fact, a 19th century British Egyptologist, Sir William Flinders Petrie, had raised such a speculation in his highly detailed study, published in 1883, *Pyramids and Temples of Egypt.*

If the engineers were correct, this discovery would turn cultural evolution theory upside down.

Gordon Tallbear immediately sent the team's findings by high security encrypted email to his headquarters at the Denver Center.

•   •   •

The Denver Center was a top-secret research facility that received grant funding from the U.S. government. The center also had created strategic alliances with a handful of well- and lesser-known high-tech companies. But the majority of funding for the Denver Center came from the center's founder, a reclusive multi-billionaire named Madison Tolles.

The Denver Center sat high in the Rocky Mountains not far from the Continental Divide. Its Executive Director, Johanna Ring, was of pure Irish descent. Tall and stunningly beautiful, with a thick mane of chestnut red hair and striking blue eyes, she turned heads wherever she went. She walked with purpose and grace. In college, her professors referred to her, behind her back, as "RR," or Rolls Royce, due to the collective opinion that she was silent, effortless, and classy, with hidden power underneath.

Johanna was born in Norwich, Connecticut, and raised in a solid Irish Catholic family. The Rings were a people with a classically Irish long memory. They had originally emigrated from Limerick, Ireland, in the late 1840s following the Great Famine. From the time she was a child, she heard the stories of her ancestors' perils and starvation in Ireland, their dangerous journey to America in the 'coffin ships,' and their eventual prosperity that followed after several of generations of grueling work in the Yankee Protestant owned textile mills. These stories shaped her view that she needed to honor the sacrifices of those who came before her and struggled to make a better life.

But she was also filled with tales of ancient Ireland – the strange people who lived there in far distant times: Druids, Tuatha da Danan, and the Ancient Kings, as well as the legends of fairies and leprechauns. She delighted in her heritage and sat raptly as her grandparents and elderly great-aunts told tales both humorous and tragic. She discovered at an early age that even the Irish wakes and funerals had their quirky moments, like the time old cousin Dinty 'succumbed to the drink.' All the priest could say at the funeral before his final blessing sent the old sod's soul on its final journey was, "Ah, Dinty. He did the best he could." Johanna, fourteen at the time, nearly convulsed in suppressed laughter and quickly fled the church. Grandma Rose said, "They were very close," at which Johanna's mother then fled the premises. Outside the church, she and Johanna had to hold each other up through waves of hysterical laughter. When the funeral was over, Mr. Ring was furious, mainly because someone from the family had to stay. He would have greatly preferred to escape with his wife and daughter.

Johanna was the eldest of four siblings, two boys and two girls. Extremely bright, she sailed through the Norwich Free Academy high school and went on scholarship to Yale. Her father used to joke that as a Catholic she would lose her soul at Yale, but her undergraduate and graduate experiences there only seemed to strengthen her faith.

Johanna was a self-contained, self-assured, and self-actuated woman. She enjoyed socializing and the occasional date, but she was very comfortable with solitude, and did not need or want to be a part of the party scene. In school, her detractors thought her snobbish and that she had a stand-off attitude, but her small circle of close friends thought of her as quick-witted and smart, and they loved her hysterical Irish stories. They were always trying to fix her up on dates, but she usually found that most of the boys she dated in college were pretty shallow. In her senior year she did develop a strong romance with a brilliant Yale medical school student, but broke it off when she discovered he was a serial cheater. She was devastated, but soon recovered from her sadness.

Graduating Magna Cum Laude, she went on to complete her graduate studies at Columbia with a master's degree in business administration. She easily landed a job with the Tolles Group, an investment banking house based in Greenwich, Connecticut. Her discretion, loyalty, brilliance and keen wit brought her to the attention of the founder and chairman of the company, Madison Tolles.

She had worked for the company for five years when Tolles asked her if she was interested in directing a new non-profit research organization that he was starting up. After hearing the details, and with the full understanding that it would mean relocating to the mountains of Colorado, Johanna readily agreed, and at age twenty-nine was named Executive Director of the Denver Center.

•   •   •

Johanna had received Gordon Tallbear's report at nearly the same time she received a report from another Denver Center team that was exploring mountains of Antarctica. That team had been on-site for two months and for the past week had been sending increasingly intriguing reports to the Center nearly every day.

From Antarctica, team leader Dr. Chuck Kinoshi's latest report indicated that his team had discovered hidden caverns in the mountains that held wonders of technology and the decayed remains of two people.

Johanna intuitively realized that the Denver Center had crossed a threshold of research. It was going to take a lot more financing and human expertise to unravel the mysteries they had found.

When Johanna read Gordon's final summary, and his unnerving discovery, she immediately went to her computer and called him on the secure video channel.

Looking into the computer screen at the face of Gordon Tallbear, Johanna was mesmerized once again. She not only thought he was the most handsome man she had ever seen, but she loved being around him for his intellect. He stirred something in her that she had never felt before, yet she always mirrored his dispassionate demeanor when they were together. Yet, as she always said to herself, he's easy on the eyes.

As Gordon began to speak, he looked at Johanna's image and marveled, as he always did, at her beauty. "I am sending you the electronic enhancements of what Badlands Bill would look like alive so you can see for yourself. They should be coming through on your printer screen right now."

Johanna looked over at her printer screen and gasped, almost against her will. Recovering quickly, she reverted to a faux Irish brogue and said, "Well, if he ain't the spittin' image of you!"

"I know," laughed Gordon. "I'm going to need some time to adjust to this." Then, more seriously, "Johanna, something inside me says that this is more than a coincidence."

"In the meantime," said Johanna assuming her center director's voice once again, "I want you back here right away. Chuck Kinoshi's Antarctica report is extraordinary. I think you'll want to link up with him on this ASAP."

"What does Antarctica have to do with Montana?" asked Gordon.

"It seems as though Chuck has found some more of your long lost relatives. Better turn your operations over to Hector Moineau. He's well-equipped to wrap up the investigation in Montana. We need you back here tomorrow. I'll send the helicopter. I'm bringing Chuck back in also so we can have a coordinated briefing. Tell the team to conduct a complete wrap-up and then pack up Badlands Bill's body and the device and get back here. And tell Hector that I want him available on a moment's notice to fill in some blanks in the briefing via teleconference."

The next thing Johanna did was to contact Madison Tolles and bring him up-to-date on the recent discoveries.

We are all one people.

The Lakota

Chapter 2

As he began packing for the trip back to the Denver Center, Tallbear reflected on the journey that led him to this recent discovery in Montana.

Dr. Gordon Tallbear was a Native American, or Indian, it didn't matter much to him what he was called. As far as he was concerned, the vast majority of people who used the term 'Indian' did so with no malice or racial prejudice. He was a Lakota, born 39 years ago about 350 miles from this remote location, on the Pine Ridge Reservation in South Dakota. He was also recognized as one of the world's leading experts on North American Indian history, migratory patterns, and culture.

Though Pine Ridge was one of the poorest regions of the United States, Tallbear came from a well-educated family that had an unquenchable thirst for knowledge.

Since the late 1800s, the Tallbear family had taken advantage of educational opportunities offered by the White Nation. Gordon's fourth great-grandfather, in the late 1800s, received a college education at Dartmouth and became a schoolteacher on the reservation. Dartmouth's original charter as "a school for Indians … and also of English Youth and any others," is not well known. In 1755, Eleazar Wheelock, a Puritan minister from Connecticut, founded Moor's Indian Charity School to educate Indians for the ministry. One of his students, Samson Occum of the Mohegans, had become a minister and had some success as a missionary on Long Island preaching to the Montauks. Inspired by this success, Wheelock went to England and raised funds for a new school. In 1769, King George III granted a charter to create an institution "for the education and instruction of Youth of the Indian Tribes in this Land in reading, writing and all parts of Learning …" Based on this mandate, Wheelock established Dartmouth College in Hanover, New Hampshire.

During its first 200 years, Dartmouth graduated only 19 Native Americans, but since then has graduated more than 500 from over 120 different tribes, more than all seven other Ivy League schools combined.

Successive generations of the Tallbear family given a Dartmouth education produced three physicians, a psychiatrist, and an anthropologist. Gordon's father, Martin Tallbear, saddened by Pine Ridge's alarming rates of alcoholism, family abuse, depression, and suicide, became a psychiatrist specializing in treating mental illness, and co-occuring alcohol and substance abuse conditions. Tallbear's mother had graduated from Montana State University with bachelors and masters degrees in psychiatric nursing. Both had dedicated their lives to serving the Lakota Nation.

Martin Tallbear initiated "Mustang Therapy" targeting at risk Native Americans with substance abuse problems, mental illnesses, troubled and at-risk youth, and Indians in the prison system facing parole within the next five years. Coupled with 12-step programs for substance abusers, therapy required each client to develop a bond with one horse, and to feed, water, ride, and groom it daily. Clients were taught to ride and encouraged to take their horses on daily excursions. Pilot programs showed an 87% recovery rate. Many who completed the program became teachers and mentors for successive groups.

While the problems of alcohol and substance abuse still plagued the tribe, several commercial initiatives in recent years had started to bear fruit for the Lakota. One was a deal negotiated with a Danish manufacturer of wind turbines. The Danes were looking for a readily available labor force to manufacture and install wind turbines to capitalize on the exceptionally windy corridor from Texas to the Canadian border. The Danes negotiated a deal with the Lakota and its family of tribes to create several manufacturing sites for turbine blades, and erected several wind towers on the reservation to take advantage of the perpetual winds in the north-central plains. In exchange, the Lakota would share in the sales revenues.

Another major innovation for both the Lakota and many of the tribes of the west and southwest was the contract signed with five different solar panel manufacturers.

In keeping with their humor, the Lakota thought it both amusing, and wonderfully ironic, that they could sell wind and sunlight back to the White Man, as the White Man was nothing more than a greedy merchant at heart.

The second initiative happened after a series of public outcries regarding federal management of the wild mustang herds. Inspired by the model program developed by Gordon's father, and because so many horses were designated for slaughter every few years, the federal Substance Abuse and Mental Health Services Administration proposed a transfer of custody and stewardship of the herds to the recognized Plains Indian tribes. The Bureau of Land Management signed off on it, Congress approved funding, and the president signed it into law.

The Tallbear family lived modestly at Pine Ridge in a neat three-bedroom ranch house. The lawn was well-kept and accented by colorful gardens mutually maintained by Gordon's parents. Their home was a happy one and very focused on itself. His parents and grandparents had instilled in Gordon and his younger brother and sister a love of learning (dinner time would find the family discussing everything from the origins of tribal customs to the complexities and ironies of Shakespearean drama), and immersed them in the language, customs, traditions and history of their people. Life in the Tallbear household was not always perfect, particularly when Gordon and his brother became enamored with professional wrestling and acted out body slams the family living room. That was the surefire way to hit their father's hot button and get him raving about raising two barbarians.

But Gordon and his siblings also developed such a strong sense of pride in their heritage and respect for themselves that they did not succumb to the temptations of drink and degeneration that plagued so many of their peers.

By his early teens, Gordon was already an accomplished hunter and horseman, and an all-around athlete of note. It seemed as though he could perform any sport with excellence.

Throughout high school he received a varsity letter every year in football, basketball, and baseball. In the spring of his senior year, his basketball coach, who also doubled as the track and field coach, approached him and said that while he knew Gordon was committed to playing baseball, he needed his help in the statewide track and field competitions. As it turned out, the statewide competition happened on a day when the baseball team was scheduled for a practice, so Gordon agreed to help. At the state event, Gordon broke the state record in the long jump and tied the state record for the high jump. But baseball was Gordon's passion.

By the age of 18, he had the physique of a world-class athlete. Beyond his good looks and athletic ability, he was popular because of his personality. Gordon admittedly, on occasion, succumbed to the temptations offered by nearly every girl in sight, yet deep down inside he remained focused on his goal of becoming an anthropologist. He wanted to learn everything about the history of his people, and more broadly, of the Native American Indian at large. His desire was to bring his expertise to the service of his people, particularly his own tribe. His goal was to create a body of knowledge that would be taught to Indian children for generations to come.

Gordon's one overriding quality that impressed everyone he came in contact with was his leadership. All he had to do was say, "I think we should do this," and everybody around him would do as he suggested. It was almost mysterious how he could lead his friends into mischief or a noble undertaking. He simply looked people in the eye and they willingly followed his lead.

Like his father and grandfathers before him, Tallbear was awarded a scholarship to Dartmouth. He graduated with honors in anthropology and went on to Harvard for his masters and doctoral degrees. By his late twenties, he had earned renown for his expertise in the history of Native American cultures.

Besides his academics, during college and graduate school he also pursued baseball, where he excelled as a power-hitting catcher, and was drafted as a second round pick by the Boston Red Sox. Despite the enormous money offered, he turned down the opportunity to become a professional baseball player, but played competitively in the elite Boston City League and the Cape Cod League, considered to be the premium amateur leagues in the country, during summers he was at Harvard.

An athletic six foot two and a muscular 220 pounds, he was the spitting image of his father. He had prominent cheekbones, a sharp hooked nose, and, most remarkably, green eyes, unusual among American Indians. Even though he was sent back east to prestigious universities to be educated, Gordon never cut his raven colored hair short and always wore it hanging straight down his back, nearly to his waist. With his chisled athletic physique, jet-black flowing locks, and piercing green eyes, he was a formidable presence in any environment.

Occasionally at college, someone would look at him and say, "Hey, Chief, how are ya' doin'?" Tallbear had mastered himself so thoroughly that all he needed to do was to look at the offender very intently, and the questioner would be numbed to silence. His young women classmates found his self-assurance irresistible, and not a few of them ended up with a Gordon Tallbear notch on their bedposts.

In high school, Tallbear did date regularly, but it wasn't until he was in college that a long-term correspondence with an old girlfriend began to develop into a full-fledged romance.

Miriam Eagle-Hawk came from the same kind of family as Gordon Tallbear. The Eagle-Hawks wanted nothing but a better life through education. Miriam was beautiful in every physical and emotional sense of the word. Standing a slender five feet five, her face was beautifully sculpted with high cheekbones and penetrating dark eyes. Gordon dated her a few times in high school, and made the classic adolescent mistake of not seeing her for who she really was. Instead, he made an inappropriate pass at her, which she rebuked. But she always saw in him what he could be. When he went off to Dartmouth, she began writing to him.

As they developed their friendship through letters, Miriam and Gordon discovered a shared strong belief in Indian education and a desire to inculcate the lore and ancient customs of the tribe into the children of the Lakotas. Miriam went to the University of Minnesota and, like Gordon's mother, earned her bachelor's and master's degrees in psychiatric nursing, which she applied back at the same clinic where Tallbear's father was the resident psychiatrist.

In addition to all the things Gordon loved about her, he also saw in Miriam a woman who would inspire the young girls of the reservation to set their sights high.

At age 25, when Tallbear graduated from Harvard with his doctorate, he came back to the reservation and married Miriam in a dual ceremony that included both the traditional Lakota marriage and the Catholic ceremonies.

Gordon and Miriam shared their souls with each other. They were both dedicated to their tribe and had given themselves totally to the advancement of their people. Often, late into the night, they would talk about their vision of what was possible for the Indians of Pine Ridge, and how they could have an impact on the future of their people.

They talked of family - a large family of boys and girls who would go on to great educational accomplishments and bring their gifts back to Pine Ridge.

Gordon initially took a job working for the state university as an anthropologist. He worked long hours, had published seminal papers on Indian migration patterns and culture, and was developing a national reputation. After he had been at the university for two years, tragedy struck. Returning home from work one evening, Miriam was broadsided by a drunk driver who ran a stop sign. She was killed instantly.

Gordon fell into a silent grief that his family could not even begin to penetrate.

Within a month of Miriam's death, Tallbear left the reservation and was not heard from again for more than three years.

He never spoke about his absence, but later occasionally dropped hints that indicated his travels took him to the far-east and India.

When he was 30, he returned unannounced to visit family and participated in traditional celebrations and ceremonies. He revealed little about his absence, but told his father that he must undertake a spiritual cleansing.

With grief at the loss of Miriam still deeply burrowed in his breast, though a few years had passed, Gordon Tallbear fasted three days, then took a very intense sweat lodge – four long immersions in a pitch-black steaming hut – with ten minute breaks about every seven minutes for recovery in the fresh air. After completing the ritual, he mounted a painted mustang and rode off into the tall wooded highlands.

Three days later searchers found Gordon sitting on a slope at the edge of a forest. He was gazing into a distance they could not see. After they brought him home, he wrote down the story of his vision, sealed it in an envelope, and gave it to his father for safekeeping.

Tallbear never told his family what he saw in his vision, but there was a change about him, a calmness and serenity that had not been there before.

Soon thereafter, he took a job with the Native American Research Foundation. There he established his credentials as a top expert on all matters relating to American Indians.

When he was 33, Gordon Tallbear was recruited by the Denver Center.

Six years before the discovery of Badlands Bill, the Denver Center invited him to come for an interview, and, based on what he saw of the center's nearly bottomless funding and technological support capabilities, he gladly took a position with them as Director of Native American Anthropological Research.

Little did Gordon know the price of his decision.

Megalopsychia: To think above and beyond one's own dreams, desires, and to be (morally) strong. According to Aristotle, megalopsychia is "greatness of the soul," and is one of the great moral virtues.

Chapter 3

Just west of the Continental Divide, at 4500 feet, positioned high on an inward curving, southern facing slope, the Denver Center overlooked an exquisite valley. The sun on this crisp fall morning turned the forest to an artist's palette of yellow, red, amber and varying shades of green. An enormous stand of aspens, their leaves rippling in the morning breeze, was a golden inland sea surrounded by green spruce and fir shores. Icy water cascaded down the mountainside, pooling at different levels until it dropped into a fast moving silvery stream flashing through the foliage on its journey to the Colorado River. Far up the mountainside eagles nested in their aeries and swooped down to the valley floor in search of prey, then rose on thermal updrafts to soar in lazy circles.

Ground access to the Denver Center was achieved by turning off a country road onto a two-mile switchback that climbed to the campus. Once past the security gate, visitors entered a compound of nearly 100 buildings spread across 10,000 acres.

The five largest buildings housed administration and research, the rest were individual residences and four-unit apartments built into the mountainside at different levels. Crushed gravel pathways connected the units. In foul winter weather, underground piping laid in below the frost line and powered by geothermal energy kept these pathways clear despite the fact that Colorado mountain snowfalls were always measured in feet. In fair weather, gazebos placed at intervals provided staff a break from intensive work and an opportunity to rejuvenate moods and minds. The solitude was amplified by bubbling streams and forest sounds.

Though designed in a rustic external architecture, comparisons to mountain lodges ended there. The entire complex tapped into a combination of geothermal, solar, hydrogen fuel cell, and wind power from towers strung across the ridgeline. In mild weather, staff travelled between buildings in photo-voltaic powered golf carts, and in inclement weather through underground tunnels on hydrogen cell powered conveyor walkways.

Ground sensors and motion-activated remote cameras provided perimeter security, all monitored from the headquarters building. Occasionally stray hikers needed to be intercepted and guided away.

Designed to look like an oversized mountain chalet, the headquarters building, with polarized floor-to-ceiling windows on all three floors, provided dramatic vistas. A helicopter pad sat one hundred-fifty-feet off the eastern side of the building.

Gordon, in field boots, jeans, and khaki bush jacket, stepped off the helicopter, walked across an open area, beneath which was a subterranean parking lot filled with hybrid electric cars, and entered the Denver Center's reception area. As soon as he stepped into the main lobby he felt right at home.

On the right-hand wall, a large natural-gas driven fireplace spread reassuring warmth. The hardwood plank floor and solid oak ceiling beams in the room gave additional comfort. On the left, opposite the fireplace, beautifully arranged and illuminated, hung four paintings, the only known copies of *The River of Life*. The originals resided on permanent display in the National Gallery of Art in Washington. American artist Thomas Cole (1801 – 1848) may have been issuing his own warning with this series. Each painting depicted a phase of life -- Childhood, Youth, Manhood, and Old Age -- and the voyage down the River of Life seeking the aerial castle of the youth's daydream. Through the sequence of paintings, nature's fury, demons, and self-doubt obstructed the traveler in his quest. Only prayer and Divine intervention could bring him to his goal. Gordon was moved each time he saw them.

At the main reception desk centered on the back wall, as he had done for the past seven years, a man sat ramrod straight in a wheelchair. Fifty-seven years old with buzz-cut salt-and-pepper gray hair, he had the still powerful arms and upper torso of a man who took his exercise seriously.

Ben Crowley, career Marine and First Sergeant, had been operations chief for the 24th Marine Expeditionary Unit deployed to Afghanistan. Two weeks short of returning home and retiring, he was caught in the middle of a vicious firefight as combat units engaged the enemy. Though badly wounded, when one of the company commanders was killed, he took over and directed deadly aircraft and artillery return fire that destroyed the attacking force. It earned him his second Navy Cross, the nation's second highest honor for bravery, and a wheelchair. He had no regrets.

"Hi, Ben," said Gordon.

"Hi, doc. What's new on the res?" said Crowley in his deep, gravelly Drill Instructor voice, honed by years of whiskey and cigarettes.

"Come on, Ben, it's been a while since I was on the res."

"I don't know, doc. I look at you and I see an Indian in desperate need of a sweat lodge. And you ain't gonna find one at the Denver Center."

"I've been working for this place for six years, Ben, and you can read me like a book every time I walk in the door."

"Well, welcome aboard again, anyway. Johanna wants to see you toot sweet, and you'd better shit, shower and shave after that 'cause rumor has it that some big shot wants you after she sees you."

"Hmm, where do you pick up all the scuttlebutt, Ben? This is supposed to be a top-secret, close-hold organization, but you have information before everyone."

"The walls are thin, son. The walls are thin," Ben growled before returning to his book, which Gordon saw was a beautiful leather-bound David Copperfield. Gordon shook his head and passed through the lobby to the reinforced steel portal that looked just like a carved oak door. He put his hand on the security screen, passed through the three-foot thick walls into the elevator, and up to the third floor executive offices. The walls are thin, he thought. Indeed.

After dropping his field case in his own office, he went down the hall to see Johanna, reflecting that for all the high-tech security and three foot thick walls, the place still had the feel of a cozy mountain lodge with its hardwood floors, fireplaces in every room, and oak-paneled walls.

Johanna greeted him warmly. "After our de-briefing, take a break and go get cleaned up. You are about to meet our prime benefactor."

Gordon looked at Johanna, his face an inscrutable mask. He thought her to be the most beautiful woman he had ever seen. Her beauty, remarkable intelligence, and dry wit intrigued him. His heart raced every time he saw her, and he recognized that his feelings for her ran deep.

He recovered himself quickly and said, "Jeepers, Ben was right."

"What do you mean?"

"When I was coming through the lobby Ben said more or less the same thing."

"That man can make you crazy. Without leaving that wheelchair or his post at the main desk, he seems to have access to all the secret doings around here. Anyway, pull up a chair."

After Gordon brought her up to date, Johanna briefed him on the Antarctica expedition.

"Chuck will be here tomorrow with all the scoop, but for now suffice it to say that his discoveries are beyond extraordinary. Madison Tolles is ecstatic. This is the fourth year in a row the Center sent an expedition to Antarctica to discover acoustical anomalies, and Chuck's team is the first one to come up with anything positive. Five thousand feet up in one mountain range about a mile from their base camp, Chuck's team discovered a pretty sophisticated secure entrance that is the gateway to an extraordinary network of caverns. Inside they discovered the apparent equivalent of a main computer storage area, and it is still functioning after God knows how many centuries. Decoding the computers is the main challenge. The written language, based on the keypad they had to decode, is in the form of strange runes. And there is more. Deep down the caverns house living quarters for perhaps 200,000 people. It's a city underground. Even deeper, perhaps a mile or so underground, they discovered a cemetery. Carvings and murals throughout the caverns depict, among other things, the Great Pyramid at Giza, the Sphinx, Stonehenge, and the Mayan pyramids. There is even a mural of the Nazca lines of Peru.

"Jesus! Who else knows about this?" asked Gordon.

"The security of this operation is exceptional. So far the press has not picked up the scent."

Gordon sat there deep in thought.

"You know," he said, "in the late twentieth century a very vocal group of apostates totally disagreed with mainstream Egyptologists on the dating of the Great Pyramid and the Sphinx. This "lunatic fringe," as the mainstreamers referred to them, insisted that both were built not at the conventionally accepted date of 4,900 to 4,500 years ago, but rather thousands of years earlier by an advanced civilization. They claimed the builders came from the legendary Atlantis, which was somewhere in the southern Indian Ocean. They further believed that Atlantis drifted far to the south on its tectonic plate and became what we now call Antarctica."

"Well raise my rent!" replied Johanna in a faux southern drawl. "It turns out that they may have been right. I had known about some of what you just said, but not about Atlantis drifting to the Antarctic. Now go and clean up because you are to have a rare face-to-face meeting with Madison Tolles. You have 45 minutes to get ready. He'll meet with you in his personal library. In the meantime, I'm going to deploy a cryptographic team from Flynn-Todd Systems to go to Antarctica and decode what Chuck's got. You haven't met Madison Tolles yet, have you?" she asked.

"No," said Gordon. "Remember, when you recruited me, I was interviewed by a search team from your board of directors. After that I met with you, but I never saw Mr. Tolles. I have been travelling around the world so much that I have never been here at the same time as he was."

"He can be intimidating," said Johanna. "When he asks questions he wants direct answers in return, even if the news is bad. He can spot a phony a mile away. To survive and thrive while working for him, you must be able to defend your position. He always wants you to back up your arguments with facts, and he's the rare leader who's willing to change his mind if your back-up data supports diversion from his original theories. I've seen people melt down in front of him. I have also seen people flourish under his leadership."

"It seems you're also doing a little flourishing, if I'm not mistaken" said Gordon.

"If I am, it's because I am very good at what I do. Now get moving. By the way, you look like you could use a home cooked meal. Come over to my place for dinner. Is 6:30 okay?"

Oh my God, I can't believe I just invited him to dinner, thought Johanna.

Gordon paused on his way out and said, "Sure, I'd like that."

Oh my God, I can't believe she just invited me to dinner, thought Gordon as he left.

Gordon took one of the electric carts back to his residence. Because of his status, his home was one of the single unit chalets. It had a panoramic view of the valley. Researchers and support staff (who commonly referred to themselves as the Jedi Knights) lived in spacious four-unit apartment complexes. Only top-level operational directors, as well as the executive director and Mr. Tolles, had private residences. Gordon's home was typical of the single unit dwellings: two bedrooms, two baths, kitchen, dining room, and living room. They were modest, but elegantly appointed. He provided his own touches with Native American art and western furnishings. It was a peaceful place to live.

At the appointed hour, Gordon, having showered and changed into comfortable casual clothes, returned to the headquarters building. Madison Tolles' personal library was on the second floor just below his executive corner office. Like the office above, it measured 25 x 25 feet. Dark wooden bookshelves lined the two inside walls. A spiral staircase leading up to Tolles' office was built near the inside corner. Centered in the room was a cozy cluster of easy chairs, couch, and coffee table. Near the windowed corner were two other comfortable chairs and a small table.

A tall, gray-haired man in his late fifties dressed in a tan corduroy sports coat, powder blue open-necked shirt, brown slacks, and penny loafers stood by the windows and looked westward down the valley. Madison Tolles turned and motioned Gordon to join him. Gordon walked across the room, shook Tolles' hand and greeted him.

"It is a pleasure to finally meet you, Mr. Tolles."

"The pleasure is mine, Dr. Tallbear."

"Please, sir, I'm 'doctor' only at conferences. Just call me Gordon, if you will."

"Very well, Gordon. Please, have a seat."

Madison Tolles was the oldest sibling born into a wealthy family from New Canaan, Connecticut. His father's private passion was American history, particularly the Revolutionary period. The Tolles children were named after great patriots: Madison James, for the principle architect of the Bill of Rights; his younger sister Abigail Adams, and his younger brother Jefferson Thomas.

After going through the excellent New Canaan public school system through eighth grade, his father insisted that Madison go to an exclusive boarding prep school. Portsmouth Abbey in Portsmouth, Rhode Island, fit the bill, and 14-year old Madison was packed off.

He actually enjoyed his experience at "The Abbey." Though quiet, and sometimes enigmatic, he exhibited talent as a persuasive leader whether in student politics, extracurricular activities, or creative mischief. Graduating in the top ten of his class, he chose to attend Georgetown University. He majored in government.

At Georgetown he took an apprenticeship with the senior senator from Connecticut and learned just how government functioned. Excelling as an undergraduate, upon graduation he dismayed family and friends alike by applying for Officer Candidate School in the Marine Corps. Stunned by his decision, as there had been no history of military service by anyone in his family, his father asked him why he was postponing a lucrative future. Madison simply said that with all the study of the Revolutionary War that he had been exposed to, he felt the need to serve in the military, just as his namesake had served in the cause of the Revolution. His father gave his blessing to Madison's choice.

Within a year, Madison received his commission as a Second Lieutenant and completed both the Officers Basic School and the Officers Infantry School. Shortly thereafter, as an infantry Platoon Commander based at Camp LeJeune, North Carolina, he deployed with a Marine Expeditionary Brigade to help quell a terrorist insurgency in the Middle East. While there his platoon got caught in an ambush in a provincial city. He was calling in artillery and air support to suppress enemy fire and get his platoon extracted when an enemy grenade exploded nearby severely wounding him. He ordered his men away to seek the safety of buildings across the street, but one of his squad leaders refused to leave him. The sergeant staunched the flow of blood from Tolles' wounds and dragged him to safety behind a wall. The enemy poured relentless fire down on their position, but the sergeant moved laterally to different positions along the wall and returned deadly suppressing fire.

While awaiting reinforcements and a medevac, the sergeant was wounded twice, but he fought on, delivering deadly fire against the insurgents. Eventually evacuated, both survived their wounds and returned to duty. The After-Action Report revealed that during the sergeant's actions to save his lieutenant's life, he had killed seventeen of the enemy and wounded a dozen more. Thanks to the recommendation written by Madison Tolles, the sergeant was awarded what was to be his first Navy Cross for his for bravery under fire.

Madison Tolles never forgot the debt he owed to Sergeant Ben Crowley. At the Center, only Johanna knew of the connection.

Leaving the Marine Corps as a captain at the end of his tour of duty, Tolles went on to graduate, near the top of his class from Georgetown Law School.

With his newly minted law degree, Tolles turned to Wall Street and cut his teeth in one of the old-line investment houses. He also lived modestly and invested a large share of his income, soon amassing a decent fortune of his own. He developed a reputation as a tough, yet caring businessman.

With a few associates he founded an investment banking house that flourished. After a few years his partners wanted to move on to other things, and Madison bought them out. He renamed the company the Tolles Group and relocated its headquarters to Greenwich, Connecticut. Soon he was branching out and investing in the world of high-tech start-ups. His fortune grew.

Tolles, now in his late fifties, was worth an estimated $75 billion. He had become accustomed to the loneliness of command. He had an enormous financial empire, and he had the Denver Center. He never let his guard down, except with his wife, Elaine, back at their estate in Greenwich. They were never able to have children, but he and Elaine had created a philanthropic trust fund, which she administered, to serve the educational needs of underprivileged children. She was his soul mate and sounding board, and she encouraged him to fulfill his lifelong dream.

Like his father, he had always loved history, but his interests led him to early Egyptian civilization. His fascination with the early Egyptians stirred a passion in him to find out how and why these ancient people built incredible structures with such mathematical precision. Like many before him, he doubted many of the conventional estimates relating to the ages and functions of the pyramids and other structures. He launched the Denver Center with his own money to find the answers to these and other questions about ancient mysteries worldwide.

He was enamored by two different unconventional theories about the utility of the Great Pyramid – one said it was used to produce nuclear fuel, and another claimed it was used to produce clean energy through chemical reactions. The conventional theory, supported by Egyptologists worldwide, was that it was a burial site for King Khufu. Tolles launched expeditions to find answers. His teams examined the Great Pyramid as well as pyramid structures of other ancient cultures, including the Mayan and Aztec.

The U.S. government became interested in these discoveries that hinted at alternative energy solutions. Various OPEC-generated oil crises of the past fifty years -- the Exxon Valdez disaster in Alaska, the BP Gulf oil spill catastrophe, and also the fact that global warming was the new reality -- persuaded Uncle Sam to offer substantial grant funding for his research efforts. That prompted the Denver Center to create strategic alliances with major high-tech corporations that supplied the center with cutting edge resources.

Madison Tolles and Gordon Tallbear settled into the comfortable chairs by the windows. All that could be heard was the ticking of a grandfather clock nestled between some bookshelves.

"I have asked to meet you, Gordon, because of the extraordinary research you have been conducting on the mysterious remains we have been finding in recent years. I am fascinated by the similarities between these discoveries and discoveries like Kennewick Man in Washington State."

"Well, Mr. Tolles, we are just scratching the surface with our examinations of Badlands Bill and the other remains discovered world-wide. In the language of anthropology, they are all referred to as "Caucasoid," which is probably not an accurate term. Caucasoid implies a connective relationship to the peoples of Europe, western Asia, and parts of North Africa. We have discovered that these unusual remains have no genetic connection to the historic residents of those areas, but they resemble them."

"Then tell me, Gordon, who do you think they are?"

"I'll elaborate a little on what I already discussed with Johanna. The academic community, in virtually every discipline, develops schools of thought. As a result, our progress in developing new theories is often hindered by these existing schools. PhD's in every discipline have staked their careers on what they have published, and they don't like any thinking that wanders, if you don't mind a touch of personal irony, too far off the reservation.

"As I'm guessing you already know, in the late twentieth century, Hancock, Bauval, Dunn, and West, to name a few, posited plausible, though controversial, theories about the origins and dating of the Sphinx, the Giza Pyramid, and the pyramid complexes of the Mayans and Aztecs. West theorized that the Sphinx was carved as early as 12,500 years ago. He makes a good argument. At that time, the monument would have been perfectly aligned with the rising of the constellation Leo, but not at 2,500 BC, which conventional Egyptologists credit as the date of the monument. Furthermore, erosion on the Sphinx indicates that it was caused by rain. That region 4,500 years ago was as arid as it is today. But long before that it was a fertile savannah with frequent rainfalls.

Coupled with West's conclusions, Hancock posited that the pyramids were built by an ancient civilization from an advanced culture, possibly the mythical Atlantis, more than 12,000 years ago. Bauval backed up that claim with computerized proof that the Great Pyramid complex at Giza is a star map. The three main pyramids are positioned exactly in proportion to the three stars in Orion's belt as they would have been aligned 12,500 years ago.

"Supporting arguments show that pyramids built by the Egyptians after the Great Pyramid complex at Giza were not nearly as architecturally sound or accurately designed. In fact, some of them began crumbling within a few years of their construction. That not withstanding, the Egyptians developed a remarkable civilization that allowed them to dominate their known world. They became the leaders in mathematics, astronomy, architecture and many other scientific disciplines. But in 2,900 BC, for all their accomplishments, they never had the technological capability to build the Great Pyramid. The precision positioning of the Great pyramid is mathematically perfect. The granite beams within the pyramid are cut to an extraordinary precision that we can only approximate today. The Egyptians of that period had no tools to cut with such precision.

"Conventional Egyptologists, of course, derided these new theories, and major foundations wouldn't fund any research related to unconventional theories. Furthermore, there is not a foundation on the planet besides yours that will grant funding to anything with the word Atlantis in it."

Tolles looked at him for a few moments and asked, "What do you think now, Gordon?"

Gordon looked into the distance before responding. "I think, Mr. Tolles, that based on what we found in Montana, and what Chuck Kinoshi apparently has uncovered in Antarctica, we are now way off the reservation and into some new and pretty exciting territory."

48

"Indeed. But once this all becomes public knowledge – and it will -- it will be a hornet's nest out there. Academics fighting for their livelihoods will be on the attack, as will theologians of all stripes. In addition, every civilized nation will want to get in on the discoveries. Are you ready for that?"

"Mr. Tolles, I think we would be making a terrible mistake not to pursue this as far as we can."

"Excellent! That's why I am appointing you in charge of all field operations relating to the archaeological and anthropological discoveries in Atlantis - I mean Antarctica. I have been continuously briefed about the Antarctic discoveries. Johanna will, of course, still oversee the whole operation. You will work closely with whoever is chosen to oversee the technological discoveries so that we have a coordinated effort."

"Of course, sir. I am honored that you have shown such confidence in me. And while the other technical team leaders you have dispatched to Antarctica are all well-qualified, I would strongly recommend that we keep Chuck Kinoshi in charge of the technical side. He is brilliant, charming, funny, one hell of an administrator, and everyone on his staff would take a bullet for him."

"Thank you. I will take your recommendation seriously. Gordon, I have been following your career since you worked at the Native American Research Center. Even before that while vacationing in Hyannis I saw you play baseball in the Cape Cod League. I was there the night you hit that guy Caruso's fastball out of the yard, what was it, 450 feet or something? Moreover, I am also not just a little interested in the resemblance you bear to our newly discovered friend in Montana. Would you like to hear my theory about that?"

"Well, yes, sir, I certainly would."

"There are many legends about Atlantis. Several indicate that Atlantis sent explorers into the world. This is reaffirmed by legends everywhere from the Greeks to the Central American pre-Columbian tribes. Even the poet-musician Donovan in the 1960s wrote a song about the explorers from Atlantis.

"You mentioned Hancock. He also proposed a pretty wild idea that the continent of Atlantis once resided in a temperate to sub-tropical zone in the southern Indian Ocean but drifted 2,000 miles south according to something called earth crust displacement theory and became what we now call Antarctica. Earth crust displacement seems to be the only plausible theory that can explain why somewhere between 17,000 and 13,500 years ago in the rapid cycle of the melting and freezing of the glaciers from the Ice Age, there was sudden extinction of wooly mammoths and other species. Why, for example, have these beasts been uncovered in arctic zones -- or even in Makoshika where you just came from -- fully intact, along with the fossilized remains of tropical trees and ferns?

"Crustal displacement theory says that the sudden melting releasing of hundreds of trillions of tons of ice, in a short time geologically speaking, caused continents to lift off their bedrock foundations. Continents suddenly shifted on the crust of the earth, much like an orange skin might slip over the surface if the skin were loose. Fairly rapidly, tropical areas rotated north above the Arctic Circle to become Alaska and the Aleutians, and formerly arctic areas rotated south into more temperate climates. New England has abundant evidence of having once been an arctic region. Formerly tropical areas like Makoshika, originally probably located in what is now southeastern United States, rotated clockwise northwest. The global upheaval was dramatic with violent earthquakes and volcanoes erupting all over the world. Devastating rains and an enormous flood followed. Hancock and others saw all kinds of connections that could be explained.

"Hancock pointed out that all over the world people share the common myth of the flood. In our Judeo-Christian tradition, we have the story of Noah's Ark. Yet the Sumerians and the Incas, as well as scores of other cultures across the world share the same myth, that one family, with animals and seeds, were saved from the flood and repopulated the world.

"Short of endorsing the idea of people from another planet building these edifices and then departing, an advanced civilization from Atlantis remains a plausible theory. And that's where I put my money.

"Whoever these people were, they left behind the most amazing structures, built with a precision that is almost beyond us today. They seem to be calling to us from 12,000 years ago saying, 'We have left behind these clues so you will know that a great civilization once existed here.'"

Tolles paused for a moment and looked out into the fading light onto the panorama of this beautiful Rocky Mountain valley. "It has been my great passion to unlock these ancient secrets. The collective genius of you, Chuck Kinoshi, and the Jedi Knights here at the Denver Center, are the keys to unlocking these ancient mysteries.

"Before I agreed to hire you six years ago, I wanted to know more about you. I sent a bright young woman to interview your parents under the pretext that she was preparing an article for an anthropological journal."

"Yes, sir. I remember my parents mentioning it."

"Your mother commented that you looked just like your father, and your father added that he looked just like his father. Now that we have you also looking just like Badlands Bill. I might be making a fantastic leap of faith, but I am surmising that Bill was one of the explorers from Atlantis. Lord knows what got him into that pit with an arrow in his shoulder. My guess is that he married one of your ancestors and that you are his descendant. Your heading of the team that examined him seems to bring us full circle. What do you think of that?"

"Mr. Tolles, I had been nursing just the same thought in my own head."

"Good. Now let's get a good night's sleep. Tomorrow Dr. Kinoshi will update us on his findings and then we will be putting together a major operational plan. Oh, and one more thing. I want you to go to the clinic tomorrow to undergo some DNA testing to see if you are really a match with our Atlantis friends."

The following morning Gordon went to the clinic in the basement of the main lodge and had his DNA tested. It confirmed that he was a direct genetic match with Badlands Bill.

My family tree has a few more branches than I expected, thought Gordon.

Not everything that is faced can be changed; but nothing can be changed until it is faced.

Chapter 4

Gordon rang the bell promptly at 6:30. Johanna answered wearing a white satin blouse and jeans. Her feet were bare. She had pulled her auburn hair back into a ponytail, held in place with a turquoise and silver band. Without a doubt, she was extraordinarily alluring. Even dressed down she looked stunning. Gordon stared at her mesmerized. Both quickly recovered. Once inside, they both felt a little awkward.

"Can I get you something to drink?" she asked.

"Any fruit juice, if you have it."

"How about a half and half orange and cranberry juice drink?"

"I've never tried that. Sounds good."

"It's a New England specialty. Coming right up."

They talked about nothing in particular while Johanna busied herself putting the final touches on her *chicken divan*. It was a marvelous concoction of boneless chicken breasts and broccoli gently spiced and oven-baked in a cream sauce. Gordon was overwhelmed. They ate in the small but perfect alcove that served as a dining room in these chalets. "That was elegant. Thanks, Johanna."

"There's more where that came from, Gordon."

Gordon felt like he was floating on air.

After dinner and small talk, they went into the living room. Gordon sat in an easy chair at a right angle to the sofa and Johanna sat near him at the end of the sofa, her legs curled under her. Through the wall to ceiling A-frame window looking out over the valley, they could see the brilliant stars of the chilly October night. The gas fireplace opposite Johanna radiated heat and cast flickering shadows across the floor. Two candles on the mantel filled the room with a linen scent. Johanna had put in some CDs of soft Spanish classic guitar music.

"Do you get back to Pine Ridge very often?" Johanna asked.

"Not as often as I'd like. I miss the seasonal celebrations and rituals. And as much as I love the sauna in my chalet, it can't compare with the power of a good sweat lodge."

"I don't think we had many of those in Connecticut. What's it like?"

"Many of my tribal brothers and sisters simply take a sweat lodge the way others would jump into a sauna, but the way to get the most out of the experience is to fast for one, two, or three days beforehand, only taking a minimal amount of water for sustenance. The purpose of the sweat lodge is to blend the natural elements of earth, air, fire, and water to work together to cleanse people inside and out and create balance. The sweat lodge itself is a completely darkened teepee-like structure. You sit down and the shaman uncovers red-hot glowing coals that have been buried in a ground trench. Periodically he will throw some green branches and water on the coals to generate moist heat. There is a vent at the top of the lodge to let the smoke out. The heat is intense, far more intense than the conventional sauna, and it's pitch black, except for the glow of the coals. It's no place for claustrophobics. You have to leave the lodge about every seven minutes to recover outside. After three or four sessions, if you're doing the complete spiritual sweat lodge, you would get on your horse and ride off to a quiet place and lie down for several hours. If properly spiritually prepared, you may have a vision."

"A vision? Like what kind of a vision? Visits from long gone relatives?"

"Possibly. A vision may be a partial viewing of something that happened in the historical past. These types of visions usually require that the recipient seek out a tribal elder to help explain what it might mean." Tallbear paused for a moment. "Or the vision might be a visit from a strange new person who foretells the future. Crazy Horse had a powerful vision like that when he was a young boy and it shaped the rest of his life."

"Really? How so?"

"When Crazy Horse was a boy, he was called Curley. His hair and skin was lighter than everyone else's and he was a quiet boy, never boasting. His father was one of the tribal shamans, or holy men. At the age of about thirteen, around 1853, he did a sweat lodge as I have described it. He did it without adult supervision, which could have been very dangerous for a boy his age, and later on his father was angry with him for doing it. After his sweat, he rode off into the hills and vanished for several days before he was found."

Tallbear's voice suddenly developed a tremor.

Recovering, he said, "Afterward, even though his father was angry, the boy told his him of the great warrior who appeared on a spotted horse and commanded him to be a complete warrior. He was not just to fight his tribe's enemies, he was forbidden to take anything for himself -- not honors or rewards -- and give all of his efforts to help the widows and orphans and less fortunate people of the tribe. He lived his life true to these values and is revered by the Lakota."

Intuiting that there was more to the story, Johanna asked, "Have you had a similar spiritual experience?"

Gordon paused for a moment, at first hesitant to tell her. As Segovia played beautiful Spanish classic guitar in the background, Gordon leaned forward, elbows on his knees, and said, "Yes, I have. And it was the most profound experience of my life. It was three years after losing Miriam and I hadn't been able to shake my grief. I had wandered the world after she died, to China, India, and Japan, seeking wisdom from Buddhist holy men, gurus, and Zen masters. It really was an enlightening experience. Finally a Zen master in Japan told me I would never be healed until I returned home and faced my grief directly. I returned home with the idea of purging myself in an intense sweat lodge. I fasted for three days, took the sweat lodge, and rode off into the hills. I was physically drained and my mind was blank. I, too, was gone for three days."

Gordon let a few moments of silence go by. "When I got back, I wrote down everything I saw in my vision. My father has one copy, sealed and stored with his private papers. I made a second copy when I came here, and it is in the safe in my quarters. In my personnel file you will find the safe combination should you need it. If anything happens to me, I want you to get it and share it with Mr. Tolles and Chuck Kinoshi. Chuck is my best friend, and Mr. Tolles may find value in what I experienced. And you, Johanna, are becoming a very special person to me as well. You and Chuck are my second family."

Johanna leaned forward, concern on her face. She touched his hand. "Gordon, why do you think something might happen to you?"

"My vision told me that I would be involved in a monumental undertaking. Based on your initial summary of what Chuck has uncovered in Antarctica, and based on the possible connection to the mysterious ancient human remains we have been studying from around the world, particularly Badlands Bill, I believe we are on the verge of a discovery that will change the planet. But in pursuit of that goal, we will be facing many dark forces that will stop at nothing to prevent our success."

Johanna reached over and took Gordon's hand in hers. After a few moments she said, "I'll pray that nothing happens to you."

They sat quietly for a while, holding hands, looking at the stars, and listening to the guitars.

Struggling inside, Gordon finally said, "It's getting late, and tomorrow should be a big day for the Center. I'll be going now." And he leaned over, pulled her hand to his lips and kissed it. She was stunned.

He rose and lifted her hand to help her stand with him. As she stood, he gave her a gentle kiss on the cheek, and left quietly.

She sunk back on the couch. Strongly sensing his absence, Johanna sat listening to the music. Slowly a tear formed, and she let it slide down her cheek.

All truth passes through three stages:
First it is ridiculed;
Second, it is violently opposed;
Third, it is accepted as self-evident.

Arthur
Schopennauer
(1788-1860)

Chapter 5

Dr. Charles Kinoshi had stepped off a plane from Antarctica just three hours earlier. Although he had showered and changed clothes, he looked exhausted. But his enthusiasm sustained him as he gave his presentation.

Chuck Kinoshi was of Japanese descent. His family had emigrated from Japan to Hawaii in the early 1900s to work on the farms. His great grandparents had insisted that their children would not work the soil, but would be educated and take their place in American society. His grandfather became a lawyer and as a young man gradually accrued wealth and position. When The Japanese attacked Pearl Harbor in December 1941, he worked closely with the ruling haole, or white, families of Hawaii, descendents of the missionaries sent there in the 1820s, to ensure that the Japanese citizens of Hawaii retained their complete American rights. This was a time when on the mainland, Japanese communities along the West Coast were being rounded up and placed in detention camps in the American West.

Chuck's grandfather and uncles soon volunteered for service in the US Army and were placed in segregated Nisei (Japanese-American) battalions and sent to fight in Europe. The Nisei battalions became the most decorated units of World War II. His grandfather rose to the rank of Captain. As an infantry company commander he was severely wounded in Italy and awarded the Army's Distinguished Service Cross, which, like the Navy Cross, was the second highest award for bravery next to the Medal of Honor.

Following his recuperation at Walter Reed Army Hospital in Washington, DC, his grandfather wanted to make himself as presentable as possible before he returned to his family in

Hawaii and went to a local barber in Washington for a haircut. Despite his heroism signified by the display of awards on his uniform, the barber said, "We don't cut Jap hair," and threw him out.

His grandfather had learned patience from his parents and vowed to get even the long way. Returning to Hawaii (after a haircut in San Francisco at a Japanese American Barber shop), he entered politics, and immediately following Hawaii's acceptance as the 50th state, was elected as one of the first two Hawaiian Congressmen. After two terms in the House of Representatives, he ran for the Upper House, ended up serving for forty years in the United States Senate, and was one of the driving forces behind the Civil Rights Act in the 1960s. While in Washington, he arranged, through a campaign contributor, investment money for a friend who opened a Japanese restaurant right next to the barbershop that had turned him away. He felt that it was the best money he ever spent.

His son, Chuck's father, became a PhD biochemist and landed a job working for a major pharmaceutical company near Atlanta.

The Kinoshi household was noted not just for the academic achievements of its children, but also for its warmth, humor, and generosity to the community. Chuck was handsome and popular in high school and claimed that he was the only player on his high school football team who understood both Einstein's Theory of Relativity and the zone defense.

Chuck went on to MIT for his bachelor's, master's and doctoral degrees. A brilliant computer engineer, he designed all the systems in place at the Denver Center. As a bachelor he lived for his work. Born and raised near Atlanta, Georgia, no matter how well you knew Chuck, it was always disconcerting to hear a southern drawl coming out of that Japanese face.

Chuck dated often, but was consumed by his work. Gordon threatened to kidnap him and marry him off to a Lakota princess if he didn't lighten up. "I'll marry when y'all do, cousin," was Chuck's defensive reply.

He had done a pretty thorough job in documenting, both in writing and with visual images, the scenes that unfolded before him in the caverns of Antarctica. His audience of 350 researchers, technicians, and administrators on the Denver Center staff awaited his briefing with eagerness.

Chuck began, "We had been examining every nook and cranny of our assigned area in the Sentinel Range in the northern part of the Ellsworth Mountains in Antarctica. This is a huge area to explore, and not much had ever been done there before we arrived. This mountain range is the highest in Antarctica and forms a chain 200 miles long and 30 miles wide. The Vinson Massif, at a little over 16,000 feet, is the highest peak in the chain, and you can see it here in the background about two miles from our base camp.

"At about 5,000 feet, we got lucky. Despite the altitude and steep terrain, we were on a reasonably flat plateau when Dr. Allison Long, our resident acoustic expert, and my number one deputy, got a reading that indicated we were standing near something that wasn't solid rock. After thoroughly searching the area, we came across some rocks that just seemed out of place. After pushing and pulling on them for a while trying to tumble them out of the way, we inadvertently moved the key rock, and the next thing we knew, the entire pile slid off to the side and revealed a solid metal door about 12 feet high and eight feet across. I'm telling you, we were totally flabbergasted.

"Off to the side of the door was what I will simply call a sophisticated key pad. Instead of the usual ten digit keypads we are accustomed to, this one had 100 rune-like symbols on it. It was time for Dr. Long to do her magic, so we sent most of the travelers back to base camp, and a handful of us set up camp in what little shelter we could find inside this entrance. In the 5-degree Farenheit outdoors, she went to work on decoding the system. Allison hooked up her computer and connected sensors to the keypad. It took three days, and we had to download some radical algorithmic programs from the Center, but finally all the tumblers fell into place and we got the right combination. Just as soundless as a mouse with cotton ball sneakers, the door slid open, as you can see on the video here.

"First thing we saw was the outer chamber. On the far wall, was another keypad. This one was easier to crack and only took us a couple of hours. Beyond that door, brothers and sisters, we left Kansas for good. We called up the rest of the gang from the base camp to join us.

"The first area we came to was what we believe to have been, for want of a better word, a 'computerized' command post. We were most pleasantly surprised to discover that it was room temperature inside once we closed the outer doors. Whoever lived here had a pretty sophisticated operation going. Actually most of the machinery in the room was still warm and humming when we got there. Sadly, the last watch standers didn't live long enough to greet us formally. Their remains are there on the floor.

"We quickly tagged 'em and bagged 'em and moved them outside to the plateau where we had camped. I had some cryogenic containers flown in to store them and eventually moved them back inside. Cousin Tallbear and his team of miracle workers can get to work on figuring out what they died of and when, and I'm sure he'll get back to you all later with that info.

"Antarctica was not quote discovered unquote until the early 1800s, although we do have maps going back to the 14th century that show a land mass down there. Never could figure that one out. What we do know, or have always surmised, is that the place was always there and was always covered with ice.

"Obviously we have to do some re-thinking. I mean no cowboy in his right mind is going to stake his claim in territory that had such a foreboding environment.

"Anyhow, here we are inside a cavern full of computers surrounded by a very cold place. By the way, we got there in late September just before the beginning of the Antarctic summer, if you can call it that, and most of the time we were outside the temperature hovered around -5 degrees. That's pretty chilly no matter how you slice it. But inside it was a comfortable 68.

"The technical team examined the machinery and after a few days of following connections, determined that it all ran on geothermal energy. The occupants had drilled way down into the earth's crust and had tapped into a source that could provide heat and electricity indefinitely. The whole place was lit with artificial lights not unlike light emitting diodes.

"Now these computers only barely resemble the Macs that y'all are all using. But there is enough of a resemblance that we can understand how data is put in and retrieved. The problem is that with what we have found, it all appears to be gibberish. But it is not so foreboding a challenge to break the code. I mean it's not like some Martian arriving and trying to figure out what the basic New Yorker is saying. It's more like some Oxford Don trying to figure out what I'm saying. It all boils down to mathematics, the common tongue of the universe.

"I think that with some of the smart old cryptologist boys and girls we just sent down there, we can have the system up and running in no time."

"Y'all got any questions about this before I continue the travelogue?"

Before anyone could speak, Madison Tolles said, "Let's hold questions until the end and hear all of what Dr. Kinoshi has to say."

"Why thank you, sir. I appreciate it very much.

"Moving along, we come to another entrance. Cracked the code on this one, too. Beyond door number two we find the entrance to the city below. In a massive network of caves, there's a city with an estimated 50,000 dwellings, all pretty basic, nothing fancy, mind you. But they all had hot and cold running water, and indoor plumbing. And it still works. The plumbing was pretty interesting in itself. Apparently with that density of people all crammed below ground, they figured out how to dispose of the waste without stinking up the joint too much. Once you flushed the john, it all went into a chamber where it was vaporized with high intensity electronic current. Damnedest thing I ever saw.

"We didn't have a lot of time to do the detailed exploring that we wanted to before I was recalled to the land of sunshine and green trees, but my team continues its work and will be sending detailed reports daily. But we did get to look at pretty near all the darned place before I left. Let me run down the basics of what we found.

"Off to the side of one of the city dweller caverns, there was door number three. Beyond door number three was another series of caverns that had a different kind of almost natural but artificial light. It was almost like stepping out into the sunlight. We determined that this was sort of their Riviera where they could go and get simulated sunlight. We're trying to figure out how they pulled that one off.

"Back in the city caverns, further along, we found door number four and that led us to their "farms," if that's what you want to call them. We discovered the most elaborate, and now hugely overgrown, hydroponic gardens we could ever imagine. I mean, there were tomatoes the size of basketballs down there. This is where they grew all their food, except for the fish. That was door number five, adjacent to the hydroponic farm. Through Door Number Five was a huge cavern that was really a major lake fed by fresh water sources, apparently from well below the surface.

"A couple of other things. On the side of the city opposite the farm, we discovered an enormous burial ground. We exhumed a couple of bodies, and lo' and behold, we seem to have come up with the same folks that cousin Tallbear has found.

"As we moved through the city, most interesting were the murals, and these weren't cave drawings either, none of that graffiti stuff you see in New York. Throughout the city were beautifully crafted murals depicting the Great Pyramid at Giza, Stonehenge, the Sphinx, Newgrange in Ireland, and a whole lot of other places. Heck, the things looked more like photographs than painted art. Damned if they weren't impressive.

"Well, I'm getting dried out talking to y'all. What questions do you have for me?"

The audience of 150 specialists sat there stunned by the images they had just seen. It took a moment before someone said, "Who the hell were these people?"

•   •   •

After the morning briefing with Chuck Kinoshi, the group broke for lunch. Johanna Ring directed them all to be back in the auditorium by 2:00 to begin the planning for the remainder of the operation.

At 2:00 promptly, Madison Tolles directed that the doors be closed and began the planning conference. He introduced Ben Crowley as the facilitator of the planning process, much to everyone's surprise.

"Ben Crowley probably has more experience than anyone in this room in planning support for big time operations. As both a Gunnery Sergeant and later as First Sergeant in the Marine Corps, his specialty assignment was Logistics and Operations Planning Chief for expeditionary units of more than 2000 Marines deploying to various parts of the globe. I am leaving you in his most competent hands to prepare a plan that will support a much larger and longer deployment to Antarctica. I will be in and out of the sessions and will be back mid-morning tomorrow to get a progress brief. Ben?"

"Thanks, Skipper," growled Ben. "Ladies and gentlemen, our mission is to launch the most comprehensive and important treasure hunt in the history of the planet. The structure for the operation is laid out for you in the folders, as well as on the computer screens in front of you. The division of our labor is as follows: Administration; Intelligence/Security; Operations; Logistics; Planning and Policy; C4 -- Command, Control, Communications, and Computers; and External Relations and Coordination. There are subdivisions in each section.

"I know each of you has been involved in planning small team deployments in support of various Denver Center interests. This is different by a magnitude of 1000. We will be sending hundreds of experts from a variety of different fields to an alien and forbidding territory. This territory, despite global warming, still has major logistics challenges for us. As you saw in this morning's briefing, it is minus 5 degrees out there, it is mountainous, and it is icy. Section assignments and roles are spelled out in the folders in front of you. Your mission is to develop a plan for each individual section that is detailed down to the last toothbrush, band-aid, toilet paper roll, and pair of socks you will need to support the overall mission.

"If your team needs experts that are not on the staff at the center, we need their names, contact information, shoe size, hat size, favorite toothpaste and every other detail you can think of. We will then begin the process to clear them for contact and subsequent invitation to join us.

"Our mission is to mount a serious expedition that will land in Antarctica no later than December 1 and stay there until the end of February. These are the optimal months for doing some serious exploration.

"Over the next few hours you will determine what your technical, logistical support, and transportation requirements will be. Medical support for the entire operation will be managed and planned for by the Logistics team.

"It is now 1420 -- 2:20 in the afternoon. Break out into your individual teams and be prepared to be back here at 2000 -- 8:00 tonight to give a preliminary brief. I will arrange for food to be sent in so you can work through dinner. Each section's presentation must be held to 15 minutes. Our goal is to have the foundation of an operational plan ready for delivery by tomorrow at 7:00 in the morning, and a final plan to be approved by noon. Remember, when you have thought of everything, there are still a hundred details you have forgotten.

" Let's get cracking."

As the group began to leave the conference room, suddenly Johanna called them back.

"Hold on group. I want you to see the latest message from Antarctica."

Everyone returned to the computer monitors to see the following message:

"WHEN DOING YOUR PLANNING, WE WILL NEED SOME CONCERT TRAINED MUSICIANS AND MUSICAL THEORISTS THROWN IN WHO ALSO ARE COMPUTER EXPERTS, PLUS AN ARTIST WHO KNOWS SOMETHING ABOUT COLOR RELATIONSHIPS. OUR INITIAL ATTEMPTS AT CRACKING THE CODE OF THEIR LANGUAGE PRODUCED A LENGTHY AUDIO. WE'VE DETERMINED THAT THEY COMMUNICATED BY SINGING. COMPUTER DISPLAYS ALSO HAVE VIVID COLOR COMBINATIONS THAT SEEM TO BE AN EXTENSION OF SOUND WAVES UP ABOVE THE AUDIBLE SPECTRUM. END TRANS."

The next morning, Ben Crowley was pleased. The initial briefings on the operational plan went fairly well. He challenged each plan to add the additional support requirements to complete the mission: travel and transportation, electronic support, communications requirements, security, food, clothing, shelter, waste disposal, medical, and a myriad of other topics.

The mid-morning's briefing to Madison Tolles went even better, and by noon, the exhausted teams had nailed down a draft of the final plan. Ben told them to get some sleep and be prepared over the next day or two for final modifications to the basic plan.

Tolles called Ben, Johanna, Chuck, and Gordon to a late afternoon meeting that same day.

"Our government masters are nudging their way into our tent. And they are bringing the rest of the world with them. We are going to have to meet with them two days from now at a secure hideaway retreat in Virginia. Apparently some observant folks from some of our traditional allies have noticed that something is afoot in Antarctica, and they want in. Ben, you must stay here and complete the planning."

Gordon said, "Well, that was inevitable."

Ben responded with, "Yeah, but at what price?"

There is a capacity of virtue in us; and there is a capacity of vice to make your blood creep.
Ralph Waldo Emerson

Chapter 6

Ambassador Sir Winslow Harrington, was everything you could loathe in a man. Born into what once was a fabulously wealthy family, he was the beneficiary of hereditary titles passed down to each first-born male child going back to the 17th century. Back then Cedric Harrington, a captain under Oliver Cromwell, slaughtered 3500 Irish farmers - men, women, and children - in a "battle" for land in western Ireland. Cedric's reward was a title and extensive land holdings in both Ireland and England.

The current title-holder faced a challenge that his forebears did not: foreclosure of the family estate in Surrey.

In simple terms, the Harrington family was broke.

The last of their estates was now rented out as a first class bed and breakfast for upscale travelers who wanted a touch of "authentic" English manor life. The Irish estates were long-gone, sold to creditors, and now owned by an American hotel chain that promised the "real Irish experience."

Sir Winslow was not amused, in fact he was incensed by the occasional snickering he heard in the halls of Parliament and at his private club (where, to add to his misfortune, he was three months behind on his dues). He discovered that his political enemies were calling him "Bed and Breakfast" Harrington, or B and B for short.

His father had squandered the family inheritance -- all, that is, save a modest but secure trust -- on a combination of bad investments and disreputable women.

Winslow Harrington had a childhood of ease and indulgence. He and his younger sister Eugenia, two years his junior, wanted for nothing, save affection. With private tutors at their disposal through age 10, they were each given a classic education. Private boarding schools followed. An endless procession of nannies ensured their good manners and upbringing while their parents found interests elsewhere.

His father, Sir Nigel, gambled, indulged himself in a succession of women, and largely kept himself absent from the remaining family estate. His mother found refuge in the company of bohemian artists, and fancied herself as a leader in London society. Their infrequent cameo appearances at home had a devastating effect on Eugenia, who at age 16 had a complete breakdown after over-indulging on sex and drugs. At age 19 she was institutionalized for her own safety shortly after her mother died as the result of years of alcohol abuse.

Winslow was not immune to emotions. When he was little he often ran off into the woods where he wept shamelessly at the neglect he felt. Unlike his sister, he hid his emotions from everyone. By the age of 10 he had begun to develop a thick skin and started to become a shrewd survivor. Raised loveless, he sought validation and approbation through rugged athletics. He excelled at soccer and rugby, playing both sports viciously, often leaving his opponents seeking medical help. At 14 he immersed himself in polo and within a few years had become an expert player.

When he was 15, his father died insane, apparently from an untreated case of syphilis. That same year Winslow had his first sexual encounter - an event that left his young partner bruised about the throat. His mistreatment of women over the next few years became more refined as he studied the methodologies readily available to him through various books and on-line resources on sadomasochism. Once he came of age, he discretely frequented several exotic private clubs in London that had a willing membership of submissive women.

When his mother died, he didn't shed a tear. He had spent years teaching himself not to.

Academics always came easily to Winslow, and never seemed to interfere with his extracurricular activities. He graduated near the top of his class and was readily accepted to Cambridge.

After Cambridge, where he majored in international relations, Winslow took his officer's commission and served in the British army on active duty for four years. Leaving the service as a Captain, and on the advice of his mother's brother, whom he respected, Winslow began his political career as a member of the House of Lords. He soon found out that he had a talent for the subtleties and infighting of politics, and rose to some prominence in Parliament.

He entered into a marriage of convenience with the heiress of a modest fortune, but was forced to sign a prenuptial agreement that limited his share of the inheritance. Nonetheless, he married her because it would be beneficial to his career.

As the Conservative Party's star was in the ascent, he won appointment to a series of ministries, and finally to the position of Ambassador to the United States. Despite the fact that Harrington was anything but diplomatic, the conservative government appointed him to this position as payback to the U.S. for not backing the Brits in their East African entanglement two years before.

Haunting his every step, however, was the specter of financial ruin. The trust fund provided not nearly enough to support his lifestyle. One day, a few weeks before he took his position as ambassador, he left his office early. As he was heading for his car, a well-dressed, but very ordinary looking man approached him. The man described himself as "an emissary of wealthy interests," and explained that his employers had been watching Harrington's career with great admiration and they were prepared to make him a lucrative offer. He asked if the ambassador would be interested in a business meeting.

Harrington was curious to know about these people and what their interest was in him, but the emissary was vague as to specifics. The man said that someone would be in touch to schedule the meeting. Excusing himself, the man vanished into pedestrian traffic.

Harrington would welcome an opportunity to become wealthy again, and was intrigued enough to want to believe that the stranger might really represent some kind of financial opportunity. On the other hand, he wondered whether the man was a crank.

Later that night, as he was leaving his mistress's flat, his cell phone rang. He looked at the number and did not recognize it. He answered with his usual abrupt "Harrington." There was a pause on the other end, and a slightly accented voice said, "If you are interested in accumulating a great deal of wealth in exchange for a few favors, get into the limousine that is pulling up in front of you." The call ended abruptly.

A black stretch Mercedes pulled up to the curb. An athletic looking young man in a dark suit got out of the passenger side, and walked to the rear door and opened it, saying nothing. Harrington paused for a second, and entered the vehicle. The door closed with a reassuring solidity, and the limo moved off into the night.

He sat in the back of the darkened limousine, having second thoughts. The opaque glass shield between driver and passengers was closed. After a few minutes he heard a voice coming through a speaker near his ear. The voice said, "We will be at our destination in about ten minutes, sir. I hope you find the ride pleasant."

In precisely ten minutes, the limousine pulled up to the garage entrance of a high-rise building. On electronic command, the door opened and the limo passed into the darkened garage. At the foot of a long ramp, the car stopped. The young man opened Harrington's door and said, "Please follow me." He walked over to a non-descript looking door along the middle of one of the garage walls. Taking out a plastic card, he slid it into a camouflaged slot. The door slid open and the young man stepped into an elevator, beckoning Harrington to follow.

The trip was soundless and smooth which only increased Harrington's anxiety. What have I opened myself up to?, he wondered. His heartbeat seemed to rise with the ascending elevator. His arrogant self-assuredness had deserted him. His escort's face was expressionless. At the top floor, the door slid open and the young man motioned Harrington to move into the suite. As the elevator closed behind Sir Winslow, he hesitantly took a few steps forward.

The suite was spectacular. The furnishings were elegant and the walls were lined with priceless art. With wall-to-wall floor-to-ceiling windows on two sides, there was a stunning vista of London at night. In a "conversation pit" area in front of a huge working fireplace, four expensively dressed middle-aged men were being served drinks by a liveried butler. A fifth man stood silhouetted in front of the windows. His motionless shadow at first gave Harrington the impression that he was a cardboard cut-out.

"Please come in, Sir Winslow," said a powerful looking man in his mid-fifties. We have been looking forward to meeting with you. My name is Peter Wilson," he said extending his hand in greeting.

As Harrington moved toward them, they all rose to greet him. "Chang Ling," said the Asian gentleman, extending his hand.

"Johan Brimmer," said the man with the accent Harrington recognized from the phone call. Maybe Swiss.

"Ephraim Fontaine," said the Frenchman.

Harrington turned to the last man who had stepped into the light of the conversation pit. The man, slender and tall, was monochromatic – black suit, shirt, tie and shoes. He had jet black hair and piercing black eyes. Harrington had no clue as to the man's age. Offering his hand, the man said, "Seth Tilcotan." When Harrington shook Tilcotan's hand, it felt like ice.

Just then the butler arrived silently at Harrington's elbow and whispered, "Bombay Gin and lemon with a touch of tonic. I understand it is your preferred drink." He handed him the drink and left the room. Harrington stood there with drink in hand, quite dumbfounded.

"Gentlemen," said Harrington, "I am just a little overwhelmed with all of this. Would you tell me why I am here?"

"You are here," said Peter Wilson, "because you smell money."

The others laughed and returned to their seats.

"These capitalists generally act harmoniously and in concert to fleece the people."

Abraham Lincoln

In fairy tales, gnomes live underground, counting their riches in secret.
The gnome has a subterranean lifestyle. He moves through the earth as easily as humans walk on it. Legend has it that if they are touched by the sun's rays, they turn to stone.

Wikipedia on-
line encyclopedia

Chapter 7

Please, Sir Winslow," said Mr. Fontaine, "Have a seat."

Harrington sat in the proffered seat, an overly soft armchair with its back to the fireplace. The chair not only seemed to want to swallow him, but also was noticeably shorter than the furniture of his hosts. He tried to pull himself forward so that he was at least sitting on the forward edge. Facing him on the couch across a wide coffee table were Chang and Fontaine. Brimmer had taken a chair to their left. Tilcotan had withdrawn to the windows where he stood as a dark sentinel. Wilson sat on a straight-backed chair to Harrington's right.

Ignoring Harrington's discomfiture, Wilson spoke. "We are the directors of, shall we say, an ad hoc consortium representing and advocating for the interests of the wealthiest international financiers and industrialists in the world. We provide our clients - and sometimes governments - with advice and guidance as to courses of action they should take to ensure ongoing prosperity for themselves and their shareholders.

"The point is that historically we have influenced the instigation of wars, and subsequently gained financial control over the warring countries through manipulation of the substantial debts they have incurred. Our goal is to ensure that the ruling elites of these countries stay in power. Where instability of governments and insurrection serve our investment purposes, we encourage it. Where peace and stability are best required, we encourage that.

"Our group thrives on inside information. There is nothing like the threat of public exposure as a most useful tool in bending one's will to our purposes. That is where we believe you, Sir Winslow, as Britain's newly appointed Ambassador to the United States, can be of service. And we, of course, will provide handsome remuneration for the right information. Your predecessor, unfortunately, lacked your, shall we say, drive for financial success. He also was not very bright, so we never attempted to recruit him. In addition to your desire for wealth, you have the sufficient intelligence to be of value to us."

"How long have you been doing this?" asked Harrington.

Again they all laughed.

"We have been doing this for centuries, Sir Winslow. We are a very secretive group, and each of us has been carefully selected to serve in this capacity by our predecessors. Our service is for life. We have been referred to, unfortunately, as the Gnomes of Zurich, a most unpleasant reference suggesting that we are evil underground creatures who hijack governments and count our money in secrecy. But all we really do is ensure that the economic wheels keep turning."

Wilson paused and looked toward Tilcotan who nodded his head for him to tell the full story.

He continued, "The United States of America has traditionally been our most serious challenge. Too much about that country is unpredictable, and the current administration is not disposed to comply with our wishes.

"From the mid 1800s through the early 1930s, we had great success in manipulating and gaining financial control over the US economy. With its great-unwashed immigrant class doing the dirtiest work for the emerging industries, our financial control was assured. The greed of the robber barons worked in our favor. But the unfortunate rise of the unions and the availability of the American stock market to the common investor created near disaster for us. We were unprepared for the sudden collapse of the market in 1929 following the rampant speculation of the masses. Franklin Roosevelt's rise to power in 1933 was a further blow to our ambitions. He was one of the rare ones who were immune to our influence. He was a disgrace to his class.

"Enamored by the fascist leaders of Europe -- Hitler, Mussolini, and Franco-- we saw their efforts as a model from which we could build our fortunes. We envisioned three global spheres of influence – Europe, Japan, and the Americas. We almost were able to organize an overthrow of the US Government in the mid-1930s and install a fascist regime. The US had 500,000 disgruntled World War I veterans who had been denied their bonus for serving in the war. When this 'Bonus Army' went to Washington to protest in 1930, they set up huge tent camps with their families and begged to meet with President Hoover. The President wanted nothing of the confrontation and turned the matter over to the Chief of Staff of the Army, Lieutenant General Douglas MacArthur, who promptly mounted up a battalion of soldiers and forcibly drove the protesters out of Washington. Unfortunately, in the general's zeal a great number of women and children were trampled and killed. These war veteran protesters were all members of the American Legion.

"We perceived an opportunity unprecedented in American history. We arranged through the very conservative heirs of the robber barons to assist in financing this potential revolutionary army to take action following an arranged political coup after the 1936 elections. We had already set the stage so that the President would be forced to resign and a more amenable Vice President would take office.

Unfortunately we chose the wrong candidate to lead this half-million man army to enforce this takeover. We knew that General MacArthur would never be accepted as the leader of our army. His actions against the bonus army assured that. Instead, we chose two-star Major General Smedley Butler, US Marine Corps, two-time Medal of Honor recipient, to lead the revolutionary army. His reputation as a troops' general made him an excellent choice, and his politics were conservative. Butler was an inspired choice for many reasons. He was twice awarded the Medal of Honor and his troops adored him. His subsequent betrayal killed our plans. To our regret he told the whole story to the House Un-American Activities Committee.

"President Roosevelt quietly contacted each of the American financiers backing our plan and told them that he was on to their game and had the power of a supportive Congress and a worshipful electorate behind him. Their financial ruin would be guaranteed if they pursued the matter any further.

"In spite of their massive greed, these kings of banking and industry thought it prudent to withdraw their support of our plan.

"We would have been delighted to have Hitler, Mussolini, and Tojo proceed with their plans for domination of their geographic spheres. It would have been a boon to our financial interests. Unfortunately Mr. Roosevelt was changing the experiment. He placed more and more economic power and education in the hands of what today would be defined as lower-middle class workers and the working poor. His decision to enter World War II threatened our position. The fact that America emerged not only victorious, but also magnanimous in victory, changed the rules of the game somewhat. We were at first alarmed by the US rebuilding both Germany and Japan. We had planned on capitalizing on their accumulation of massive debt. But our organization is nothing, if not flexible.

As it turned out, we greatly benefitted from these emerging economies, though not as much as we would have following German and Japanese victories. Our fortunes ebbed and flowed in the post-war years. In the 1960s, the Kennedy brothers and Martin Luther King would have put far greater economic power into the hand of the working class. We had to remedy that. But things ultimately began to look up.

"From 1981 through 1992, we thrived on the policies of the Reagan and elder Bush administrations. Deregulation was a boon to us and our growing clientele in both the carbon-based and nuclear industries. In the 1990s, President Clinton frustrated our ambitions by building a huge surplus after years of deficit. In 2000 our hopes rose again when we manipulated the electoral results in Florida thereby engineering the election of another conservative. That was a low cost investment for us that paid off handsomely. The new president was sufficiently dull intellectually, but had all the right intentions as far as we were concerned. Unfortunately he didn't have the political capital to implement them. We simply gave things a nudge by facilitating the funding of the Al Qaida attacks of 2001. As a result, by the end of the first decade of the new century, the US political system was almost totally controlled by the ruling elite. America was borrowing money from the Chinese to buy oil from the Arabs. US debt went right through the roof, and the fortunes of our clients did, too. Yet there were still the wild cards - the college dropouts who went on to become high-tech and dotcom billionaires. We have little influence with them as much as we have tried.

"The most recent administration has developed economic policies that stand in the way of our plans. That is why we must get ahead of the curve of American thinking.

"Our proposition, Sir Winslow, is simple. As ambassador to the United States, you will be privy to a wealth of political and economic information that would serve our interests and those of our clients. All you must do is provide us with the information we need, and in return, there will be a generously endowed, virtually bottomless, numbered off-shore account, completely untraceable, at your disposal for the foreseeable future. And as our gift to you just for having this meeting, we have cleared all your outstanding debts – to your club, to your tailor, and to the landlord of your mistress' apartment. Additionally we will gladly provide you with an endless supply of the kind of submissive women you prefer, as well as discreet locations where you can pursue your unusual pleasures.

"All we need is your solemn oath of loyalty, first and foremost to our organization. Then you will swear to eternal secrecy about our activities."

78

Sir Winslow Harrington was totally caught off guard by the final twist on their proposal. He realized immediately that he was compromised. The threat of public exposure would ruin him. And these men had the power to eliminate him. But they could restore his fortune.

He accepted their proposition.

A few days later, after some detailed instructions from his new masters, Ambassador Sir Winslow Harrington flew to Washington to assume his duties.

*Treat all men alike. Give them all the same law. Give them all an
even chance to live and grow. All men were made by the
Great Spirit Chief. They are all brothers.*

Chief Joseph of the Nez Perce in Washington, DC, 1879

Chapter 8

North America, 8,000 YEARS AGO

*Palen Golendar awoke with a terrible headache. He was
in an eight-sided leather hide shelter measuring about fourteen
feet across. There was a fire in the middle of the floor that vented
through an opening at the top of the shelter.*

*Across the shelter from him sat three men – one elderly
man and two younger men. They were all clad in what appeared
to be deerskins, and carried clubs in their leather belts. One of
the younger men brought a bowl over and placed it next to him.
Palen picked up the bowl and saw that it was some sort of soup
with vegetables and wild rice in it. He took a sip and was
immediately grateful.*

*Seeing his bag next to him, he pulled it over and opened
it. The translator device was still inside along with some other
items. He pulled the translator out and pushed a button. He sang
his thanks to the men for the soup.*

*Looking at him, they were surprised. They obviously
didn't understand him and spoke rapidly among themselves. His
translator device hummed quietly. One of the young men said
something directly to Palen. The translator converted it to
Palen's language. "Who are you and where do you come from?"
sang the translator in Palen's language. The men across from
him backed up in shock.*

*Palen sang, "I am Palen Golendar. I come from a land a
long journey many months to the south and across wide oceans
from here. I have come to seek your friendship." The translator
spoke his words in his captors' language, and the men were
amazed.*

80

After a while they gradually lost their fear and the conversation picked up speed. The men wanted to know what he saw on his journey and if he meant any harm to them. Gradually Palen started picking up the rhythm and cadence of their speech. As each of the teams deployed from Atlantis were composed of people who had a facility for picking up new languages, Palen sensed that he would be able to master their tongue in short order.

He said to them, "I have seen great beauty and great wonders, and I bring no harm to your people."

He was kept in this shelter for three weeks and questioned each day. When he indicated a need to relieve himself, they allowed him to do so. Taking him outside to the edge of the encampment, they always had him under the supervision of a young warrior.

While he waited, he communicated to his other two teams that he was a being held by one of the tribal groups and that they must obey the command to return to Atlantis without him. After sending that transmission, he received an alert on his communications device to switch to his family frequency.

He switched to the frequency and sent the coded signal. His father's voice came through the communicator singing to him the bad news that the people of Atlantis were to go underground for what might be centuries. He told Palen, "Within the next two weeks we will be sending the coded signals that will destroy our orbiting satellites. We are to leave no clue to our technologies on the surface so that the people of the earth can gradually develop on their own. The remainder of our technological legacy will be hidden in our mountain caverns to be discovered someday by one of the civilizations that has advanced itself. You must stay where you are and survive. Above all else, find an opportunity to destroy the communications device. If you are accepted into the culture of your captors, find a wife and have children. We must have someone to tell the story of our people."

They said goodbye, and Palen wept.

Soon Palen was able, on his own, to speak some basic words and simple sentences in the language of his captors. But he did not want to press the indentations on his communications device that would cause its destruction. He hoped on hope that he would hear from his family again.

Palen was a total mystery to these natives. Among the things that confused his captors was the fact that whenever they brought him food, Palen only ate the greens, fruit and tubers. He always left the meat in the bowl. At the end of his third week of confinement, Palen was brought from his shelter to a much larger lodge. He was being scrutinized by a council of tribal leaders.

"Palen Golendar," said one of the elders, "we do not know what to do with you. We have never had such a strange visitor come to our lands. Some in our councils say we should kill you and be done with you because you surely must be an evil spirit. Others suggest a more patient counsel. They want to know more about you and the strange land you come from."

Palen, speaking in a broken, yet understandable version of their language said, "Respected elders, I come only in peace. I have been sent by my people, the First People of the world, who have lived longer than all the people on earth. My mission is to know you and understand you, and to find ways where our knowledge can help you."

"Do not trust him!" shouted one young warrior. "When in our experience has anyone ever come to our lands except to kill our game and steal our women? He can be no different!"

"Be patient, Running Elk," said one of the other elders. "There will be plenty of time to kill him if we must. But even you, our most impatient warrior, must see that this man is different."

Palen responded, "I thank you for your counsel, Elder. In my land we revere the wisdom of our elders, we love our women and children, and we have learned to refrain from war making. As a result, my people have become great and live well and in harmony with the Earth. I ask only that I stay with you for a time to learn about you. Then someday I will return to my people and tell of the wonders I have observed. For what I have seen so far is that your land has an abundance of natural beauty, plentiful food from the earth, and clear waters that will last you forever."

One of the elders who had remained silent began to speak. Palen could see the deference that the others gave him. "I have three questions for our visitor. When you were captured, you were heard to be singing. You also sang when we first asked you questions. Why did you sing then and why not now? My second question is why, when we offer you food, do you not eat the meat of the deer and the rabbit? And third, do you, Palen Golendar, believe in the Great Spirit who we believe gives us such abundance?"

Palen answered, "To your first question I can only say that singing is the natural means of communications for my people. We have always sung our words even going back to generations that cannot be counted. As far as I know, that is the only way my people have ever communicated. We believe that song is the first language of the world, and that someday, all peoples will sing to communicate. But some of us, like myself and the people I have travelled with, have a gift for learning the other languages of the world. Now that I can speak a few words of your language, I do so to show my respect, put you at ease, and to let you know that I am a friend.

"To answer your second question, I say to you that my people only eat fish, vegetables, nuts, and fruits. Over several thousand years, our bodies have become so accustomed to this diet that the eating of animal flesh sickens us. As that is my custom, I must refuse the meat you give me. I mean no disrespect. I am grateful for your offerings, but I am simply unable to eat such food.

"As to your third question, yes, Oh Great One. We believe in the Creator who has given all good things to all the people of the world."

"Then you, Palen Golendar, may stay among us and be our guest for as long as you wish."

No act of kindness, no matter how small, is ever wasted.

Aesop

Chapter 9

Upperville, Virginia, is horse country and a rural playground of the rich. It is also home to three of the most secure safe houses in the world. All belong to the U.S. government.

Madison Tolles, Gordon, Johanna, and Chuck were housed in a beautiful French Provincial mansion. With a more than one-mile long driveway leading up from the two-lane country road, the estate sat on a hillside overlooking a pond bordered by a grove of trees. Behind the mansion was a beautiful Olympic sized pool, the walls of which were dark green veined marble. To the left of the pool, slightly downhill, was a sauna.

Beyond the pool, starting at about twenty feet up the hill on the right and flowing downhill to the left, was a seven-tiered garden. Each tier was bordered by carefully constructed stone walls. Down to the left the gardens culminated in a greenhouse full of exotic plants. At the very top of the highest garden on the right, a hot tub overlooked the gardens and rolling hills beyond the mansion.

About 300 yards to the west of the mansion was a stable where two young women and a middle-aged man were currying and feeding several horses.

The mansion had a staff of two men and two women who provided various housekeeping duties. The main kitchen was the domain of a cordon bleu chef and his assistant.

After settling in on a Thursday evening, the Denver Center group refined the presentations that they would be giving the next day at another nearby safe location.

At dawn on Friday, Gordon, dressed in blue jeans, a flannel shirt, and real moccasins -- calf high, soft buckskin leather crafted back at Pine Ridge -- was relaxing by wandering around the estate. It was a cool October morning. Leaves were just starting to turn their fall colors. In a few days this valley, like the one in Colorado, would be cloaked in shades of yellow, orange, and red. Gordon was up very early as was his habit, and he wandered over to the stables. He entered and asked if he could spend some time with the horses. The man who seemed to be in charge said, "Sure. Would you like to ride?"

Gordon quickly assented and they saddled a horse for him. It was an English style saddle, which Gordon had never used before, but he took the horse outside and mounted him and went off into the hills at a gallop. About a half-hour later he returned feeling renewed. It had been quite a while since he had ridden. He dismounted and stroked the horse, speaking to it in the Lakota language. The horse nuzzled him in turn and after a while he returned to the mansion.

On his stroll back to the mansion, Gordon enjoyed the beauty of the land and mused on the differences between the rolling hills of Virginia and the towering mountains of Colorado. After a while he entered the residence, took a quick shower, and joined the others for an Eggs Benedict breakfast.

Chuck Kinoshi observed, "Just like back on the res, isn't it, Tallbear?"

"Yeah, right," Gordon laughed.

Madison Tolles informed them that there would be a meeting of the minds at 10:00 at another mansion a few miles away, but it was to be an informal meeting and they were to remain in their casual clothes.

At ten o'clock a government driver brought them to the other safe house. They were guided to a large conference room. Awaiting them were the Secretaries of State, Defense, and Domestic Protection (the new title for the formerly ill-named Department of Homeland Security), the Directors of the CIA and FBI, the Canadian, Mexican, British, French, German, Italian, Russian, Chinese, Indian, and Japanese Ambassadors, four Senators, four Congressmen, and ten other people.

The meeting was hosted by the Vice President of the United States, Thomas Pemberton.

Chuck looked around the room and whispered, "Cousin, I think we've crossed into another dimension."

"Indeed we have, brother Kinoshi," whispered Tallbear, "indeed we have."

The vice president asked everyone to be seated and asked that each participant introduce him-or herself. When Gordon stood to introduce himself he could hear the British ambassador say to his nearest companion in a stage whisper, "Rather primitive looking chap." Gordon's face was inscrutable, showing no sign that he had heard.

Following introductions, the Vice President thanked everyone and turned the floor over to Madison Tolles who stood and said, "Thank you, Mr. Vice President. Honorable ladies and gentlemen, we are here today to present an extraordinary briefing on a discovery that could well change the world - *if we are wise enough to realize what is at stake*. This isn't about a private discovery, or an American discovery. It is about a discovery to benefit all mankind.

"For those of you who are unfamiliar with the Denver Center, or who know something about it but had to speculate on the rest, I will now share with you what the Center really is.

"The Denver Center is a Top Secret research facility, privately built and partially funded with federal grants. The Center's mission is to conduct research into the mysteries of our planet's past. My passion has been the mysteries of history. I have been fortunate in convincing both our federal partners and selected partners from corporate America to co-fund our efforts. I personally have invested a small fortune into this organization. An interesting by-product of the Center is that we hold many patents on new technologies we've developed that help the Center to be more self-sufficient and less reliant on outside funding.

"As an amateur historian by myself, I had, when I was much younger, learned of the great joint effort of Britain and the United States to create an espionage organization to defeat the Nazi regime. Our British friends had established a unique intelligence center at Bletchley, a research facility north of London. They brought brilliant minds together and unleashed them for the sole purpose of breaking the Nazi 'Enigma' code.

"Using Bletchley as my model, over the years I assembled a magnificent team of geniuses from many different disciplines, gave them broad guidelines as to what I was seeking, gave them the most sophisticated tools imaginable, swore them to eternal secrecy, and turned them loose.

"This, many of you will realize, is the equivalent of what we Americans call a "skunk works" -- an organization dedicated to simply finding new and interesting ideas, concepts and innovations. Our leading high-tech companies and many others have done just the same thing, and they have produced marvels of technology.

"I was seeking marvels of technology, make no mistake about it. But I was seeking more. My burning issue was to apply innovative thinking and technology to de-code the mysteries of the past, for I believe that there are great secrets there that can guide us into the future.

"As some of you may know, the Denver Center has spent much of the past few years analyzing information related to unusual archaeological and anthropological discoveries. First I will have Dr. Gordon Tallbear tell you about the recent discovery of the completely mummified remains of a man who was not of this continent, but who roamed this land nearly 8,000 years ago. Dr. Tallbear."

Gordon gave an eloquent presentation about the discovery of Badlands Bill as well as his team's study of the other 27 unclassifiable remains discovered worldwide. "The origins of these people have baffled anthropologists for years. But in the past few weeks since the discovery in Montana, we have determined where these wanderers came from, and more. As you will see in Dr. Kinoshi's upcoming presentation, an advanced people left its imprint on this planet more than five thousand years before what we traditionally consider early civilization.

As he concluded to respectful applause, he sat and Madison Tolles took the floor again.

"I know that the main reason you are here is to find out just what we have been doing in Antarctica. A month or so prior to the discovery in Montana, for the fourth year in a row, we had deployed a thirty person team to Antarctica to heretofore unexplored mountain areas. Dr. Charles Kinoshi will now brief you on that mission. Dr. Kinoshi."

As usual, Chuck overwhelmed the audience with both his folksiness and the stunning array of images he brought back with him from Antarctica. He concluded his remarks with the now confirmed DNA evidence that the remains of the cavern's inhabitants were a genetic match for Badlands Bill and the 27 other previously unidentified remains. The crowd response was overwhelming with people applauding and shouting questions.

Tolles motioned the crowd to silence saying, "The bottom line, ladies and gentlemen, is that we are on the cusp of discoveries that can change the world. What their full import and impact will be is anyone's guess at this point, and obviously just the fact that an ancient civilization lived on this planet with advanced technology is mind boggling. We are happy to share with you what we have discovered thus far. As Dr. Kinoshi has indicated, these people had made major advances in science, energy efficiency, and hydroponic agriculture. The fact that they have harnessed geothermal energy so efficiently as to heat and power a city of 200,000 is a quantum leap beyond what we are capable of doing today.

"The implications are enormous. We have uncovered connectivity between Antarctica and the discovery of ancient human remains worldwide. As preposterous as it may sound, Antarctica may be the lost continent of Atlantis. The unusual human remains may be explorers deployed from Atlantis to explore the world. Ancient myths claim this, and now we may be able to find the link that separates myth from reality.

"The real issue is, of course, the technologies we are discovering and what applications they may have for us today and in the future."

The Russian ambassador rose, "What is to become of all this technology you are discovering? Is it not to be shared with the world?"

Madison Tolles paused for a second before answering, "The short answer is both yes and no. The long answer is that if my research team in Antarctica is correct, the capabilities of at least some of the technology could be two-edged. What I am saying is that there is staggering potential for its peaceful uses, and there is also staggering potential that the discoveries could also be used for belligerent purposes. We must be very cautious about what is to be shared and how it is to be shared."

And that unleashed a firestorm of shouted questions. The vice president finally rose and held out his arms to quiet everyone down. "Ladies and gentlemen, please, please take your seats and ask your questions in an orderly fashion. And keep in mind that much of what is discussed today will not be resolved for weeks, maybe even months. This is new territory for all of us."

Gradually they all resumed their seats, but then, suddenly, the British ambassador stood up.

Winslow Harrington said, "Can it possibly be that our American friends are going to keep this all to themselves? Can it be that America will only dole out its discoveries like a miser handing out pennies to the needy? Perhaps it is time for America to realize that she cannot treat her allies in such a cavalier fashion. I propose that we set up an international commission, led by the British because of our traditional sense of fair play, and we will decide the best use of these discoveries."

Immediately the French ambassador objected and demanded immediate access to all the discoveries.

The German ambassador suggested that the French would hand everything over to the Saudis because the Saudis would threaten to cut off the oil supply to the French.

The French ambassador hinted, not too subtly, that too much power in certain hands could de-stabilize the world.

The meeting threatened to degenerate into chaos until the vice president once again gaveled the meeting to order.

Harrington shouted, "Hear! Hear! Gentlemen, this is the obvious reason that the British should have a leadership role. It is hardly seemly that the disposition of such marvels should be left to the discrimination of our American friends, no matter how well-intentioned are Madison Tolles and his esteemed, if rustic, American Indian colleague from … South Dakota."

"That is certainly enough, sir," said the vice president. "And I am not sure I like the tone of your comments, Mr. Ambassador."

"My humblest apologies, sir. I certainly meant no offense to our learned colleagues."

"Very well," said the vice president. "I would like to meet privately this evening with the American Congressional delegation. Tomorrow afternoon at our next session, we move this discussion forward. And I do mean forward, ladies and gentlemen. I will not tolerate the outbursts we had today. And furthermore, ladies and gentlemen, if one word of this meeting leaks to the press, the United States of America will close off all discussions and proceed unilaterally as it sees best."

With that, the chastised delegates left the meeting and went their separate ways. After the room emptied, Tolles asked the Vice President and the directors of the FBI and CIA if they could see him in private for a moment.

When they were alone, Madison Tolles made an astonishing suggestion. "Gentlemen, we are dealing with the most delicate issues here. I believe that the discoveries in Antarctica can be of great benefit to the world. However, I believe also that there will be no shortage of attempts to breach our security. Secrecy is our most valuable ally here, and until we delve deeper into the mysteries of Antarctica, we must proceed with utmost caution. We must be assured that the participants in this conference, and any conferences we have in the future, do not share their information with anyone else."

The FBI Director said, "Are you suggesting, Mr. Tolles, that we monitor ambassadors and leaders of Congress?'

"Yes sir, I am saying just that."

The Vice President interrupted the conversation and said, "Madison, what you are proposing is a serious breach of protocol. With certain noted historical exceptions, we don't usually bug ambassadors' residences. As for members of Congress, there will be a firestorm of criticism, not to mention the threat of cutting funding, if we bug their residences. Let me take this up with the President. For now, good day gentlemen." And with that he ended the meeting.

Fear is the path to the Dark Side.

Yoda

Chapter 10

Sir Winslow called the number that he had memorized following his first meeting with the 'Gnomes.' When the phone was answered, he simply said, "We should meet to talk about polo." The voice at the other end said, "I look forward to it." Winslow waited 15 minutes until his phone rang. He let it ring twice, and waited. No third ring.

He took a cab to Union Station, got out, went inside, left by another entrance, and took a different cab to Arlington to what locals referred to as 'The Lagoon.' The Lagoon is the public park just beyond the 14th Street Bridge in Arlington across an inlet at the north end of the Washington Reagan National Airport main runway.

He got out and walked to the designated picnic bench, sat down and waited. Within five minutes a portly, slightly disheveled man in khakis, dirty running shoes and a windbreaker walked casually down the bike path and sat down in front of him.

" You have something for us?" the man asked.

"Yes, I most certainly do," replied Sir Winslow.

With passenger jets in their final approach down the Potomac passing just above their heads in the North-South landing pattern, Harrington leaned close to the stranger and related everything about the top secret briefing in Virginia regarding the Antarctic discoveries.

The man listened to every word, not taking any notes or asking any questions. When Sir Winslow was finished, the man said, "Wait here for five minutes. A cab will come for you." And with that, he walked away up the bike path and out of sight.

Sir Winslow was sweating even though it was not a hot afternoon. In five minutes, a cab pulled up and the driver called over to him, "Need a cab?"

Back at the embassy, Sir Winslow spent the next several hours trying to keep busy with official paperwork. By late afternoon he had cleared up most of the paperwork. He returned to his quarters where he showered, shaved and changed into evening attire for the reception he was to attend at the French ambassador's residence.

At 7:30 Harrington called for his driver and proceeded to the reception. Upon his arrival he went through the usual formalities with the other attendees and had just begun to sip at his champagne when a strikingly handsome woman came up and introduced herself to him.

"I believe you are Sir Winslow Harrington?" she asked.

"Yes I am, and how have I managed not to meet you in the three months since I have been posted here?'

"I am a busy woman and don't usually get around to many of these functions. Why don't we find someplace quiet where we can get acquainted?'

"That would be my pleasure."

And with that she slipped her arm into his and guided him out onto the terrace. They walked for a few moments in silence when abruptly she turned him toward a set of French doors. He opened the door and she led him into a beautiful library. She turned to him and said, "I'll be back for you later," and exited through a door next to the fireplace.

Suddenly a voice behind him said, "Your first report was quite remarkable, Sir Winslow. Now we must determine what it all might mean."

Harrington turned to see Peter Wilson standing there.

Peter Wilson was a formidable presence. At age 58 he was still in top physical condition and was a man who was accustomed to his orders being followed to the letter. Just under six feet, his command presence made him appear much taller.

"Mr. Wilson, I did not expect to see you here."

"Sir Winslow, when we believe that there is some serious significance to the information we receive, we take immediate action. Otherwise we would schedule a more suitable and discrete meeting place. There is some risk to meeting with you here, but I believe the risk to be justified.

"We did a quick analysis of your Antarctica report and concluded that there is a potentially severe risk to the stability and continued growth of our oil, coal, and nuclear power clients and their investors. That would be very bad news indeed for our group. If all of this is to believed, these ancient people had power sources that were limitless.

"You are to stay as close to this situation as possible and keep us informed."

Peter Wilson turned and walked through the door by the fireplace. In a moment, the beautiful woman reappeared and escorted Sir Winslow back to the reception where she silently relinquished his arm and walked away.

Aggressive fighting for the right cause is the noblest sport the world affords.

Theodore Roosevelt

Chapter 11

Madison Tolles sent Chuck, Johanna and Tallbear back to the Denver Center to prepare for the next phase of the operation. He wanted Chuck and Tallbear to leave for Antarctica as soon as possible to oversee the explorations. Johanna was to remain in Colorado to coordinate the needs of the technology and anthropology teams. Tolles stayed in Washington, initially to be present for the second day of the conference. Nothing was resolved, and all parties agreed to wait and see what further discoveries would be forthcoming from Antarctica. They agreed to a follow-up meeting in the spring unless something urgent would require a conference in the shorter term.

His other mission in DC was to work out the details of funding requirements with the senior Congressional leaders. He would return to the center later in the week.

The Vice President had his hands full with the foreign delegations, trying to keep them at bay until some final planning could be done. As a prudent measure, he and Tolles met with the secretaries of State and Defense to plan out worse case scenarios in the event that other nations would attempt to encroach on the discoveries in Antarctica.

Back at the Denver Center, Tallbear and Chuck briefed their respective teams, screened new members recruited for specific technical purposes, and briefed them on the entire scope of discoveries to date. Tallbear again gave the newcomers a detailed briefing on the discovery of Badlands Bill and the mysterious device he carried. Chuck dazzled them with the Antarctic discoveries. Finally the teams were told to get ready to move out on 24 hours notice. Thirty members of Chuck's team were still in Antarctica, and another 15, including a music composer and an artist would go with Tallbear, Chuck, and

Johanna from the Center. Other augmentees to both teams would arrive within the next two weeks. They met with the logistics support team, now under the direction of Ben Crowley, and made two plans – one for a short-term 30 to 60 day deployment, and one for a year-long deployment.

As the departure day approached, Chuck was weary of all the preparations. While sitting at yet another planning meeting with Johanna, Tallbear, Ben Crowley and Madison Tolles, who had arrived five days after they did, he said, "Hey, I'm about filled up to here with all this planning. Before we all head to the frozen wasteland to the south, how 'bout we all get out of here for an evening and go get us some nice thick steaks. There's a great road house about five miles down the highway that grills a steak you could cut with a fork. It being a Tuesday evening, we should get good service as few people will be there."

"That, Dr. Kinoshi, sounds like the best idea of the day," said Tolles. "Ben? You in?"

"Steak and a beer sounds great to me, Skipper," growled Ben. He was the only person at the center who routinely referred to Mr. Tolles as 'Skipper.' "I'm getting bleary eyed with all these details."

Gordon and Johanna agreed, and early that evening Gordon and Chuck got into Johanna's hybrid four-wheel drive and headed out of the compound. Tolles and Ben got into Ben's specially equipped van and followed them. After making their way down the switchback, they turned right onto the two-lane country road. As they moved toward their destination, two vehicles with their lights off pulled out from a side road to follow them.

Within ten minutes they pulled up to the Silver Lode Tavern, a log cabin styled emporium sporting neon window signs promoting a popular regional beer. When they got out of their vehicles, Tolles and Ben discovered a minor technical problem with the van's chair lift. Ben said, "Go on in and get a table, we can fix this thing in a minute."

96

None of them paid much attention to the two vehicles that pulled in right after them. Six very rough looking men got out and entered the restaurant.

Tallbear, Chuck and Johanna went into the nearly empty tavern and proceeded to pull two tables together. A waitress came over with menus, placemats, tableware and napkins. "How y'all doin'?" she asked cheerily, while casting a suspicious eye on Tallbear. She had never seen an Indian in the place before. "I'm Melissa."

Melissa looked to be about forty. Probably a divorced single parent, Johanna thought, not unkindly, just as a simple observation.

"We're just fine, Melissa," said Johanna. "I hope you don't mind us pulling these tables together. We're expecting two other gentlemen, one in a wheelchair, in just a couple of minutes."

"Well, you just holler when you're ready to order," the waitress said as she walked away.

Chuck immediately started scrutinizing the menu while Tallbear and Johanna chatted. Suddenly their table was surrounded by the six tough guys.

"What's this?" said one of them. "A Jap and an Indian? It's bad enough we have to put up with the niggers, but no way should we have to share this place with a Jap and an Indian."

"I suggest you and your friends back off," Tallbear said quietly.

"Shut up, Tonto. When we want your opinion we'll ask for it."

"Now how about we buy you guys a beer and forget about everything?" said Chuck in his usual cheerful style.

""You can shut your yap, too, gook. And what about this tramp? What kind of whore goes out with a gook and a redskin?"

97

"Hey, hey," shouted the bartender. "Knock it off or I'm calling the police."

"You and the waitress stay out of it or you're going to get your asses kicked as well," the apparent leader shouted back. "And don't even think of picking up the phone." One of his confederates moved close to the bar to ensure that the orders were followed. The leader turned back to Tallbear, Chuck and Johanna.

Tallbear stood up and quietly said, "That's enough. Okay, bozo, what do you want? And leave her out of it."

"No, Gordon, forget about it. Let's go and find another place," said Johanna.

"Shut up, bitch. You ain't going nowhere until the redskin apologizes - to me and each of my friends."

Tallbear squared himself to the leader and said in a deadly quiet voice, "All right. I apologize to you, and I meant no offense to your scum sucking, slobbering, flea-bitten pack of white trash dogs."

Immediately, one of the men took a swing at Tallbear, who ducked the swing and brought the heel of his open palm down on the guy's nose. With the sound of crushing cartilage and a spurting of blood, the man at first backed away, and then charged Tallbear who stood motionless. As the man tried to deliver a right-hand punch, Tallbear suddenly spun in one smooth move, grabbing the man's right wrist. As the man's momentum carried him forward, Tallbear twisted his wrist clockwise and flipped his assailant over his head. As the man crashed down on a table, Tallbear did not relinquish his grip. The man's arm snapped like a branch and he tumbled, along with the remnants of the shattered table, to the floor in a howling heap.

While Tallbear dealt with the first man, Chuck leaped to his feet and kneed the second man in the groin. He dropped to his knees in agony.

Johanna backed away just as Madison Tolles and Ben Crowley were coming through the doorway. She grabbed a saltshaker and threw it at one of the men moving toward Tallbear. The man suddenly dodged and the projectile glanced off the side of Tallbear's head. She shrugged her shoulders as Tallbear gave her a bewildered look.

In the meantime, the other four split up so that there were two on Tallbear and two on Chuck. Tallbear started to duck away as one man feinted a punch. That was the signal for the other man to catch Tallbear on the side of his face with a solid blow. His ring left a deep gash along Tallbear's right cheekbone. Tallbear turned and hit the man in the solar plexus and the man went down on one knee. As he was struggling to his feet, Johanna grabbed a chair and brought it down his back, finishing him.

Chuck fell to the floor after one of his assailants hit him on the side of the head. Chuck lay there, struggling for consciousness while his two attackers started moving in on Tallbear who was circling to keep them from rushing him all at once. One charged him and bulldogged Tallbear to the floor. The others immediately pounced and dragged Tallbear to his feet. One man held him while the other delivered a cascade of punches. Another man pulled out a knife.

Suddenly the knife wielder went flying backwards in an almost complete flip. Ben Crowley, propelled by a lunging push from Madison Tolles, had gotten up to speed in his wheelchair and smashed into the man from behind. At the same time, Ben grabbed the belt of the man who was punching Tallbear and spun him to the floor. Ben rolled out of his wheelchair and proceeded to beat the man senseless.

Madison Tolles grabbed the one that Ben had flipped, kicked the knife away, and violently stomped on the man's instep, producing a howl of pain. Pulling the man up by the hair, he punched him in the throat. The man dropped, choking and gasping for air.

Tallbear swung the one holding him until he crashed into the end of the bar and slipped to the floor. He grabbed the other one and unloaded a solid punch to the man's face that left him unconscious. The other one got to his feet and squared off against Tallbear, who feinted a right hand jab, then delivered three solid lefts to his face. The man staggered back, blood streaming from his nose as Tallbear moved in and delivered a right to the man's jaw that spun him down the bar. Then a second right and the man was barely clinging to the bar. The third right drove the man straight to the floor where he lay unconscious and bloody.

Chuck had come around and was just standing up when the man he kneed in the groin grabbed him and tried to pull himself up. In a flash, Chuck brought the sides of his hands straight down breaking both of the man's collar bones. With the man's arms hanging uselessly at his sides, Chuck grabbed him by the shirtfront and dragged him to his feet. Balling his right fist with the thumb sticking upward, Chuck jabbed him in the solar plexus and the man went once again to his knees. A solid right to his jaw dropped the man to the floor.

The whole incident was over in a few minutes.

Tallbear, Chuck, and Tolles picked up Ben and lifted him back into the chair that Johanna had righted.

The bartender gave Johanna a towel and some ice, which she applied to Tallbear's cheek.

By then the police and the EMTs had arrived. As soon as the fight started, Melissa had dialed 911. It took a half-hour or so, but with the testimony of the waitress and the bartender, the police sorted it all out and cuffed the six men and took them away – three of them to the hospital. The leader shouted at them, "We'll sue your asses for this."

Chuck shouted back, "What? You're going to sue a computer programmer, an anthropologist, a man in a wheelchair, a woman, and a middle aged executive for kicking your asses? Piss off, you white trash summmbitches."

Before the police left, Madison Tolles had a long talk with the officer in charge. They saw Tolles give the officer his card.

A medical assistant with the EMTs repaired the gash on Tallbear's cheek with several stitches. He also applied salve and bandages to Ben's and Tallbear's knuckles, and stitched up the gash inside Chuck's hairline. He gave Chuck and Tallbear booster tetanus shots.

The tavern owner had been called, and when he arrived, he said, "What the hell happened here, and who is going to pay for the damages?"

Madison Tolles stepped forward and said, "I will pay for everything..."

Gordon and Chuck immediately interrupted him. Tallbear said, "No, Mr. Tolles. *We* will pay for everything, me and Chuck."

Ben growled, "Hell, let's just split the tab four ways. We all had a part in it."

Tolles laughed, and turned to the tavern owner. "Will that be all right?"

"Don't forget me," said Johanna.

"Okay, five ways."

The tavern owner shrugged his shoulders and said, "Sounds all right to me as long as your checks are good."

"All right, then," said Tolles. "Now, while we go and wash up, is there any chance of getting a good steak and a beer?"

Johanna said, "I can't believe you guys. You were just involved in a major brawl and you still want your steak and beer."

"Welcome to guy world, Johanna," said Ben.

The four men went to clean up, and as they were headed for the restroom, Ben asked, "My only experience has been with Marines. Do all you PhDs fight like that?"

Without missing a beat, Chuck said, "Look at this face, Ben. Don't you think I might know something about the martial arts? And despite what you Marines might think, MIT and Harvard are no places for sissies."

101

"And what about you, Doc?" Ben continued looking at Tallbear. "Did you learn all that at Harvard Yard?"

"I used to watch a lot of westerns, and I picked up a lot from the bar fight scenes," Tallbear blandly answered.

Ben shook his head realizing it would be useless to press the issue further.

While they were gone Johanna righted a couple of tables and chairs. When the men came back, Melissa came over once again to set them up with menus, placemats, tableware and napkins.

"I sure am sorry about what happened," she said. "And I am particularly sorry, ma'am for what they said to you and to you two gentlemen. And, guys, I am embarrassed that you should be insulted because of your ethnic background. I have seen you here before, sir," she said to Chuck. "You come in here with the computer guys every once in a while. It has always been a pleasure serving you all. You computer guys are a little crazy when you come in to let off steam, but you are well-behaved. The locals like you, too, because whenever you come in you always buy a round or two for the house."

"Melissa," said Tallbear, "you are a real lady. Thank you for your concern."

Melissa blushed deeply and said, "Can I get you all something to drink?"

"Beers all around," said Ben.

"Not for me," said Tallbear. "Just some lemonade or iced tea."

"Sorry, Doc, I forgot," said Ben.

"Not a problem."

They ordered their steaks, and while they waited, Madison Tolles filled them in.

"I asked the officer in charge to be sure to get fingerprints and contact the FBI. From what both the bartender and Melissa said in their statements, these guys were not from around here. This is a place for locals. I'll talk with our FBI friends in the morning, but all of this looks like a set up. I think we are being targeted."

When they left, they combined to give Melissa a $500 tip.

In the parking lot, Johanna stopped them and said, "You all were magnificent. I felt like a princess whose honor was being fought over." She turned to Tallbear and, offering her hand, theatrically said, "This, Sir, you have won so nobly on the field of honor."

"Thanks, Johanna, but when you hit me with that salt shaker, I was beginning to wonder which team you were on."

They all had a laugh and got into their cars.

•   •   •

The following morning Madison Tolles briefed them.

"Our assailants last night were definitely not local. In fact, they barely knew each other. It turns out that they come from six different states. Their vehicles were rented under false names with bogus charge cards. In their motel rooms are pictures of the four of us. Their prints indicate that they are all known mercenaries. Early this morning lawyers showed up for all of them. High priced lawyers from one of Denver's largest firms. The FBI will take it from here. Now we need to alter the plan a little. I want all three of you out of the country as soon as possible. The next time our assailants will be chosen more carefully. Johanna, you can run the Denver Center and coordinate the teams' needs from down there."

It's never too late to be who you might have been.

George Eliot

Chapter 12

In a dark chamber, deep underground below a building in a major European city, a man dressed completely in black – mock-turtle neck shirt, sports coat, slacks, socks, and shoes – knelt, head bowed to the floor before a hideous winged effigy. Behind him thirty-four men stood expressionless despite the clammy dark coldness that permeated their bones. They had long ago cast their lot with Seth Tilcotan and his dark master in exchange for the promise of eternal life and riches beyond counting.

After a long period of obeisance, Tilcotan raised his head and nodded.

In a dark, ugly language that none of the others understood he said, "Thy will be done, Master. My adversary is near, and I welcome his threat. Soon I will destroy him and his followers and your darkness will be complete. We will watch the world turn itself into a cinder and the work of twelve thousand years will be complete.

"I am yours. I am yours. I am yours……"

He slowly turned and faced his associates. Rage smoldered deep inside of him as he focused on one man. His soul was filled with a dark ice that grew and grew, and grew …

"YOU CHOSE THESE CRETINS FOR THIS JOB!!' he screamed.

Johann Brimmer fell to his knees and stammered, "I – I – I just followed standard protocol, Mr. Tilcotan. I assumed that these were professionals and that they would deliver the appropriate message."

"YOU ASSUMED," screeched Tilcotan. 'You allowed a bunch of academics – and a woman, I might add – a supposed bunch of limp wristed academics, and a man in a wheelchair, no less -- to beat up on professional mercenaries. You failed completely! I am not happy, Mr, Brimmer, and the Master we serve decrees that you do extreme penance for your incompetence!"

Brimmer dropped to his knees in abject terror.

As Mssrs. Wilson, Chang and Fontaine looked on dispassionately, Seth Tilcotan leaped on Brimmer and tore his throat out with his teeth.

Rising from the shredded remains of their former colleague, blood and cartilage dripping from his mouth, Tilcotan began chanting in the dark tongue. The room got colder than ice, and his remaining colleagues dropped to their knees and placed their heads on the floor in complete fealty to the dark master to whom they had sold their souls.

After a short period of time, Tllcotan, stained with Johann Brimmer's blood, turned to his colleagues and calmly said, "This must never happen again."

•   •   •

That night, Tallbear awoke from a horribly graphic dream, simultaneously sweating and freezing. He knew his adversary was near, but neither place nor time was within his reach to tell him when or where he would strike.

At the same time, Johanna came out of a deep sleep and sat up straight in her bed feeling a terrible dread.

Madison Tolles and Chuck slept through the night, but with dreams of demons and unseen terrors that they could not escape.

.   .   .

Within a few days of the basement horror the defections began. Among the 30 second tier disciples who were in that underground chamber there was no shortage of greedy men. As amoral as they were, once Tilcotan slaughtered Brimmer and devoured his flesh before their eyes, several immediately decided to execute long contemplated escape plans.

Eleven of them had secret numbered offshore accounts across the globe ready for their use at just such a moment. Eight of them had plans to secretly disappear and live off their loot in exotic seclusion. Three were simply terrified to their core and made other plans.

One went to a Shinto temple in a remote area of Japan. One went to a Buddhist retreat in the mountains of northern India. The third found a remote Catholic monastery in Peru. When each made his case for sanctuary and explained the reason why, he was told that he would be accepted and forgiven if he gave up all his treasure to the poor, renounced Satan, turned to a spiritual life, and willingly embraced a life of poverty and prayer.

Only one accepted.

In the following weeks when Tilcotan realized that his following had been diminished he became consumed with rage. He vowed that before he had taken care of the Denver Center menace he would track these men down and make them pay dearly.

As the other ten would soon discover, you can't outrun the devil. And he left a messy trail.

The technology of any sufficiently advanced civilization is indistinguishable from magic.

Arthur C. Clarke

Fools rush in ... and get the best seats.

Alfred E. Newman, *Mad Magazine*

Chapter 13

By mid-November, with wounds now healed, Tallbear, Chuck, and Johanna were aboard a flight of two massive Air Force C-17F transport planes contracted from the federal government and headed south to New Zealand with their teams and 60 days worth of supplies. In New Zealand they unloaded cargo and transferred to the new, upgraded Hercules-3 CH-230 transports that were better equipped to land on the shorter airfields in Antarctica. They took enough essential supplies to last them two to three weeks and transferred the rest to two waiting ice-breaker cargo ships, which would arrive within two weeks at McMurdo Station, Antarctica.

Located on the southern tip of Ross Island on the shore of McMurdo Sound, the combined research and logistics station is 2,200 miles due south of New Zealand. It is operated by the United States through the U.S. Antarctic Program, which is a branch of the National Science Foundation. It is the largest community on the continent, and had recently been expanded to support up to 2,500 residents. Most residents are there during the Antarctic summer, and only 200 to 400 residents remain through the winter. It is the main U.S Antarctic science facility, and it provides logistics support for half the continent.

The station became the center of scientific and logistics operations for the continent during the International Geophysical Year, a scientific research effort that spanned from July 1957 to December 1958. A collection of agreements officially called the Antarctic Treaty Systems (ATS) became official in 1961, and had been re-ratified by all signature countries, plus China and the Federation of Russian States, in 2012.

At McMurdo Station, with the daylight of summer in its early phases, they transferred everything to waiting Condor jets. The Condor was an amazing plane in that it could take off and land vertically or horizontally. Its wings rotated 90 degrees from vertical to horizontal and could do so while in flight. The aircraft was the offspring of the Osprey used by the Marine Corps and Air Force. It was the perfect vehicle for accessing narrow landing sites in the mountains, and the Denver Center had contracted with the Seahorse Aviation Corporation for their use on the continent.

Capable of mid-air refueling, the latest modifications of the fully loaded craft enabled it to fly at close to 500 miles per hour and carry 30 passengers, plus an external cargo of four tons slung beneath the aircraft.

Thirty-four hours after leaving Colorado, and within a couple of hours after their departure from McMurdo, Tallbear, Chuck, and their teams stood at the entrance of the mountain complex. The temperature outside was five degrees above zero, but Chuck assured everyone that once inside, it would be shirtsleeve working conditions. Chuck put in the code, and the anxious new arrivals were relieved to walk into a pleasant interior atmosphere.

Chuck's team was delighted to see him. As the new group passed through the computer center, they saw a dozen technicians busily patching interface connections into the Atlantean equipment.

Off to the left of the computer center the new arrivals were brought into a unique conference room. The chairs and table were made of a composite material that defied, for the time being, any analysis. They all took their cold weather gear off and settled in around a massive table.

Chuck said, "All right, y'all. I've been gone a week. Now what's the latest scoop?"

Dr. Allison Long, acting as Chuck's deputy during his absence, stood up and began her briefing. Allison was 29 years old and had once been a scholarship soccer star. At five foot seven, with short dark hair, she moved with the confident stride of a natural athlete. She had penetrating dark brown eyes and a sculpted face, with prominent cheekbones, a sharp jaw line and a wide, dazzling smile. After a knee injury ended her soccer career in her junior year at the University of North Carolina, she focused on getting her Electrical Engineering degree. She now held a doctorate in computer technology, specializing in acoustics. Offered huge sums of money to become a retained consultant to one of the biggest music recording labels in the world, she turned that down and jumped at the chance to work for the Denver Center. She never regretted her decision.

Brushing her hair back behind her ear and pushing her reading glasses up on her nose, she began, "I broke the team into three sections. One twelve person team continues to work on the computer system, another team of twelve continues to explore the cavern complex, and I have been leading a six person team outside doing acoustic tests around the mountain chain to see if we can uncover more caverns.

"The computer team has been making progress with a translation program, but we will need the assistance of your music expert. The internal cavern team has discovered a few more passages and cavern complexes that you'll find very interesting. My outside team has been doing acoustic testing on sites up to five miles away, and we believe we've found four promising possibilities to explore. That'll have to wait until we get a lot more help down here"

"What's the progress on the computers?"

"Well," said Allison, "we've been able to access their programs, but their written language has so far defied our attempts at deciphering it. Where we've had the most success is in accessing the audio version of their song-language. Again, we don't have a translation, but we have some real sharp minds on the problem. The contractor team from Flynn-Todd Systems is working on breaking the code."

Just then the music composer, one of the new additions recently arrived from the Denver Center, spoke up. He was a middle-aged man with a greatly receding hairline and what appeared to be a permanent smile on his face. "Dr. Long," he said, "My name is Adrian Vanderwiel and I am a music composer with an expertise in computer systems. Have you taken their song-language and run it through a spectrum analyzer? Once we determine the relationships between various frequencies that a human speaker uses to make vowel sounds, we can correspond that information neatly with the relationships between notes of the 12-tone chromatic scale. That may help us unlock, via mathematics, some of their linguistic secrets."

"No sir, not yet. We thought about attempting that before you arrived, but even though some of our people are trained musicians, the consensus was that a more gifted musical talent should guide us. You're to link up with the Flynn-Todd group to get working on that."

"How soon can we get started?" asked Vanderwiel.

"As soon as we're done with the briefing," she replied.

"Okay, let's move on," said Chuck.

Allison continued, "Of particular interest to Dr. Tallbear will be the lab we set up for him and his team. The remains of the two watch standers and three other bodies we exhumed from the cemetery are in cryogenic containers shipped to us this week. Beyond that, depending on your individual schedules, we'll make small group tours available to you so that you can see the cave complex first-hand.

"That pretty much wraps up the initial briefing. Are there any questions?"

Having received an overall briefing back in Colorado, the group was anxious to get to work. But one person raised his hand and asked where they were to sleep.

Allison said, "Ah, glad you asked. Over here against the wall are some team members that've been assigned to get you to your living quarters. I believe you'll like the accommodations.

Each of the newcomers was escorted through "door number two" to the living quarters area. To their great surprise and pleasure, they were brought to spacious apartments, sparsely furnished, but comfortable. They unpacked their gear and within an hour were working within their designated team assignments.

Remaining behind after the briefing, the artist approached Chuck and introduced himself.

"Sir, my name is Brendan Pell. We didn't get a chance to meet personally before this, and I just wanted to get an understanding of what my role will be on this expedition." Recruited and interviewed by Johanna for the expedition, Brendan Pell was thirty-two years old, a little over six-feet tall and with the build of someone who works out relentlessly, he had a thick head of long, nearly black hair pulled back into a queue. He also had a thick mustache flecked with a little gray.

"Pleased to meet Y'all," said Chuck. "Our expectation is that you will work with Mr. Vanderwiel, as he explores the relationships of sound as it pertains to the Atlantis song-language. We want you to take it up the spectrum and do the same with color, because one of the first programs we were able to access on their system began with a middle "C" note and kept going up an octave at a time, until it was past the range of human hearing. At that point the computer monitor showed a line climbing at octave intervals. Many octaves up from middle "C", the computer began to display light and colors. We will be exploring hundreds of octaves up from there where we believe electronically compressed music turns into energy. So tell me about your expertise in color relationships."

Brendan responded, "That's cool. I graduated from the Rhode Island School of Design 15 years ago and did my post-graduate work at the Sorbonne studying the impressionists. Since then I have been working with some cutting-edge technology and experimenting with some pretty far-out color-sound relationships. My work has gained national recognition. My background might help you understand how I can help the expedition.

"In the mid-1800s an interesting discovery was made by Michael Eugene Chevreul, a French scientist, born in1786. Working for a tapestry factory analyzing its wool dyes, he discovered that the infinite shades of visible hues are nothing more than the three primary colors mixed in different proportions. He demonstrated that placing a colored fiber adjacent to another color modifies the perception of the original color. His findings were summarized in "The Principles of Harmony and Contrast of Colors."

"In what may be significant to this expedition, his discovery contributed to the later emergence of the Impressionists school of art. In 1859, Georges Pierre Seurat was born, and as he grew up, he discovered his talent as an artist. In 1883 he began a major work of art, *Bathers at Asnieres*, which incorporated Chevreul's belief that color juxtaposition, rather than color blending, yielded a more faithful portrayal of nature. To achieve this, Seurat applied his oils as finely placed dots of primary color rather than conventional strokes of blended colors. This became known as *pointillism*, and was adopted by a growing school of artists such as Cassat, Cezanne, Degas, Gauguin, van Gogh, Monet, and Renoir. In current parlance, what we see displayed in high definition on computer monitors and television screens we call pixels, which is nothing more than electronic pointilism. Is that cool, or what?

"Now from what I understand about this project when you recruited me a few weeks ago, you are going to explore the relationship of harmonic musical notes to color relationships to radio frequencies to power generation at the highest spectrum. Am I correct?"

"So far so good," responded Chuck.

"Well fortunately my family had insisted on classic piano lessons for me from the time I was eight until I went off to college. They're vision was that I would do something in the classic tradition of music. They nearly disowned me when they discovered that I was covering my personal expenses at college playing keyboards in a rock band. We focused on 1950's and 1960s early Rock and Rockabilly music. That fortunate blend of music and art made a lot more sense to me when I started studying color relationships. The two-part harmonies of the Everly Brothers, a remarkable late 1950s and early 1960s popular duo, who harmonized mostly in thirds, parallels the relationships of color. Listen to their music and you would be convinced that there are more than two singers.

"Just as Chevreul and Seurat realized that juxtaposition of two colors produced a third color in the mind's eye, so it goes with music. As you pointed out, if you take middle "C" on a piano and raise it up a few dozen octaves, you get color. But that is just a single note. Now a musical chord is a minimum of two notes played simultaneously. And just like with two colors producing a third in the mind's eye, when two notes are played together, the ear, or the brain, really, hears a third note. I would imagine that the same relationship exists with radio waves, and further up the spectrum, with the power sources you talked about. The big question in my mind now is what happens when you combine four, five, or six notes – or colors - together at hundreds or thousands of octaves above the range of human hearing.

"Another aspect to the relationship between music and color is a neurological phenomenon called *synesthesia*. The word comes from the ancient Greek and means 'together' and 'sensation.' Synesthesia is an occurrence in which the stimulation of one sensory pathway causes an involuntary response in another neurological area. About one in twenty-three people have this capability. They are called synesthetes. Many well-known musicians perceive the notes they hear or play as colors. Now this is really far-out. Jimi Hendrix would drive his sound engineers crazy when he would say things like, 'No, I want that to sound a darker shade of blue.' I once saw a video of a Paul Simon rehearsal, and he said to the bass player, "No, I want it to sound more brown." Is that weird, or what?

"Somehow these people of Atlantis had the ability to perceive how the value of relationships of notes could have technical applications. I believe that based on what you have briefed us on so far regarding the device that was discovered with the remains of Badlands Bill, we will have to re-discover the narrow band-width, or widths, way up the scale that can produce laser beams and lifting capabilities. What that might mean is anyone's guess."

"Brendan, you'll do just fine. What you have been telling me dovetails neatly with what some of my technicians have been saying. After working with Adrian Vanderwiel, and when you get your feet on the ground, tell me what cutting edge technologies you need to carry the study further. Whatever you need, we'll get it."

Over the next several days, the various teams settled into their work. By the end of the first week, all the newcomers had had a chance to tour the entire chambered complex, and to a person were awestruck. But still, the computer teams were unable to break the language code.

•   •   •

On the eighth day after the arrival of the newcomers, Allison Long returned from one of her outside explorations with a huge grin on her face. She walked right up to Chuck Kinoshi in the conference room and handed him an exact copy of the device found with Badlands Bill three weeks before.

"Dr. Kinoshi," she announced with the mock formality of a bow, "I present you with the key to the kingdom."

Chuck did not know what to make of this pronouncement as he took the device into his hands. Then Allison said, "Don't push that middle indentation or you might kill one of us. Just push the one on the lower right quadrant, say a few words, then push the same indentation again."

Chuck pushed the indentation and said, "This is Chuck Kinoshi and I am standing in a cavern six hundred miles from the South Pole, and my team and I are struggling to unlock the secrets of the Atlantis computer system." He pushed the button again, and the device began to sing in a strange language.

"Jumpin' horny toads!" he exclaimed. The light went on in his mind and with a huge grin he gave Allison an enthusiastic hug and kissed her on the forehead.

"Allison, you just gave us the shortcut we need to get into this computer system. This is a translator device, as well as God knows what else. We can now talk to the computer in plain English and find out what it contains."

Gordon interjected, "That's amazing. Back at the center we have been carefully studying the identical device that Badlands Bill carried, but we have been focusing on is destructive capabilities. We haven't gone so far as to experiment with the different indentations."

"Dr. Tallbear, we just started fiddling with it rather than take our time trying to deconstruct it carefully. I suppose we should have brought it back for a more careful scientific scrutiny before we started toying with it."

"Nonsense," Tallbear answered. "The most brilliant discoveries in history were made the way you did it. You deserve our congratulations as you have probably short-cut what might be months of careful scrutiny. I admire your initiative. And for heaven's sake, call me Gordon."

Allison beamed. "Yes, sir!"

Chuck said, "I agree completely." He went on, "Let's figure out how this thing can help us. We probably should start by speaking short sentences into it that will, of necessity, elicit short predictable answers. That way we can back our way into a full translation of their language. Where the hell did you find this?"

"This is the best part! As I mentioned, my team had found some promising sites that acoustic readings indicated

116

might be caverns. We finally found the entrance to one of them. Like this complex, there was an artificial rock pile blocking the entrance. After some careful scanning and testing, we found the key rock to move so that the entrance was exposed and applied the same program we used for the main complex to key the entrance door open. Basically what we found was at least one of the garages to this mansion. Let me show you. Jim, can you transfer that video to the main screen here? Good, let's just show them."

Jim tapped a few commands into his iPad and the video came on to all the individual monitors and to the large screen at the end of the conference room. They could see the massive entrance to the cavern. The door must have been fifteen feet high and another 20 feet across. It was much larger than the door to the complex they were in.

"As you can see, the entranceway to this complex is quite large. Once past the door, the cavern opens up to be about forty feet high, one hundred fifty feet deep, and about one hundred forty feet across. Inside we found out why. There, over to the right you will see twelve large, for want of a better word, vehicles. Notice the cockpit and passenger areas. They can seat up to twelve people. But there are no wheels, and the four wings, if you can call them that, project only two feet or so from the body. See, there are two sets of these wings, one pair near the front of the vehicle and one pair about three-quarters of the way back. So we initially figured that these things might be undersea vehicles.

"The vehicles are identical. Each is more or less eggshell white in color, approximately eight feet tall and twenty-five feet long, and a little over eight feet wide, with large, darkly tinted glass or plexiglass windshields running nearly from the roof to the floor. The vehicles sit on an eighteen-inch thick frame of a slightly darker material. The front and rear of each vehicle, as you can see, is slightly rounded. The windows, also darkly tinted, begin at waist level and go up until the curve into the roof, which is only about four feet wide. Where the windows met the vehicle body, there's no apparent seam. It just morphs from glass to solid frame as if it were one material.

"The doors were not evident at first, but as one of the technicians ran his hand along the sides of the vehicle, he encountered a slight indentation. Pressing it caused the entire side to lift open like an old gull-wing Mercedes. When we closed the doors, the glass simply resealed leaving absolutely no seam. Once the doors were opened, the interior revealed twelve individual recliner bucket seats, two side-by-side in the cockpit and five on each side of the cabin. There was also a large console in the middle of the cabin and a storage area behind the last seats. In the front cockpit area you can see what appears to be a computer monitor and instrument panel.

Chuck exclaimed, "Looks like the Atlanteans had soccer moms, too." That drew a laugh and a recognition that the vehicles did resemble, if vaguely, a minivan.

"There's Jack Walton going over to sit in one of the cockpits," continued Allison. "Watch as he starts pushing buttons. There, you see? The next thing we knew he was levitating and starting to drift around inside the cavern. He finally got the thing to land and was grateful he didn't crash it.

"Looking around the cockpit he noticed this device ensconced in a holster of sorts. He pulled it out, got out of the vehicle, and while he was fiddling around with the indentations, he began talking to us about the brief flight. He must have accidently hit the right combination, because the next thing we knew, the device made a chiming sound and suddenly was singing to us. We began experimenting with the buttons, or, more accurately, indentations, and look, you can see the darn thing fired a burst of energy into the wall. It's a good thing none of us were in the line of fire.

"From that point on, we carefully documented our efforts at making it work again. We finally got it right and you can see the few tests we did with it. Among other things, it is a sound analyzer that translates what is being said, most likely into the Atlantean language. We also took it outside the cavern, just in case the damned thing went off again, and after a few other experiments, it projected an electronic beam that had the effect of a high-powered rifle. After experimenting some more, we found that it also could project a continuous beam that cut rock like you would slice an apple. Now watch this. Jack is holding it

118

pointing downward at about a 45 degree angle. When he touched a certain combination of buttons, the device started humming quietly. We didn't realize it at first, but soon realized that it was emitting an invisible a beam that cut through the ground at our feet! Here are two halves of a rock we just cut less than an hour ago."

She reached into her pack and brought out the two rock halves and passed them around for everyone to see. Where they were cut the surfaces were completely smooth as if they had been sliced with a precision, high-speed granite-cutting saw.

"And we discovered another amazing capability of the device. At certain settings, which we uncovered by trial-and-error, you can point it at a heavy object and it emits some sort of energy beam that will lift the object. Watch the monitor to see Jack lifting a huge stone not far from the garage entrance.

Allison continued. "We still need to do a lot more experimenting with this device to divine its full capability."

"Allison," said Tallbear, "when you get a minute please send a full report on this to the engineering team back at the Center. As I mentioned, they have been proceeding cautiously on the unit discovered in Montana. This should give them a chance to experiment more fully with its capabilities while we concentrate on other matters."

"Will do, Gordon."

"All right," said Chuck. "Let's get this thing talking to the computer system. And Allison, I want you to take me out to the garage."

Before he got more than a couple of steps, Brendan Pell moved to Chuck's side and said, "This is in keeping with what I spoke to you about a week ago. If we can get a detailed analysis of the device's capabilities, we may be able to understand whether musical notes and chords are critical to its functions. This is soooo far out!"

.   .   .

Over the next several days, Brendan found that while everyone worked at a rapid pace constantly, they all worked hard at keeping a friendly and cooperative work atmosphere. Surrounded by an extraordinary array of talent in multiple disciplines, he could see that each and every person was enthusiastic, dedicated, and focused on the mission at hand. He also noticed that there was very little supervising being done. If anyone needed some additional technical support, they just asked Chuck or Gordon for it and it was provided on the next flight in. This was a totally self-motivated group. The entire team reflected the combined leadership styles of Tallbear, Chuck, and Johanna. Most places where Brendan had worked, superiors were always looking over your shoulder. Not here. Brendan was quite happy to be with this remarkable assembly of talent even though they were in Antarctica and umpteen thousand miles from the Dockside Bar in Providence where he used to jam nightly.

After putting in long hours working with the computer team on the significance of color relationships extending from sound relationships, Brendan realized he needed a break to clear his head. Late one afternoon when the team finished its work for the day, he wandered down into the underground city. Other than the initial tour, he had not had a chance to scrutinize the wall art depicting the great and mysterious constructions of early man.

Stopping in front of the massive mural depicting the Great Pyramid, he examined it in detail. The rectangular mural had been measured at 22 feet by 33 feet. Discerning no brush strokes, Brendan studied it from a distance as well as up close. Going along the base of the mural he stopped at a corner and looked at it from a severe angle trying to determine whether the picture was done in some form of oils or acrylics. Near the corner

120

of the picture he noticed three indentations. He ran his finger over them and pressed one to see what would happen.

Suddenly the picture vanished. A moment later something happened that the artist never expected.

We must exceed our own expectations.

Nelson Mandela

Chapter 14

Atlantis, 12,500 Years ago

Goro sent a second quarry team more than 500 miles away to precision-cut the granite beams for the interior chambers. The specifications on these beams were precise and there was absolutely no margin for error. They were to be cut to twenty-seven feet in length, their ends, sides and bottoms were to be cut to .001 inch of tolerance, and their upper sides were to be rough-hewn.

The beams were to weigh exactly 70 tons each. Along with the quarry team was a team of musicians whose job was to direct the fine-tuning of each beam so that each and every one of them resonated precisely in Earth's musical key. Under their direction, members of the quarry team chipped away parts of the rough upper surfaces and even bored holes in these beams until they all chimed precisely in unison.

At the appropriate time during the construction, these seventy-ton beams would be lifted by silent, magnetic-levitation aircraft, transported the 500 miles to the construction site, and gently guided into place.

As the pyramid construction reached its first level of completion, the first granite beams of what would be later called the Queen's Chamber were laid in place.

Goro had decided that virtually every measurement of the pyramid must reflect a measurement of the earth, the solar system, and the starry universe.

Gradually the pyramid would gradually climb higher and higher – 201 stepped tiers of blocks tghat measured in staggering weight. Exterior construction on the great pyramid had to be halted periodically at each tier as the lower shafts, the lower chamber, the passageways, the slanted resonance chamber, the upper anterior resonance filter chamber, the fuel resource chamber, and the main chamber were constructed using the granite beams. Great care was taken in the laying of the stones through which four uniquely designed shafts would pass, particularly the one with the copper fittings at the upper end of the north-facing shaft in the lower chamber.

We feel most alive in the presence of what is beautiful.

John
O'Dona
hue,
Irish
poet

Chapter 15

Everyone stood about fifty feet back from the mural while Brendan pushed one of the indentations. The mural went blank and everyone gasped. In a few seconds, the wall lit up again with the picture of an empty savannah. As they watched the scene, presented in nearly three-dimensional high definition, dozens of Atlantis aircraft moved into the picture, each one carrying crates of quarried stone blocks. The aircraft moved in a coordinated fashion as if directed and timed for arrival, conceived and directed by a master logistician. Gradually the scene evolved and scores of Atlantean teams could be seen using their hand-held devices to lift individual stones and place them carefully.

Over the next several hours, the research teams watched as the Great Pyramid took shape and rose from the grassy savannah. They saw the careful arrangement of the massive limestone exterior and the careful placement of granite beams to form what is now called the Queen's and King's Chambers, the shafts and passageways, and the construction of the Grand Gallery. They also saw the hand held devices cutting limestone and high speed tools slicing granite sections. Finally came the completion of the exterior to the pinnacle, and the placement of the highly polished limestone cladding, and the laying on of the gold plates casing the upper third of the structure.

The 'movie,' for want of a better word, did not show the laying of every single piece of stone, but rather showed a flow of the construction. It apparently was constructed in stages over a period of years. At the very end, the Great Pyramid and its two sisters stood as we see the complex today, except that it sat amidst a sea of grass and not a desert.

The *coup de main*, however, was toward the end of the movie just after aircraft lifted in the gold plates. Then came a strange scene in which hundreds of Atlanteans could be seen standing some distance from the Pyramid. One raised his hand in signal. In a few minutes the ground began to shake as evidenced from the jittering of the camera. After the shaking stopped and smoke began to drift from the structure, the man with upraised hand ran like he was on fire toward the pyramid, and the scene ended.

Next came almost a repeat of that scene, but following the same man's hand signal, a steady beam emerged from the King's Chamber shaft at the southern side of the pyramid and went out into space. There was an interval of about thirty seconds and the 'video' resumed showing the removal of the gold plating to leave a limestone cased structure. That was the last "frame" of the movie, and the one that the explorers initially discovered on the wall when they first discovered the underground city.

Over the next several days, the teams went around the caverns to the different murals and watched and recorded the carving of the Sphinx, the construction of Stonehenge and Newgrange, and the etching of the Nazca Lines in Peru.

The Sphinx, carved out of a natural limestone rock formation, with a lion's head initially, was constructed during a period when the region received heavy rains. An interesting aspect of the carving of the Sphinx as a gigantic lion was the chamber dug between the paws. The video showed people excavating and lowering granite beams down into the excavated passageway, and then the entire area between the paws was filled in and re-sodded with turf lifted from elsewhere on the savannah. Undoubtedly over the years, the erosion of the rain weakened the head structure of this limestone behemoth causing parts of the lion's head to break off. It was apparent that later generations of the desert dwelling Egyptians re-carved what remained into the head of a pharaoh.

After viewing and recording every one of the 'murals' with multiple back-up copies, at Johanna's order the teams distilled the entire collection into selected groups of slides that could be used in briefings. Johanna wanted Mr. Tolles to see the whole recording, but knew he would need the condensed versions of all these remarkable constructions for any future briefings.

There are three types of leaders: Those who learn from reading, those who learn from observation, and those who still have to touch the electric fence to get the message.

Anonymous U. S. Marine Colonel

Chapter 16

Shortly after arriving in Antarctica, Gordon had his deputy, Hector Moineau, break the thirty-two person anthropological group into four teams: a biological team, a socio-cultural team, a linguistic team, and an archeological team. While archaeology is considered a separate discipline outside of the United States, it was in keeping with the American "holistic," or "four-field" approach to anthropology that the group be structured this way.

It has been argued extensively over the years as to whether it makes sense either theoretically or pragmatically to take the holistic approach. The proponents of the method consider anthropology holistic in two senses. First, it is concerned with all human beings across times and places, and studies all dimensions of humanity (i.e., evolutionary, biophysical, sociopolitical, economic, cultural, linguistic, and psychological). Second, taking this four-field approach provides a more comprehensive understanding of the culture studied.

The opponents of this approach argue that the four-field approach pushes anthropology across the border into realms of science that should be handled by other academic disciplines.

For Gordon, the four-field approach was perfect for the environment they were about to examine. The biological team would focus on the remains of the cavern's inhabitants. They would seek an understanding of the evolution of this distinct human group, and learn about their adaptability, the genetics of the population, their evolutionary history, their nutrition, susceptibility to diseases, and so on.

The socio-cultural team would be looking for the clues to their culture and social organizations, and delve into the economic and political organization, their laws and conflict resolution, family structure, gender relations, childbearing, religion, and mythology.

The linguistic team, in conjunction with the computer experts, would work to understand the inhabitants' communications processes as well as the relationship between language and culture. Given the potential age of the Atlantean culture, this team would also examine evolutions in their language and work closely with the computer teams dissecting the song language.

The archaeological team would search the cavern for artifacts with the intent of discovering the development and social organization of the Atlanteans. Among their activities would be cavern surveys, excavations, radiocarbon dating, and laboratory analyses.

While each of these fields has a number of subfields, such as ethnomusicology and medical anthropology, the individuals on the team that Gordon assembled each had expertise and experience in several other disciplines as well. On top of that, there were medical experts and music experts on the larger team under Chuck Kinoshi's direction. If Gordon required additional expertise, he needed only to ask for it. That allowed him to utilize economy of effort, prevent unnecessary personnel from getting in the way, streamline activities, and reduce costs for the expedition.

Each afternoon at 5:00 Gordon listened as team leaders summarized progress. At the end of each week, Gordon briefed the entire team to keep them aware of the other ongoing discoveries.

The first big breakthrough for the entire expedition was the breaking of the translation code. The translator device had proved invaluable. Before they applied it directly to the computer system, a working team had spent a few days brainstorming and testing questions and answers among themselves to finally come up with thirty questions that required a known answer. For example, "What is the relationship of any circle's circumference to its diameter?"

The answer, of course, had to be 3.14159, or *pi*, as we know it. The big risk was if the computer translated the question literally and gave an answer that went on into infinity like the infinite answer to pi. By fine-tuning a series of questions, making sure, on the advice of the linguists, to use as many phonetic sounds as they could in forming the questions, they hoped to evoke some standard responses that would lend themselves to translation.

After several days of trial and error, the team refined their questions and were ready to begin.

Speaking each of the questions into the translator evoked a singing response that the linguistics experts analyzed. Using Adrian Vanderwiel's suggestion, they processed the answers through a spectrum analyzer to determine the various frequencies Atlanteans used to make vowel sounds. With a combination of mathematics and the known answers to the questions, they gradually unlocked the secrets to the structure of the language. Shortly they were able to produce credible translations to the basic answers. To double-check their accuracy, they read the translated answers back into the translator device but in a question format. For example, "How can you confirm that the relationship of the circumference of a circle to its diameter is 3.14159?"

To everyone's relief, the translator produced answers that lent themselves to translation into English. Once this was done, the computer technicians, with the assistance of the linguists, were able to affect the process of translation directly with the main computer.

By the end of their second week, the computer translations were producing dramatic discoveries. Gordon invited the technical group under Chuck to attend the anthropological briefing. After he called the weekly meeting to order, the revelations began to mount up.

"The linguistics team," Gordon began, "was the driving force behind the discoveries of the other teams. After uncovering the secrets of the language, the computer records produced amazing revelations.

"The socio-cultural team has determined that the Atlanteans, at least since their confinement in the caverns, had adhered to a strict "zero-growth" approach to the population, that is, no more than two children per married couple. The team also discovered that the Atlanteans had a "town hall" approach to self-governance. Disputes were resolved fairly and amicably, and there appeared no evidence of crime in their culture. That, in itself, strained credibility.

"The archaeological team found no evidence of any system of confinement – no jails or prisons. The only possible answers were that either the society had no crime, or the society simply banished criminals to the outside to meet their fate, and left behind no records of transgressions or punishments.

"The biological team confirmed through autopsies that the people subsisted on fatty fish rich in Vitamin D like salmon and herring, as well as fruits, vegetables, and simple grains. This was doubly confirmed by the hydroponic farms. The team also uncovered why the population died out. Despite their efforts in growing their own food in underground caverns in artificial light, despite their consumption of fatty fish, and despite the area that Chuck had labeled "the Riviera," over successive generations the people suffered from a lack of natural sunlight.

"They apparently were getting their vitamin D through their diet of fatty fish, and that generally would mean that they would have high bone density and a more natural resistance to some cancers, like colon and breast cancer. However the biological team made fascinating discoveries when they exhumed remains from the cemetery.

"Before beginning the removal of the remains, the team studied the layout of the cemetery and determined which were the newest graves and which were the oldest. By collecting a representative sampling from each section of the cemetery, they discovered the causes of mortality among the population.

"Among the oldest remains, and that would have been the people who were the first inhabitants of the caverns, the evidence was overwhelming that, except in the cases of accidental death, the cause of death was usually old age - really old age. Initially the team had to keep revising their estimates upward as to people's ages. It was not uncommon to find these earliest remains to be well over two hundred years old at the time of their death."

Chuck interrupted asking, "Now how in the dickens did you figure that out? Did you cut them in half and count the rings?"

That brought a laugh from everyone.

"No, Chuck," Gordon answered, "we actually abandoned that method a while back. Now we use a number of techniques, including radiocarbon dating of bone marrow samples."

Gordon continued. "As best as the team could determine, the last Atlanteans died only 600 years before we recently discovered the caverns. These people died only slightly before the discovery of the Americas by Europeans. Most of the adults from that period were now dying in their 50s. Their bone density had diminished, and there is strong evidence of several types of cancer that had not existed among the earlier inhabitants. Our teams are still trying to determine exactly when the Atlanteans had entered the cavern system ..."

Chuck was busy whispering to one of his people who had just slipped into the conference room. Suddenly he said, "Sorry to interrupt your briefing, cousin, but we've got something really remarkable for y'all to see. If you will come with me to the computer center, I think you'll love the surprise."

"Why do you doubt your senses?"
Jacob Marley's ghost to Scrooge, from
Charles Dickens, *"A Christmas Carol"*

The whole problem can be stated quite simply by asking, "Is there a meaning to music?" My answer would be, "Yes." And "Can you state in so many words what the meaning is?" My answer to that would be, "No."
Aaron
Copeland, American composer, (1900 – 1990)

Chapter 17

One of the computer experts looked up at Chuck from her console with wonder in her eyes and said, "Stand by." She hit the 'Enter' key. Suddenly, in the middle of the room that had been labeled the 'Computer Center,' with forty-five researchers standing around the walls wearing earbuds, an image began to form. Within a few seconds a hologram appeared and began to sing. Simultaneously in everyone's earphones a translation began.

For the next hour, the entire research crew stood or sat mesmerized by the tale that unfolded.

The hologram image was of a tall, bearded, green-eyed man dressed in flowing robes. He had pale skin, a slightly hooked nose, and a powerful -- almost ferocious -- gaze. His dark facial hair was more than a goatee, but less than a full beard. Over his shoulder was another hologram of a world map.

"My name is Kulen Golendar, and I am Exploration Master of Atlantis. As I tell you our story, it has been 8,500 years since the beginning of the great thaw of the ice and glaciers.

"We of Atlantis are the First People. Our civilization, like all civilizations, spent its first five thousand years developing gradually. But we discovered that we advanced rapidly thereafter. We call the first five thousand years the First Era. In the first thousand years of the Second Era, the end of the age in which ice covered much of the earth, we developed rapidly. That was a little over five thousand years from the time we could trace our civilization. We believe that we were placed here on earth by the Creator and we gradually, after many severe trials, came to the belief that our mission is to bring good works to the world. But we suffered many challenges and difficulties before reaching that conclusion.

Pointing to a location in the southern Indian Ocean, he said, "Our island nation once sat in a sub-tropical location with a temperate climate, even with the ice covering so much of the earth's northern hemisphere.

"Given what we have learned in the past 8,500 years, it is evident that we had accidentally uncovered some key secrets of the universe. In our early history there was a great man of Atlantis named Ison Davol who discovered that our song language held mathematical principles. Furthermore, through mastery of mathematics he taught us to behold the infinite secrets of the universe.

"As a result, we leaped over the evolutionary development commonly associated with the peoples of the rest of the planet.

"About 4500 years ago, our people came under the control of men who were determined to dominate the world. They at first shared our technical knowledge with the people in the emerging regions hoping to overawe them and convince them to do the bidding of their masters in Atlantis.

[*Golendar's image turned slightly and he swept his hand across China, India, and what was then the ancient area of Mesopotamia, Greece, and North Africa*]

"Things began to go wrong almost immediately. Technology as advanced as ours in the hands of unsophisticated people led to disaster. Soon there were skirmishes wherever our people would go. Gradually these skirmishes escalated to full-blown war, and our misguided leaders struck back with all the power they had at their disposal. They warred on the people of these regions to bring them into submission.

"Many of our weapons had been stored in these lands, and in some cases, our enemies, aided by dissidents who had fled the tyranny of Atlantis, broke into the storage facilities and stole them to use against us. These weapons were devastating. We had unlocked the secrets of the atoms and taught ourselves how to turn these discoveries into weapons of unthinkable destruction. Using missiles, our morally corrupted leaders launched these weapons indiscriminately. Where they were used, their explosions were of such heat and fury that sand turned to glass and people by the hundreds of thousands were vaporized.

"These wars burnt the forests of the world and brought global darkness, and eventually rain that soaked the planet for many years. The great flood caused by these rains nearly wiped out the population of the world. Under the pretext of protecting ourselves and our technology from our enemies, a faction of more visionary leaders had hollowed out caverns in our mountains where we could hide. We were forced to live underground in these caverns for the years of rain. Our men of vision wisely used the time underground to plan.

"Fifteen years after our underground exile, eleven years after our people emerged at the end of the rains, our men of vision were planning the actions that would be necessary to drive the evil ones out of power. But in the meantime, the leaders of Atlantis bent on hegemony were planning their next move.

"From the time over four-thousand years ago, when it was discovered that the fate of our land is to drift to the coldest reaches of the planet, a movement grew within the hearts of some of our people that led them to plan the evacuation of Atlantis. They wished to settle in the world among the newly emerging cultures.

"Amon Goro, Master Architect of Atlantis, had been secretly meeting with colleagues over a two year period to see if they could design a massive power plant that would beam electrical energy across the planet. Discovered in his secret endeavor, the Elders of Atlantis summoned him to explain what he and his colleagues were doing in secrecy. Facing charges of treason, Goro convinced the leaders that the secret meetings were intended to find a solution to the Elders' plan for exploitation of the world's resources. He was given the go ahead to build this machine in Atlantis, but Goro convinced them that it would be a monument to the legacy of Atlantis if it were to be built at the center of the earth's land mass.

"On the fertile plains of this area [*here he pointed to Giza*], our world domination-bent leaders directed that Master Architect Amon Goro build the great pyramid power plant that they believed would be their signature for the ages to admire. To Goro's credit, he used every element of our technology to design and create a structure of incredible precision, the purpose of which was to provide an unlimited energy source to support the world colonization plan.

"The top section of the pyramid was covered in gold and the remainder clad in highly polished limestone. The entire structure was designed to tap into the vibrations of the earth and beam energy from the source of the earth's heart out to our satellite hovering stationary above the earth's surface. From there, the energy was to be beamed down initially to energy collection stations in Atlantis, and later to the areas we would colonize. Those subjugated people throughout the world would be enslaved and forced to work in mines to produce raw materials for their masters in Atlantis. Those of our ancestors who had wisdom and vision could see where this would lead the people of the earth: to certain destruction.

"Shortly after its construction, the time for revolution was ripe, and our leaders struck at just the right time. The initial test of the Great Pyramid had failed – nearly catastrophically. A minor miscalculation on sound input caused mostly internal cosmetic damage. But after repairs, the next tests proved successful. We feared it would lead to the same situation we faced when we sought shelter in the caves.

"Our ancestors chose that moment to strike. The evil leaders of Atlantis were arrested, trials were held, and they were executed. Unfortunately for us, and for a burgeoning civilization just north of the isthmus separating two great continents far to our west, the most evil of these men, Tezcar Tilpocan, whom we believed had gone totally mad, escaped and found his way to an emerging population in this region [*here Palen Golendar pointed to the region of southern Mexico above the Yucatan Peninsula*]. He taught those indigenous people that the world would come to an end if they did not follow his commands. He taught these people that the world could only be saved by the ritual blood sacrifice and cannibalization of their enemies. He wrought terrible destruction to an area that we thought held great promise for mankind, simply to gain power for himself and the even darker evil one he served.

"Earlier our expeditions to that region had born great fruit. These were a people who were receptive to our teachings of mathematics and study of the stars. We taught them to construct calendars that would not only teach them about celestial events, but that also would be used as a guide for their agricultural development. But these people were being brought to ruin by Tezcar Tilpocan.

"Back in Atlantis, every single atomic weapon, and every single technological weapon of any kind, save one, was destroyed and the parts scattered to the deepest parts of the oceans around the planet. We also destroyed all the instructions for making them. The only weapon remaining to us was the hand-held communications device, which also has the capability of being used as both a tool and a weapon. This was to be considered a weapon of last resort as our impact was felt upon the world. If the weapon were to be used to take the life of another, our law was absolutely clear and severe: the person who used this device for such a purpose must forfeit his life.

"We had come to the realization that the pyramid could be used for peaceful purposes if we were careful. From the time it was built nearly 4,500 years ago, we have used the power generated from this monument to operate our machinery, light our homes, and power our building projects, always ensuring that we applied this resource for peaceful purposes. It is only within the past months, when we finally accepted that the fate of Atlantis was irrevocable, that we dismantled its technology.

Our new leaders recognized that there was always the possibility that our culture would not survive forever. Famine, pestilence, or the intervention of a huge comet might end our civilization forever. The earthquakes and gradual drift of Atlantis to the southern arctic regions confirmed that our time as a great civilization was coming to an end. Therefore they ordered, for future generations to discover, the construction of a star map that would say, '*Once there lived here a great and technologically sophisticated generation of people who understood the principles of mathematics, the structure of the earth, and the relationship of the earth to the rest of the universe.'"*

Recognizing that our island nation was drifting into the frigid realm of the southern pole, Goro suggested that we could leave a defining monument for future generations to discover. He proposed building a star map around the great pyramid that would reflect the constellation of the Great Warrior. Given the go ahead, adjacent to the great pyramid, he built two other pyramids scaled to the relative size of the star cluster of the warrior's belt as it appeared on the horizon at the time the great pyramid was built. We also built several other pyramid structures reflecting the other major stars in that constellation, albeit with some haste. I hope they have survived the ravages of time. But the original pyramid and its two sisters were built with great precision.

"They also carved the great lion that symbolically reflected the constellation just rising above the horizon in the same era as the original pyramid was constructed. This idea was suggested by our astronomers who felt that such a marker would further pinpoint exactly when the great pyramid was built.

"Our leaders were finally convinced that the people of Atlantis must leave their homes and settle, initially, along this great river. That would be the platform for further colonization of the earth. With that in mind, the great pyramid served to capture the earth's energy and serve our needs. The remaining pyramid structures were placed mainly to prove what a great civilization we had been.

"After we executed the evil ones and destroyed the weapons, the people of Atlantis spent the next ten years developing and refining a new system of government that would be accountable to the people it governed. More importantly, we developed of a philosophy of life that we believe is in keeping with what the Master of the Universe intended for us. This philosophy has been ingrained into every child of Atlantis from birth. Our philosophy is simple and at the same time irrevocable. We must only do good in the world, and our mission was to nurture the communities that were emerging from the ruin of the Great Flood. We forbade ourselves to give people the technologies that we had developed. For us, that became a crime punishable by instant death.

"We the people of Atlantis have explored the earth and planted the seeds of mathematics, astronomy, and agriculture to enable emerging cultures to learn to live in harmony with the earth and the cosmos. We have each year sent seven teams of twelve explorers each to carefully interact with the other societies of the world. Each team would spend seven years exploring and building solar and lunar calendars of stone. It has been our hope, with what we taught about agriculture and how to read the calendars we constructed, that the cultures we touched would begin the slow process of maturation. At the end of each seven-year cycle, the teams would return to Atlantis for well-deserved rest and to give fully detailed reports on the progress of the emerging cultures.

"Each team that has been sent out for the last 4,500 years has lived by one of our strictest codes not to intimately involve itself with the cultures they studied. That means that they could instruct, but not socialize or intermarry. We feared that such intimacy might alter the natural evolution of cultures.

"We knew that emerging civilizations would eventually figure out the significance of the stone formations and pyramid cities reflecting the cosmos, and dedicate themselves to mastering the cycles of the cosmos and advancing their civilizations.

"We deliberately left behind none of the technologies with which we built these amazing structures, as there is a tendency among some of humankind to use technology for evil purposes. We know this from our own sad experience. Our hope was that emerging civilizations would do better to evolve gradually.

"By mastering agriculture, people would eventually congregate in communities. From these communities other disciplines would naturally emerge as the art of learning took hold. Eventually the people would evolve to develop their own sciences and technologies. We know that this process takes thousands of years. Atlantis has taught itself to be a patient society. We have learned from early mistakes in our own civilization that the advancement of humankind must be a slow, evolving process. We had hoped that by this gradual evolution of progress, we would develop a harmonic relationship with all reaches of the globe, and from that point reach out to the stars.

"Our study of the cosmos indicates that the earth evolves in cycles. We are now at the middle of a 5125 year cycle. Five of these cycles represent the complete astronomical evolution of the twelve constellations that appear on the eastern horizon, beginning with the great lion. That cycle is characterized by the slow emergence of cultures. When this current cycle is complete, the emerging cultures will begin to define themselves. We believe that before the next 5,000 year cosmic cycle is complete, or early into the following cycle, most of the people of the planet will be ready to take this step with us.

"I speak now at the beginning of the end for my people. Atlantis, our home, is drifting ever southward to the coldest reaches of the planet. We have known this for the past 4,000 years. Soon our land will be covered with ice and glaciers, for how long we cannot predict. Even now the ice has covered most of our land.

"We have left a gift that can be used for good purposes. That gift is the great pyramid complex and the carved lion. It tells future generations when we existed, exactly when the pyramid complex was built, and how mathematically advanced we were.

"The struggle had been great between the faction advocating relocation and those of us who are convinced that such a plan goes against the natural order of human evolution. That argument is moot now. The matter of our future has been decided by the council of our senior leaders. They have decreed that 250,000 of us will go to live underground. The balance of our population will remain above, but without any of our technologies, and that is their own choice. They will sail for the continents to our north and settle there. We expect that the majority, maybe 90% of them will die in the attempt. But for those who survive, the gift of exploration will remain.

"Over the past 2,500 years we have done all we can to prepare for this time. We have continued to hollow out the caverns inside the mountains of Atlantis and placed inside almost all of our technology, all of our knowledge. We have built dwellings underground to house our people.

"I am preparing this message for a future generation that, hopefully, will have benefitted from the seeds we planted and grown into an advanced culture like Atlantis.

"If you are watching my image now, you have indeed unlocked a number of our secrets. I trust that you have the wisdom to use prudently what you have discovered, and what you will discover.

"As you have already learned, the keys to understanding Atlantis are mathematics and our song language. You will also discover through mathematics what happened in the lands we have touched. Mathematics and music are the only true constants. Languages evolve and are greatly different from each other, but mathematics and music remain constant through the ages. And the music is all around you. The rustle of leaves, the singing of birds, the crashing of the ocean waves, and the gentle flow of a small stream all have something to tell our minds.

"For you who are watching me, your mastery of these areas will enable you to rapidly unlock many secrets.

"Through the language of music and mathematics, we have discovered how the earth can provide its people with perpetual energy for their technologies. The precise dimensions of the Great Pyramid are no accident. They mirror the dimensions of the earth, the moon, the changing of the seasons, and the measurements of our solar system. Therefore the Pyramid becomes the harmonic conduit from which mankind can draw on the resonance of the earth for its energy.

"Master these discoveries well, and lead the Earth to a new and great era, for the earth itself is the great gift of the Creator for us to use in peace.

"The gates to our world have now been closed. All people of Atlantis who will live underground are now saddened because we have to say goodbye to the beautiful land above. But that is what must be done to preserve what we hope will be of great value to future generations. It is the final gift of our philosophy.

"The last of our teams have returned. There was much promise to be found in the two continents with the narrow isthmus joining them, the part of the planet we called Hourglass. Team leader Veran Cocha who explored the upper part of the lower continent and the lower part of the upper continent, as did generations of his forebears, did much to help trigger the cultural development of those people by introducing them to agriculture, mathematics, and calendars.

[*Golendar again indicated the area of Peru, Central America, and southern Mexico just to the north of the Yucatan Peninsula.*]

"He and his teams also constructed many pyramid cities in the region north of the isthmus. These pyramids not only reflect the constellations of the heavens, but also reflect many of the mathematical details of the Great Pyramid complex at the center of the earth's mass. This precision was meant to tell future generations that might not find our technological center here in Atlantis that a great civilization preceded them and left clues for them to unravel.

"But Veran Cocha encountered major difficulties in this region.

"It seems that our evil nemesis Tezcar Tilpocan, had spawned generation after generation of evil doers. Veran Cocha managed to convert the people of this region away from human sacrifice while teaching them the arts of civilized cultures – how to live in communities and raise families, how to avoid war - but he ran afoul of a descendant of Tezcar Tilpocan. After ten years of struggle against him and his followers, Veran Cocha finally escaped with his life to return to his final fate here. I fear for the people of this region, for they know not what they have unleashed for themselves. The descendants of Tezcar Tilpocan, it seems, have unleashed the dark power of the Great Demon who opposes the Creator. The people now routinely practice cannibalism. Following ritual sacrifices, they strip the skins off their victims and wear them, running through their villages and terrorizing everyone.

"Hopefully the people living in fear in this region will finally rid themselves of this evil. But it is too late for the people of Atlantis to help them.

"As for the team that just returned from the northern of those continents, I particularly am saddened because my son, Palen Golendar, could not return with them and remains outside. I have told him to violate our rule of non-intimacy with the outside world. He is the last survivor of an exploration team searching in the north center of the little populated continent north of the equator, thousands of miles north of our dying world ... [*here Golendar pointed to the area that is now eastern South Dakota*]. When last we spoke, he had traversed the long river north of the great gulf, and had been captured by a tribe of natives. They have allowed him to live with them as long as he wishes. I hope he finds peace, solace, and a family to lead as he continues on his journey.

"As you, my discoverers, unravel more secrets, you will see the maps of the earth we have prepared and the routes of all the teams we have sent out, and when we sent them. Look to the route of the last team and you will see where my son will finish his days.

"May the Creator guide you in your quest."

And with that, Kulen Golendar's image faded from view.

•   •   •

Music is what language would love to be if it could.

John O'Donohue, Irish poet and philosopher

Chapter 18

That night Johanna called a team leaders meeting and also invited the music composer to join them.

"Okay, now that we have been walloped by our friend in the hologram, who wants to go first?" Johanna asked.

Tallbear interjected, "I think at first we should hear from Mr. Vanderwiel about the musical properties of the language."

"Very well, Gordon. Mr. Vanderwiel?"

Adrian stood up scratching his bald head. "While you were all focused on the translation of the language, I got focused on the music of Golendar's language. I did not read the translation, nor did I listen to it, until after it was over. During his speech, his emotions varied. He was alternately serene and serious, joyful and sorrowful with a touch of tragedy, and he was powerful and visionary. As I listened to his speech a second time, I read the translation on one of the computer monitors rather than listen to the oral translation.

"I discovered in Golendar's musical speech melodic elements similar to Grieg's *Hall of the Mountain King*, Beethoven's *Ode to Joy*, J. S. Bach's *Cello Suites*, Shubert's *Ave Maria*, Mozart's *Piano Concerto Number 24,* and Gershwin's *Rhapsody in Blue*. Emotionally, he was all over the lot. What I can conclude from that is that the great composers I just mentioned must have been channeling the music of Atlantis. I am sure that with further analysis, I will pick up strains of Lennon and McCartney.

"A generation or two ago, several well-known psychiatrists posited theories about the human brain being hard-wired for music. As Golendar said, music is the natural means of communication.

"I must study this a bit more before I come to any major conclusions, but I will tell you this: the mathematics of music is absolute and undoubtedly played a key role in their technological development."

Johanna thanked Adrian and recognized Gordon.

Tallbear paced back and forth as he spoke. "I don't know much about music, so I will move to another facet of the speech. We know that the great ice melt lasted from around 17,000 to 12,500 years ago. Based on what friend Golendar has told us, I did the math. He must have made that recording approximately 8,000 years ago. Added to our dating of Badlands Bill, who more than likely was Kulen's son Palen, that makes sense. This time of great upheaval is reflected in the myths of nearly every culture on the planet. It is said in many of the myths, that following the time of darkness after the flood, great strangers came to teach farming, architecture, astronomy, science, and the rule of law.

"One thing Golendar said, or sang, has been rattling around in my head. After his briefing I went to do some homework on the internet to refresh my memory about the history of the natives of Central America. Golendar referred to one of the teams that came back as having explored the northern part of the southern continent and the southern part of the northern continent, and, of course, he pointed to northern South America and southern North America. The team leader he was referring to was named Veran Cocha. Here's a short course on Central American mythology.

"The Inca, Maya, and Aztec shared a common creation myth with slight variations. They believed that a light-skinned, bearded man with beautiful emerald green eyes came to their lands. Before his arrival, they were cannibalistic savages, but he taught the people how to farm the lands and how to behave peacefully as humans. He also taught them about the earth, the planets, and the stars.

"The Inca called him Viracocha, the Mayans called him Kukulkan, and the Aztecs called him Quetzalcoatl. He is represented in the art of the three cultures as a feathered serpent god.

144

"The Incas had great technology at a time when Europeans were still barbaric nomads. The Incas claimed that their technology was taught to them by Viracocha.

"Their legend has it that Viracocha rose from Lake Titicaca before there was light in the world, and that he brought light to the world. Viracocha was considered both a storm god and a sun god, with thunderbolts in each hand, tears running from his eyes as rainfall, and wearing the sun for a crown.

"He is said to have wandered the earth disguised as a beggar, weeping at the plight of the creatures he had made. Displeased with his first creation, he destroyed everything with a flood and began his creation anew. Then in his wanderings he taught his new creations the basics of civilization and also performed many miracles such as curing the sick and raising the dead.

"Eventually, as the Incan legend has it, Viracocha disappeared across the Pacific Ocean by walking on water. It was taught to every generation that Viracocha would return in the future during times of trouble.

"The Mayans called the creator Kukulkan and claimed that he lived some twenty centuries ago. They believed that he was the creator of all empires in ancient America. Their legend says that he descended from the sky as the god of life and divine wisdom, and brought love, penitence, and exemption from the usual ritual of blood sacrifice. Their legend also has it that Kukulkan was light skinned, bearded, and with green eyes.

"Kukulkan, like Viracocha, was a mystical man who could heal the sick and bring the dead back to life. He was also said to have met with people from distant lands. When he departed, he traveled east across the ocean on a raft of serpents, promising to return one day. Many have speculated that this was Jesus who appeared in this hemisphere around the same time as He lived in Galilee. Many North American Indian tribes, including my own, have a similar myth about Jesus.

"In Aztec mythology, Quetzalcoatl, a light skinned man with a beard and green eyes, was the Lord of Intelligence and the Winds who came to earth from the heavens above. In their lore, Quetzalcoatl said and did many of the things that the Incas and Maya claimed for Viracocha and Kukulkan. By the way, Quetzal is the name of a plumed bird in the Aztec language.

"In the Aztec myth, Quetzalcoatl, after ten years of struggle, suffered defeat at the hands of an evil doer named Tezcatlpoca who advocated ritual sacrifice to postpone the end of the world. Subsequently Quetzalcoatl set off to the east over the water, promising the people that he would return.

"When Hernan Cortez landed in Mexico in 1519, he was believed, to the eventual regret of the Aztecs, to have been the reincarnation of Quetzalcoatl. Moctezuma thought that since the Spanish had come from the same direction that Quetzalcoatl had last been seen, and also because the Spanish wore the same type of beard, that Cortez might be the returning god. They came to believe that because of the humiliation Quetzalcoatl had suffered, he was now returned to destroy them.

"Nonetheless, they entertained Cortez and his troops with 'tchocolatl,' which Quetzalcoatl had taught them to cultivate, and then, of course, the Spanish slaughtered them.

"Two of the legends say that Viracocha/Kulkulkan/Quetzalcoatl came from the heavens to earth. Because of that, in all three cultures, he was represented as a feathered serpent. He was thought to be half man and half god in one being. The bird represents heaven, the serpent represents earth.

"The three cultures - Aztec, Mayan and Incan – were, by all standards, considered advanced in many ways. The architecture of their individual buildings was amazingly precise, as were the designs of the cities in all three cultures. Their understanding of astronomy was vast and is reflected in the way their cities were laid out to reflect the Solar System and constellations, particularly in the Inca and Aztec realms. Their calendars were amazingly precise, and their art was incredibly advanced. Supposedly the god known as Viracocha or Kukulkan or Quetzalcoatl was credited for giving these crafts to the Incas, Mayans, and Aztecs.

"Some have theorized that the existence of this god can be attributed to the Vikings, who seemed to get around a lot; or to aliens from outside this world; or to people from Atlantis.

"Based on what Kulen Golendar has told us, we have an overwhelmingly strong case for claiming that the man from Atlantis, Veran Cocha, and the Inca's Viracocha are the same guy. Furthermore, in the Aztec legend we have an evildoer named Tezcatilpoca, which sounds like our evildoer from Atlantis named Tezcar Tilpocan."

With that, Gordon stopped his wandering around the conference table and found his way back to his seat.

As his audience was stunned into silence, Gordon again rose from his seat and said, "Going back to our approximation of when the pyramid was built, there is supporting evidence from some late twentieth century discoveries. In the early 1990s, an amateur Belgian astronomer named Bauval finally realized that the three major pyramids in the Giza complex are aligned exactly to mirror the configuration of the three principle stars in Orion's Belt as they were aligned in 12,500 years ago – not the conventionally reported 2,500 BCE date commonly ascribed to their construction. At that earlier time Orion hovered low on the horizon, and its belt stars had a slightly different relation to each other. The pyramids are not in the same alignment as the 2,500 BCE configuration of Orion's Belt, which was much higher in the sky at that time. Bauval has essentially proved his claim through computer simulations of the relative configurations of the stars in that earlier epoch." With that, Gordon resumed his seat.

"Thank you, Gordon," said Johanna. "Sometime in the next few days I think the three of us need some face-to-face time with Madison Tolles. In the meantime, let's keep digging. I think there is a lot more to find around here. And I would suggest that we reinforce Allison Long's team to explore those other potential soundings. A place of this size should have more than one garage."

Chuck added, "And I want to find out more about these aircraft. I went down to the garage this morning with Allison, and it was an amazing thing to see them lined up. Each one of the twelve is still fully functional. Allison's team has tested every one of them and they all fly. More than likely they run on some sort of nuclear fuel, so we have to be careful about taking them apart."

"We can give Mr. Tolles a general idea about what we have uncovered so far," said Johanna, "but with so many people in on part of this secret already, and I am referring to both the U.S. and foreign delegations from the Virginia meeting, we must be more circumspect in our communications. I am willing to bet that there are a bunch of hackers already trying to break into our communications channels." I will remind the teams of our security requirements in the morning. Meantime, let's get some sleep. We have a lot to accomplish tomorrow."

When once you have tasted flight, you will forever walk the earth with your eyes turned skyward, for there you have been, and there you will always long to return.

~

Leonardo
DaVinci

Chapter 19

No one thought they could top the discoveries of the past weeks, but the next few days surpassed all expectations.

First thing in the morning Johanna assembled the entire team and reinforced the doctrine of maximum security. She told them everything about the meeting in Virginia and the likelihood that there would be sabotage attempts on the security of their communications channels. Therefore they had to be circumspect when communicating with the Center about any additional requirements. Henceforth all communications, even routine non-sensitive messages, must be encrypted.

After the briefing, Johanna got back to Chuck and Gordon and said that Madison Tolles was still in Washington, and if they felt that an urgent meeting was required, then he would be glad to see them as soon as they could get there. Chuck told her that there were a few things they needed to do over the next few days, but that they would try to get out soon from McMurdo.

Just then Gordon got a funny look on his face. "Johanna," he began, "I think I have the makings of an idea. Can you get back to Mr. Tolles on a secure direct hook-up?"

"Sure thing, Gordon. He's got a late morning meeting scheduled, but I think he is free right now. Stand by while I contact him."

After a moment they had Tolles on screen. "What can I do for you, Gordon?"

"Mr. Tolles, I'd like a favor. Would you contact the CEO of Seahorse Aviation and ask if he can arrange to detach two of the most experienced Vertical Take Off and Landing pilots at McMurdo to work directly for me and Chuck?"

Chuck gave him a puzzled look - then it registered.

Tolles said, "It is a strange request, but I am sure you have your reasons. If you want it, you have it. Stand by while I make a call or two, and I'll get right back."

Fifteen minutes later Tolles was back on line and gave them the names of the two pilots. Retired Marine Lieutenant Colonels Jones and Ross would be expecting Gordon's call.

Gordon immediately videoed McMurdo and asked to speak to either one of the pilots. Jones got on the line and said, "Brad Jones, Sir. I understand you want me and Lucien Ross to come work for you for an indeterminate time?"

"That's right, Colonel. How soon can the two of you get dropped off here?"

"Dropped off, sir? Don't you need the aircraft?"

"Dropped off. Pack your gear and plan to stay for a while. Now how soon, Col. Jones?"

"We'll be out in three hours, sir. The CEO personally directed us to do everything you want, so we'll be right on our way."

"Good. See you in a few of hours," said Gordon, and signed off. "Okay, Allison, how far are the other sites from the garage?"

"The garage is closest to us. The other three sites are within a half mile of it," she responded.

"Good," said Gordon. "I think we should augment your team with a few engineers from the computer center. Chuck, would you arrange that? I think what we may find in the other sites could be of high technological value. Now let's get ready to go as soon as the pilots get here."

Three hours later, the noisy Condor aircraft settled on to the hard packed ice surface. Chuck, Gordon, Allison, and her augmented team approached and entered the craft using the rear ramp. Gordon had been in contact on their inbound leg and asked the pilot to ferry them all to the nearby garage site.

Once aboard the aircraft Chuck and Gordon greeted Brad Jones and Lucian Ross, the only two passengers besides the crew chief. Both were initially taken aback by Gordon. The long, flowing hair and that fierce, green-eyed visage made an imprint on them. Gordon smiled at their reaction. He was reassured when they both made eye contact and gave him a firm handshake. Chuck introduced them to Allison and her team. Allison moved forward to the cockpit to direct the pilot to the new site. Within a few minutes, they lifted off and shortly were settling in near the garage. Gordon thanked the Condor pilots for the lift, and they all de-planed with their gear.

After the aircraft lifted off to return to McMurdo, Gordon turned to Jones and Ross and, in a command voice, said, "What you are about to see is of the highest importance to our national security. It, and the other things we will reveal to you, must be considered Top-Secret, Close-Hold. No One Period No One must ever be told about what you see until it is cleared with us. Understood?"

"Yes, Sir!" they replied.

With that, the team led the pilots up to the garage and keyed in the security code. Once inside and with the door closed behind them, Chuck, Gordon, and their teammates immediately shrugged off their Arctic outerwear. Jones and Ross slowly began to drop their parkas and stood there awestruck at the enormous cavern, the lighting, and the normal room temperature.

Stripped of all his Arctic gear, Jones was a rugged looking man with blond, close-cropped hair, who stood about five foot nine and looked like he was the model for someone's statue. The guy must work out all day, thought Chuck.

Lucian Ross, an African-American, was taller, about six feet one, and with a leaner muscular build. He had a laconic, gunslinger demeanor, as if nothing in the world could faze him. Good quality to have in a combat pilot, thought Gordon. Both pilots were in their early forties.

They looked over along the wall and saw the dozen vehicles. For a moment they were silent, then they looked at Gordon. Lucien Ross spoke first. "Just where the hell are we, sir?"

Gordon grinned. "Oz, my friends, Oz. Dr. Kinoshi and I will give you the full briefing later, but first I want to explain why I asked you to be detached from your regular assignment to join us here. We represent a private research institution that is partially grant funded by the U.S. government, and we have been conducting explorations down here for the past two months. We discovered a series of caverns hollowed out inside these mountains, and are bringing in additional experts on a regular basis to assist with the discoveries. You two are the latest experts to join our ranks because of your enormous experience flying vertical-take-off-landing aircraft. Against that wall is your research project. Allison?"

Allison directed Jack Walton to demonstrate what he had learned about the aircraft. The two pilots were bug-eyed when the vehicle lifted off the floor and just silently hovered there. Jack set it down gently and got out. He motioned the two pilots over to show them what he had figured out thus far.

Jones and Ross were as excited as kids as they tested out the craft in the garage. After a short time, Gordon directed them to hold up for a bit.

"Here's your new mission, gentlemen. No pressure, but you have the entire afternoon to figure this aircraft out. I want to know how high, how far, and how fast it will fly. Each of these aircraft is obviously capable of carrying 12 people. From what we know, they should also be able to carry heavy external payloads. Have fun and don't kill yourselves. While you are testing them, we are going to figure out what makes them run. Questions?"

"Who built these things?" asked Jones.

"Men from Atlantis, sir. Men from Atlantis. We'll give you a full briefing tonight, and then you will be as smart about all this as we are."

"And you don't know what makes them run?" asked Ross.

"Chuck is guessing a nuclear power source, but I heard Allison suggest that it might be a form of magnetic levitation. Chuck and Allison are going to dissect one of them right now to see what we can discover."

Jones and Ross proceeded to the aircraft and began examining every inch of its surface. After doing that, they looked at each other and Ross produced a coin from his pocket. He flipped it in the air and Jones called heads. It came up tails, and Ross got a huge smile on his face. "Gotcha! Now don't look so upset. Somebody has to be Neil Armstrong, and I guess it's gotta be me. There's plenty of room in the cavern, so I'm going to take her up about eight feet and hover. You examine the underside and document what you see.

"Dr. Kinoshi," Ross called, "can we have the services of a camera to record our efforts?"

"No problem. And call me Chuck. And you can call him Gordon or Tallbear, he ain't too fussy. Allison, can you spare one of your people?"

"Sure, Chuck. How about it Jack? Want to advance the cause of aviation for the afternoon?"

Jack Walton was only too delighted to oblige. After about fifteen minutes of hovering and maneuvering inside the cavern, Jones asked for the hanger door to be opened. The three of them tossed their cold weather gear into the craft and proceeded out into the Antarctic daylight. They soon disappeared over the horizon.

Soon, under Chuck and Allison's direction, the engineers had figured out how to get into the hull of the aircraft through the console in the center of the cabin. The console was about eight feet long and three feet high and opened, no surprise, at pressure on indented buttons.

Indented buttons, thought Chuck. Atlanteans used them on everything.

Examining the remaining aircraft, they concluded that they operated on a magnetic levitation principle aided by an extensive series of gyroscopes in the hull of the aircraft.

Later on, after more exhaustive testing, the engineering team concluded that the power system for the aircraft was made up of a linkage of hundreds of small gyroscopes and a sophisticated magnetic suspension system in which electromagnetic force is used to counteract the effects of gravitational force. Basically, the principal involves two magnetic forces repelling each other, much the way that two magnets having their polar norths placed side by side will repel each other. This was a technology that was under development, and achieving great success, particularly in Japan and Germany, to operate maglev trains. The maglev technology allowed trains of extraordinary weight to hover a few inches above a surface and be propelled at high speeds. Somehow the people of Atlantis had mastered the technology and been able to create aircraft, based on what everyone had seen on the moving art displays in the caverns, that could fly at much greater altitudes.

Adrian Vanderwiel and Brendan Pell determined that the frequency of the electromagnetic force was in a narrow band well above the levels of common radio waves. Atlanteans had discovered anti-gravity. They knew how to reflect electromagnetic force against the gravitational force of the earth so that flying vehicles could naturally go to incredible heights with no resistance. Using a basic computer model created by Adrian, they determined that the heart of the system involved multiple harmonic notes in the audible scale electronically compressed and projected to electromagnetic levels thousands of octaves higher. This created the magnetic oscillations necessary to counteract the earth's natural gravitational pull. As Brendan and Adrian later explained to Chuck, it was more complicated than that, but simple explanations are always better.

The interlude while the specialists were figuring out the power source and the pilots were testing the aircraft proved invaluable for Chuck and Tallbear.

Tallbear said to Chuck, "Brother, we are deep in foreign territory. Our operational plan was designed to get here and conduct explorations. Mr. Tolles will need some idea about where we go from here. We can't just pack up, scratch our asses, and head back for the Center. There are too many obstacles. We need to come up with a course of action. You and I need to think this thing through. I wish Ben Crowley were here to facilitate the discussion. We are probably going to skip over some of the things we should be doing." And for the next four hours they brainstormed courses of action.

The aircraft returned late in the afternoon and the pilots couldn't wait to brief the team. Gordon and Chuck put away their laptops and gave them all their attention.

"Dr. Kinoshi, Dr. Tallbear," began Jones, "this is the most remarkable aircraft ever to fly over this planet. Once we went out and started putting it through its paces, we discovered that the aircraft apparently has no limits. The markings on the instrument panel were gibberish to us, so we couldn't get exact airspeed or altitude, but suffice it to say that without pushing it too hard, we crossed the entire continent in 40 minutes without even pushing it to its limits. The cabin automatically pressurized as we passed above 10,000 feet. I also have a GPS app on my cell phone, so

155

we also timed our travel between two fixed and well-known points on the continent. At one point I believe we exceeded 4,000 miles per hour at an altitude of 40,000 feet. That's faster than either of us has ever flown by a great magnitude. As for maximum altitude, my handy-dandy watch with all the whistles and buzzers on it said that we had taken the aircraft up to 80,000 feet. I didn't want to push it any more than that. We thought it best to come back here and fill you in on what we have discovered. Jack, however, did use the video to document everything we did. We also had him record every change to the instrument panel as we put her through her paces and matched that with recording the data on our wristwatches and cell phones. Hopefully that will help in translating the information. As to the weight carrying capability, that test will have to wait for another day, although our initial examination of the undercarriage revealed a hooking device."

"Well done, gentlemen. Now let's gather the team together and get back to our main cavern," said Gordon. He contacted Johanna and asked her to arrange for Ben Crowley to come down to help them plan the next phase of the operation.

A few minutes later Johanna got back to them and said, "Ben Crowley has suggested, in so many words, that your Ivy League education has been wasted and that you both have taken leave of your senses. I wrote this down so I wouldn't miss anything. He said, 'Nothing could be crazier than trying to bring a man in a wheelchair to a mountain slope in Antarctica. Tell those two knuckleheads to start using their gray matter. For all of their advanced education, they have a lot to learn. They have two retired Marine pilots down there who should have a pretty comprehensive knowledge of the operational planning process,' end quote. Anything else I can do for you two?"

"Ah, no, Johanna. Thanks."

Gordon and Chuck looked at each other, and finally Gordon spoke, "I really hate it when he's right."

If you don't know where you're going, you'll end up someplace else.

Yogi Berra

Chapter 20

Back at the main cavern Gordon, Chuck, Johanna, Jones and Ross gathered in the conference room. Before their meeting, she had directed Brendan Pell to show the pyramid video to the aviators to help bring them up to speed. After grabbing some food, the team briefed the pilots on Badlands Bill and the anthropological and the technological discoveries made thus far. Johanna gave them a full briefing on the Denver Center and Madison Tolles' vision and leadership. She also outlined the roles played by their business and government partners. Chuck and Tallbear caught them up on everything in the caverns, and showed them Kulen Golendar's hologram message.

Johanna finished by summarizing the Virginia conference and the potential international political considerations.

After answering many of their questions, Gordon said, "Ladies and gentlemen, this brings us to the main matter that we hope colonels Ross and Jones can help us with. Johanna is the Director of the Denver Center, a hugely responsible position requiring her to direct all administrative and operational activities. Though Johanna has authored strategic plans for the center, the scope of what we are dealing with here is pretty exceptional. Chuck is a computer technologist extraordinaire and part-time stand-up comic. I am an anthropologist with a specialty in American Indian culture. The issues we are dealing with have global and far-reaching implications for the human race.

"What we are faced with is the need to develop both short- and long-range plans and recommend the best courses of action to Madison Tolles. The one thing we can be sure about is that Mr. Tolles expects us to be able to answer all the hard questions about our plan. Our challenge is that we have never attempted something of this magnitude. The director for logistics for this operation in Antarctica, Ben Crowley, is a retired Marine who suggested that you would have the expertise to help us.

Frankly, we are all in foreign territory, both literally and figuratively.

"As you have discerned, we currently believe that all roads lead to the Great Pyramid at Giza. The question is how do we get there, or are there alternatives we haven't considered?"

Lucian said, "Both Brad and I are graduates of the Expeditionary Warfare School and the Command and Staff School at Quantico, and we both graduated from the Naval War College in Newport, Rhode Island. In our studies we had to develop an expertise in national policy and strategy at the four-star and presidential levels. En route to the big plans, though, we first have to do a thorough estimate of the situation, or what we call a Commander's Estimate. Before we can define our mission, we must determine what the desired end-state should be. We will work our way to a modified mission based on the commander's, that is, Mr. Tolles', intent, and examine the domestic and foreign political considerations. En route we will brainstorm all the courses of action available to us as well as all the obstacles that may lie waiting in our path. We will "war Game" all the courses of action against each obstacle. It is essential that we fully document our discussion."

Johanna said, "No problem. I'll record everything on my laptop and it will be simultaneously projected on the big screen here."

"Okay, let's get started."

In short order they all agreed that the original mission was research and exploration, and now they were moving to the practical application of their discoveries.

"The fact that the hologram revealed the Great Pyramid to be a power plant capable of supplying an endless stream of clean energy means one of two possible things," said Gordon. "Either we need a plan that will lead to the re-activation of the pyramid at Giza, or we need a plan to build one of our own. Standing in the way of finalizing any type of plan is the fact that the data contained in the Atlantis computer system has not yet been fully accessed. Undoubtedly the technical specifications required for any plan to be put in place needs to be clear and precise. We'll have to wait until the computer people gain full access to all the Atlantis data. But we can still move forward with the basics."

Brad Jones and Lucien Ross were masterful at facilitating the discussion, and seemed to instinctively know when the group was getting mired in the weeds of detail, or going off the main track of the discussion. After several hours they had examined a huge range of obstacles that they potentially would encounter.

"Good Lord," Chuck exclaimed. "There are a ton of things standing in our way. We have international demand for sharing the wealth as well as international resistance to any action being solely controlled by the United States. We also have the potential religious turmoil that might ensue following the publication of the anthropological data and the technical discoveries that predated human history as the world knows it. Traditional Egyptologists will raise a big stink about that. And Egypt is not exactly the locus of stability at this time. In addition might be their perception that the western powers, mainly the United States, is attempting to denigrate Egyptians' contributions to history by claiming that it was not Egyptians, but Atlanteans who gave these gifts to civilization. You also know there's going to be a firestorm of obstacles thrown our way from the carbon producing industries. And let's not forget our own political situation. Each of our two political parties will oppose anything the other favors."

"Yes, Chuck," said Johanna, "but we can't let all that bog us down. Whatever we come up with, it has to be something that will be so compelling that only the most obstinate will criticize it."

For each obstacle they had to come up with several courses of action to counter and overcome the obstacle, and then choose the most appropriate one. After selecting courses of action, which ranged from political approaches to public relations campaigns to implementation of clean energy solutions, the group struggled with the new mission to recommend to Madison Tolles.

Among their chief considerations were the revelations about the technology. Moreover, security for all of it had to be considered. If the technology were to be removed, if the aircraft were to be removed, where would it all go, and how would it be either protected or shared?

They spent some time just talking about the aircraft. On the one hand, the magnetic levitation technology would be a technological boon for the world. On the other hand, the wrong people could use its potential for weapons systems.

There were no simple answers.

"Once we have all the information from the Atlantis computer system, our planning must include the nearly preposterous suggestion that we build our own pyramid on American soil to the exact same standards of the original," said Gordon.

By midnight they were all getting a little punchy and agreed to get a good night's sleep and begin the refining process over the next several days.

In an instant, a treasure of incalculable value lay gleaming before us.

Edgar

Alan Poe: *The Gold Bug*

Chapter 21

Allison Long had been pushing her team hard. They had three highly significant acoustic readings of hollow rock under the ice-encrusted mountain just one-half mile from the aircraft cavern, but they couldn't find any entrances.

One of her four person technician teams had gone on a scouting mission to check out an area that previously hadn't been looked at too closely, mainly because it seemed inaccessible. It required the team to climb a rocky outcropping and then descend into a narrow defile. They ascended the outcropping, and at its peak radioed back to Allison that she better bring the rest of the team up. Well-equipped to make the ascent, they all arrived at the top to see something they did not expect.

Below them, down the defile, was a roughly circular flat area about one hundred feet in diameter. Allison said, "I don't see the significance of that open area other than that it's symmetrical."

The team leader said, "Not down there, look across and up."

Allison shifted her gaze to see where he was pointing. Beyond and to the right of the open area the "mountain" they were looking at had a symmetrically shaped dome. They were definitely not expecting symmetry in such a place. Allison said, "Take the team down to the open area and see what you can find. In the meantime I'll see if we can get one of the pilots to fly over and examine the landscape."

As soon as the team began descending the slope, she got on the radio and called Chuck with her request. Within fifteen minutes a silent aircraft was over her position. It slowly descended to an open spot and the door opened.

"Dr. Long, would you like a lift?" asked Brad Jones.

"It is Ms. Long to my friends," she replied with mock haughtiness. Then she added, "Only if you are going my way."

"Yes, Ma'am. Just tell me where you want to go."

Allison scrambled aboard and the ship lifted off.

"Just there, over to the right. I want to examine that dome."

"Got it, Ma'am. How close do you want to get to it?"

"Ideally only a foot or two above it. I'd like to scan the whole surface. I'll be running my acoustic instruments to find out what we are seeing. And please call me Allison."

The craft began a slow descent and began its close-up fly-over. After about 25 minutes, Allison's radio began to crackle.

"Where are you, Allison?" excitedly asked her team leader.

"I'm hovering right above the dome on the far side, southeast, away from the outcropping where we started."

"Okay, but have your pilot lift off away from the dome a bit. We found an entrance to a cavern. It has a huge doorway, bigger than the one at the hanger cavern where the twelve aircraft are stored. We ran a quick test and got the code for the keypad. Once the door opened - oh, Lord, you are not going to believe this – we're in a place that trumps everything we have see so far! We discovered a second keypad that I think will open the dome. Stand by, and be sure you have your sun glasses on."

Allison looked at Jones and said, "I wonder what he means by that?"

Jones just shrugged his shoulders and moved the aircraft about 150 feet above the dome. Slowly the dome opened, and as the low-slung Antarctic afternoon Sun's rays crept into the opening, gradually a glow developed until Allison was looking straight down into a sea of gold.

"Holy Mother of God!" she exclaimed. "That's incredible!"

A short time later, in the symmetrical area near the opening of the new cavern, Johanna, Gordon, Chuck, their team leaders, and pilots Jones and Ross stood alongside Allison and her team looking at a most extraordinary sight. The entire cavern was stacked with rows upon rows of gold plating in varying square, rectangular and trapezoidal sizes. It was mind numbing to see this much gold in one place.

Just to the left of the main entrance to the 'golden dome' was another massive door. In short order the crew had it open and they walked in to see sixty more aircraft waiting silently. Adjacent to this aircraft 'hanger' was another room, much smaller, but with what looked like slanted architect's tables and scrolled acetate-like documents in cubby holes along one wall. Tallbear quickly went over to the wall and began pulling out large documents and spreading them out on one of the tables. He soon found what he was looking for. Motioning Johanna and Chuck over, he pointed to a spot on the thin, opaque, plastic-like map. The place he was pointing to was approximately east-central South Dakota. Clearly indicated was the location of the last of the Atlantis explorers and the route that brought him there.

"I'll be wanting my team to spend some time here," Tallbear began, "and I want to study this map some more. I believe we have found Badlands Bill."

Johanna said, "Just when I think my awe quotient has hit maximum, another door opens and I am stunned again. There can't be more than we have uncovered already. Can there?"

"I don't know, Johanna," said Tallbear. "It is going to take years to unravel all of this."

"Amen, cousin, amen," said Chuck.

After documenting everything on video, they closed the caverns and returned to their base.

At the command center, they brainstormed the implications of this latest discovery.

"This gold, without a doubt, was the plating for the top section of the Great Pyramid at Giza. To what end and for what purpose it served, we don't know just yet. But Kulen Golendar's hologram gave a clear message. The plating they had applied to the Great Pyramid had to be removed before the people of Atlantis moved underground. If we are talking about the application of these discoveries, we are going to have to deal with the reality that the gold is going to have to be placed back on the pyramid eventually. That will mean dealing with a sometimes intransigent and politically unstable Egypt and its Bureau of Antiquities to get permission. We will also face a firestorm of protest from the Egyptologists worldwide. They do not like to change their thinking on anything."

All the people who couldn't get dates on Saturday night are now running the world.

A political analyst on Bill Clinton winning the presidency in 1992

Chapter 22

Damien Cooper, PhD., one of Chuck's mathematics/computer wizards, had the lead on compiling all information available on the construction of the Great Pyramid at Giza. He had done enormous research through contemporary resources, and was now extracting translations of the pyramid specifications from the Atlantis computer database. Awaiting the information download, he reflected on the staggering amount of both factual data and speculative lore available just through open internet resources.

The more he found out, the more he wanted to know.

Brendan Pell and Adrian Vanderwiel joined him as he stared at the Atlantis data display and listened to English translations. They were mesmerized by the graphic display indicating that this advanced civilization had used music to cut and move rock weighing tons.

The principles were fairly simple. The people of Atlantis would take anywhere from two to six notes that are in harmony with each other - a musical chord - and electronically compress them, to hyper-intensive levels, and bring them up selected scores of octaves to achieve different technological wonders. Brendan and Adrian wondered at the infinite mathematical permutations of combined musical notes.

The challenge that Denver Center technicians were dealing with was "what happens when two harmonic notes, or three, four, five, or six notes are digitally compressed and accelerated up thousands of octaves to where the compressed Herz rates are converted into thousands, millions, or even billions of cycles per second?"

Radio frequencies range from 3 Herz (3Hz) to 300 Giga Herz (300GHz). In between is everything from Ultra Low to Ultra High frequency bands of varying widths. Included somewhere in the middle are AM, VHF, FM, and Short Wave radio bands. It appeared that using the hand held device to increase harmonic groupings of notes up to the radio frequency bands enabled a person from Atlantis to communicate world-wide if needed. Going beyond the radio frequency bands one potentially could achieve engineering marvels.

The data that flowed from the Atlantis computers affirmed that using the hand-held device with pre-programmed note combinations, the operator could increase the compressed note combinations up an infinite number of octaves and either communicate, cut rock, lift great masses of stone, project energy pulses as a weapon, and who knows what else. They were going to have to create a number of computer simulations until they found the key to the secrets of these ancient people.

In order to confirm the data, Brendan and Adrian went back to their quarters and sat down at their own computers to start building mathematical music models.

Damien stayed in the computer center and entered his own calculations into the Atlantis system.

While he worked on some possible models that would explain how music worked into the technology of Atlantis, the translations of the Atlantean information began to flow. With a growing sense of awe, he absorbed the architectural data. When he saw the mathematical calculations of the Great Pyramid and its two sister pyramids, along with the schematic diagrams and footnotes, he nearly yelled in delight at not only the precision with which they had calculated, but at the mathematical meanings behind the precision of each and every feature.

A lanky six-foot two inches with slightly stooped shoulders, Damien Cooper always looked, in the words of one of his friends, like a homeless person. The combination of the shaggy goatee, long ponytail, and shabby clothes gave him the air of a lost hippie transplanted from the 60s.

Damien was simply a product of his own creation. Born with an extraordinary intellect, he excelled at mathematics and science, and by the age of thirteen had become mesmerized by the world of music. Damien had no real friends growing up, though he longed for them. He was born and raised just outside of Buffalo, New York, to solid working class parents. His father was a baggage handler at the airport, and his mother a line worker in a company that made carburetor filters for the automobile aftermarket. They loved him unconditionally, and were incredibly supportive, but they could not grasp the depth of his brilliance. Part of that was because their son had difficulty communicating.

Damien suffered from an incredible stammer that for years made him the victim of taunting by his classmates. Whenever he tried to speak, his mouth and face contorted and the slow process of forcing words out left him humiliated and exhausted. Despite therapy his parents arranged, he made little progress.

Though skilled in academics, he was once ridiculed by his eighth grade English teacher, Agnes McGann, a thin, black haired, hawk-nosed, bony- faced spinster of a woman. She was all edge, as Dickens would say, and she had a voice that could split rock. Early in the fall semester of eighth grade, in front of the entire class, she called him a "stupid, stupid boy," because he could not get out an answer to one of her questions without painful stammering. Damien never forgot that shame at age 14, a difficult time in any boy's life. At that age, an adolescent boy would never ask for help. His parents knew that he suffered from the taunting of bullies, and they tried to compensate by showing him unlimited love and support. But they were unaware of the torment he endured from one of his teachers. Despite his grades on quizzes and tests, Miss McGann kept her relentless attack on him through the academic year. She often bragged in the teachers' lounge that she would 'cure' him of his stammer one of these days even if it killed her. One wag said, "Whatever it takes, Agnes, whatever it takes."

In January of that year applications were entertained for the entrance exams for a Jesuit day preparatory school. Damien's parents, always concerned for his welfare, asked him if he was interested. Damien laughed, and with Agnes McGann in mind, thought of a Weird Al Yankovich song that had the lyric, 'I would rather spend an eternity eating shards of broken glass than spend one more minute with you.' He nodded vigorously. His parents contacted his 7th grade English teacher, Mrs. Farrell, whom Damien liked very much, to see if she would tutor him in the Humanities for the entrance exam, particularly in the areas of English Lit and History. As brilliant as Damien was in math and the sciences, the humanities were never his strong suit. She readily agreed, and tutored him so successfully that he easily aced the entrance exam.

After nearly a whole academic year enduring Miss McGann's relentless attacks, desperately anticipating his entrance to the prep school, he finally received his letter of acceptance in the spring of his eighth grade year. Agnes McGann told him, in front of an audience of his classmates of course, that he would be a complete failure at the prep school, and that he should reconcile himself to quitting school at sixteen and getting a job in a factory. He was surprisingly buoyed up by a former teacher, Mr. Norton.

Mr. Norton was a tall, bean-pole of a man who had taught seventh grade history, but then took ill. Damien, while greatly enjoying Mr. Norton's class, had always thought of him as Ichabod Crane. It turned out that Mr. Norton had terminal brain cancer. He came back to school in late spring of eighth grade following unsuccessful neurosurgery, with a shaved spot on his skull covered by a medical dressing. One day he was walking down the hallway and saw Damien sitting in geography class. He interrupted the class and asked the teacher if he could speak to Damien for a minute. The teacher was a good friend of Mr. Norton's and would deny him nothing under the circumstances. He excused Damien to go out in the hallway. Outside the classroom Mr. Norton said, "I understand that one of my colleagues has been giving you a hard time." Damien's eyes watered as he bowed his head in shame. Mr. Norton took him by the chin and lifted Damien's face so he could look into the boy's deep brown eyes. "You are a brilliant young man. Now go out and show that rotten bitch she's wrong."

For the first time in his life, Damien felt like he was not alone. He threw his arms around Mr. Norton's waist and became wracked with sobs. Mr. Norton slowly pushed Damien to arm's length and said, "Now go and do it. For you and for me." Damien got a radiant smile on his face and became filled with resolve.

Mr. Norton passed away the following fall, and Damien never forgot that kindness from a man who certainly had a lot more to worry about than the troubles of an eighth grade kid. He faced life with a new determination and made a solemn promise to honor Mr. Norton's memory.

The scholarship ride through MIT brought him a BS degree, two masters degrees and a PhD in computer science by the age of twenty-five. He received a waiver on his orals. Fuck Agnes McGann.

But despite his academic talents, Damien's main interest in life was his Martin guitar. An uncle's collection of old blues records, discovered in the winter of eighth grade, made him fall in love with the rhythms of Robert Johnson, Leadbelly, Josh White, and Blind Lemon Jefferson. It became his life's passion to play the blues like the old masters. He largely succeeded. And he had discovered by the summer after his escape from eighth grade, that when he first tried to sing, his stammer vanished. Soon he developed his singing voice and found an incredible joy at being able to get in front of people and communicate with them through song. After a few performances in the annual high school talent contests, he started to develop friendships.

By the time he went to prep school, after mastering the art of playing a modestly priced acoustic guitar, he went about the process of discovery that would lead him to the perfect guitar. He went from music store to music store and tried out every different guitar he could get his hands on. Finally he discovered the exact sound he was looking for.

For the next three years, he scrimped and saved every dollar he could get his hands on through after school and full-time summer jobs until he had amassed the $3000 he needed for a Martin D-16 Rosewood acoustic-electric model. That guitar represented a lot of snow shoveling and lawn cutting. The problem was that there was little market for a talented, white,

Buffalo-based suburbanite in the blues world. But when he got to MIT he played all the open mike venues in Boston, and occasionally was asked to sit in with various blues bands. Reaching deep into his own torments, he captured the depths of the blues and gave all that he had to his audiences. He easily picked up enough in tips every week to comfortably meet his living expenses through college and grad school.

Upon completion of his doctoral dissertation at MIT, he was personally recruited by Chuck Kinoshi to work for the Denver Center. Chuck also provided him with a list of all the blues clubs in Denver and its surroundings. Chuck did all the talking and simply asked Damien to nod his head if he wanted to join him in Colorado. The situation suited Damien perfectly. He would have the solitude of the mountains to do what he was trained for, and the relative convenience of getting into Denver on weekends to play the clubs. In his living quarters at the Denver Center, he set up one room just for his music. In it he had a Fender acoustic amp, a state-of-the-art sound system, and a computer system dedicated to making recordings.

He took a less expensive guitar to Antarctica, fearing what the cold might do to the perfectly crafted Martin, but after discovering the ideal climate inside the mountain caverns, he emailed Ben Crowley and asked if his Martin could be shipped in a temperature controlled container. Ben, who had a fatherly affection for this odd young man, emailed back that this indeed could be done as there were several computer servers that had to be sent down in a temperature controlled environment. He would arrange for it on the next shipment.

While Damien was basically shy in his interpersonal communications, he was a natural entertainer and provided some terrific musical diversion for the research crew in the caverns of Atlantis. He linked up with Brendan Pell, who had arranged for his Yamaha keyboard to be sent down, and the two of them rocked the caverns between shifts. Occasionally Brendan would throw in a classical piece, and Damien discovered that he could finger-pick incredible improvisational backgrounds.

. . .

English and Humanities majors always marvel at the mathematics geniuses and wonder how they can get so excited about numbers. Let's face it, they think, numbers are just numbers. They are not thoughts or feelings. What is there to get excited about?

Damien knew what to get excited about, particularly since he had been reading alternative theories on the pyramids and their measurements from contemporary sources. Now he was seeing the actual Atlantis data and schematics on the construction of the Great Pyramid and its sister pyramids flowing from the font. With the data, came many explanatory paragraphs elucidating the reasons for the measurements.

While many conventional Egyptologists had speculated that these measurements were coincidental or accidental, and insisted that it was the Pharaoh Khufu's burial chamber, Damien could see that these numbers were intentionally calculated into the design of the pyramid for another reason.

But that raised some significant questions.

Did the data mean that it was essential for the pyramid to be built with this extraordinary precision because such precision was critical to the structure's functionality, and was the pyramid itself therefore harmonically integrated with the planet because of these precision measurements? Or was this degree of perfection calculated into the structure a way of this advanced civilization simply telling future civilizations that an exceptionally advanced culture once lived here? Or was it a combination of both?

There was a pause in the flow of information coming from the Atlantean computers. Then it resumed, and the full mystery of the pyramid was revealed. Damien had the answers right in front of him.

It definitely was not a burial chamber, and it truly was a power plant, as had been speculated on by a number of people before the hologram affirmed it. The structure was designed to convert hydrogen to energy using the earth's resonant harmonics.

It was a massive energy machine with no moving parts. And it ran on music from the earth.

Damien wept.

A cool head and a light hand are as important in an office as they are in a cockpit.

Anne Marie MacDonald, "The Way the Crow Flies"

Chapter 23

Tallbear and Chuck had been meeting privately with Damien for more than three hours. Damien had sent them text messages to have them come to the computer center where he could share the new information privately rather than try to explain it himself before the full body of technicians. But once again his stammer was preventing him from telling the story.

Tallbear finally leaned forward and gently touched Damien's shoulder. Speaking softly he said, "Damien, try singing it to us."

At first Damien wasn't sure if he was being mocked, but then he saw the sincere concern on Tallbear's face. He smiled and thought a minute. Then he had it. He would model his revelations on Kulen Golendar's hologram speech. He thought about it for a minute, took a breath and began to sing, at first in musical scales, then in more elaborate musical patterns. He forced himself to control his enthusiasm or he would have sounded like Bach on steroids.

"Brendan and Adrien are analyzing data from the Atlantis computer system that affirms music as the baseline for almost all Atlantean technological achievements. They will be able to tell you what musical note combinations produce the capabilities of communicating, cutting, and lifting at various levels above the basic audible music scale. They are working on computer models as we speak."

For the next three hours, Damien held Tallbear and Chuck in thrall as he reaffirmed through downloaded data on what contemporary theorists had only speculated. Damien sang an amazing tale, interrupted only periodically with a question or request for clarification from Tallbear or Chuck. He started by telling them about Amon Goro, Master Architect of Atlantis, and the story of why he designed the pyramid complex and how it works. His improvised singing told them the full history of the pyramid and the purpose behind its precise measurements.

"Master Architect Amon Goro gave a decisive design feature the Great Pyramid – and only to the Great Pyramid – which was the slight indentation that ran from the peak to the base down the middle of each of the four sides, making the Great Pyramid the only eight sided pyramid in the world. The enormous pressures that would be placed on the interior walls from the vibrations would necessitate a natural reinforcement of the structure."

Next, he told them about the dimensions of the Great Pyramid, reaffirming some things already calculated by contemporary theorists.

"The number 365.24, the exact number of days in a year, crops up all over the place. The length of the sides converts to 365.24. The perimeter of the base divided by 100 equals 365.24. It is also deliberately calculated into the length of the internal ante-chamber, the Grand Gallery, the King's Chamber, and many other places as well."

He sang of the 1:43,200 ratios that were built into the pyramid to reflect the earth's measurements. "This is not groundbreaking news," he sang. "We have known for some time that 1:43,200 reflects not only the radius of the earth, but the polar radius of the earth as it related to the pyramid. We did not know why such accuracy was built into the design. The measurement ensures that the pyramid is in perfect balance with Earth's forces."

"The number 43,200 is not a random number," Damien sang. "Curious variations of the number occur in various ancient myths, and, oddly, which may be of interest to Dr. Tallbear, in the modern game of baseball."

At this, Tallbear perked up.

"In India there is a myth about the length of the gods' years being equivalent to 432,000 years of man.

"In ancient Norse mythology, the final apocalypse will have one cataclysmic battle in which the number of soldiers was to be 432,000.

"The earth migrates around the band of the zodiac signs at a rate of one degree every 72 years, and 30 degrees, or one complete zodiacal constellation, every 2160 years. Precession through two zodiacal constellations takes 4320 years.

"Now for something that is really off the charts, and which will interest Dr. Tallbear in particular. For years, people have touted the mystical precision of baseball. They most often center their concentration on the frequent use of threes and nines in baseball. For example, three strikes becomes an out, three outs ends an inning. As for nines, there are nine players on a team and nine innings in a game. There are twenty-seven outs in a game, which is evenly divided by both three and nine. Pointing out the more ethereal, theoretically, a game of baseball could continue to infinity if the score were tied at the end of each inning after the regulation nine innings had been played. But those enthusiasts may have missed something important. I remembered reading something a while back, and I confirmed it today, that in Major League Baseball, the most difficult feat - and the one most rarely accomplished - is the pitching of a perfect game. A perfect game happens when a pitcher faces only 27 batters in nine innings and none of them ever reaches first base. This is so rare an occurrence that in Major League Baseball it happens on average only once approximately every 43,200 games played. And 43,200 is also equally divisible by three and nine."

Tallbear and Chuck sat stunned at this bit of information.

"This may just be a coincidence," continued Damien, "but it is sure interesting. It makes me wonder just how significant the number 43,200 is in relation to everything in the cosmos.

176

Damien sang on speculating about the question of whether there was an ancient knowledge about the ratio of the pyramid in relation to the measurements of the earth and the heavens that was encoded in these timeless myths.

He concluded this portion of his exposition singing, "It is a remarkable cultural curiosity that so many ancient cultural myths reflected the numbers found in the zodiacal precession as well as the ratio of the great Pyramid's circumference and height to the earth's circumference and polar radius.

Damien went on at length about the incredible precision of both the exterior and interior design. "Such precision is astonishing. A present day architect would not be required to build with that level of accuracy if he or she were constructing a skyscraper in a modern city.

"But a question is begged by such precision, and that question has not been answered yet by the translations of the data. As we have seen, the perfections of measurement have a meaning. They tell us that the builders had a mastery of global and celestial dimensions. My question is, when we see imperfections – miniscule though they may be - such as the slight deviations in the lengths of the pyramid sides, are these tiny imperfections telling us something else? Were they deliberate? Do they have meaning as well?"

Damien's song continued in its description of the pyramid's structure. He sang about the choice of the site of the pyramid at close to the 30th parallel telling us that the builders knew exactly where the geographic center of the earth's landmasses lay. An extraordinary calculation by today's standards. In the measurements of the sides of the pyramid, Damien went on to sing about the miniscule error rate represented by the measurements of the base of the pyramid. He pointed out that the north side is slightly shorter than the south side, an error representing a minute fraction of one percent based on an average of over 9000 inches per side.

He speculated that there is a purpose to this exceptionally small error.

"If we were to draw two lines following the ever-so-slight angles of the west and east facing sides, would those lines converge at a significant point on earth? Say magnetic north as it was positioned 12,450 years ago? Or might they converge above the earth's north pole pointing to the north star of the era in which the pyramid was built? As with the affirmation that the three pyramids reflect the relationship of the three stars in Orion's Belt 12,450 years ago, might the imprecision of the side measurements of the Great Pyramid be actually another precise confirmation of that date?

"These people seemed to do nothing without a purpose. If the accuracies represent certain significant phenomena, might not the inaccuracies, such as the exact location of the center of the pyramid, also have a purpose?

"In the early 1880s, a Professor Smyth surveyed the latitude of the center of the Great Pyramid. His measurements have been confirmed by modern satellite surveys and images.

"Smyth's survey put the center of the pyramid at 29 degrees, 58 minutes, and 51 seconds of latitude, or 29.9809833 in decimal form. Initially everyone was impressed with how nearly exactly the ancient builders had come to the 30th degree parallel latitude of the earth. It was considered a most impressive feat of engineering. Ultimately, many pyramid analysts realized that we in the modern era had used a lack of imagination in analyzing this measurement. There is a greater significance to this number.

"The speed of light in decimal form is 29.9792458 times 10 million meters per second. Einstein used this number in his famous 'Energy equals Mass times Speed of Light squared' equation. This number corresponds very closely to the number Professor Smyth came up with, but not exactly.

"The number 29.9809833 ties energy and matter together in the universe. Dividing that number by 10,000,000 apparently converts light speed to latitude near the center of the pyramid. This is seems another of the precise gifts these people have left us, but we have not yet unlocked the primer enough to fully understand the exact meaning of these relationships.

"This light speed-latitude number doesn't pass through the center of the Great Pyramid, but rather it is a position right between the Great Pyramid and the second pyramid. Some theorize that this location is the exact spot marking where there is an underground hydrogen storage chamber that feeds the pyramid engine.

"There is another possibility that may offer a simpler explanation. The speed of light in decimal form is 29.9809833. The location of the center-line of the structure, 29.9792458, rounds off to 29.980. Maybe the location is not a miniscule mistake keeping it slightly below the 30 degree latitude mark. Maybe it is both the precise center of Earth's landmasses and a clue that they completely understood the speed of light. And why shouldn't they given the discoveries we have made.

"The precision measurements built into the pyramid are deliberate. Some may have a lot to do with its functionality, some are clues to the extent of their knowledge, and others are purely ornamental," Damien sang. "We are being told that an advanced civilization once lived here, and that there are mathematical clues as to when exactly this civilization built this extraordinary structure. All the calculated measurements reflect the dimensions of the Earth, Moon and Sun, and accurately reflect the mathematical relationships each has with the others.

"The data also confirms that the precision cutting of the granite blocks within the internal passageways and chambers is calculated to ensure the introduction of acoustical vibrations at a specific frequency level. While we know that granite has great resonant qualities, the granite used in the Great Pyramid contains 55% or more quartz, which enhances resonation.

"The smooth cuts on the sides and bottoms of these granite beams indicate that they were cut to 0.0001 of an inch of accuracy. But the data also confirms that the irregular contours of the top surface of the beams in the Weight Relief area above the King's Chamber were shaped so that each individual 70 ton beam was finely tuned so that if you struck it, it would resonate in the key of 'A'. These beams were sculpted on their upper surfaces so that each beam was completely in tune with all the others. And they were sculpted more than 500 miles away from the actual site of the Great Pyramid complex at Giza.

"The Grand Gallery, which is made of granite, was originally lined with resonators, according to the recently downloaded data, and designed to re-channel the key of F# vibrations of the earth into the King's Chamber at a new rate of 438 cycle per second, or the key of A, through the coffer in the King's Chamber. This is the precise rate at which hydrogen gas can be stimulated and be converted into pure energy.

"In short, Music equals Mathematics equals Vibration equals Energy.

"The upper external levels of the Great Pyramid were capped with sheets of gold, and that is another stroke of genius. Gold is highly resistant to corrosion, and is an excellent reflector of electromagnetic radiation such as infrared and radio waves. That's why we use it on many artificial satellites as a protective coating. The pyramid gold cap serves a unique purpose. Hydrogen gas flows into the King's Chamber and accumulates waiting for a catalyst to convert it into microwave energy. It needs to be enhanced. Microwave signals created by atomic hydrogen, which bombard the earth constantly, are channeled down the pyramid's northern shaft. The gold cladding simply bounced microwave signals to a reflector above the northern shaft. The microwave signals reflected down the shaft where they hyper-stimulated hydrogen atoms accumulating in the King's Chamber coffer, channeling them to beam out of the southern shaft as pure energy.

"One of the last mysteries of the Great Pyramid is the mortar that seals one block of stone to another. Researchers over the years have ascertained the chemical breakdown of this substance, but no one has been able to reproduce the mortar, despite exhaustive attempts. Thanks to the data dump, we now have the mortar recipe. It may be one of the most important secrets that we have uncovered.

"And one other thing. When we watched the video of the pyramid being constructed, when the initial signal was given to activate it, there was a panicked response as smoke began coming out of it. The data dump revealed that on the first test, the baffles that channeled the earth's resonance in the key of 'F' into the Grand Gallery where the baffles converted the musical key to 'A' and channeled the sound into the King's Chamber, were not aligned properly. That created the frantic response we witnessed. The data dump revealed that the first test was a failure, and that has been confirmed by recent discoveries that there was a chemical reaction inside the pyramid that caused some cosmetic structural damage."

At this, Damien slumped back in his chair, exhausted by the effort of singing the tale of the pyramid. He felt like he had done a non-stop concert in a stadium filled with 60,000 fans.

Tallbear nodded, reached over to Damien and put a reassuring hand on his shoulder, and said, "You have done a remarkable service to this expedition. Your research is the key to its success, and we are forever grateful."

"Amen to that," said Chuck. "Damien, you have unlocked some extraordinary secrets that have only been speculated on for years. Thank you, my friend."

Damien nodded and began to think of how he could impart this information in a Blues format. It gave him a lot to think about as he went to sleep that night. It would make one hell of an epic Blues song. Atlantis Rhapsody. Maybe even better than Gershwin's *Rhapsody in Blue*. He must talk with Brendan Pell and Adrian Vanderwiel about it.

All labor that uplifts humanity has dignity and importance and should be undertaken with painstaking excellence!

Martin Luther King, Jr.

Chapter 24

Atlantis, 12,500 Years ago

A unique design feature Amon Goro gave to the Great Pyramid – and only to the Great Pyramid – was the slight indentation that ran from the peak to the base down the middle of each of the four sides. The enormous pressures that would be placed on the interior walls from the vibrations that the structure would be subjected to necessitated a natural reinforcement. The slight indentations were the perfect design feature to accomplish this.

The curvature designed into the faces of the pyramid exactly matches the radius of the earth.

Goro directed the workers in the careful process of laying the casing stones. The Great Pyramid alone was covered by 144,000 highly polished, slant faced, white limestone casing stones, or cladding, that formed a smooth shiny surface. These hard limestone units were 100 inches thick and weighed 20 tons each. This limestone was like marble, but superior in hardness, and would be extremely durable against the elements. The cladding was visible on the bottom two-thirds of the Great Pyramid. The upper third was dressed in solid gold plate above the limestone cladding.

When the pyramid was completed in just under five years' time, Goro reflected on the measurements he had calculated into the construction.

The pyramid was 481.3949 feet high. The height exactly reflected two things: one, the average height above sea level of all the earth's landmasses, and two, the ratio between the radius and circumference of a circle as if the circle were drawn around the base of the pyramid.

As Goro smiled to himself, he realized that someday someone would realize that the construction was founded on the universal mathematical principle of *pi*. Someday, he thought, someone will figure out that the ratio of the great Pyramid's circumference and its height reflects the earth's circumference and polar radius.

The circumference at the base of the pyramid multiplied by 43,200, is the exact circumference of the earth.

The height of the pyramid multiplied by 43,200 is the earth's polar radius.

The length of each side of the pyramid is approximately 9131 inches. That represents 365.24 pyramid cubits, which is the number of days in a year. The perimeter of the base divided by 100 equals 365.24. The length of the internal antechamber used as the diameter of a circle produces a circumference of 365.24. The ratio of the length of the granite portion of the antechamber's floor to the main upper chamber translates to 365.24. The ratio of the lengths of the angled resonance gallery to the solid diagonal of the main upper chamber times 100 equals 365.24.

There are numerous other measurements related to the height and other dimensions of the pyramid that reflect exactly the distance to the Sun. Other measurements translate into the radius of the Earth's orbit around the Sun and other celestial phenomena.

Ah, thought Goro, life is wonderful. Tens of thousands of years from now, people will know that a greatly advanced civilization had once mastered the mysteries of the earth and the cosmos.

Oh, I have slipped the surly bonds of earth and danced the skies on laughter-silvered wings; Sunward I've climbed, and joined the tumbling mirth of sun-split clouds...and done a hundred things you have not dreamed of ...

Wheeled and soared and swung high in the sunlit silence. Hov'ring there,I've chased the shouting wind along, and flung my eager craft through footless halls of air.

Up, up the long, delirious, burning blue I've topped the windswept heights with easy grace where never lark, or even eagle flew. And, while with silent, lifting mind I've trod

The high untrespassed sanctity of space, put out my hand, and touched the face of God.

High Flight by John Gillespie Magee, Jr.

Chapter 25

It had been six weeks since everyone had departed for Antarctica, and Johanna had been sending updates on their progress every four hours to Madison Tolles. She had sent Tolles the edited videos, and he was elated with the remarkable discoveries. One morning, Johanna contacted him on the first of her regular daily briefings.

"Mr, Tolles," began Johanna, "We are coming up to give you a pretty comprehensive briefing. Can you get us a highly secure location where we can land and meet you away from prying eyes? And also, can you get us advanced clearance from air traffic control? We are going to bring a couple of the Atlantis aircraft up, and we need to do this so securely that no one will ever know about it."

"Certainly, Johanna. I'll get on that right away, but the Air Traffic Control people will need to know your flight plan."

"You may have to pull a rabbit out of your hat to make this happen, but I'll put one of the pilots on with you and he will give you the details," she replied.

Ross got on the video and told Tolles what their plan was. "Good morning, sir. My name is Lucien Ross, and I'd like to thank you for putting Brad Jones and me on this assignment. Our plan for later today is to fly up over the center of the Atlantic Ocean at an altitude exceeding 80,000 feet and at airspeed in excess of 4,000 miles per hour. Flight time should be about three hours and forty-five minutes. We will be in two aircraft."

"What?" said Tolles. "Say that again, Col. Ross."

Ross repeated it and added a little explanation about the aircraft.

When Tolles heard the plan and the details of the flight, he had to contain his emotions. "Stand by, Colonel, this is going to take a few calls for me to set up. Sit tight and I will get back to you ASAP."

Tolles immediately called Vice President Pemberton and asked to see him about an extremely urgent matter. The VP cleared his calendar in anticipation of the meeting. When Tolles outlined his request, along with the flight details, the Vice President, at first slack-jawed, insisted on being there for the briefing. Vice President Pemberton said, "I recommend the Patuxent River Naval Air Station in Maryland as probably the most secure location. Pax River is the Naval aircraft test facility and has excellent security."

After making several more calls, he received confirmation that it was all set up. The Vice President said, "Wait here, Madison. I need to catch the President up on all this. After your people meet with us, we'll come back to the White House and give him the full briefing."

After the VP updated the President on the situation, Tolles got his approval. He connected back to Johanna to give her the green light. She said, "Thanks Mr. Tolles. We'll see you in a few hours." Tolles sat back resisting the urge to gloat about what would finally be revealed to the president.

Shortly the Vice President said, "Our ride is here," and led Tolles out to the waiting Marine helicopter.

•   •   •

Johanna said, "We need to split into two groups for this trip. We will be flying in aircraft that we are not that familiar with, even though Brad and Lucien have been putting them through their paces. I've duplicated everything we have discovered down here, from the complete videos we have taken to the abbreviated presentation we will be giving to Mr. Tolles and the Vice President. Each aircraft will carry a set of these records. Allison Long and Hector Moineau each have a complete set, and there are five other sets sealed in secure containers should a worst case scenario ensue."

"You are painting a grim picture, Johanna," said Chuck.

"We have to be realistic, Chuck. When we fly up there, Gordon will be with me in Lucien's aircraft, and you, Damien and Brad will be in the other aircraft. We can't afford to take chances."

After making the final arrangements with Madison Tolles, they arrived at the garage where Lucien gave the final instructions before boarding.

"What Brad and I are going to do is rapidly accelerate once we lift off. We'll head across the Weddell Sea and angle northward up the Atlantic. We'll ramp up the speed and altitude until we reach a little over 80,000 feet with airspeed of about 4,300 miles per hour. Welcome aboard and please be sure your seatbacks and tray tables are in an upright and locked position. Next stop, the Twilight Zone."

With that they got into the aircraft and glided out of the garage. Once clear of the garage, both aircraft began the gradual acceleration and lift that would bring them to their cruising altitude.

Austrian physicist and philosopher Ernst Mach once came up with a formula that reads 'M' is the speed number equaling Velocity relative to the medium, divided by the velocity of sound in the medium. Essentially, the formula defines the speed of sound. The speed of an object traveling at Mach 1 will depend on the fluid temperature around it. At 36,000 feet the speed is about 655 miles per hour. As the two aircraft from Atlantis passed through 36,000 feet and broke the speed of sound, through the rear windows they saw the Prandtl-Glauert singularity, a puff of disk-shaped cloud. Few people had ever seen this phenomenon, and the pilots and passengers in these two remarkable aircraft were duly impressed.

Soon they were up at their cruising altitude of 83,000 feet and coasting along at slightly above Mach 6.5, 4,300 miles per hour. In all of aviation history, the experimental X-15 aircraft flown by test pilots in the late 1950s and 1960s, the SR-71 spy plane that was in service from the late 1960s to the late 1990s, and the space shuttle returning to earth from orbit were the only manned aircraft to reach such speeds inside the earth's atmosphere.

Lucien was all business up until they reached cruising altitude, then he sat back, and with the joy-stick in his hand, looked over to Brad Jones' aircraft, cruising 150 feet off to their starboard, and gave the thumbs-up signal.

Johanna looked at the ocean below as they blazed over the Atlantic in total silence. She unconsciously reached across the console to take Gordon's hand.

187

Gordon took her hand, looked at her and said, "Your ancestors who sailed in the coffin ships, mine who rode ponies across the prairies, and Lucien's who came to America chained in slave ships could never have conceived of this. They existed so that we could be here doing this incredible thing." He gave her hand a reassuring squeeze. They gazed upward through the thin atmosphere to the indigo sky above and then looked downward to the white puffy clouds and blue ocean below, sharing the moment.

Johanna squeezed his hand and said, "Now I know why I exist."

After a while, Lucien Ross asked if either of them wanted to take the controls. They looked at him like he was insane. He said, "It's no sweat. This is the simplest aircraft that has ever been flown. It is more difficult to fly a kite. Just sit here and hold the joy-stick. Once we figure out just how high these things will fly we might be on the threshold of space and earn ourselves some astronaut wings. This is close enough for now, but I'd sure like to take a shot at it."

Gordon stepped forward and, taking the seat next to Lucien, guided the craft along on its journey. He could only think of his ancestors, and his vision. After a while he beckoned Johanna to take his place, which she gladly did. As she guided the aircraft through the silent ether, she thought of starving Irish potato farmers from generations past, of a conquered Native American people, and of Africans brought to America against their will. She bowed her head and asked for their blessing.

In the other aircraft, flying parallel with them, Chuck said to Brad, "Summbitch, if this isn't the damnedest thing I've ever done." Brad soon relinquished the controls to Chuck, and he was in seventh heaven. "Imagine me doing this, and I didn't even have to take my belt and shoes off before I got on board."

Damien Cooper just stared into the ether and improvised some extraordinary licks on his guitar.

After twenty minutes or so of flying, Chuck handed the controls over to Damien. Damien looked like he was seeing a vision of heaven itself.

As they flew, the pilots told them just when to turn so that they stayed dead center over the ocean between the continents.

When they entered the latitude of southern Florida, both pilots took back the controls. Communicating with each other over the radios that they had placed in each craft, they coordinated their approach to Pax River with the carefully selected air traffic controllers. The controllers guided them into a descent that would bring them over the least populated area. The public relations people at Pax River were already preparing stories about swamp gas for anyone who claimed to see a UFO.

In less than four hours from the time Tolles spoke to Johanna in Antarctica, the two aircraft rapidly approached the air station. Dropping down steeply from their cruising altitude over the mid-Atlantic, the aircraft glided across the rural fields of coastal Maryland, and across the air facility tarmac, hovering their way quietly into an open hanger. The hanger doors were quickly secured as the passengers deplaned. Most of the military and civilians had been cleared out of the area during the past hour. Among the few people to witness the arrival of these strange craft were the Vice President's Secret Service detail and the forty-two men of the Marine Reaction Platoon that had just been flown in from Quantico. All the Marines had Top-Secret clearances and had served on protective Presidential details at Camp David and elsewhere. They knew how to keep secrets.

Johanna introduced Tallbear, Chuck, Damien Cooper, Brad Jones and Lucien Ross to the Vice President. With the hanger surrounded by armed Marines, they got into a van and proceeded to the Commanding Officer's conference room for the briefing.

Two hours later, a visibly moved Vice President Pemberton was trying to get a grip on the implications of all these discoveries. "If this information were made public all at once, the world would be thrown into a turmoil. Every adventurer on the planet would be trying to get to Antarctica in rowboats to loot these treasures, not to mention certain governments who would be deploying warships for the same purposes. I like the courses of action you have come up with, but we are going to have to proceed with great caution. It's time to go the White House and brief the President. He's expecting us."

•   •   •

Entering the Oval Office, Chuck quietly commented, "Cousin, in the past few weeks we have uncovered the treasures of the ages, traveled as no one in known history has ever done, and now it looks like we have crossed yet another threshold. We're in the Oval Office. Never thought I'd be here."

In a moment, President Richard Moore entered the office and they all rose. The President, 54 years old, handsome and graying slightly around the temples, stood about six feet three inches tall and carried himself with the bearing of someone who is comfortable with the power he held. A former governor of California, he was facing reelection the following year.

"Please be seated, madam and gentlemen."

The Vice President conducted all the introductions, concluding with, "And of course you know Madison Tolles."

"Good to see you again Madison. It has been a couple of years."

Chuck, Johanna, and Gordon all glanced at each other, amazed at Tolles' connections to power.

The Vice President said, "Ms. Ring, please begin."

Johanna proceeded to give the President the overview and background for the explorations, and then turned the briefing over to Gordon, who succinctly summarized the anthropological side of the discoveries, including the discovery of Badlands Bill. Chuck filled in all the blanks on the technical revelations they had uncovered, including the aircraft and the hand held devices. Johanna had placed her laptop on the coffee table so the President could see the slides summarizing the building projects of Atlantis. They saved the Pyramid construction slides for the end, and for the grand finale showed him the cavern of gold.

Gordon introduced Damien Cooper as the man who unlocked the key translation code of the Atlantis computers, and Brad Jones and Lucien Ross as the test pilots for the aircraft and facilitators of the development of the courses of action that they would be presenting. The two officers conducted a concise briefing about the capabilities they had discovered thus far on the aircraft.

President Moore sat in quiet contemplation for a moment before speaking.

"I am not the wisest person in the world, and I wish that person were here with us now. What I do know is that now we need wisdom more than anything. What does this remarkable discovery mean, and what do we do about it?"

"Mr. President," said Gordon, "if I may, I would like to throw in a couple of other considerations. Right now we have a full translation of the materials related to the construction and function of the Great Pyramid. So far we have confirmed that the pyramid was intended to be a power generation plant, as well as the reasons why that might have been needed those many thousands of years ago. We know that such a marvel would be of tremendous value today. The principle of its operation is simple.

"Mr. President, have you ever been to a basketball game where a player shoots the ball and misses the rim completely?"

"Dr. Tallbear, you are touching an area close to my heart," the president responded. "I was not a great athlete, but I was a second-stringer on my high school varsity basketball team. Yes, I know the feeling of completely missing a shot."

"Mr. President, if that happened to you, what did the crowd do?"

"They chanted 'AIR BALL' at the top of their lungs. Anything else you'd like to drag out of my past, Dr. Tallbear?"

Gordon grinned. "What you probably never knew, Mr. President, was that the crowd didn't just chant 'AIR BALL.' They chanted 'AIR' in the key of 'F' and they chanted 'BALL' in the key of 'D.' That is a constant that has been studied in high school and college gymnasiums all over the country. All crowds chant 'AIR BALL' from 'F' to 'D.' Add in another factoid. Almost all automobile horns are tuned to the key of 'F'. My point is that without our knowing it, music and musical harmonies are a part of our very existence. We have discovered from our friends from Atlantis that music is the fundamental building block for everything from basic communications to visual art to energy production."

"Based on simple principles of acoustic resonance, the Great Pyramid at Giza is designed to generate a chemical reaction that will produce raw energy. The entire process is triggered by initiating vibrations from the granite interior chambers of the pyramid. That produces a harmonic response from the earth itself which resonates in the key of "F#" at a constant rate."

Gordon summarized the chemical reaction process that would lead to pure energy beaming to earth collection stations.

"The Great Pyramid is a marvel of mathematical excellence."

He proceeded to elaborate on the mathematics of the pyramid, confirming a myriad of mathematical measurements. He requested that a formal inquiry be made to the Egyptian Bureau of Antiquities to allow a Denver Center team of engineers and acoustic experts to confirm acoustical data.

"Now we don't know yet whether the latitude of the earth is significantly essential to the location and function of the pyramid. We are analyzing that data now.

"What we know is that some of this information is absolutely significant when considering the function of the pyramid, and other information is significant only in that it tells us of a remarkable culture existing here long ago. They left us detailed clues to their advanced skills. They tied the dimensions of the earth, Sun and moon into the design of this great structure.

"Global climate change, depleting energy resources, and the vulnerability of transporting these resources across the globe leaves us with little choice. We must either re-activate the Great Pyramid at Giza, or replicate the feat on our own to produce and distribute an unlimited source of clean energy to the rest of the planet.

"I am not optimistic about reactivating the great Pyramid for two reasons. One is that there has been significant internal damage done to the pyramid over the last two centuries by well-intentioned explorers, and that will make reactivation a difficult challenge. Only a close scrutiny of the pyramid will confirm or deny that. The second consideration must be the political one. Egypt has, in recent years, undergone revolutions. The results of that are, for now at least, indeterminate. The perception of the new government may be that once more an imperial power will be seen as exploiting the national treasure of a sovereign nation for its own gains, or so our adversaries both globally and in this politically unstable region would portray it.

"In proceeding further, we need all the resources of the American intelligence organizations to ensure that our plans are not compromised. I can only imagine that after the first conference in Upperville, Virginia, British *MI6*, French *Direction Generale de la Securite*, and all the rest of them -- the Chinese, the Russians, Germany, Japan, and everyone -- are working overtime to try to get ahead of our thinking. And I am sure that, compounding our problems from this point forward, the industrial espionage experts of the world's biggest energy corporations are hacking away at our computers. I've been told by our experts at the Denver Center that there are at least 38,000 attempts daily to hack our computer systems.

"Finally, we must have an alternative course of action. I would strongly advise that we consider the second alternative we have presented. If we cannot access or reactivate the Great Pyramid, we must consider building our own full 1-to-1 replica. The reason I propose this is that everything we do on foreign soil compromises our position."

"And how, Dr. Tallbear," responded the President, "might we do that? The Japanese attempted to build a scaled down version of the Great Pyramid several years ago and completely failed. I also read somewhere that the best guess of the Egyptologists is that it took at least twenty years to build the Great Pyramid. We don't have twenty years to build a pyramid."

"We don't need twenty years, sir. We can do it in three to four years."

There was a collective gasp around the room.

Chuck threw in, "Y'all might want to give yourself a little wiggle room, cousin."

Gordon continued, "We mustn't forget that the Japanese attempt was based on conventional knowledge. They attempted the feat using manual labor. We are well past that, Mr. President. No, if we initiate action right now, we only need three to four years with the technology at our disposal, but that also depends on certain other preparatory considerations. Damien Cooper here, one of the geniuses in the Antarctic cavern, worked out the math after breaking down the 'movie' we saw of its construction. A later download of data containing the genesis of the pyramid construction from its designer, Amon Goro, confirms my estimates. His own notes on the construction revealed that 12,500 years ago they built it in five years. I also consulted with one of the logisticians to do a rough estimate of the lift capabilities we would require. The seventy-two Atlantis aircraft we have at our disposal, with their seemingly limitless capabilities, coupled with all the ground, air, and rail transportation resources we have here in America, means we can do this in a relatively short time and under conditions of maximum security. Those are resources the people of Atlantis did not have on the ancient savannah of Egypt."

"What 'certain other preparatory considerations' are you suggesting, Dr. Tallbear?"

"We have been so focused on end results that we have not given enough consideration to the blindingly obvious. One of the main conditions is that we begin quarrying limestone and granite at an unprecedented rate. And we start doing that right now. We will need a total of just over 600,000 blocks of limestone, and granite of weights varying from two to 70 tons, in precision cut shapes, and with a fifty-five percent or greater quartz content. Everything else we already have," Tallbear responded. "What I am suggesting is industrial mobilization on a wartime scale. It's not just the labor at the quarries. It is also the manufacture and servicing of advanced precision cutting tools and other support apparatus that will supply these quarries. We must also ensure that our rail infrastructure in particular is capable of delivering precision cut limestone and granite at the pace of construction for at least four continuous years."

"If I could jump in here, Mr. President," interjected Madison Tolles, "I would offer that I have already begun this undertaking on a slightly smaller scale. Ten months ago the Denver Center, through subcontractor companies, engaged in contracts, only recently signed, with eight different quarries across the country for nearly 200,000 precision-cut blocks of limestone and granite. We need only to change the specifications on size of the individual blocks and total volume of the purchase. We also need to enter into a major contract with the railroads to start hauling the rock. Our other major consideration will be labor. I was doing some calculating while Dr. Tallbear was speaking, and I figure that we will need a force of about 25,000 laborers initially at both the quarry sites and the construction site. They will be expected to place slightly over 300 blocks a day. But that block placement will be more of a guiding rather than muscling into place. We have the aircraft and hand held devices to actually do the hard work. The hard part will be the heavier blocks of the base. Once the structure goes up in height, the number of laborers will be reduced and the weight of the individual blocks will decrease."

"And where," asked the President, "do you propose to build this American Great Pyramid?"

Gordon responded, "There are only two general locations in the continental United States regarding the 30 degree latitude site. The 30th parallel crosses northern Florida from just below Jacksonville, Florida, to the northern Gulf of Mexico. It crosses through southern Louisiana at New Orleans, then passes through Texas just above Houston and below Austin. From there it crosses Texas high country, skims north of the Mexican border, and then crosses through Big Bend National Park before going into northern Mexico. Louisiana has to be ruled out because the terrain is too wet and marshy to support the pyramid's weight. That leaves northern Florida and a number of sites across Texas. Each region has its advantages. A Florida site would mean that what we send from Antarctica, as well as what we quarry in the United States, can be delivered in ships or by rail to Jacksonville, Florida, and shipped short distances overland by rail to the building site. Proximity to the sea, however, means vulnerability to sabotage parties coming ashore at an almost infinite number of spots along the Atlantic and Gulf coasts.

The Texas sites are more elevated inland and would require a heavier reliance on rail access. Proximity to the state capitol may bring with it a lot of political anxiety about the safety of the project in relation to nearby population centers of Austin and San Antonio.

Another consideration regarding the site we choose is that it should be on a solid bed of granite just as the Great Pyramid is to capitalize on the earth's natural resonance. I don't know whether the Texas and Florida sites have a granite base.

As for a third locale, should the 30 degree latitude location not be a show stopper, we could build in any number of places. My personal recommendation would be in or near Pine Ridge Reservation in South Dakota," answered Gordon. "It is extremely geologically sound, and it will be a relatively easy place to safeguard. Regarding security, it will be unlikely that an Islamo-facist terrorist will go unnoticed in South Dakota, which should make it easier for our domestic security forces to protect the site." And with that he glanced over at Madison Tolles and

Johanna, who were sitting side-by-side on a couch, and saw them nodding approval.

"Okay, Dr. Tallbear. You have made a good case, and you have done your homework. But if Pine Ridge is to be chosen, full buy-in by the Indians is necessary. How much of a problem will that be?"

"If they don't buy into it, we have the other sites I mentioned. If the 30 degree latitude is not necessary, I will do all that is in my power to make it happen on Pine Ridge, Mr. President. But all unemployed Native Americans should get first priority on jobs. Additionally, the Lakota family of tribes, and maybe all the documented Native American tribes in America, should share in the profits of selling energy to the world. As a matter of fact, whatever site is chosen, the natives of America should be given a priority as to labor and return on investment. I know I may be speaking out of turn, and guilty of promoting a personal agenda, but I think that it would be suitable, if not beautifully ironic, that our native populations who once lived so closely in harmony with the earth should benefit from selling the earth's energy back to the white man."

At this the president gave a hearty laugh.

"If you are correct in your predictions of power generation, there will be plenty to go around," answered the President. "It will be interesting to see whether Congress and the Indian tribes can come to an agreement. And now I will leave it to the Vice President to set everything in motion for a new conference."

The life I touch for good or ill will touch another life, and that, in turn another, until who knows where the trembling stops or in what far place my touch will be felt.

Frederick Buechner, Protestant minister and writer

Chapter 26

In late March, the vice president scheduled the second conference. Between early January and late March there had been endless meetings with the CIA, State Department, and Department of Defense officials. Johanna, Gordon, Chuck, and Madison Tolles had spent weeks in endless planning sessions designed to apply to any possible contingency. Tolles was also holding numerous teleconference meetings with his team of mechanical engineers and architects back at the Denver Center. Tolles had also applied for a patent on the mortar for the pyramid and entered into a contract with a company to manufacture it. Additionally, he arranged for a geological survey of Pine Ridge to determine the granite content below the soil.

Surprisingly the media had been kept at bay. The only thing they knew was that the Smithsonian and National Geographic were planning to make a big announcement in mid-April regarding some new discoveries. It had not been revealed where these discoveries were located.

Out at the Denver Center, Ben Crowley was putting the finishing touches on a logistics plan to remove the gold and the aircraft from Antarctica. He was also coordinating the continuous flow of food, which was minimal due to the hydroponic gardens, and supplies to the Antarctic teams.

Down in Antarctica, the discoveries mounted. In the cavern near the gold, where the other sixty aircraft were stored, a door was discovered leading into what the team labeled 'The Tool Shed.' The place was a mechanical engineer's dream. The initial inventory included hundreds of granite cutting saws and hand-held communicating devices as well as the acoustic resonators that would fit into the Grand Gallery of the Great Pyramid. These latter were tuned resonators much like the Helmholtz resonators (a hollow sphere with a round opening that

198

is 1/10 to 1/5 the diameter of the sphere) in use today; and schematics and architectural plans for the construction of the Great Pyramid.

On three separate occasions, Gordon, Johanna and Chuck had been able to slip out of the country and return to Antarctica to stay on top of the work being done. Madison Tolles had finally had a chance to see, first-hand, what he had sought these many years. He was awestruck as Allison Long guided him from one discovery to another. In addition, Gordon had gone twice, but by commercial air, to Pine Ridge to begin negotiations with carefully selected key members of the tribal council who were sworn to absolute secrecy. If they would remain silent about these negotiations for the next six months, Gordon told them, then the proposal had a chance to work. If they went public with any of it, the US government would dismiss them as crackpots. Total secrecy was paramount.

The Sioux were amazed by the scope of Gordon's proposal, and justifiably skeptical, based on their previous well-documented, horrible experiences with American treaties, about the promises contained in the preliminary draft agreement. There was also the complaint that, should the white man's promises be true, it would also mean their sharing the wealth with all the other Indian tribes of the country. The American Indian was not accustomed to this type of arrangement, although it did have several precedents among certain tribal groups.

Gordon put his most persuasive talents to that argument. He reacquainted the Indian leadership with what they already knew from their history, that there had been a thriving Iroquois nation that included the northeastern United States and southern Canada, including New England, upstate New York, Pennsylvania, Ontario and Quebec. Founded by five tribes, the Confedercy handled all external matters, such as trade and conflict resolution with other nations, while allowing tribes to retain internal autonomy.

Gordon reminded them that the Confederacy had existed from the 13th century and that all tribes participating in it thrived. As a result of their joint agreement to cease warfare among themselves, they became one of the strongest collective forces in seventeenth and eighteenth century northeastern North America.

Gordon held long discussions with his people about the Iroquois Confederacy and the value of having the American Indian tribes consider a similar arrangement in light of the proposition he was making to them.

He told them to think of it as purely an economic union similar to Europe. Wealth would be shared proportionately, but tribal integrity would remain intact. The wealth could be used only for building and staffing schools, hospitals, and health care centers; building infrastructure and housing; creating education and scholarship programs; social development; and development of programs that would bring further economic livelihood to the tribes. It gave them a lot to think about.

In the end, they agreed to the proposal and began plans to have Gordon facilitate a series of meetings with the leaders of all Native American tribes to refine the structure of the agreement.

But elsewhere the forces of darkness had been working diligently on plans to stop the Denver Center in its tracks.

We honor ambition, we reward greed, we celebrate materialism, we worship acquisitiveness, we commercialize art, we cherish success, and then we bark at the young about the gentle arts of the spirit.

Russell Baker, 1987

Chapter 27

The phone's incessant ringing roused Gordon from a deep, dreamless sleep at 5:30 in the morning. He and Chuck, now housed in a fairly luxurious condo in Rockville, Maryland, had been up late brainstorming the next phase of the operation, and they had not gotten to bed until 1:00 in the morning.

He reached over and picked up the receiver.

"Hello."

"Gordon? Johanna." Johanna was residing in a small, but elegant, apartment near DuPont Circle that was owned by a close friend of Madison Tolles who wanted her in proximity as he dealt with the various departments of federal government and the layers of federal bureaucracy.

"Don't you ever sleep?" asked Gordon.

"Not this morning," Johanna answered. "I just got a call from Mr. Tolles. All of us need to meet with him at the FBI headquarters downtown no later than 7:00. If you two start getting organized right now, I'll have a driver in front of your condo at 6:30. The driver's name will be the same as our composer's, and he will know something that only you know." And then Johanna hung up.

Gordon was fully awake now. They had been briefed by both the FBI and the CIA about the potentially mounting security risks, and told to work out a code so that in emergency situations where a stranger might be involved, the answers could only be something that one of them would know. They labored long and hard coming up with things that would be unique, yet not showing up on any of their background checks.

Gordon threw on a pair of sweat pants and went down the hallway to bang on Chuck's door.

Chuck was not happy with the rude awakening, but he saw Gordon's seriousness and quickly got up. They both had time for a shower and a bowl of cereal before going down in the elevator. Chuck got off at the third floor and Gordon at the second floor. They went to the stairways at opposite ends of the corridors to arrive in the lobby about thirty seconds apart. No one was there and they quickly exited as the limo drove up. An athletic looking young man got out of the driver's side of the vehicle, walked over to them and said, "I am Adrian. You are Drs. Tallbear and Kinoshi?"

When they answered in the affirmative, 'Adrian,' almost in a whisper, said, "Dr. Tallbear, I understand that you played baseball in the Cape Cod League. Do you recall your batting average?"

"Refresh my memory," answered Gordon.

".465," responded Adrian, and Gordon nodded.

"Man," said Chuck, "you were a prospect!"

"Yes, but I had other things to do first."

As they got into the back of the car and Adrian sped them downtown, Chuck could not contain his curiosity. "Were you drafted?" he asked.

""Yes, brother Kinoshi, I was drafted in the second round by Boston."

"Cousin, you could have been a multi-millionaire and had your own baseball card. What were you thinking when you chose anthropology instead?"

"It seemed like a good idea at the time."

At the FBI building they entered the lower garage and were deposited near the elevator where an agent escorted them to a seventh floor conference room where Johanna and Madison Tolles awaited them.

Almost immediately, a coffee service was brought in, followed shortly by two women. They introduced themselves as agents of the FBI and CIA and showed appropriate credentials. The CIA agent was in her early fifties and could have easily been mistaken for a woman on her way to a garden club meeting. Slightly overweight, but comely in appearance, with salt and pepper hair and a rosy complexion, she had a matronly air and a gentle way of speaking.

"My name is Eleanor Thomas. I am sorry for the inconvenience of bringing you in so early, but this information just would not wait. Have any of you ever heard of the Gnomes of Zurich?"

Except for Madison Tolles all shook their heads no.

"Mr. Tolles, what do you know about them?"

"I only know some of the common lore about them. Google 'Gnomes of Zurich' and you will find speculation about their deeds going back 200 years or more. They are the dream children of the delusional and conspiracy theorists - the international bogeymen. The Gnomes, at least in the minds of these true believers, are apparently responsible for the assassinations of Lincoln, McKinley, Archduke Ferdinand, Ghandi, and Pope John Paul I, as well as both the Kennedys and Martin Luther King. They are alleged to have engineered the Spanish American War, mid-eastern terrorism, 9/11, and any number of other events that have altered the course of history. The people who see black helicopters everywhere are convinced that the Gnomes are behind it all."

"I hate to disillusion you," Ms. Thomas answered, "but some of that speculation may be real."

Tolles looked shocked. The group exchanged glances.

"At the CIA we look into everything, and I mean everything," Ms. Thomas continued. "We have a desk devoted to the Gnomes of Zurich. They aren't gnomes, and they aren't based in Zurich, although they once were. Their history goes back even further than 200 years. Their group isn't even named the Gnomes of Zurich. That's just their legend. They have no name. This is an incredibly secretive cabal that, at present, numbers thirty-five people. They meet with an unpredictable frequency, and rarely with all thirty-five members at once.

"They have subordinates to provide 'services.' These subordinates operate on the cut-out system. For example, if the group wants research done, it is done through layers of subordinates in such a discreet way that the researchers do not know whom they are working for. No one in the chain can identify anyone other than the person who gave him his orders, and sometimes not even then. Even the next layer down from the top of the organization does not know whom it's working for. Everything at that level is done through untraceable messages. For example, a person may receive an untraceable email directing them to book a room in a particular hotel on a particular day. That person is to go to the room and stay there, never leaving until the next message is received. A courier may knock and slide a sealed envelope with instructions under the door. The courier might only know that some non-descript person had delivered the envelope to the courier service with the appropriate fee and instructions to deliver the envelope to that particular hotel room. The recipient, after looking at the instructions may even bring the package to another delivery service for further delivery to another cut-out.

"This group thrives on secrecy. They have managed election fraud both here and abroad. The same is true for assassinations. The number of heart attacks and fishing and hunting excursion accidents that take place among top executives of major corporations world-wide defies actuarial charts.

"These people are all brilliant, devoted to the accumulation of wealth, and totally heartless. Their equivalent would be the sociopath who can squeeze the trigger without remorse. They are relentless in the pursuit of wealth for themselves and their clients. They are handpicked generation after generation to serve the cause of the group 'until death us do part.' They all seem to be recruited from the international ranks of the financial community. The candidates for membership in the organization are apparently scrutinized over a period of many years during which they are psychologically screened to fit the profile desired: possessed of insatiable greed, amoral, monogamous, focused, multi-lingual, and brilliant at analyzing geopolitics.

"They have no allegiance to ideology of any kind, save that which can line their pockets. Nor are they allied to any political agenda – only that which serves their purposes.

"Historically they served the needs of the bankers, robber barons, and industrialists of the nineteenth and first half of the twentieth century. Their present clientele includes an international family of investment bankers, industrialists, oil, nuclear, and coal industry investors, and selected members of the international energy producing nations, to name a few. Their services include investment counseling, political manipulation, the stirring – and quelling - of insurrections, and assassinations. When Ian Fleming invented S.M.E.R.S.H. and S.P.E.C.T.R.E., he, knowingly or unknowingly, was on the track of the Gnomes of Zurich. Fortunately he had James Bond to save the day.

"We are not James Bond, either individually or collectively, but we are here to save the day - hopefully."

Madison Tollles responded, "All right. So what does that mean for us?"

205

"It means, Mr. Tolles," Ms. Thomas responded, "that right now you and your key people have bulls' eyes painted on your chests."

In a sotto aside, Chuck said, "I knew I should never have gotten into computers. Makes you rethink your position on professional baseball now, doesn't it?"

Gordon just laughed.

Johanna spoke up. "Ms. Thomas, how are you so certain of the existence, not to mention the structure of this organization?"

"Thank you for asking that question, Ms. Ring. I will tell you what I can. Since its inception in 1947, the CIA has looked into the aspects of target, time, and opportunity to place someone inside this organization. A few years ago, after decades of frustration, we finally had an incredible, one-time-only opportunity to place one of our people inside the inner circle of this organization. Our operative, interestingly, is a man who is an accomplished actor who, on a lark between extended periods of unemployment, explored work opportunities with the CIA. Thank God for us that this guy, no matter how talented, couldn't find work in his chosen profession.

"What we know now we have learned from our deep cover source. He has provided us with an extraordinary amount of hard intelligence. Thanks to him we know that of the thirty-five principal players in the organization, five of them do the heavy lifting and final decision-making. And he tells us that you are right in their crosshairs.

Madison Tolles then asked, "How long has he been undercover, if I may ask?"

"He has been under cover for almost four years, Mr. Tolles. And that is much longer than we like. The longer an under cover operative stays in his or her position, the more likelihood that either of two things will happen. One, the operative will simply crack from the strain, have a breakdown, and become useless. The other is that he or she will be compromised.

"This is where my part of the briefing ends. You are now in the hands of the domestic branch of our intelligence services, the FBI. Gretchen Tokata, Senior Special Agent, will continue the briefing."

Gretchen Tokata, a Japanese-American, was stunningly attractive. She appeared to be about thirty-five years old, and had a serious air about her. She cleared her throat and began to speak. "At the request of Mr. Tolles some months back, the President issued a secret executive order allowing us to monitor each of the participants of the conference in Upperville, Virginia. We were not surprised that the majority of the foreign attendees have been doing everything in their power to gather information about your explorations and discoveries. But they have, for the most part, been staying within the accepted parameters and unwritten rules of state sponsored espionage. And they've had no luck so far.

Tolles interjected, "My IT security experts tell me that our systems have seen an increase in cyber attacks from an average of 38,000 per day last year to 70,000 per day since the conference, and that the attacks are becoming both more relentless and more sophisticated."

"I'm not surprised, Mr. Tolles. We have discovered that one of the attendees is an agent of the Gnomes, and they seem to have unlimited resources at their disposal.

"The Gnome operative is the British ambassador, Sir Winslow Harrington. Here are the unedited transcripts of his background and meetings with the Gnomes. You may read them here, but they cannot leave this room unless they are in my possession."

They all sat there stunned. Then Tolles spoke. "I knew that Sir Winslow was a pain in the ass and a potential thorn in our side, but I never suspected ..."

"That's all right, Mr. Tolles. Even the most jaded of us have expectations of proper behavior at that level. Let me go on to give you the particulars."

Senior Special Agent Tokata proceeded to give the details of Harrington's background, upbringing, and career, including the financial difficulties he was facing before he was recruited by the Gnomes. She quoted extensively from the psychological study that the FBI profilers had compiled.

"I apologize in advance to anyone who would be offended, but the respected ambassador is a sexual sadist. He began his adventures in private clubs in London and elsewhere when he was in his teens, and the older he has gotten, the more violence he has used to achieve sexual gratification. His most recent encounter left his victim requiring private hospitalization.

For the next half-hour, Johanna, Gordon, Chuck, and Madison Tolles read the dossiers with increasing disbelief.

The most current information they had was of Sir Winslow's meetings at the lagoon and later that evening at the French embassy with the mysterious Mr. Wilson, followed by his clandestine encounter not far from his own embassy.

When Special Agent Tokata was finished, they all were speechless.

Finally Chuck broke the silence. "So why haven't you busted this cartel before this?"

"It is not that simple, Dr. Kinoshi," she answered. "The trick has been to place their fingerprints on a crime. Thus far, no crime has been committed. There have been unpleasant conversations and even more unpleasant activity between supposedly consenting adults, but nothing to bring down the power of the Justice Department or the International Court at The Hague. We have to catch them in an act of actual espionage or worse before we can do anything."

"And in the meantime, we are the bait," said Gordon.

"Yes, Dr. Tallbear, you are the bait. But as we speak, there is no clear consensus about how you can bring these bottom feeders closer to the surface. They have their own timetable. You have another international conference coming up. Perhaps something will happen there that will drive them to action."

Madison Tolles asked, "Special Agent Tokata and Ms. Thomas, your report mentions a Mr. Wilson. Is he one of the five or one of the thirty-five? And who are the five?"

Eleanor Thomas paused for a moment before speaking. "The FBI has already done background investigations and each of you now are cleared for Top Secret/Close Hold information, so it won't hurt you to know."

Then she gave the five names of the inner circle of Gnomes, including Mr. Wilson's. When she said that one of the five was named Seth Tilcotan, Madison Tolles looked shocked. She asked, "Why are you so startled to hear the name, Mr. Tolles? Do you know him?"

Madison Tolles said, "No, Ms. Thomas, I don't know him, but when I tell you a little story, you may think I am crazy or that the connection is a complete impossibility."

Tolles got to his feet and began pacing the room. "You know all about the nature of our discoveries in Antarctica. Now let me back up about twelve thousand years and tell you some history. From our translations of the Atlantean language, we have learned, among other things, that following a period when evil leaders of Atlantis nearly brought ruin to the world, wise people of Atlantis plotted against and finally overthrew their rule. The leaders were arrested and public executions were held. But before the executions were completed, the most evil of the leaders, one *Tezcar Tilpocan*, escaped, later to be found in Central America where, apparently, he, and his descendants, had made a pact with the devil and was teaching the people that cannibalism and human sacrifice were the only way to stave off their eventual demise at the end of the world.

"Jump forward a bit, about 8,000 years ago. For the previous 4500 years, Atlantis had sent thousands of 12 person teams to explore the world. Among the last teams returning to Atlantis before they sequestered themselves in the mountain caverns, a team leader named Veran Cocha returned to say that in Central America he had run into direct conflict with a man named Tezcatlpoca, a descendant of Tezcar Tilpocan. Veran Cocha was defeated by this evil person who was still teaching the tribes the dark arts of cannibalism and human sacrifice.

"It gets better. Now jump to Egypt and its ancient written records. In the Egyptian mythology, Osiris was the great leader who taught the population to be civilized and to stop practicing cannibalism. He taught agriculture, mathematics, and the study of the stars. But he had an evil brother named Set who ultimately killed Osiris and had him dismembered and his body parts scattered throughout Egypt.

"There is more to the myth, but that is not the point. In Egypt there was an evil person named Set. In Central America there was an evil person named Tezcatilpoca, a descendant of Tilpocan. Leading the Gnomes is a person named *Seth Tilcotan*. Could this person be a descendant of these twin myths?"

Eleanor Thomas looked at Tolles with wonder in her eyes. "You raise a most interesting question, Mr. Tolles. What makes it interesting to me is that despite the most exhaustive research over the past three years, and despite the fact that we have his fingerprints and DNA on file, we have not been able to come up with a biography on Seth Tilcotan. It is like he appeared in the Gnomes leadership group fully formed with a blank resume behind him. You have given me much food for thought, Mr. Tolles. I will be in touch with you."

210

As they wrapped up that briefing, Chuck moved over to Gretchen and said, "Well, I assume you have our numbers if you need to get in contact with any of us."

She gave him a bemused smile and said, "Certainly, Dr. Kinoshi. We will be in touch."

"...this empire has been acquired by men who knew their duty and had the courage to do it, who in the hour of conflict had the fear of dishonor always present to them, and who, if ever they failed in an enterprise, would not allow their virtues to be lost to their country, but freely gave their lives to her as the fairest offering which they could present at her feast."

From *Pericles Funeral Oration* (Thucidides "*The Peloponesian War*")

"... So that if tomorrow is the great getting up morning, if that tomorrow we have to meet the Judgment Day, O Heavenly Father, we want to let our folks know that we died facing the enemy! We want 'em to know that we went down standing up!"

Morgan Freeman's character, *Glory*

Chapter 28

Ben Crowley had spent long days and endless hours coordinating additional logistics requirements for removing all the discoveries from Antarctica. He also spent a great deal of time teleconferencing with Madison Tolles in Washington. Tolles, having been given the green light from Eleanor Thomas, filled him in on the Gnomes. Ben, characteristically, told Tolles, in response to this new information, "Christ, Skipper. Why is it that the good guys have no fucking shortage of enemies? Now there's one more fucking problem we've got to solve."

On this particular weekday evening, it was already 8:00 pm and he was as hungry as a bear, so he decided to go out to the Silver Lode for a steak and a beer. He got one of the computer guys to go with him for company.

At the restaurant, as he was lowering himself from his van to the parking lot, three men in suits approached him. Their leader was dressed entirely in black. He seemed to hiss his words as he spoke.

"I am Seth Tilcotan and I represent the interests of men who do not want to see your venture succeed. Madison Tolles and his friends are out of my reach for the time being, so you have the honor of becoming the message I will soon deliver to him," the man said.

Exiting the van ramp, Ben glided toward them and rolled to a stop just a couple of feet from one of the men. In his classic gravelly drill instructor voice Ben barked, "I know who you are, you miserable sons of bitches. Get the hell out of my way you horrible fucks!"

The man nearest Ben pulled out a Colt .45 caliber semi-automatic pistol. Ben was just close enough that with a slight lunge out of his chair he was able to grab the man's wrist. His momentum dragged the man down. Ben twisted the pistol from the man's hand as he pulled his assailant to the ground. Grabbing his assailant's pistol, he shot the other henchman in the chest as the man was drawing his pistol from a shoulder holster.

Turning his attention to the first man, Ben was about to shoot him when he felt a strange clammy coldness and a sudden stabbing pain in his right arm. He dropped the pistol but retained his grip on his assailant with his left hand. He knew in his soul that in that moment he was doomed, but he was damned if he would just surrender. Releasing his grip on the man's wrist, he grabbed the man's right ear and squeezed with all the strength he could muster in his powerful left hand. The man screamed in agony. Ben shouted, "I'm going to give you something to always remember me by!"

With that he ripped the man's ear off. Adrenalin pumping and screaming in agony, the man scrambled a few feet away from Ben. Tilcotan glared at his maimed henchman and hissed, "My followers carry out their assignments." Propelled by his black boot, the pistol skittered across the pavement to his maimed henchman. He looked up to see Tilcotan's very disapproving face. He grabbed the pistol and shot Ben with the five remaining bullets.

Mercifully, Ben was dead with the first shot, which penetrated his heart and left lung.

Tilcotan turned to the one surviving henchman, "Sometimes you really disappoint me."

Leaving their dead colleague in the parking lot, they sprinted to their vehicle and made a hasty withdrawal.

By the time people rushed out of the restaurant, the two men had disappeared in their black SUV.

Ben's dinner companion had been frozen in his tracks next to Ben's van, held to the spot by a strange clammy coldness that penetrated his bones. As Tilcotan sped away, the Denver Center techie suddenly was freed from his paralysis and rushed to Ben's side. As the sirens approached the roadside restaurant, the computer expert dropped to a sitting position on the parking lot and cradled Ben's head in his lap. Rocking back and forth with silent sobs racking his body, he finally calmed himself and slowly pulled his cell phone from his pocket. He called Chuck Kinoshi.

In their apartment in Rockville, MD, a very shaken Chuck repeated the story to Gordon and called Madison Tolles to tell him the sad and stunning news. As Tolles slowly closed his cell phone, he sank down in his chair in complete shock. Memories flooded him and reached into his soul, leaving him spent and drained. Recovering himself, he called Johanna. He also called the FBI.

•   •   •

Three days later in Ada, Oklahoma, population 16,000, the funeral was held at a church where a standing room only crowd came to pay their final respects to Ben Crowley, US Marine Corps, Retired; two Navy Crosses, Silver Star, Bronze Star, three Purple Hearts. In addition to Madison Tolles, Johanna, Gordon and Chuck, there were four Marine generals and a host of active duty, retired, and former Marines, and, it seemed, half the population of the town. Most of the technical staff in Antarctica flew up for the funeral to join nearly the entire staff from the Denver Center. Skeleton crews remained in both locations. Because Ben's murder was deemed a matter of national security, the FBI deployed a tactical force to the Denver Center to lock it down in their absence.

Once everyone was inside the church, with ritual solemnity, six muscular, well-decorated Marines in dress blues escorted the coffin down the center aisle in slow cadence. At the altar, they gently positioned the casket, took one step back, slowly raised their right hands in salute, held the salute for a long

214

moment, and just as slowly returned their hands to their sides. Making deliberate precision movements, they solemnly returned to the rear of the church where they stood at parade rest behind the last pew.

The elderly minister was a long time friend of Ben's family and spoke of the pride that the whole community had for Ben.

Toward the end of the service, Mr. Tolles gave a moving eulogy that told not only of Ben's combat heroism, but also of the compassion he felt for both his Marines and the people at the Denver Center. Ben, he said, was one of those rare people who arrive on earth and write a check that pledges everything, up to and including their lives, for the betterment of their fellow man. He haltingly told of the time in combat when Ben saved his life disregarding his own safety. Tolles had to interrupt himself several times when he became overcome by emotion. When he was finished, there was a moment of silence.

Gently from the choir loft, on a nylon string acoustic guitar, came the opening notes of Shubert's *Ave Maria*. Damien Cooper, tears running down his cheeks, played the instrumental version of this timeless classic with deep passion and all the skill and sensitivity he could muster. Everyone wept.

When he concluded, the Marines formed up and began their slow march down the aisle to retrieve the casket. As they processed toward the altar, Damien, accompanied by Brendan Pell on the organ, began playing a moving version of *Eternal Father*, the Navy Hymn, that is played at all Navy and Marine funerals.

The saddened crowd followed the casket out of the church. Outside, as the casket was being placed in the hearse, Damien Cooper walked up to Madison Tolles and stammered, "H-h-h-he a-a-a-always t-t-t-treated m-m-me w-w-w-with … kindness."

Tolles put his arm around Damien's shoulder and drew him into a hug.

A lengthy funeral convoy formed up for the fifteen-mile trip to the veterans' cemetery. At the burial site, the Marines reverently carried the coffin to the grave. Following the final prayers of the minister, they completed the slow ritual of the folding of the flag until it was a tight tri-corner. A squad of Marines in dress blues, standing away from the site, fired a volley of three rounds. A bugler played taps. The team leader turned and gave the flag to the senior three-star general who in turn went down on one knee and presented it to Ben's elderly mother with the thanks of a grateful nation. Before she left the site with her family, the elderly woman grabbed Tolles' hand and said one word, "Courage."

When everyone else had departed the site, Madison Tolles and the entire Denver Center staff stayed behind.

A late morning sun cast a glow on the white marble grave markers. Gentle breezes stirred the trees bordering the burial ground and caused a shimmering wave across the yellow fields of grass just outside the cemetery.

Gordon Tallbear stood a little apart from the rest of the group with his arms folded across his chest, staring off into the gently rolling hills.

A weary and saddened Madison Tolles stood before them, seeming much older than he had been a few days before. "I never thought our project would come to this," he said. "Maybe this all is not worth it. Nothing is worth the loss of a man like Ben Crowley. I am responsible for putting all of you into danger, and none of you signed on for that. I am considering sealing up Antarctica and putting the entire project on hold. I will not hold it against anyone who wants to leave."

"Now hold on there, Mr. Tolles," Chuck interjected. "With all due respect, sir, I think if Ben Crowley heard you talking like this, he would, in no uncertain terms, tell you to get your head out of your ass."

That was the emotional catharsis they all needed. They all broke up laughing, including Tolles, who, laughing, said, "You're probably right."

Gordon stepped forward and began speaking softly, yet clearly enough so that everyone could hear him. "Amen, brother Kinoshi. Ben was a brave man and he went down facing his enemy with courage in his soul. He lived the core values of the

216

Marine Corps, which, I believe, are *Honor, Courage, and Commitment.* Like Ben, all of the rest of us believe in your vision, Mr. Tolles. Each one of us knows in our hearts that our individual bits of expertise are somehow going to contribute to make this planet a better place to live. Brendan and Damien would someday like to give outdoor concerts where the crowd doesn't have to cut the air with a knife. And you, Allison, would like to see your daughters grow up in a world where playing soccer does not mean running the length of the field gasping for oxygen.

"Our unified commitment means that our children and grandchildren will never have to face darkening skies and dead oceans.

"If we give up now, we'll not only make Ben's sacrifice meaningless, but we'll nullify all the sacrifices we have made to get where we are. I would hate to face him in the hereafter with that on my conscience.

"No, Mr. Tolles, we are not giving up. We are going to re-double our efforts to bring the project to its conclusion."

With that, the entire group crowded around Tolles to shake his hand and reaffirm their commitment.

Unnoticed by the Denver Center people, a very large, black SUV with darkly tinted windows sat parked on a road about a half-mile away. A man with a surgical dressing on his ear sat at the wheel. Next to him Seth Tilcotan put down his powerful binoculars. "Those stupid people are not giving up. It appears that their commitment is as strong as ever. That Indian bastard Tallbear is holding them together. No matter. He'll live to regret it."

*Neither charm nor patience nor endurance has ever
wrested power from those who hold it.*

Frederick Douglas

Chapter 29

North America, 8,000 years ago

Several months had passed and Palen Golendar had
mastered the language of his hosts. He no longer thought of
them as his captors. His first awkward moment came early on
when he refused to go out with a hunting party. Again he told the
people that killing, handling, and eating meat was forbidden by
the people of Atlantis. Some of the younger warriors, led by
Running Elk, began to mock him as a coward until the elders of
the community forbade them to do so. One of the most
respected elders, Eagle Claw, told them, "This man is the guest
of our tribe. He has traveled through many lands and faced many
dangers to be here. He is a brave traveler who has his own
ways, and we must respect that."

In gratitude for Eagle Claw's intervention, Palen offered
to provide fish for the community and took several of the older
children to teach them how his people caught fish with both
spear and net. His willingness to provide food for the Lakota
bonded him to their community.

In the early fall, as his second winter with the tribe was
approaching, Eagle Claw told him the tribe would move south
and west a good distance looking for new winter quarters. He
told Palen that they were being encroached upon by tribes to the
north and east and that game was becoming scarce. Palen saw
the efficiency with which the tribe broke down their homes and
packed their goods on animal skins stretched between two
poles. Everything was dragged or carried to the new destination.

After several days of rough living out in the elements,
Palen learned much about the native fruits and berries such as
chokecherries, plums and currants. He learned also of the
bounty the earth had to offer in the way of wild squash, onion,
and potato. Two weeks into the march, the longest movement

218

the tribe had ever made, as the tribe approached a large north-south running river, scouts indicated to Eagle Claw that they had arrived at their new camp. During the trip he came to respect and admire the simplicity of these people he had come to love.

Palen recognized early on that these nomads were not ready to make the move to agriculture. They subsisted largely on meat – buffalo, deer, elk, rabbits, birds – and wild rice that grew in abundance in this region of the country. He knew that he must learn their ways and customs. Perhaps in a few years, after he taught them about the stars and the Sun and how they could live more fully by planting crops and not be so reliant on game, they would be ready to begin the transition to permanent communities.

One day he told them of the great pyramids standing in the middle of a vast savannah half a world away. When asked who had put the pyramids there and why, Palen told them that his own people had built the great pyramid to capture the energy of the earth, and the other pyramids to show a star map.

This confused his hosts. "Why would you take energy from the earth? Would not that offend the Great Spirit who created the earth?"

Palen replied, "You ask the great question. My people, the First People, believe that the Creator gave us the earth as His gift, and that we, like you, were to use its resources prudently. My people have become advanced in many ways. We have learned, like you, to take from the earth only what the Creator has given us. As a result, we can build vehicles that allow us to fly over the earth. I myself have flown over vast oceans and looked down upon great mountains and forests. We have made tools that allow us to lift great stones and build permanent communities for us to dwell in. For this we need a source of energy, which the Master has given us from the earth.

At this, the people laughed. "No one can fly but the birds," they said. "You are making up stories to entertain us."

At this, Palen himself grinned. Such a story must sound absurd to these nomads of the plains. "What I tell you is true," he said, "but I have no way to prove it. Someday I will figure out a way to explain this to you."

The people loved to hear his tales of far away lands, and he became a favorite of both the adults and the children. The women especially enjoyed his stories because their work was endless. They bore the children and raised them; they gathered the rice grains; they skinned the animals brought back from hunting expeditions; they cooked all the meals; they cured the hides and stitched them together to make both clothing and shelter. In the evenings, while mending moccasins or making clothing for their children, they got a chance to relax and listen while Palen told stories about the people who lived in the mountains, deserts, and rain forests of the world.

One young woman in particular was fascinated with Palen. She was Morning Star, granddaughter of Eagle Claw. Her father, Standing Bear, had been killed while hunting buffalo long before Palen arrived. Her mother, Anpaytoo (Radiant One), had never recovered from her grief and could be seen about the encampment talking to herself and breaking into tears. She survived on scraps tossed to her by families that had not suffered the same sorrows. Palen took pity on the old woman and asked Eagle Claw if he might care for her. Eagle Claw arranged for a small dwelling to be made for Palen and Anpaytoo. Over a period of months, Palen patiently cared for Anpaytoo, and she gradually abandoned her grief. When she began to become more self-sufficient, she started preparing meals for Palen and mending his clothes.

Morning Star's grandfather and grandmother raised Morning Star and loved her, but they were frustrated that she would not consider any of the tribe's warriors to be her husband.

Morning Star was pretty and slender and had large brown eyes, and moved with more grace than any of the other young women. Every unattached warrior sought her favor, but she rejected all of them, especially Running Elk, whom she particularly did not like. One day she got into a big argument with her grandfather. He told her, "But for you I would be a great-grandfather by now. You are too particular in what you expect from a man. I should force you to marry the next man who comes to our lodge."

"But grandfather, I already know who I will marry," said Morning Star.

Eagle Claw looked at her in surprise. "Who is this warrior? I must meet him and see if he measures up to you. This is the best kept secret in our community as you seem to have rejected everyone."

"I will marry Palen Golendar," said Morning Star. "He is unique among men, and the only one I will consider. I will marry him or I will marry no one."

Eagle Claw looked at her and realized that this stubborn independent woman was not going to change her mind. She was, in her stubbornness, just like her father. He also knew that her selection of someone outside the tribe could possibly have severe ramifications for the tribe's internal harmony.

"For now, Morning Star, speak of this to no one. I will talk with your grandmother and then seek the counsel of the elders. After that, I will give you my decision."

"Yes, grandfather. I will abide by your wishes … for now."

Later that night Eagle Claw sat down to talk with his wife, Star Dancer, about Morning Star's decision. When he told her of their granddaughter's firm stand on the matter, Star Dancer laughed. "That girl is just like her father, hard headed and determined. Does Palen Golendar know of her feelings?"

221

"I do not think so," answered Eagle Claw, "but I know he follows her with his eyes. As a newcomer to the Lakota, he is too polite to say anything. I am sure that he would be delighted to know of her feelings, but that is not what concerns me. I have no objection to her becoming his wife. I think it would be a good idea to bring new blood into our tribe. Too many families are related. We have had outsiders from other tribes take our maidens for wives before this. My bigger concern is the effect it will have on the tribe to have an outsider who is not of our coloring and characteristics take such a prize as Morning Star for his wife.

"Like you, I have no objection," said Star Dancer. "I also admire Palen Golendar very much and believe he will do our tribe no harm and will be a good husband to Morning Star. But your concerns are justified. Talk with the other elders and seek their counsel." The next day Eagle Claw called the elders to a private counsel and ordered all others away from the shelter where they met. After hours of discussion and much smoking of the pipe, the other elders gave their blessing, but warned that the biggest problem would come from Running Elk, and that he must be warned against taking any action after the announcement was made.

That afternoon, when most of the young men of the tribe were out hunting, Eagle Claw approached Palen as he was coming out of his lodge. "Palen Golendar, I must talk to you now about a matter of great importance."

"What is it, Eagle Claw? What concerns you?"

"My friend, it has been noticed that you look with loving eyes at Morning Star. Wait. Do not interrupt. I also came to tell you that Morning Star looks lovingly upon you. Will you consent to take her for your wife?"

Palen was stunned. Indeed he had looked longingly at Morning Star, but he did not wish to offend his hosts by pursuing her as a suitor.

"My heart has betrayed me, Eagle Claw. I had tried to keep my feelings about Morning Star to myself as I had no wish to offend you who have given me shelter and a home. I know *many of the young men have asked her to become their wife, and I did not want to offend them as I am an outsider. If that is a problem, I will leave the tribe. To see Morning Star and not have her as my wife will become too strong a feeling for me to bear. Yes, Eagle Claw, I want her to be my wife, but will she have me for a husband?"*

"That will not be a problem. She has already told me that her desire rests in you and she will have no other. Then it is settled, Palen Golendar. And you shall have a new name as a member of our tribe. You will be called Tahatan, which means White Hawk in our language, because your skin is white and you say you can fly."

That evening, when everyone had returned from the hunt, Eagle Claw announced that the new visitor, who now had the new name of White Hawk, would become the husband of Morning Star. Most of the village rejoiced. Some of the young men were disappointed, but they accepted the news because they had come to admire Palen Golendar and his stories. Moreover, they always knew that they never stood a chance with Morning Star.

A few of the warriors, led by Running Elk, were not so accommodating. As Running Elk rose to protest, Eagle Claw silenced him and told him that the decision was final and had been approved by the elders. He told Running Elk that he was either to accept the decision or be banished.

In a rage, Running Elk ran off into the hills. It was many days before he returned.

Life went on in the community.

But Running Elk kept his own counsel. He plotted. He waited. Soon, he thought, his time would come, and he would be rid of Palen Golendar forever.

These rulers are afraid of ideas, they fear friendship, and they fear passion.

Unknown

Chapter 30

Vice President Pendleton called the international conference to order and introduced Madison Tolles. There was nearly triple the number of participants as the last conference, with most of the ambassadorial attendees bringing along technical and political experts to assist and advise them.

Tolles looked over his audience realizing that he was about to produce revelations that would stagger them. Clearing his throat he launched into his presentation. "Since our last conference my people have been very busy in Antarctica. They have broken the translation code so that we can now decipher everything in those computers. What has been revealed is astonishing. Briefly let me hit the high points and then I will go back and amplify what each of these discoveries means.

"First, Antarctica really is Atlantis." At the shocked response of the audience, he held up his hand for silence. "Second, the unusual skeletons discovered worldwide, and particularly the most recent remains discovered in Montana, were explorers from Atlantis. We even know Badlands Bill's real name - Palen Golendar. Third, the wall art displays in Atlantis are not just still paintings. They are moving art just like our motion pictures. They reveal that people from Atlantis built Stonehenge and the Great Pyramid at Giza, not to mention many other ancient phenomena."

Gasps and murmurs greeted this revelation.

When the audience quieted, Tolles went on. "Fourth, there are flying vehicles down there – 72 of them we have discovered so far – that operate on principles of magnetic levitation and can travel many times the speed of sound even to the upper reaches of our atmosphere. Fifth, there is an entire cavern filed with the gold plates that once clad the upper third of the Great Pyramid. Sixth, there is a cavern loaded with high-speed granite cutting tools, and a map room with detailed depictions of every square inch of the earth as well as star maps. And seventh, and most important of all, is the definitive proof from Atlantean computer records, that the Great Pyramid was once a power plant capable of beaming energy to the farthest reaches of the earth."

Tolles kept having to increase the volume with which he spoke to be heard over the increasing astonishment of the crowd.

Madison Tolles stood his ground. "Mr. Vice President," and then louder, "Mr. Vice President and distinguished guests. Please," he shouted, "the Denver Center has undertaken," and the crowd settled down a bit, "the enormous task of sorting out all that has been discovered.

"We have studied the great ancient structures and stone formations to discover their purposes and origins. Our goal was to see not only how these remarkable structures were built, but also how they were so precisely measured, and to discover what was their intended function.

"Massive and enigmatic, the Great Pyramid of Egypt, and its two smaller companion pyramids, stood silently awaiting someone to unlock their hidden codes. For nearly two-hundred years, explorers and scientists of all stripes and colors have uncovered a clue here, a clue there. Occasionally there have been break-through theories that have peeled back a layer or two of mysteries, but never a complete unveiling of their purpose or their exact age.

"The Great Pyramid draws most of the attention because of its exact symmetry, its exact measurements, and its mysterious chambers and vents which are not found in any other pyramid. But early scientific examinations left their mark in unintended damage to the interior. It is only in the period of the mid- to late-twentieth and early twenty-first centuries that the Egyptian Bureau of Antiquities has gained control and cautiously limited detailed examination to all but the most qualified explorers. Whether that is because of suspicion of outsiders or fear of discoveries that would contradict traditionally accepted conclusions is debatable.

"The Great Pyramid is the most remarkable man-made structure on the face of the Earth. Externally, its precision measurements have not been matched in any structure built since its original construction. Until the late 1800s it was the largest and tallest man-made structure on the planet. Its silent presence at the geographical center of the Earth's landmasses at nearly precisely the 30th parallel, has begged three particular questions that modern man has not been able to conclusively answer.

"Who built it?

"When was it built?

"For what purpose was it built?

"That was the basic start point for the Denver Center to launch its explorations.

"Conventional thinking Egyptologists have insisted that it was built by the Egyptians between 4900 and 4500 years ago. Most Egyptologists believe it was a tomb for Fourth Dynasty Egyptian Pharaoh Khufu, or Cheops in Greek. The problem is that there is no evidence that the Great Pyramid was used as a tomb. This is one of the areas where the mavericks differ from the mainstream Egyptologists. It is odd to think that this civilization should suddenly spring up out of nowhere fully equipped with such engineering capability. The blindingly obvious flaw in this thinking is that Egypt had virtually no history before that time, no evidence of advanced mathematical capability; and the Egyptians of that era did not possess the wheel or any evidence of cutting tools that could carve limestone and granite with such precision. Today, with all our advancements in technology and machine tools, we still can't cut with that level of precision. The mortar used to bind the huge building blocks together holds to this day. It has been analyzed and we know its properties, but until now we have yet to figure out how to make the mortar ourselves. The massive area covered by the Great Pyramid's base would provide enough parking space for ten jumbo jets.

"What is seen today is the underlying core structure. The Great Pyramid originally was covered by 144,000 highly polished, slant faced, white limestone casing stones, or cladding, that formed a smooth outer surface. These stones were 100-inch thick, 20-ton blocks of hard limestone. Much like marble, but superior in hardness, this limestone was very durable against the elements.

"The original peak of the pyramid was four inches wide and the upper portion of the pyramid was gold plated. No one knew when the gold plating was removed, or what happened to it.

"In AD 1301, the outer casing stones were loosened by a massive earthquake. In 1356, on the orders of Bahri Sultan An-Nasir-ad-Din al-Hasan, many of the outer casing stones were carted away to build mosques and fortresses in and around Cairo. Later explorers doing continuing excavations cleared away from the base of the pyramid most of the rest of the rubble of the casing stones that had broken away from the pyramid. Today near its base there still can be seen many of these casing stones.

"All four sides of the Pyramid are very slightly and evenly bowed in, or concave, creating what is really an eight-sided pyramid. The Great Pyramid, and only the Great Pyramid among all the pyramids of Egypt, has eight sides. This effect, which cannot be detected by looking at the Pyramid from the ground, was discovered around 1940 by a pilot taking aerial photos to check certain measurements. As measured by today's laser instruments, the radius of the triangle formed by this concavity is equal to the radius of the Earth.

"The mathematics, alone, that have been built into the Great Pyramid, belie any speculation that the structure could have been built by the early Egyptians. The mathematical calculations imply that the builders knew the exact dimensions of the earth, the distance to the sun, and a host of other earthly and celestial measurements that were beyond the capabilities of the early Egyptians.

"Also, every pyramid that the Egyptians *did* build after 2500 BCE has flaws in its architecture, and in many instances, began crumbling soon after they were built.

"Based on the information we have downloaded, it is evident that prior to Atlantis drifting into the Antarctic region, massive numbers of its citizens took to boats and sailed for this region of the world. They were the original Egyptians. Deliberately denied the technologies of the Atlanteans, they settled into the coastal areas of the Mediterranean Sea.

"So back to the three questions.

Answer number one is that it had to have been built by a nameless advanced civilization that significantly preceded the Egyptians. That is the only possible answer based on the physical measurements and other physical properties that we will cover later.

"Secondly, it was most likely built 12,500 years ago. The reason for this is simple, but it had only been discovered in the 1990s. The Great Pyramid complex consists principally of three pyramids – the Great Pyramid itself, its adjacent somewhat smaller sister pyramid, and a much smaller third pyramid.

"These three pyramids are not aligned exactly. No one could make sense of this until 1993 when an amateur Belgian astronomer named Robert Bauval noted and proved that the three pyramids constituted a precise terrestrial map of the three stars in *Orion's Belt*. The intriguing part of his discovery, proven through computer simulations of the relative skies of each period, was that the alignment did not reflect the relationship of the three stars in *Orion's Belt* to each other in the Fourth Dynasty, 4500 years ago, but rather exactly with the three stars' relationship to each other in approximately 12,500 years ago, when the constellation Orion hung just above the horizon. Over the course of millennia, the stars we see in the sky move ever so slowly in relation to each other. The precision of the alignment of the three pyramids *only* reflects the three stars in *Orion's Belt* 12,500 years ago.

"Our downloads of the Atlantean data confirms that after the construction of the great Pyramid, the other pyramids and some remote sites were constructed to create a star map that

228

would tell us about when this great civilization existed. The Sphinx was also constructed to give us a time frame reference for this great civilization.

"Another claim by the orthodox Egyptologists is that the southern shaft leading from the King's Chamber of the Great Pyramid was lined up with the star Osiris in 2500 BCE. It is evident, as will be shown later, that the builders knew about the rotation of the stars over time. Regardless of the talent and skill of the designers and builders of the Great Pyramid, why should they put so much effort into building a pile of stones – more than 600,000 of them ranging in weight from two to seventy tons – that would line up with one particular star for a very short period of time?

Tolles paused for a moment before continuing. "The answers to my questions," he continued, " have now been confirmed by the data from Antarctica.

"Translations of the Antarctic computer data, coupled with a remarkable hologram presentation from Kulen Golendar, father of Palen who was discovered in Montana, tell of an originally aggressive advanced culture hell-bent on dominating the world. The desire was to excavate the planet's resources using primitive slave labor worldwide to serve the technological needs of an advanced culture. The problem was how could the island nation of Atlantis provide power for the technology to extract ore from remote locations around the world?

"The solution was provided by a man named Amon Goro, Master Architect of Atlantis, who conceived of the most massive, and simplest machine imaginable to accomplish the task. In his design for this great power plant, he imbedded all the significant measurements of the Earth, sun and moon, and the precession of the equinoxes, which were intended to be clues for us to discover when we had advanced far enough technologically."

Tolles paused for a dramatic moment. "But the big, blockbuster answer that came from a translation of the data was that this incredible structure is, in fact, a power plant capable of producing an endless supply of clean energy to the planet."

At this, there was collective murmuring from the audience.

"So what does this all mean, ladies and gentlemen? And what relevance does it have to Badlands Bill and Antarctica?"

All eyes were riveted on him.

"The answer appears to lie with our friends in Antarctica. These people who have left to us the discovery of their technologies, were the people of Atlantis, the lost continent, to whom Plato referred in his writings over two thousand years ago. They sent their own explorers out to the remote regions of the world. Badlands Bill, or Palen Golendar, was one of these explorers.

Tolles, supported by a slide presentation, showed the recent discoveries including the moving wall art, the 'garage' with its aircraft, and the cavern of gold. This brought gasps from the audience. Chuck then gave a more technical explanation of the wall art and computer translations as well as the description of the aircraft and their apparent use of magnetic levitation principles. Gordon elucidated on the cultural and historical findings of his forensic anthropological team. He held forth on the remarkable discoveries about the people of Atlantis and their culture, and concluded his briefing giving them a synopsis of the message from the Kulen Golendar hologram.

Sir Winslow Harrington leaped to his feet. "*Doctor Tallbear*," he began in a disdainful voice, "you expect us to believe this rubbish about an advanced culture that lived during the melting of the last Ice Age? Are we to accept, unchallenged, the assertion of an American Indian anthropologist that these people had weapons that could cause destruction much the way our nuclear missiles can today? And that they subsequently developed a utopian culture after they 'vanquished the 'evil ones' from their society? I think we all would have to take a speculative leap of faith to accept your theories."

With that, Madison Tolles stood up and, using all the force of will at his command, stared down Sir Winslow Harrington and said in as firm and strong a tone as he could, "Sir Winslow, if Gordon Tallbear says that the moon is made of green cheese, that is all I need. I trust his word. How dare you, Sir Winslow, accuse this learned man of creating a fiction?"

Sir Winslow then made another one of his 'Sorry, I didn't mean to demean the accomplishments and discoveries of our learned colleague from... South Dakota' apologies.

Gordon stood there a moment, unexpressive, and then, nodding to Tolles, resumed his seat.

Yet Harrington continued unimpeded, repeating his earlier proposal to put the British in charge of the entire research program, and that British scientists should be allowed to examine what has been found in Antarctica. In his argument he reaffirmed the traditional British sense of fair play. His further dismissal of the potential for developing an unlimited energy source for the planet, coupled with his impassioned plea to protect the vital interests of the fossil fuel industry, was nauseating to the Americans. Harrington rambled on about the loss of jobs and economic impact that would be caused by the destruction of the fossil and nuclear fuel industries, but he only got murmurs of support from the various delegations.

Madison Tolles brought his briefing to a close by saying, "Ladies and gentlemen, with the information we now have, we can confirm without reservation that the pyramid complex is, in fact, a power plant designed to harness the energy of the earth perpetually. It can produce, according to the translations we have made, enough wattage that - coupled with the solar, wind, and geothermal technologies that we have developed thus far - we can permanently eliminate the use of every coal fired, natural gas powered, and nuclear powered plant on the planet.

"What we are witnessing is a perpetual energy source for the entire planet."

•   •   •

That evening the Denver Center group sat in the library of the French Provincial mansion doing a post-mortem. Finally Madison Tolles called a break and said, "We are going to drive ourselves crazy sorting out the dynamics of today's meeting. My discussions with the State Department confirm your worst fears that attempting to reactivate the pyramid at Giza would be a disaster. The damage done to the Great Pyramid over the years by well-intentioned explorers complicates any of our attempts to bring it back to life. But the biggest problem comes from the political instability in the mid-East. We would need several hundred thousand soldiers and Marines poised off-shore to go in there at a moment's notice to provide security for the operation in the unlikely event that Egypt would grant us permission to proceed with our primary plan. I do, however, believe that we can get permission to send a team to conduct advanced acoustical testing in the Great Pyramid.

"I have had enough discussion about the conference. A little while ago I notified our chef to prepare a supper for us. I think he is going to do some magic with salmon. Now let's go down to the dining room."

As they were eating, Chuck spoke. "This afternoon was worse than the first conference. I thought we were going to have to pull that German off the Frenchman when the Frenchman said that the Germans lacked the subtlety to appreciate this great discovery. I mean, that German was about to chew him up like a Doberman with a cornered rabbit."

"Yes, my friend," said Madison Tolles, "it was a dicey moment. Thankfully the Vice President brought some order to the chaos. But the one I am worried about the most, of course, is our friend the British ambassador. I have never witnessed such a sense of entitlement. He is as arrogant as anyone I have ever met, and he makes my blood boil. His defense of the carbon producing industries was particularly appalling."

Tallbear said, "Tomorrow should be interesting. Harrington approached me after the meeting broke up like I was a long lost chum from Eton."

"Yes, I saw you talking together," said Tolles.

In a near perfect imitation of Harrington, Gordon said, "He said something like, 'No hard feelings Dr. Tallbear. Politics, you know. So you're a Sioux Indian anthropologist, eh? One doesn't see much of that, now, does one? I suppose as an Indian one must be able to ride a horse then?'"

"And I said, 'Sure. You know how it is. All of us Indians ride.'"

"And then he said, 'Jolly good. Why don't you join us for a few chuckkers tomorrow afternoon. There's a polo club nearby that I frequent, and my British team is scheduled to play in a match. Be a good chap and join us.'"

I said, "Wouldn't miss it for anything, old boy."

Chuck chimed in, "Y'all gotta be kidding, cousin. When was the last time y'all ever played polo?"

"Never." said Tallbear. "But I just Googled it and read up on it."

Johanna nearly jumped out of her chair and exclaimed, "Are you mad? Do you remember the briefing on his Lordship? Harrington has played polo since he was a boy. You can't do it. You'll get killed."

"Never happen," said Tallbear, with a slight grin, "Never happen."

Then Tolles said, "Well, I'll tell you something, Gordon. If you kill yourself out there, I'll never forgive you. If you kill Harrington, I'll give you a bonus."

There was a great pause, and then they all laughed, as it was the most unexpected thing they could imagine Madison Tolles saying.

Tolles went on to add, "I will be meeting privately with the principal American players tomorrow morning. After your polo match, we'll gather at dinner to plan the next move.

That night Tallbear suddenly awoke, having had a most interesting dream about a black horse with a white star on its forehead.

The grace of God is found
Between the saddle and the ground.

Irish

proverb

Chapter 31

It was a beautiful, crisp, early spring day, and wonderfully mild for late March. Daffodils were blossoming, and the dogwoods and cherry trees were near their peak. Shortly the tulips would be out covering every public park in Washington, DC. The city was already awash in tourists for the cherry blossom festival.

Out in the horse country of Virginia, about forty-five miles South, an FBI driver delivered Johanna, Gordon, and Chuck to the polo field. Well-manicured, a lush green, and 300 yards by 200 yards, it was a standard regulation-sized polo field. The parking lot was more interesting, with very few cars in it valued at below $100,000. This truly was a rich man's sport.

Nearly a thousand people had shown up for the polo match. British nationals arrived to cheer their boys on, along with a significant American delegation practicing that time-honored tradition of tailgating, albeit with champagne and caviar from the trunks of luxury automobiles, to prepare themselves for the rigors of cheering for their underdog team. No barbequed ribs or fried chicken for these folks.

Tallbear was an imposing presence. A thin white scar, the remnant of the bar fight the previous fall, crossed the top of his right cheekbone. He was wearing faded blue jeans, a hand–tooled leather belt with silver buckle, a buff-colored, loose-fitting long-sleeved western style shirt with scalloped pockets and snap buttons, and calf-high moccasins. He also wore a thin leather strap tied around his forehead to keep his hair from blowing in his face. And for reasons known only to him, behind his right ear in a thin braid, he had tied a small quartz stone. He looked every bit a modern day Sioux warrior rather than a PhD anthropologist.

He, Chuck and Johanna were talking when Johanna quietly said in an Irish brogue, "Ah, the things you see when you don't have a gun." Tallbear and Chuck followed Johanna's gaze.

Approaching them was Winslow Harrington in full proper polo attire – white pullover open necked short-sleeved shirt, tight white riding pants, helmet, and knee-high boots. Harrington greeted them with false heartiness. Barely acknowledging Chuck and with a discomfiting leer at Johanna, he said to Tallbear, "I've taken the liberty, old boy, of selecting your mounts for you, if you don't mind."

"No, I don't mind," said Tallbear. "Where are they?"

As Harrington led them to the horses, a BBC television crew was unloading equipment from their van. Taking note of them, Harrington said, "I asked them to come and cover the match today. Thought it might be a pleasant diversion from the usual fare for my countrymen."

When they got to the horses, one of them, Tallbear noted, was probably 15 years old and appeared docile. The groom, struggling with the other horse, pointed to the first one and said, "Her name is Jasmine. This one is called Taboo, for obvious reasons."

Tallbear reached up, whispered into Jasmine's ear, and stroked her. Jasmine nuzzled into Tallbear's chest. The horse the groom struggled with was a three-year-old stallion, nearly jet-black, with a broad, muscular chest and a white star on its brow. He appeared to be barely broken.

Gordon looked at the black stallion and immediately felt a strength surge through him remembering both his vision and his dream of the night before. Gordon smiled at the sight of the animal. The stallion was fighting the groom with ferocity, bucking and yanking the reins trying to free himself from the man's grip. Both horses appeared to be about 14 hands high, a hand being four inches as measured from the ground straight up the forelegs to the withers - the high point of the horse's shoulders. Tallbear noted that all the other polo horses were at least sixteen hands high.

Tallbear smiled and walked slowly toward Taboo and stopped about ten feet away. "Let him go," he said to the groom. The groom, in a natural Irish brogue, said, "If I do, sir, he'll bolt and we won't see him 'til he slows down in Tennessee. He's not named Taboo for nothing."

Looking the groom steadily in the eye, in a firm, low voice, Tallbear said, "Let him go."

Taboo suddenly froze at the sound of Tallbear's voice.

Chuck and Johanna looked at each other. They felt the power of Gordon's command.

The groom paused, stunned for a moment, looked at Gordon and dropped the lead line. The horse paused, and then skittered about 50 feet and stood in profile to Gordon pawing the earth. Tallbear walked slowly toward Taboo until he was about twenty feet from the horse. He slowly squatted down and focused his gaze about a foot in front of Taboo's nose. After a few minutes the horse took a step forward to Tallbear's left trying to make eye contact. As he did, Tallbear again shifted his gaze to the left to a point about a foot in front of the horse. Gradually a rhythm took shape until finally Tallbear slowly rose and with his eyes was leading the horse in a continuous counterclockwise circle. Around and around they went with Tallbear's eyes leading the horse in a slow trot. After three or four revolutions, Tallbear abruptly shifted his gaze to a position behind the horse. Taboo suddenly turned and again kept moving, now in the opposite direction, trying to establish eye contact.

Back and forth they kept this up for about 15 minutes until Tallbear turned his back on the horse and slowly squatted down to the ground.

Taboo snorted and shook his head. He looked away, then back, his lead line dragging on the ground. After a few minutes, Taboo began a slow zig-zag walk that brought him toward Tallbear. Finally Taboo bowed his head over Tallbear's shoulder. Tallbear reached up and stroked the horse. He stood up, taking the lead line in hand, and began to talk quietly to Taboo while stroking him gently. He said to the groom, "Do you have a western saddle? I'm not real good with the English style saddle."

Totally in awe of Tallbear, the groom responded, "As a matter of fact I do, sir, I do. I'll go get it."

Tallbear kept stroking the horse and speaking quietly to it. Johanna was mesmerized, and Chuck said, "Hey, cousin, they used to burn people at the stake for doing stuff like that."

Harrington glared at Tallbear for a moment, but recovered himself quickly and said, "Time to meet your new teammates." Tallbear handed Taboo's lead line to Chuck and said, "I'll be right back."

Chuck was bewildered. "What am I supposed to do with him?"

"Tell him some jokes."

Tallbear turned to Taboo and raised his hand, giving the air a gentle patting motion indicating that Taboo should stay where he was. The horse stood silently, slightly turning his head to look at Chuck. Chuck stood there dumbfounded holding the lead line loosely in his hand and looked in wonderment at Taboo. "So why the long face?" he asked. Taboo shook his head violently and Chuck elected silence as his best ally until Tallbear came back.

Harrington had arranged for Tallbear to play for the American team and brought him over for introductions.

"Jonathan," he said abruptly, "This is the gentleman I spoke to you about. Dr. Tallbear, this is Jonathan Sloan. Jonathan, please be good enough to let him play a bit during the match." And he promptly turned and walked away not waiting for an answer as if his words were nothing less than an imperial command.

Jonathan looked skeptically at Tallbear and asked, "Doctor Tallbear? Are you a physician?" Tallbear replied, "I am an anthropologist, and you can just call me Gordon or Tallbear. Either is fine. And how about all of you?"

Jonathan said, "I am an investment banker, Phil Taylor is an attorney practicing international law, and Darrell and James are the co-founders of Flynn-Todd Systems which is some sort of high-tech software company. I believe they are under contract to the National Security Agency. They say little about their work, which is not surprising."

At the mention of Flynn-Todd Systems, Gordon remembered that code breakers from Flynn-Todd had been in Antarctica assisting Denver Center technicians in breaking the translation code.

Jonathan explained that he, Phil, Darrell, and James had played together for the past five years, but, lacking extra players, had struggled mightily since the season began, particularly against the new Brit team. Their friendliness and quick acceptance of him made Tallbear like them immediately.

Phil asked, "What brings you to our sport today?"

Tallbear carefully responded, "The organization I am working for is having an international conference in the DC area and one of the participants is the British ambassador. He invited me to come along and see if I could handle a polo match."

"Have you played before?"

"No, but I am a very experienced rider and know my way around horses."

Darrell said, "Apparently so. That was an impressive thing you just did with Taboo."

"That notwithstanding, if I know anything about Harrington, he is trying to set you up," said Jonathan. "Selecting Taboo for one of your mounts is the height of his typical nastiness. The man is a sadist. That horse would have a lot of potential if he weren't nuts, but he is too high-strung and unruly. Despite what you just did with him, he will be impossible to handle. And Jasmine is at the end of her career as a polo pony. She is very good, but she is losing her stamina. I would be happy to delay the match and help you select some other mounts. The four of us are all co-owners of the stable, so we do have some clout around here."

"No," said Tallbear, "That won't be necessary. I have already met Jasmine and Taboo. And I would prefer to beat the good ambassador using the mounts he chose."

Sloan took a hard look into Tallbear's eyes and was reassured by what he saw.

Smiling warmly, Sloan told Tallbear that he would use him as a substitute periodically during the match, probably starting in the third chukker. He wanted to go with his most experienced players for the beginning of the match. Tallbear said that would be fine, and shortly the match started.

The groom had returned with the western saddle and Gordon introduced himself, Johanna and Chuck. "Joe Delaney," said the groom, "and I'm very pleased to meet you all." As Gordon went to warm up his mounts, Joe took one look at Johanna, looking radiant in white slacks and a Kelly green blouse, and said, "By all the saints, if you are not a vision of Irish loveliness." Johanna blushed and, with eyes smiling and hands on hips in a saucy attitude, said, *"Exci go raibh maith agat.."* Joe laughed and, bowing, said, *"Nil a bhuiochas ort or ta failte romhat."*

Chuck said, "What kind of gibberish are you talking?"

Johanna laughed and said, "I simply said 'thank you,' and Joe responded 'you're welcome' in the Irish language which you might know as Irish or Gaelic."

"It still sounds like gibberish."

"And Japanese doesn't sound strange to western ears?" Johanna replied.

"Don't you worry yourself, Mr. Kinoshi," Joe said. "Half the Irish don't understand it either. And how did you, darlin', manage to become fluent in the old tongue?"

Johanna proceeded to tell Joe of her Irish ancestry.

In his early 50s, white haired, and with a slight limp, Joe was an Irishman right from the 'Ould Sod' and had been around horses all his life. In his thick brogue he said, "Mr. Sloan was a frequent visitor to our stables in Ireland and took a liking to me. He sponsored my immigration. He's the one that took a fancy to Taboo and bought him from his owner, who was only too happy to see him go. Mr. Sloan believes that somewhere inside that horse are the makings of a fine polo pony.

Johanna turning to see what Tallbear was up to, said, "Well, will you look at that." They looked over to where Tallbear was working with his mounts. Sitting erect on Taboo, with the reins loosely in his left hand and with no apparent visible movement from either his hands or legs, Gordon had the animal going forward, backward, sideways, and turning in tight circles in each direction. After a few minutes he switched the saddle to Jasmine and did the same thing. He looked like he was part of the horse.

Riding Jasmine and leading Taboo, Gordon returned. As he dismounted, Joe asked suddenly, "Would it be that ye'r an American Indian?" Gordon, smiling, told him that, indeed, he was a Lakota. "Ah," said Joe, "you're a blessing to me. I'll have a pint on that. One of the main reasons I ever wanted to come to America was to see the Indians." Gordon's smile widened, and as Joe helped him get the blanket and western saddle on Jasmine, Gordon told him about the Mustang therapy program on Pine Ridge. Joe was fascinated by the information and said,

"Imagine that. Horses used for therapy. Half the time after working with them, I'm the one who needs therapy. For all the work I do with them, I really never understood the beasts." Gordon invited him to come out and see the program in operation. Joe thanked him and said he'd love to, but right now they had better concentrate on the business at hand. He said that Jasmine was an experienced polo mount, but that Taboo had never been in a polo match, and only a few of the most accomplished horsemen had attempted to ride him, all without success.

"Well, then," said Tallbear, "when it comes to polo, Taboo and I have something in common."

"You've never played polo?" exclaimed Joe, his voice rising in shock. "Jaysus, Mary, and Joseph! Harrington will kill you out there. Now you listen to me, young man. He's vicious, that one, and vicious doesn't go far enough. Winning isn't enough for him. He isn't satisfied unless he humiliates his opponents."

"Not to worry, Joe. Know the story of the Little Big Horn?"

"Aye, but It's your funeral," Joe replied, and then, after a pause, added, "and I'd be proud to sing at your wake."

Johanna laughed at this charming Irishman, and Gordon just grinned. Chuck didn't know what to make of it all. He was expecting his friend to be killed.

While Gordon spent time with the horses, Joe looked at Johanna and asked, "Darlin,' I've been watching you watch him and him watch you. Does he know you love him so much?"

Johanna was at first taken aback. "No, Joe, he doesn't. Not yet."

"Then grab him soon, darlin'. By his look, his heart aches."

"You tell her, Joe," said Chuck. "Where we work, everyone says that they're a perfect match, but the two dimwits keep up this front. It's about time one of them got something going."

"Thank you, Dr. Kinoshi," said Johanna frostily, "I had no idea that among your talents was your skill at giving advice to the lovelorn."

"All part of the service, ma'am," said Chuck with a bow.

"He's right, you know," said Joe. "Don't wait for it to happen. Make it happen. You can take that as Gospel truth from a thoroughly repressed Irishman."

Johanna laughed. "I'll keep that in mind, Joe."

Gordon watched from the sidelines for the first two of six chuckkers, or seven-and one-half minute periods. During this play, each team scored once. At the beginning of the third chuckker, Harrington was competing with James Todd for possession of the ball when he pulled off one of the oldest tricks in the book. He maneuvered his horse to position himself alongside Todd, and while appearing to be struggling toward the ball, lifted his knee under Todd's thigh and unhorsed him. Todd slipped right out of his saddle and crashed to the ground. The sickening snap of his breaking leg made even the most jaundiced observer wince.

Harrington just sat on his mount and looked down disdainfully while the EMT's rushed over. He looked at Gordon, smirked, and turned his horse away.

As the EMTs took James Todd to a nearby emergency clinic, Jonathan Sloan signaled Tallbear to come onto the field.

"It looks like you're in to stay, Gordon. You'll be in the number four position. Your main job is to prevent them from scoring. You're kind of a goalie, though you can leave your position if an opportunity arises to get possession of the ball. The main thing is to knock the ball to one of us, preferably to Darrell, as he is our best scorer and is in the number two position. Phil is the number one and will be covering your opposite number. I'm the number three, and will be trying to feed the ball to Darrel or Phil. By the way, I hope you are right-handed as the game requires that you hit the ball with the mallet in your right hand. You ready?"

"Let's do it."

Gordon Tallbear grabbed the horn of the saddle, smoothly swung up onto Jasmine, and entered his first polo match. Joe had to struggle with Taboo to keep him from chasing after Gordon.

Play against these Brits was pretty rough, and Harrington was the roughest -- and dirtiest -- of the lot. After a few collisions, Tallbear was beginning to get the hang of it. Jasmine was exceptional in anticipating every move and responding to his commands. She was obviously a thoroughbred cross horse, and was accustomed to a rider with one hand on the reins. She responded immediately to Tallbear's leg and weight cues as he handled the mallet with his right hand. The hand-eye coordination honed from years of hitting a baseball came back to him quickly. He had no trouble hitting a ball in motion. Jasmine's quick responses enabled him to block three shots on his goal.

At the end of that third chukker, Jasmine was showing the effects of the effort. Sloan said, "All the horses need a break at least at the end of each chukker, Gordon. Sometimes more. While we all change horses, you should know that you are about to give Taboo his baptism of fire. I hope he responds well to your commands. He's a pretty independent horse."

"No problem, Jonathan. Taboo and I will get along just fine."

And Taboo did very well in the fourth chukker. He responded instantly to every command Tallbear gave. He and Tallbear became one moving and flowing entity. What Taboo lacked in height, he more than made up for in speed. At one point Tallbear drove the ball down the field. Taboo sped for the ball like lightning and Tallbear angled the ball downfield. Evading his pursuers and swinging around behind Harrington, the opposing number four, he closed on the ball and whacked it with his mallet only to see that his aim was off and the ball missed the goal by a few feet.

Right after that the fourth chukker ended and it was time to give Taboo a rest.

In the fifth chukker, Jasmine started out well, but toward the closing minutes she noticeably slowed down in speed as well as responses to his leg and weight cues. Mercifully, his teammates made up for Jasmine's slowness and Tallbear's inexperience, and chukker number five ended with the score still tied at 1.

During the break to change horses, Tallbear – and everyone else, for that matter - could hear Harrington down the line berating his teammates. "Why can't you manage to get a clean shot on goal against this savage?" he shouted. So much for ambassadorial diplomacy, thought Tallbear as he switched the saddle to Taboo. It was obvious to all that even the British ex-pats were offended by his tirades. As he was finishing with the saddle, Tallbear had to grin when he heard one Brit mutter, "Bligh lives on."

Jonathan Sloan came up to Tallbear and began to apologize for Harrington's insult. Shaking his head, Tallbear just held up his hand and gave an enigmatic smile. He spoke a quick word in Lakota and Taboo launched into a gallop as Gordon grabbed the pommel, pulled himself slightly up, then dropped his feet to the ground and used Taboo's momentum to spring up into the saddle for the final chuckker.

The sixth and final chukker was characterized by Harrington's pressuring his team to play more aggressively. By the fifth minute the match was threatening to degenerate into an undignified brawl. An umpire finally shouted a warning to

Harrington that he would be penalized for unsportsmanlike conduct if it continued.

The crowd was really getting into it, and instead of rattling the ice in their drink glasses, the majority of them were actually clapping and cheering for the American team.

In the waning seconds of the chukker, Tallbear spotted an opportunity. Leaving his defensive position, he needed little effort to get Taboo up to speed to intercept a pass close to his goal. He swung his mallet and drove the ball between two opposing mounts. Moving quickly to make his follow-up shot, he swung his mallet too low and snapped it off about 18 inches from the mallet head.

Dropping the useless handle, and with knee commands and a shifting of his weight, he spun Taboo on the spot and sped back to the broken mallet. Bending down nearly vertical over the side of Taboo and at full speed, he snatched the stub of the mallet from the ground and used the reins to turn Taboo toward the ball. One of the opposing players got there first and attempted a pass to his number two. The ball had only traveled about fifteen feet when Tallbear and Taboo intersected the angle like a blur.

Hanging down off the side of the horse with the stub of the mallet in his hand, Tallbear smacked the ball downfield. He looked for Jonathan, but he was behind Tallbear. Phil and Darrel were blocked by the Brits and trying to work themselves free.

With his long hair flowing behind him and his moccasin clad foot hooked over the horn of his saddle, he was an amazing vision of athleticism and courage as he drove the ball downfield with his stump of a mallet -- a warrior at the top of his game.

Suddenly Phil and Darrell broke to the inside of their defenders. Tallbear hit the ball over to Phil on his left. As one of the Brits began closing on Phil, he knocked the ball across to Darrell forward of Tallbear on the right. As his opposite number tried to block him, Darrell shot the ball to the middle. Tallbear urged Taboo to top speed and drove the ball up field.

Right in his line of fire blocking the goal was Harrington. Taboo was now running flat out, his flanks shiny with sweat, muscles rippling with effort of doing what he was born for, and the thunder of his hooves throbbing right through Tallbear's veins.

From the sidelines he could hear Johanna over the crowd. "GET HIM, TALLBEAR!! GET HIM!"

The crowd's roar went up a notch.

Harrington held his massive horse firmly, determined not to move in the face of Tallbear's headlong charge. It's all a bluff, he thought. Then in the micro-seconds that showed Tallbear not deviating from his collision course, Harrington's mouth went dry and his bowels turned to spaghetti. Never, until this day, this moment, had he experienced sheer, unmitigated terror. He couldn't move if he had to. Approaching him at full speed on an undeviating course, was the single unit of man and animal, an incarnate force of honor and integrity he could never possibly comprehend.

In one flashing move, Tallbear, hanging nearly vertically off Taboo's right flank, hit the ball hard, driving it right between the legs of Harrington's mount. Almost simultaneously he swung upright in the saddle. He and Taboo were closing on Harrington like lightning, but Harrington was frozen to the spot.

With an extraordinary leap, Taboo and Tallbear soared over the neck of Harrington's horse. As Taboo landed, Tallbear dropped down to the side, and with a gentle whack drove the winning goal home while the seconds ticked off the clock. As he slowed Taboo down and turned, his teammates were crowding in to congratulate him and it was then that Tallbear heard the screams of the crowd. People were dancing up and down and high-fiving and hugging each other.

Johanna threw her hand to her mouth and began shaking. Then she began to weep.

Chuck just stood there on the sidelines and mumbled over and over, "Summbitch! Summbitch!"

Joe Delaney made the sign of the cross and said, "Holy Mary, Mother of God!"

When Tallbear got to the sidelines he gracefully eased his leg over the saddle, dismounted, and whispered a Lakota prayer into Taboo's ear. The horse nuzzled him in appreciation. Tallbear began walking the horse to cool him down. As he passed the British team, Harrington gave him a look that would turn other men to stone. Tallbear stopped and simply looked him right in the eye and said, "Thank you, Sir Winslow, for choosing my horses for me. It was your sense of fair play, no doubt." And then he and Taboo moved on. Harrington grew livid. His jaw tightened. A vein in the side of his neck throbbed. He was a man totally consumed by unadulterated rage.

Joe Delaney ran over as fast as his bad leg would let him and said, "Sir, I have been around horses and polo since I was knee high, and I tell you I have never seen anything to top that. That, sir, was an extraordinary display of horsemanship – and courage. Little Big Horn indeed. You did all but bring home his scalp, if you'll forgive my saying so. You have my congratulations, sir, and I will consider it an honor to care for Taboo."

Smiling at Joe's comment, Tallbear said, "No offence taken, Joe. Take special care of Taboo for me, for this is one remarkable horse." And with that he stroked Taboo one more time before Joe, with no difficulty from the horse, led him away.

By then most of the spectators, the Brits included, were crowding around him wanting to congratulate him. He looked over the crowd and on its periphery saw Johanna and Chuck. Johanna, her eyes now dry, gave him a radiant smile as he nodded to her. He had to grin when he saw Chuck mouth, "WOW."

During the lengthy period of handshaking with strangers, and while signing a few autographs, one fan grasped him by the hand, leaned in close, and said, "Welcome to the world of bait. I think you have successfully pressed for a confrontation. Be extremely careful. We'll be in touch."

When he was finally able to get back to his teammates, he thanked them for letting him join them. Jonathan Sloan, eyes moist, then said, "Thank us? Thank *us*? I speak for us all when I tell you that it was our greatest pleasure and deepest honor to have you on the team. We have struggled all this season against that lot, having to put up with their dirty play and his Lordship's antics. This was the first time we walked away victorious, and boy does that feel great! Please join us for some celebratory champagne. And, by the way, where in hell did you learn to ride? I know I speak for us all when I say that none of us has ever seen such brilliant horsemanship."

Gordon modestly replied, "I am a Lakota, born and raised on Pine Ridge Reservation in South Dakota, and was trained in all the traditions of my people, including the taming and riding of horses."

Jonathan replied, "Well, Gordon, we consider it a deep honor that you have been a part of our team today."

Tallbear said, "Thank you, Jonathan. And as for that offer of champagne, well, I don't drink, but while you down the bubbly, I'm happy to toast you with a bottle of water."

"So be it, good friend. Join us."

They all stood together basking in the glow of their victory, and with the men's girlfriends and wives looking at Tallbear like the exotic wonder he was, Johanna and Chuck approached the group. Johanna walked right up to Tallbear, threw her arms around his neck, and gave him a deep, long kiss and hugged him. Tallbear became a little flustered at that, but couldn't resist returning the kiss. They slowly parted, looking deep into each other's eyes. He quickly regained his composure and made introductions.

As exotic as Tallbear was to the women, the men couldn't take their eyes off of Johanna.

Chuck, going into full grit mode, spoke his piece. "Ah was hopin' someone would pin the ears back on that arrogant summbitch. And man you should have seen the look on Harrington's face when cousin Tallbear went airborne. I bet Harrington pooped his panties. You talk about tall in the saddle. Hell, he had the same look on his face as Custer when ol' Crazy Horse nailed his ass to the wall."

At that everyone broke up laughing.

Darrel said, "James will be furious that he missed the end of this one. I don't think we could describe it to him accurately."

"Not to worry," said Jonathan's wife Angela. "I've got it on video. Plus the BBC crew had two cameras covering the action." At that they all crowded around to see the replay on her iPad.

Johanna spoke up. "Angela, if it's at all possible, could you send me that video?"

"Me, too," said Chuck.

Phil spoke for everyone when he said, "We'll send it to everyone, and to the British embassy as well!"

At that they all roared. Tallbear smiled, but had a calmness about him that Johanna noticed. They locked eyes knowing that this was just a small step toward a bigger victory.

Gordon went to Angela and quietly asked her to be sure to send the video to Joe Delaney. She said she would be happy to do so.

Finally the post-mortem began to wind down, and Johanna exchanged email addresses with Angela Sloan. As Tallbear, Johanna, and Chuck were leaving, Tallbear said, "If you will excuse me, I want to say goodbye to Taboo and Jasmine."

With that he walked off to the barn, his hair blowing gently in the wind, the little stone swaying behind his right ear.

They all stared after him in silence.

At the barn, Joe was just finishing currying Taboo and Jasmine. Both horses were being well-fed and watered. Tallbear walked up to the two horses standing side-by-side and stroked their necks. "It has been a while since I rode, and may be a while until I do so again," he said quietly to the horses. "Thank you my friends, for caring for me on the field."

And after several moments of silence with the horses nuzzling him, he whispered something into each of the horses' ears, spent a little extra time with Taboo, finally saying to him, "You and I will meet again for a great adventure," then turned and shook hands with Joe and walked slowly out of the barn.

"The wind at yer back, son," said Joe quietly, "the wind at yer back."

People cannot be subdued unless they lose belief in themselves.
Introduction to

Crazy Horse: Strange Man of the Oglalas

Chapter 32

Tallbear, Johanna, and Chuck arrived back at the safe house drained. After showers, they met in the library. A little later Madison Tolles came in and enthusiastically reported that there was some good news to come out of his meetings in Washington.

In Congress, there was growing bi-partisan support – a rare occurrence indeed -- for the plan to build the pyramid on American soil, and the Secretary of Defense and the Joint Chiefs were directing respective staffs to develop plans for security contingencies. The Secretary of State indicated a growing sense of cooperation in the international community.

"I see Gordon is back here alive, so he must have survived his polo match. How'd it go?"

Johanna said, "See for yourself." She pulled out her iPad and cued the video to the break where Harrington went into his tirade. Handing the device to Mr. Tolles she said, "This was sent from Angela Sloan, the wife of Gordon's polo team Captain." Excusing herself, she left the room. Tolles sat and watched enraptured. He leapt out of his chair when Gordon and Taboo flew over Harrington's mount.

Tolles just stood there for a moment and then said incredulously, "Gordon, I can't believe what I just saw!"

Chuck interjected, "He did more than that. He nailed that summbitch good and solid on the sidelines when he thanked the good ambassador for his 'sense of fair play' in choosing his mounts for him. I thought his Lordship was going to bust a gut. I mean his face was red and you could see the vein throbbing in his neck. He was wound up tighter than a golf ball."

Just then Johanna came back in and said, "In ten minutes we will be able to see some of the BBC footage of the match on ESPN's Sports Center. And at 10:00 on the BBC channel we can see the whole match."

They all moved to the recreation room to catch the coverage on the big screen TV. ESPN made it the Number One play of the week and repeated the video segment several times. The broadcasters were falling all over themselves in their excitement.

When the coverage was finished, Madison Tolles stood up shaking his head. "I saw it and I still don't believe it. Hot damn!" He looked at Gordon in wonder.

Gordon spoke up. "After the match, as people were crowding around me shaking my hand and asking for autographs, a man shook my hand and welcomed me to the world of bait. He said to be careful and that he would be in touch. I assume he was FBI. Is this the time for their move?"

Tolles thought a minute and said, "I'm not sure whether the polo match would be the catalyst for the Gnomes taking some action, but their window of opportunity is closing, and we can expect something to happen soon anyway. They will undoubtedly come after you, Gordon, maybe all of us.

"This is the only shot they will get at eliminating us. It is well known that in late April National Geographic and Smithsonian will be making a major announcement about breathtaking discoveries that were 'uncovered in their joint venture.' We have been secretly prepping the key people in both organizations for this. As we speak, their photographers and film crews are in the caverns documenting everything and are under a strict edict not to communicate with the outside world. Once that announcement is made, the project cannot be stopped. In the meantime there are a few weeks in which the Gnomes can create mayhem – with us from the Denver Center, and with threats and intimidation, if not more, to the principal players from National Geographic and Smithsonian, and to the political leadership of Congress. Lord knows that there's no shortage of members of Congress with skeletons in their closets. They will crumble under threat of exposure. And without you, Gordon, to bring the Native American nations together, it could get dicey.

"I don't think even that will stop the project, but without the four of us leading it, it could face a lot more hurdles."

Johanna asked, "What about increasing security for us? Right now we have an adequate security plan, but it doesn't cover us from a determined group of people out to kill us."

"You're right about that, Johanna," Tolles agreed. "I am going to ask the FBI for a meeting tomorrow to develop a beefed up security plan. We already had increased our security coverage after Ben's murder, but we are going to need more. Now let's turn in. I know Gordon needs a break, and the rest of us need to get ready to turn this project into action. By the way, Gordon, you didn't kill him, but what you did was better. I haven't forgotten about that bonus."

"Forget it, Mr. Tolles. It was my pleasure. And I have an idea for our security you might be interested in.

With that Gordon began his narrative.

"During that point of balance when the white man was stymied in his advance into the Great Plains, all the mounted tribes of the west used the same tactic to lure soldiers to their deaths. While the tribes of the Sioux Nation used it pretty effectively, the Comanche, the most masterful horsemen of the West, were absolute geniuses at it, and kept western expansion of the white world in check until the early 1870s. From Nebraska to Texas, from the beginning of the Plains in the east on out to the Rockies, their tactics were consistent. A battle would be engaged with a few Indians against a superior force of white cavalry. The Indians would withdraw, luring the cavalry to chase them further and further from their main lines of support. At an appropriate time, the withdrawing Indians would disperse leaving the cavalry in the middle of a well-prepared ambush by the main Indian force.

"Here's how I think we can lure the Gnomes into a trap."

And for the next fifteen minutes, Gordon drew up an interesting plan. "The key," Gordon said, "lies in letting the Gnomes think that we are oblivious to their threat. We keep to fairly set routines, varying them just enough to let them know that we are conscious of the need for security. The moment will come when they are confident that they can take us. They'll send goons, just like at the Silverlode Tavern. But this time they will send in real pros. I'm betting our lives on a hunch, but I believe that the Gnomes are not going to settle for our death by underlings. They'll want to do the job themselves. Now my plan will need a lot of resource support from the FBI."

When he was finished, they all agreed to give it some thought until they could meet with the FBI and flesh out the details.

As their meeting broke up and Gordon and Chuck were heading up to bed, Johanna said, "Mr. Tolles, If I might have a word before you turn in?"

"Certainly, Johanna. Goodnight Gordon, Chuck. See you in the morning."

"Good night, sir," they both replied.

After the two men left, Tolles turned to Johanna. "Now, Johanna, you seem ready to give me all the background information on today's events."

"Sir, it was all so incredible." And Johanna proceeded to give Madison Tolles all the information that was not covered in the videos. She told him about Harrington's "gracious" offer of selecting Gordon's mounts; about Taboo and his total wildness; about Gordon's seemingly miraculous taming of the horse. She told of the graciousness of Gordon's polo team; of the shifting support of the crowd. She tried to capture the emotion of Gordon's final confrontation with Harrington. She told about Gordon's humility in victory.

She left out any reference to Joe Delaney's personal observations.

·   ·   ·

The next day, they went to the FBI office and outlined their plan. It was enthusiastically accepted.

Chapter 33

The next evening the phone call, while not unexpected, left Sir Winslow with a sense of dread. He quickly changed into slacks and a sports jacket and slipped out the rear entrance of his quarters. One block away a limousine was waiting for him. It was a twenty-minute ride to an upscale high-rise condo complex in Crystal City, not far from National airport in Arlington, Virginia.

Following a routine similar to the one he experienced in London, he was quickly brought up to the penthouse level. Again he walked into a beautifully furnished apartment. The same butler served the same drink and retired.

But this time there was no time for amenities.

"That was a pretty inept performance on the polo field," Peter Wilson began softly. "Your arrogance and conduct brought unwarranted attention to yourself. The amateur video taken by one of your opponent's wives of your humiliation at the hands of an inexperienced American Indian, has gone viral on the internet. YouTube has already had more than two million hits. The performance is Number One on ESPN's Top Plays. On top of that, there was a BBC film crew there – at your instigation, I might add – who went public with this on their sports broadcast last night. And for Christ's sake, the pro-British crowd shifted their allegiance to Tallbear and his team, **I AM REALLY HAVING SOME TROUBLE WITH THAT!!** .

And your friends in the BBC also caught your tirade in which you referred to Dr. Tallbear as a savage. **BRILLIANT STATESMANSHIP, YOU USELESS TOOL!!** Undoubtedly you will be hearing from Whitehall on this. Our organization thrives on having no profile at all, **AND YOU HAVE SPLASHED YOURSELF ALL OVER THE MEDIA AND CONNECTED YOURSELF WITH ONE OF OUR MOST DANGEROUS ADVERSARIES.**

YOU MUST BE THICKER THAN A PLANK IF YOU CAN'T SEE WHERE THIS COULD BE HEADED!"

This opening salvo sent a trickle of sweat down Harrington's spine, not to mention that his armpits were a mess.

"Hell, we couldn't have interfered with the broadcast of the BBC video if we wanted to! ESPN instantly got the right to broadcast it. But you will not be receiving an official reprimand from your government, only an unofficial one. We will take care of that. In the future, Mr. Ambassador, you **WILL** be more discreet!" Wilson hissed. "Do we understand each other?"

"Yes, Mr. Wilson, I understand," replied Harrington. "But I want Tallbear dead!"

"Lash yourself to the mast, Sir Winslow! If and when it suits our purposes, Gordon Tallbear will die. But you will do nothing – **REPEAT NOTHING** – in regard to that. Is that understood? Rest assured, Sir Winslow, the leadership of the Denver Center will not be allowed to proceed with their plans.

"Yes, Sir."

And for the next twenty minutes, Peter Wilson spelled out in excruciating detail the potential for financial ruin that they all could expect if the U.S. government and the Denver Center decided to put all their money on the potential universal solution to the world's energy problem.

"Hell," Wilson said, "Madison Tolles has enough money to finance this whole thing personally and still have enough left to be one of the richest men in the world!

"Buggy whips!" he railed. "Buggy whips is what our clients may as well be manufacturing if that goes through. The internal combustion engine ended the buggy whip industry, and this Great Pyramid idea will do the same to our clients. If that happens, Sir Winslow, it will be no more country estates for you, no mistresses, and certainly none of your aberrant recreational activities. You will be on the street like the rest of us. **AND WE WON'T STAND FOR THAT, NOW WILL WE?"** Wilson concluded, bellowing in Harrington's ear.

Harrington was beside himself with worry. He was in so deep that he couldn't think straight. After some more of Wilson's tirade, he was dismissed and told to stand by for further orders. He was returned to the same corner in Washington, quickly went up the block and slipped into his quarters, and made himself a drink.

Harrington's agitation was severe. He had placed himself at the disposal of these powerful strangers and despite attempting to work with them, he was ridiculed for his humiliation on the polo field. He could feel his rage rising. He paced his apartment for hours. Shortly before midnight his cell phone rang.

The seductive, accented female voice said, "If you are having trouble sleeping, perhaps I might be able to relieve your tension." Harrington felt himself being swallowed up in her voice. She gave him an address near his embassy. "If you are not here in 30 minutes," she said, "this address will no longer exist." That was the end of the call.

Harrington got in his car and went to the address. It was an old Victorian mansion just a few blocks from Embassy Row. A very muscular man in a tight fitting black T-shirt and blue jeans opened the door and silently escorted him to the basement. It was a perfect dungeon equipped with all the accoutrements of torture. Against a far wall was a beautiful raven-haired woman suspended by chains from a rafter. Her legs were spread and anchored at the ankles by chains attached to floor rings. Naked except for her stiletto platform heels and a spiked dog collar, she was covered in a sheen of body oil.

Harrington moved forward slowly removing his clothes. On a rack to his right hung a cat-o-nine tails. He reached for it. The woman had a look of sheer terror as he approached her.

After an hour of his favorite recreation, he was able, with some difficulty, to relieve his tension. The woman submissive, however, required some serious medical care when he was done with her.

Five days later, when she had recovered well enough at a carefully chosen private clinic, she was given a generous cash settlement and placed on a private jet back to her native country.

When the plane landed, she was not aboard.

Rage, rage against the dying of the light.

Dylan Thomas

Chapter 34

There are various sub-cultures in America, but one of them, constantly overlooked, is the mercenaries. America, however, can't claim exclusive rights to the mercenary class. The world is crawling with them.

The mercenary has no political agenda. He loves the profession of arms, and is not too fussy about who hires him to do a job. He is amoral and only in it for the pay and adventure. Idealism and nobility of cause have withered as motive as far as he is concerned. Just pay him to quell an insurrection, or start one. It doesn't matter to him. He works out to keep his body in the same peak condition it was in when he was in Delta Force, or Navy SEALS, or Army Special Forces or Rangers, or Marine Force Reconnaissance.

He watches the classified ads in selected publications for the coded message that might send him to an African village or the mountains of Paraguay for action and substantial pay. Who and why don't matter to him, just where and how much. Who he works for is not important. What the job is, well, that's not important either. What the pay is, and what the adventure is, that's what counts.

Often this man simply responds to a phone call from a respected colleague who has landed an unwritten contract. He is told what the mission is and packs appropriately. He arrives at the rendezvous point cocked, locked, and ready to go.

Following the bungled attempt to terrify the leaders of the Denver Center in the confrontation at the roadside bar and grill in Colorado, the Gnomes reassessed what would be required to bring the matter of the Denver Center to a successful conclusion. On the orders of Seth Tilcotan, they brought in an exceptionally talented group of professionals to execute a stunning plan.

A message was delivered to thirty-three men in various parts of the country. They were to arrive in Baltimore, Maryland; Washington, DC; and Richmond, Virginia, on March 30 at staggered intervals, and they were to check in at thirty-three different motels in Maryland and northern Virginia. They had been sent false identifications and credit cards allowing them to rent cars and pay for lodging, and they were told that nine-passenger vans would pick them up at their motels on April 1 at pre-designated times.

Each of the thirty-three men was a sniper-trained marksman who could put a bullet through a silver dollar at up to 1000 yards. They all were experts in a wide variety of small arms, hand-to-hand combat, explosives, and communications. Each one could pick any lock manufactured anywhere in the world in less than 30 seconds. All were raid experts who had completed mountain, jungle, and desert warfare schools. They were SCUBA trained. All were jump qualified and had been certified in HALO jumping. HALO is High Altitude Low Opening parachuting, which involves jumping from a plane at 43,000 feet, free-falling, popping the parachute at 800 feet, and walking away from the encounter without wetting their pants. They could lie silently in a hide site for three days without moving, eating, or sleeping, and many had done so in combat operations. All were combat veterans.

The thirty-three contractors arrived at a farmhouse near Dale City, Virginia, ready for instructions. A man in his late 40s, very fit with close cropped blond hair and a strong military bearing, was there to welcome them. When all had arrived and been given box lunches, he outlined the plan.

"This is going to be a smash-and-grab operation targeting four key people. They are to be brought here to this farmhouse in pristine condition, un-harmed and unmarked. You are to deliver them here, bound and blindfolded, and turn them over to a different security team. Once the targets are delivered, you will be brought back to your hotels and return from where you came."

He brought out a map of the DC metropolitan area. "These four people are currently in three different locations. Two of them are in a luxury condo in Rockville, Maryland. One is in an apartment in DC near DuPont Circle. And one is in the Watergate apartments near the Kennedy Center. They are to be snatched at exactly the same moment. Security in each of these three buildings is high. FBI agents are closely watching the Rockville and DuPont Circle locations. The Watergate already has extensive private security due to the fact that so many high profile individuals live there. Because of the particular profile of the target at this location, a separate team of federal agents is also monitoring the site. They will need to be neutralized, but killing is to be avoided.

"I have procured most of the necessary tools you will need to accomplish this task. Here is a full list of what I have acquired thus far, including vehicles, weapons, and clothing. In the next 24 hours, we will refine the elements involved and rehearse each aspect of the three operations. Should you require any additional tools to complete the mission, I will get them. For each of you the pay will be $50,000 to be deposited in accounts you have named following your initial contact. Any questions?"

No one had questions, and the refinements to the plan began. Pictures of Johanna, Tallbear, Chuck, and Madison Tolles were given to each man. They were told that these people were definitely being watched and shadowed by federal agents 24-7, and that the targets were certain to have their own security precautions in place. This was not to be considered to be a routine operation.

Based on prior military rank, experience and specialty, each man was assigned to one of the three raid units. Each raid unit was divided into an assault team, a security team, and a command team.

The command and security teams were each composed of three men. The assault teams had five men each. The security teams were to neutralize, and preferably not kill, the federal agents shadowing the targets. The assault groups were each tasked with the actual smash-and-grab mission.

One man in each command group would be in charge and make all final decisions for his team. The other two would monitor surveillance videos and maintain secure communications with the farmhouse and the other teams to ensure coordination. Each of the three teams in each operation had several people trained and experienced at handling medical emergencies in the event of casualties.

They were briefed on the irregular schedule maintained by each of the targets, and an appropriate time was selected to effect the execution of the operation.

The next order of business was a reconnaissance by each of the command group leaders. First was the map reconnaissance. Routes of ingress and egress were mapped out, backed up by alternate routes. That night, after midnight, the three command groups each embarked in ordinary looking SUVs with tinted windows to do their site reconnaissance. They timed the routes to the second and conducted a thorough surveillance of each of the target areas. Later they would analyze the photographs they took and plan for contingencies.

The security and assault groups, meanwhile, inventoried everything they would need to accomplish the mission and brainstormed to uncover all of the hidden or forgotten problems that would arise. They came up with alternatives to neutralize every possible unforeseen contingency.

The security and assault teams went outside and conducted walk-through drills on how each target would be neutralized. They came back in and practiced the actual kidnapping part of the operation in rooms in the spacious farmhouse. They compared notes, revised estimates, added to the shopping list of things needed, and, as every military planner has known since the beginning of time, still realized that there were probably 1000 things that they hadn't thought of.

The leaders of the command groups came back and they walked through the rehearsals multiple times. Team leaders got their men prepared for the first equipment and "uniform" inspection. Each man fell out dressed for his role and equipped with what he would need to accomplish the mission. The middle-aged man who initially briefed them, along with the three unit commanders, inspected each man and their equipment and armament.

By this time, more than 24 hours had elapsed. It was now 7:00 PM on April 2. The targets would be taken after midnight on April 4. In a barn adjacent to the farmhouse, a temporary barracks had been established. Following final briefings, and with little chatter among the men, they each settled down with their own thoughts and slept through until 5:00 AM.

Following 'reveille', they went through final rehearsals and inspections. The man in charge gave them their final instructions.

"In the event that your mission is compromised before you take the hostages, you will break contact, split up, make your way back to your hotels, and from there return home. In the event that the mission is compromised after you take the hostages, you are to release them unharmed and do your best to get away. Should the operation be compromised, this location will be evacuated immediately so that the FBI will have no useful information to get from you. If you are caught and arrested, appropriate legal counsel will be provided to obtain your release. Now move out."

They were ready.

The vans left at coordinated times and delivered the men to predetermined locations in Virginia and DC around mid-day.

•   •   •

Over the course of a two hour period, no one particularly noticed the athletic looking men who got off the trains at seven different Metro stops in Washington and Rockville, MD. Some were casually dressed, some wore blue jeans and T-shirts, some were wearing suits, and a few were wearing blue blazers and gray trousers. All carried gym bags. But in the DC area, men with military haircuts and dressed that way drew little notice. Half the military in Washington wore civilian clothing to work, and for military officers, blue blazers and gray slacks are the ultimate in civilian attire. It was late afternoon and people would assume they were probably coming from their government offices and headed to fitness centers for a daily workout.

At the high-rise condo in Rockville, from two different Metro stops, over a one-hour period late that afternoon, five of these men entered the target building. Two entered the front of the building along with some innocent residents. From a distance these men appeared to be friends with the residents by the way they bantered with and held doors open for them. The other three, having carefully observed where the likely FBI watchers were, slipped into the garage. All five men rendezvoused on the top floor, neutralized the alarm on the fire exit and headed to the roof. They stripped their clothing, stuffed it into equipment bags, changed into black tracksuits, and applied camouflage paint to their faces and hands. They checked their weapons and equipment and settled in silently to wait.

A similar scenario was conducted at the Watergate. At DuPont Circle, the scenario was slightly different, but with the same results. That location was a small luxury apartment building only four floors high with two apartments on each floor. As one of the residents was approaching the building with an armload of groceries and struggling while opening the door, two well-dressed men approached her and offered to help. Once inside, she was ordered to take them to her apartment. There she was subdued, her keys taken. She was bound, blindfolded, and gagged in her apartment. One of the men stayed with her while the others went down to a rear entrance and let the rest of the assault team in. When all were back in the apartment, they calmed the woman down and assured her that she would be treated well and that no harm would come to her.

From that point on, they all waited in total silence. The team leader took the woman's hand in his and spoke gently. He told her that what was happening wasn't about her, but they needed her cooperation. Whenever she needed to go to the bathroom, she would be escorted and afforded as much privacy as possible. Should she need food or drink, they would get it for her. His voice calmed her.

Periodically over the next seven hours, when the woman needed to go to the bathroom, she was escorted and given as much privacy as could be allowed under the circumstances. She got to the point where she was comfortable with the intruders. They were acting like gentlemen.

Just as in Rockville, the men changed into black track suits and applied camouflage to their faces and hands.

Shortly after dark the command and security teams arrived about two blocks from each target. Leaving their gear in the vans, and dressed in dark tracksuits, the security team members dispersed, only to reappear as random joggers. Coming from different directions toward the target buildings and at varying intervals over a two-hour period, they took everything in. These men had been trained to observe. When they first went to sniper school, they were walked through a large room to a classroom. The instructor handed each of them a piece of paper and a pencil and told them to record everything they had seen in the room they had just passed through. Most did not do well on the first quiz and were sent back to their units right away. But a few of those who had a talent for observing details were kept on, and they were further trained to scan and mentally record everything.

At each site the teams easily picked out the cargo van that was probably FBI surveillance.

Also at each location, there were various men and women either jogging or walking dogs. Some of these dog walkers returned to their nearby apartment buildings and weren't seen again. In other cases, the same dogs were seen later being walked by different people. Each site surveillance team made note of this and identified which nearby buildings and which windows in those buildings potentially housed observers.

At strategic locations like low walls and the sides of mailboxes, the joggers would fake a loose shoelace, bend over as if to tie it, and place cameras.

Well after dark, and in staggered order, the men returned to their vans knowing how to take out each target.

Each of the security teams contacted their command team. The command teams slowly moved into place in their vehicles.

Later that evening, around 10 o'clock, at each of the three locations a woman in her mid-sixties walked her dog. In Rockville the dog was a toy poodle. At DuPont Circle, the dog was a Pekinese. At the Watergate, the dog was a terrier. Each was discounted by the security teams. Women of that age with dogs like that were part of the landscape.

In Rockville, the dog-walking woman began to cross the street in front of the parked security team van. As she stepped out to cross the road, a boy coming down the street on a skateboard deliberately wiped out to avoid hitting her. Pulling himself off the ground he cursed her and she gave back as good as she got. The men inside the van got a good laugh out of the scenario. Finally the kid went under the van to retrieve his skateboard, still cursing her with every breath. While he was under there he planted a magnetized GPS tracking device.

This also happened at DuPont Circle and at the Watergate.

·   ·   ·

Tallbear and Chuck arrived back at their condo just after 10:00. As they entered the building and headed for the elevators, a man in a dark tracksuit was approaching the door. Suddenly he stopped and snapped his fingers. He said, "Damn." He looked at them and said, "Forgot my heart beat monitor." He turned with them and went back to the elevators. As he entered, he asked, "What floor?" Chuck said, "Nine," and the man pushed the button. He pushed 12 for himself and nodded to them as they got off the elevator. When they exited and the doors closed, he spoke into the silence of the elevator, "Got that?"

Through his earpiece receiver he got an answer in the affirmative.

Outside, the three observers on the security team watched the building from different angles. Soon one of them saw a light go on in one of the apartments on the ninth floor. He spoke softly to the command team, "Ninth floor east end of the building, second apartment from the end." The command team looked at the floor plan of the building and relayed the information to the assault team. "Apartment number 924." A similar scenario was being played out at the Watergate.

For Tallbear and Chuck, it had been another mentally exhausting day. Loads of technical questions needed answers. Would the placement of the pyramid at higher latitude require that the angle of the shaft from the King's Chamber be modified? Using the levitation technology of Atlantis, could the energy beaming from the pyramid be directed to low earth orbit satellites, or would it have to be beamed to high orbit satellites more than 22,000 miles above the equator? They had architects and engineers at the Denver Center working out the numbers on modification of the southern shaft should they need it.

Political considerations complicated matters as well. The Secretary of State briefed them that some of the allies were showing signs of cold feet. As regards internal security, the Secretary of Defense and the Justice Department were dealing with the delicate legal area referred to as *posse comitatus*.

The Posse Comitatus Act of June 16, 1878, has the intention of restricting federal power regarding the domestic use of the military for law enforcement. The Act, as amended in subsequent years, legally denies members of the U.S. armed services – the Army, Navy, Air Force, and Marines, and also the National Guard – from exercising law enforcement, police, or peace officer powers on non-federal property within the United States except where authorized by the Constitution or Congress. The Coast Guard, which was now under the command of the Department of Domestic Security, was exempt from *posse comitatus* because by charter it already had law enforcement mandates.

If the pyramid were to be placed on Pine Ridge Reservation, would Congress approve of that as a federal property entitled to protection by the military services? And if it did, would the Indians agree? Or would that open up another can of worms? The lawyers were hashing that out. It was just another headache for the leadership team of the Denver Center.

By the time Chuck and Tallbear got back to their temporary home, they were in need of a good night's sleep. Chuck quickly disposed of a bottle of Guinness, and Tallbear had a glass of half cranberry -- half orange juice. They went to their rooms exhausted from the day's activities.

Johanna was similarly fatigued. For days on end she had been Madison Tolles' eyes and ears at a variety of secret congressional hearings as well as meetings with the secretaries of State and Defense and the directors of the CIA and FBI. In all her spare time she coordinated information flow between the Denver center, Antarctica, and Washington. She arrived back at her apartment at DuPont Circle drained of energy. As she switched on the light, outside watchers easily identified which apartment was hers. They relayed the information to their colleagues in the building.

Johanna poured herself a glass of Merlot, sat down at her computer to answer a ton of emails. As soon as she was done with that, she threw on an old sweatshirt and sweatpants, switched off the light, and crawled into bed for a good night's sleep.

Madison Tolles was feeling the full burden of trying to bring his life's dream to fruition. Dealing with a bureaucracy that moved at glacial speed was taking its toll on him. He remembered one of Dickens' novels, *Little Dorrit*, where extended members of the Barnacle family held complete control of the bureaucracy of mid-1800s England, and their job was to thwart progress of any kind. The hero was constantly referred to the *Circumlocution Office* for resolution of any problems. Tolles felt his pain.

Tolles poured a shot of Glenmorangie single malt Scotch and turned on some classical music to relax. When he finished the drink he showered and went to bed.

At exactly 1:10 a.m., the mercenary teams struck all three locations.

Each assault team moved silently down the corridors of the respective buildings. The electronic locks were easily decoded. Putting on night vision goggles, the teams slipped quietly into the apartments. One mercenary stood by the door while the others proceeded to the bedrooms. Each of the targets was quietly awakened and assured that struggle meant instant death. "Just get dressed and come along quietly." The targets each fumbled in the dark to find their clothing, occasionally assisted by one of the night-visioned assault team members who could see clearly. Already in sweat gear, Johanna simply put on socks and running shoes.

The only hitch in the proceedings occurred when they awoke Tallbear. He began to comply with the request to get dressed when one of the kidnappers prodded him in the back with the business end of his assault weapon. Quick as a flash Tallbear spun to his left and jabbed his elbow into the man's solar plexus. He spun quickly to his right in a complete 360 turn and with the edge of his right hand nailed the mercenary just below the ear. The man was unconscious before he hit the floor.

"That will be enough, Dr. Tallbear," the team leader forcefully said as he chambered a round into his weapon.

"When your dog wakes up, tell him he didn't need to prod me," answered Tallbear, who calmly proceeded to get dressed, "I am fully aware of the situation."

As this was going on, the security teams neutralized the FBI watchers by throwing tear gas grenades into their vans and slashing their tires. They kept a wary eye on the adjacent buildings to ensure that no one came out in pursuit. On signal at both Rockville and the Watergate, the security team leaders drove their vans into the underground garages. They used the electronic decoding equipment to open the garage doors. At DuPont Circle, the van simply pulled up in front of the building.

Within minutes, three vans and their blindfolded and bound human cargo were headed to the farm in Virginia. The woman in the apartment at DuPont Circle was rendered unconscious when a small open bottle of ether was passed under her nose. She was untied and placed on her couch. She woke up several hours later and called the police.

In their van on the way to the farm, Chuck said, "I bet the Red Sox are looking like a better alternative now."

At that, Tallbear and Chuck got laughing, which intrigued their captors. These two laughing men acted like they were in control of the situation.

Arriving at the farm shortly after 2:00 am, there was a new security team in place to receive and take control over the hostages. The thirty-three mercenaries were directed to change back into their own clothes, wash off the camouflage, gather their gear, and get in the vans to be returned to their motels.

The four hostages were guided to the basement of the main house, and, with hands bound behind them, were placed on straight-backed wooden chairs. Their blindfolds were removed and they were offered water. Soon they heard footsteps above, and two well-dressed men, one completely in black, the other in a dark suit, came walking down the stairs followed by two athletic looking men carrying M1911A1 modified Colt .45-caliber semiautomatic pistols. One of the security guards had a surgical dressing on the side of his head where his ear would have been. The second well-dressed man dismissed the other security guards and the two henchmen took up positions behind the hostages.

Gradually, each of the hostages felt a sensation that it was getting colder in the basement. The temperature was definitely dropping and a cold clamminess gripped each of their hearts. They felt themselves suddenly close to despair.

Johanna, sensing the pure evil nature of this coldness, recalled a family reunion years before. At that outdoor picnic, she took an opportunity to speak with her great uncle, Fr. F.X. O'Reilly, formerly a missionary priest in equatorial Africa. He was quite along in years and was living in semi-retirement and helping out on an Indian reservation in rural California. She asked him to tell her about his experiences in Africa. Against a background of adults laughing, children playing, and burgers sizzling on the grill, F.X. told his story.

"Well, young lady," he began, "you ask a question that covers my twenty-two years of experience in that fascinating place. As a newly minted priest, I went there a year after my ordination in 1938 following an immersion course in the culture of Tanganyika, now Tanzania, and its language, Swahili."

"I had been ministering to a family of five villages of rudimentary farmers over a fifteen square mile area for about three years. Basically I had been 'riding circuit,' much like the judges of early America. Early one morning, as I was travelling with my porters to one of the remote villages through the stifling jungle heat, a runner from one of the other villages caught up with us. He was nearly totally spent. We gave him water, and though exhausted, he managed to deliver his urgent message.

"It seemed that in one of the villages I had converted the wife of the village witch doctor to the Catholic faith. She subsequently had become pregnant, and according to the message bearer, had given birth. The infant was sickly and on the verge of death. This woman had requested my presence back at her village to baptize the infant and prevent her husband the witch doctor, from capturing the infant's soul for the devil.

"I could not refuse. So I redirected the porters to head for this particular village. We arrived just before dusk to find that the villagers had formed a semi-circular cordon about thirty feet away from the witch doctor's hut.

"The villagers parted when they saw me coming, but they would not approach the witch doctor's hut. I said a hasty prayer, put myself in God's hands, and proceeded through the gap that the villagers had provided. As I drew within the perimeter of the hut, I could feel the temperature dropping. Now keep in mind that this was equatorial Africa where the average temperature during the day was about 115 degrees. I had started off self-assured, but as I approached that hut my steps became labored. I felt like I was dragging my feet forward. When I reached the entrance to the hut, I swear that the temperature was in the low forties, maybe lower, damp and clammy.

"I pushed my way into the hut, and it was nearly freezing inside. Despair began to fill my heart. Everything in my being said for me to run. It was a tremendously compelling and seductive temptation to do just that. But from somewhere I mustered my faith in God. I knew I was in the presence of pure evil. The witch doctor was chanting incantations over the child, who by now was in extremis. The witch doctor looked at me and backed away. He respected my 'magic' as I respected his. The mother of the infant was in the corner of the hut squatting down on her haunches. She had a look of terror on her face that I never want to see again.

"I walked over to the child, baptized him with holy water, anointed him with holy oil, and administered the final sacraments. As I did so, the temperature seemed to return to normal. I took a final look at the child, who appeared at peace as his life ebbed from him; then at the witch doctor, who looked at me in wonder; and finally at the mother of the child, who managed a grateful look; and I backed out of the hut.

"I am certain that I had been in the presence of Satan himself."

Johanna recalled the feeling that she had been transported to equatorial Africa by his story and could almost feel the cold. Time and place stood still while he spoke, the sounds of the picnic fading into the distance, only to return when he finished his story.

"Good evening Mr. Tolles, Dr. Tallbear, Dr. Kinoshi, and Ms. Ring," said the man dressed completely in black. "I apologize for the inconvenient hour, but I trust you had a pleasant journey to our farm. I am Seth Tilcotan. I am, shall we say, the business agent of Mr. Peter Wilson here. We have been watching the progress of your little venture, and are not amused by the potential outcome."

"Well that just tears us all apart, Mr. Tilcotan," Chuck forced himself to say, dripping with sarcasm. "We sure hope we haven't inconvenienced y'all, you horrible summbitch."

"Ah, yes, the well-known humor of Dr. Charles Kinoshi," hissed Tilcotan. "I once attended a conference in Zurich at which you spoke about the potential benefits and dangers we faced as an increasingly technological society. You were quite amusing."

"Well, anything I can do to please the troops. Have you heard the one about the group of murderers who are planning the earth's destruction?"

"Rave on, Dr. Kinoshi. Your time is limited."

Before Chuck could say anything more, Madison Tolles, feeling constriction in his chest, forced himself to be calm and struggled to speak. "So what are you going to do with us, Mr. Tilcotan?"

"We intend, Mr. Tolles, to prevent any further development or implementation of your plan to harness the earth's energy. The group I represent has certain clients in a broad range of carbon producing industries that would not like to see their fortunes diminish. I am under no illusion that your future silence on these matters can be bought. You have inconvenienced us greatly, and undoing your initial work will cost us dearly. But I believe we can contain what has been started. For years we effectively slowed down and limited the development of successful hybrid technologies for the automobile industry. Witness the crippling of the Big Three American automakers in the early 2000s. I am sure we can fix this problem as well.

"The group I represent has arranged for your presence here because I do wish to tell you to your faces, before I amuse myself with your deaths, that I actually admire what you have nearly accomplished. You, Mr. Tolles, made an investment that almost caused any number of orthodox Egyptologists to realize that their life's work was rubbish."

"Yes," Tolles responded, "but unless those people are completely unstable, no lives will be lost because they came up with the incorrect academic conclusions."

"True, Mr. Tolles. You do have me there. But I expect that those same academics will not weep when they read your obituary this week. And what a loss for your colleagues. There is no one else who will be able to drive forward with your resources to make your plan come true.

"And I am truly sorry you had to be included in this Ms. Ring. You are a truly beautiful woman, and I hate to see such beauty die. I personally would prefer to use your beauty for my own purposes. But I fear that you might be a worthy successor to Mr. Tolles and just might influence a number of positive actions on the part of the U.S. government."

Johanna, said a short silent prayer, then let him have it. "Ahh, you could bring a tear to a glass eye with your sweet talk, Mr. Tilcotan. We have never met, but I know you and who you really work for. Your soul is forfeit and you are pure evil, but I look in your eyes and see that your power is waning. We can all feel that. I'm not impressed. Piss off, Mr. Tilcotan, and take the devil with you. You are living proof that if you lie down with dogs, you get up with fleas. By the way, dress lightly as it is going to get real warm where you're going."

Tallbear, Chuck, and Tolles looked at her in wonder.

Tilcotan looked genuinely shocked. "You are apparently immune to my charms. You are not afraid of the force I can muster to crush you right now?"

"Not a chance. None of us fear you or your dark master."

Tilcopan's eyes glazed slightly. The room got even colder.

"Let me tell you something, Ms. Ring," Tilcopan hissed. "My dark master has put the world at my feet. For hundreds of years, I have manipulated the earth at will and been handsomely rewarded, just like generations of my forefathers. Do you think that the near genocide of the American Indian was an offshoot of Manifest Destiny? I was behind that very policy. Whenever I wish, I can crush the soul right out of you."

Recovering himself he said, "But I have a few things to say to your colleagues first. Then it will give me great pleasure to hear you scream for mercy as I reach in and tear your heart from your chest."

After a moment, he shifted his eyes and, ignoring her, and moved on. "Dr. Tallbear, I also must commend you on your lifetime of accomplishments. You may have single-handedly revolutionized the world of anthropology, and you certainly have been instrumental in your discoveries about the origins and migrations of the American Indian. Or should I say Native Americans?"

"Suit yourself, asshole. You have the floor." Tallbear appeared unaffected by Tilcotan's menacing manner or the dank cold of the room. Chuck, Tolles and Johanna Looked on in wonder.

"Now that is uncharacteristic of you, Dr. Tallbear."

"You caught me on a bad day."

"I had no idea your comedic talents were the match of your colleague, Dr. Kinoshi."

"Chuck taught me everything I know. Are you planning to talk us to death?"

"All in good time, Dr. Tallbear. All in good time."

With that, Tilcopan turned toward Madison Tolles, who was seated just to the left of Tallbear. Tilcotan pointed a finger at Tolles, and began to chant in a dark and unknown language. Tallbear suddenly leaped out of his chair and put himself between Tilcopan and Tolles. The guards turned, but seemed frozen. It happened so fast that Tilpocan looked shocked and lost his composure for a moment. Wilson stood off to the side with a confused look on his face.

Suddenly from above, there was a burst of gunfire, a groan, and the sound of a body crashing to the floor. As everyone's eyes went upward to the sound, Tallbear caught Chuck's eye and nodded his head backward toward their guards.

Chuck straightened his legs and drove this chair backward into the guard standing behind him. The guard was driven straight back into the wall. His head hit the stone foundation and he slid to the floor. Chuck smashed his chair against the wall and freed himself. He rolled backward and in a clean, fluid movement shifted his bound hands around his rump and up the backsides of his legs until he was able to get his hands in front of him.

Tallbear's luck was not as great because of his awkward angle, and while he did knock his guard over, the guard was still conscious and groping for his weapon while Tallbear did as Chuck did and quickly maneuvered his hands in front of him. He grabbed the guard who had the medical dressing on his ear, and punched the man into unconsciousness.

Tilcotan suddenly turned and pointed his finger at Tallbear and chanted a curse. Tallbear clutched his chest and dropped to his knees. Reaching into his shirt he wrapped his fist around the quartz stone hanging from a leather string around his neck. He quickly felt his strength return and squeezed the stone as hard as he could. He looked at the smashed remains of the chair Chuck had destroyed and picked up one of the rear legs that extended up the back of the chair. Standing up straight he looked Tilcotan squarely in the eye.

Tilcotan looked shocked, but recovered himself. "That should have killed you," he hissed.

"It will take more than you have to kill me," Tallbear responded.

As Johanna looked on, there was a glowing aura surrounding Gordon. He seemed to stand taller and stronger than she had ever seen him. She could have sworn that she momentarily saw the figure of a white robed man on a black horse standing behind him. She blinked her eyes and the vision was gone, but not the glowing aura surrounding Gordon.

Tilcotan raised his finger pointing at Tallbear and began another incantation, but Tallbear's aura seemed to expand and block Tilcotan dark magic. They stood in a timeless tension until gradually Tallbear's aura exhausted Tilcotan's efforts.

One last time Tilcotan began to raise his finger toward Tallbear, but he was too slow. Gordon flicked the chair leg down quickly, breaking Tilcotan's forearm. The man screamed with pain. Tallbear slashed the chair leg at his face, breaking his jaw. With his jaw contorted and blood flowing from his mouth, his arm dangling uselessly at his side, Tilcotan had a strange look of wonder in his eyes. The last thing he saw was Gordon Tallbear, former baseball star, assuming a batting stance. Tallbear shifted his weight to his back leg and began his pivot, turning his back foot and straightening his front leg. The home run swing landed squarely on the front left side of Tilcotan's forehead shattering his skull in five places. The impact drove him backward. He bounced off the wall, slumped to his knees, and toppled over dead. As Tallbear looked on in wonder, Tilcotan's body transformed before his eyes until it was a shriveled husk of a man, wrinkled and aged beyond count of years.

While this was happening, Wilson broke for the foot of the stairs.

Chuck dove at Wilson, driving him into the side of the stairwell. Managing to get his arms over Wilson's head, Chuck pulled the plastic ties binding his wrists to cut off Wilson's breathing. Chuck applied pressure fighting against an unanticipated strength emerging from his adversary. Slowly Wilson's strength ebbed and he sank to the floor,

A female voice from the top of the stairs called out, "FBI! Freeze! Nobody move!"

Chuck called up the stairs, "Hey, Gretchen! Yer late for our date. C'mon down and join the party."

Gretchen Tokata, in an FBI windbreaker over a bullet-proof vest, edged down the stairs with her weapon scanning the scenario. "Geez, it's freezing down here." Suddenly she spun slightly to her left and squeezed off a round. They all turned to see the guard with the ear bandage drop his weapon and sink slowly to the floor, blood seeping out of a wound in the middle of his chest. The other guard had regained consciousness and started to raise his weapon. Gretchen shot him in the shoulder.

"We need a medic here!" she shouted.

Tilcotan lay in the middle of the basement, blood seeping into a pool around him, eyes wide open and fixed. Wilson was barely alive. It turned out later that he suffered permanent brain damage from his near strangulation. Nonetheless, he was raving incoherently as he was bound and loaded into an ambulance.

"And I'll wear a red dress and dance at your funeral, you bastard!" shouted Johanna as Wilson was being wheeled out of the farmhouse.

Chuck and Tolles looked at her in amazement.

"Well, I meant it," Johanna said. And the three of them began to laugh. Suddenly they realized that Tallbear was not laughing with them. Gordon had dropped to his knees clutching his chest.

"Gordon!" screamed Johanna. "What is it?"

It was a while before Gordon came to his senses. He sat up and they slowly began to bring him to his feet.

"I feel like a large truck drove straight into my chest," he said. "When Tilcotan pointed at me and spoke in that dark language of his, I felt a terrible pain in my chest. The pain is subsiding now, but I fear the devil worshipper might have left a mark on me."

They were all solicitous of him, and after the medics examined him, he was cleared to stay and give his statement, but they advised getting him to a hospital for a more thorough diagnosis as soon as possible.

It turned out that the GPS tracking devices did their job well. The FBI SWAT teams intercepted the various vans carrying the 33 mercenaries before they got to the highway. The mercenaries were currently being held in a secure location on Marine Corps Base, Quantico, pending initial federal charges of kidnapping and assault.

As planned, FBI SWAT teams had enveloped the farm and moved in with stealth. They had neutralized the external guards and took the farmhouse cleanly.

As dawn was nearing and coffee was being passed around, Tallbear, Chuck, Johanna, and Madson Tolles sat at the farmhouse kitchen table being debriefed by Gretchen and her primary team.

Gretchen began, "Before you recount your individual and collective experiences, I have one bit of news that is just about to be released to the media. Our friend Sir Winslow Harrington was found dead just before midnight last night. Following an anonymous telephone tip, his body was discovered in a sado-masochistic basement torture chamber. Preliminary evidence shows that he apparently was whipped severely and then his heart was torn from his chest. It seems that his murderer also took a few bites out of his flesh before he died. It sounds to me like the handiwork of our friend Tilcotan. The media will be told that he died in his sleep, apparently of natural causes."

"Lord have mercy on him," said Johanna. "I loathed the S.O.B., and I might have even wished him a short illness and a quick funeral, but I'd never wish such a death as that on him."

"Okay, folks," said Gretchen. "Now let's hear each of your stories about last night. Let's start with Mr. Tolles. If you would, sir."

After relating the individual experiences regarding their capture, and telling their stories of the experience in the farmhouse basement, Johanna told them about her great-uncle Fr. F.X.

Tallbear, Chuck, Tolles, and the FBI people sat there in the kitchen, totally mesmerized.

"When Seth Tilcotan came down into the basement, I began to experience what Fr. F. X. had told me that day many years ago," said Johanna. "The dropping of the temperature and the presence of something totally evil is something I will never forget. I said a quick prayer asking F.X., now long deceased, to intercede with God to give me the strength I needed, and then I was ready to confront this devil's disciple," she concluded.

"And you just about spit in his eye in spite of everything," said Chuck. "I can't believe how calm you were. I began shaking in my boots as the temperature dropped, and I began to feel a despair choking my heart. All I wanted to do was die."

"Johanna, you inspired all of us to fight that force of darkness," said Tallbear

.

"I have been in combat and been wounded and faced death," said Tolles, "and I never felt that level of terror. It was a vice-like compression of my chest. I believe our own experience and Johanna's story about her uncle gives credibility to our knowledge of Tezcar Tilpocan, and later his descendant Tezcatlpoca. They sold their souls to the devil. Undoubtedly, their present day descendant, Seth Tilcotan, had done the same thing."

"Must run in the family," said Chuck.

That gave them all a chuckle that broke the spell.

As they were getting ready to get into the vehicles the FBI had provided to transport them back to their respective quarters, Madison Tolles caught Tallbear's eye. He motioned with his head that he obviously wanted to talk with Tallbear privately. Tallbear picked up the signal and walked over to where Tolles was standing.

"Gordon," Tolles began, "I have to ask you a question. Why, in the world, with the incredible evil that we all felt permeating our souls, did you place yourself between Seth Tilcotan and me?"

Gordon answered, "Sir, there are a couple of things I should tell you. First, I, too, had the same feeling that gripped all of you. A few years ago I once fasted for three days, took a sweat lodge, and rode off into the wilderness where I had a vision. In my vision, that same kind of despair came upon me before the answer to such evil was revealed to me. My vision told me to reach down deeply inside myself, hide my fears, and share my courage with others.

"Second, you stood tall for me at the international conference, in what I saw as an amazing validation of my contributions to your vision. I had no choice, in my soul, but to stand for you in your time of need."

"Gordon, I have had friends before. And I have had people who honored me with sacrifice, like Ben Crowley, who saved my life. But no one I know has ever been willing to sacrifice his soul for me. That is beyond my comprehension. I am eternally in debt to you."

"There is no debt, Mr. Tolles. There is only the love and respect we all have for each other. Chuck forced himself to make wisecracks in the face of pure evil. Johanna carried all of us along with her courage and the celestial support of her uncle. We all believe in each other and the vision of the future we share. That is why each of us would give our lives for each other. You owe me no debt, Mr. Tolles. We all owe you so much."

With that, Madison Tolles began to weep. Gordon put his hand on his shoulder and gave a reassuring squeeze. Then he walked away to the waiting van.

Suddenly Gordon doubled over and fell to the ground.

Chapter 35

Gordon was rushed to the George Washington Medical center in DC. After undergoing an extensive battery of tests over a three-day period, there was no conclusive diagnosis for the pain in his chest. But it persisted and came in waves. He would feel fine for a few hours, and then the pain would return. Chuck and Johanna had spent most of the last three days at his side.

The doctor came in on the third day and said, "His diagnosis is beyond our reach. He has no evidence of heart damage or anything else. In fact, he is one of the most incredible physical specimens I have ever seen, solid muscle structure and no anomalies in any of his organs. All his vitals are perfect. It's a mystery why he is exhibiting these symptoms."

Mr. Tolles said, "We understand. Just discharge him to me and I will assure that he has 24 hour care."

When he was discharged, they took him back to the apartment in Rockville. In addition to professional full time nursing care, his friends made sure one of them was always with him.

A week after his discharge Tallbear, Johanna, Chuck, and Madison Tolles sat in the same FBI briefing room as before. Tallbear was weakened, but he insisted on being there. Eleanor Thomas and Gretchen Tokata handed each of them a "Top Secret" folder.

"We thought you would want to know the latest information," began Ms. Thomas. "Peter Wilson has been medically confirmed as permanently brain damaged. With no one stepping forward to represent him, he was assigned counsel for his competency hearing. He has been declared unfit to stand trial and has been committed to the forensic psychiatric unit in a maximum security federal prison in Pennsylvania for what may be forever. He will be re-examined on a regular basis in case his status changes, but I guarantee you that he will never see daylight again.

"His two surviving colleagues from the Gnomes inner circle, as well as the other thirty members of its executive council, have been taken into custody, extradited from their native countries to the U.S., and are being charged in federal court under the RICO statutes. Interpol has been terrific in assisting us. RICO stands for Racketeer Influenced and Corrupt Organizations Act. Under its provisions, those found guilty can be fined up to $25,000 and/or sentenced to 20 years in prison per racketeering count. In addition, the racketeer must forfeit all ill-gotten gains and interest in any business gained through a pattern of racketeering activity. This will put billions into the US treasury.

"We immediately arranged for the cremation of Seth Tilcotan. On your advice Mr. Tolles, because Tilcotan's blood had been spilled there, we soaked the basement of the farm in gasoline and burned the building to the ground. Not to be superstitious, but any evidence of that man's existence must be eradicated. The other Gnomes will never get out of prison, I assure you. Thanks to our undercover man, we have recordings of every meeting they have held for the past three years, and enough evidence to hang them, so to speak.

"Their arrests have triggered other responses from our State and Justice departments resulting in meetings with CEOs and board members of a number of domestic and foreign energy producers. A few of these visits will result in total housecleaning of these companies, and in some cases lesser charges of conspiracy. Unfortunately, most of the guilty culprits are investors in these corporations, but we will root them out eventually.

"As for the lesser players, the surviving basement guard is charged with conspiracy to commit murder and kidnapping, so he'll be away for a long time. The mercenaries hired to kidnap you are also charged with kidnapping and conspiracy to commit murder, as well as a host of other charges. They, too, will be doing a lot of prison time.

"We have, thanks to you, effectively broken the back of the Gnomes of Zurich. Gretchen, anything to add?"

"No, you've covered it pretty well. Do any of you have any questions?"

Tolles asked, "What about your undercover agent? Can you give us an update on him, or is that still classified?"

"Glad you asked that, Mr. Tolles," said Gretchen. "Ms. Thomas has assured me that he is safe and ready to reassume his real life. In case you were wondering, the butler did it. He has been assured a well paying, starring roll in a high budget film that is to be completed next year. Four years ago we carefully staged a near accident where Mr. Wilson, a man of disciplined habits, was crossing a street at the same time he did each day. He was almost hit by a car driven by one of our agents. Our actor friend quote saved his life end quote by pushing him out of the way. We had rehearsed that scenario for months until we had it down to the split-second. After expressing his gratitude, Wilson asked our man about himself. He answered that he was a combination butler and valet, currently between assignments. After checking our carefully prepared references, Wilson hired him to be his valet.

"You just tell him, Ms. Tokata and Ms. Thomas, that whether a career in acting works out or not, he will never lack financial security. I will ensure that he is taken care of for the rest of his life. Just tell me how we can set this up. He has served his country, and the world, in a most admirable fashion, and his courage is something we must reward."

"Thank you, Mr. Tolles," said Gretchen, "I will help you set that up. Are there any more questions? Chuck?"

"Have you ever had dinner on a three-hour flight to Antarctica?"

Chapter 36

The next months proved to be grueling in their intensity for the Denver Center leaders.

Madison Tolles continued working with the State Department to spearhead the diplomatic and domestic political coordination that ultimately brought the principal world leaders into a cooperative alliance. Not surprisingly, the British government, having appointed a more enlightened ambassador to the United States, became an enthusiastic supporter of the American initiative.

Tolles also was given permission by the U.S. government to patent the epoxy that held the pyramid blocks in place. He contracted with a manufacturer for production and arranged for a percentage of the profits from this patent be applied to the operational expense budget of the Denver Center. The balance of the profits were, after the manufacturer's share, to be distributed among the entire staff of the Denver Center.

Johanna divided her time between forming strategic alliances with various sectors of the federal government and coordinating the activities of the Denver Center. The well-trained staff at the center took over the major role of overseeing the research team activity in Antarctica.

Once the National Geographic and Smithsonian revelations had been made, Tolles, Chuck and Tallbear were in demand on all the news and talk shows. Madison Tolles was, as always, reticent despite the media's insatiable thirst. Tallbear was earnest in his interviews and considered a uniquely exotic example of America at its best. But Chuck was the darling, always charming and folksy. None of the three could wait until the media frenzy abated.

Chuck managed to split his time between the caverns of Antarctica and Washington, DC. He and Gretchen spent as much time together as possible. She even took some vacation time so he could fulfill his offer of dinner on a three-hour flight to

Antarctica. They also discovered mutual interests in art, music, the creation of Japanese gardens, and, of all things, ballroom dancing. Visits to each other's parents -- his in Atlanta and hers in Seattle -- pretty much settled the issue. A date was set, invitations went out, the banns were published, Gordon was asked to be best man, and they were married in Seattle within a year. Madison Tolles paid for the whole thing, including first class travel and lodging for Chuck's family.

Because of his recurring pain and weakness, Gordon turned over most of his operational responsibilities to Hector Moineau and focused on putting together the American Indian Strategic Alliance to manage the building of the pyramid complex and the sharing of a percentage of the wealth among all the American Indian tribes. He also was instrumental in coordinating the infrastructure support required to bring raw materials to the Black Hills. Though still weakened by the basement encounter, he was determined to see the project through to its completion. He and Johanna were developing their romance.

Although they went to the center periodically, and he frequently travelled around the country meeting with Indian leaders, her work kept her in Washington most of the time. Gordon could have based himself at the Denver Center, but he didn't want to miss any more time with Johanna, so he too based himself in DC. They found a beautiful home to share in the Aurora Hills area of Arlington, Virginia. It was outrageously expensive, but they were both well compensated by the Denver Center, so they mapped out a plan to pay the mortgage. When Madison Tolles heard of their plans, he went to the bank and bought the house outright for them. He told Gordon that it was a modest bonus for his actions on the polo field and for much more. Gordon understood and accepted the gift, but in his Indian tradition, a gift from someone meant that a gift should be given in return.

"Johanna," he said, "what can we possibly give him in return?"

She paused before answering, "How about naming our first child after him?"

Gordon smiled. "I think he would value that gift above everything."

As busy as Johanna was, after dinner every evening she insisted on an hour of privacy in a room they had designated as their library. Gordon could not figure out what she was doing and she wouldn't tell him other than to say it was a surprise.

Often in the evenings when they were sitting quietly listening to music, while Gordon was reading Johanna would take out a lap table and spend a lot of time writing letters to her various family members. Gordon was both surprised and delighted. His parents had insisted that he and his siblings be able to take pen in hand and write letters. At Dartmouth, and later at Harvard, he lived for the long letters his parents and brother and sister would send him, and he knew they counted on him to fill their mailbox as well. As far as he was concerned, email could never replace thoughtfully crafted letters.

Shortly after Chuck was married, Johanna invited Gordon to Connecticut to meet her family. Gordon wanted to meet them, but also he was apprehensive. He said, "Johanna, there are three things working against this visit. One, we are, I would imagine in your parents estimation, 'living in sin;' two, I am not Irish; and, three, in case you have not noticed, I'm an American Indian."

She looked at him in wonder and said, "Gordon, in case you have not been paying attention, you have just saved the world from an incredible evil, and all those letters I have been writing to my family were not about exchanging recipes. They know the whole story of your incredible heroism in destroying an agent of the devil himself. My family is liberal in its outlook, and their tolerance and understanding have no bounds. Finally, I just happen to be the shining light of the family and they are grateful that any man would be willing to make an honest woman of me. They will love you because I love you. Matter settled."

"You said all that about little ol' me?" Gordon asked in a credible imitation of a southern plantation belle. Johanna pounced on him, laughing. "I think you will drive me nuts one day," she said.

One Friday they flew to Hartford, Connecticut, rented a car, and drove down Route 2 to Norwich. Much to his relief, Johanna's family was terrific. They embraced him and made him feel as comfortable as if he were in his own home. Almost from the moment they arrived, all her brothers wanted to do was talk baseball, and her sisters and their families thought he was the most exotic thing they had ever seen. Her youngest sister's little girl, six-year old Bridget, shyly came up to him and stared. He looked down at her and said, "Hello, beautiful." She just looked up at him and said, "Mama says you are an American Indian. What's an Indian?"

Laughing, Gordon said, "Come here and I will tell you." He reached into his shirt and squeezed the quartz stone as he bent down to pick her up and set her on the arm of an easy chair. He sat down in the chair and began to tell her, in as simple terms as he could, about the Lakota. After a while he looked up to find the rest of Johanna's family mesmerized by his tale.

"You'll have to forgive this lot," said Johanna. "In the Irish tradition, the story teller, or shannachie, travelled around the country. He was the repository of all the Irish legends and lore, and wherever he was given lodging, friends, family and neighbors gathered to listen in rapt attention as he unfolded tales of the past. You are a Lakota shannachie, so you will have to put up with their endless questions."

For the rest of the week, Gordon held court every evening and told of the great warrior leaders – Sitting Bull, Gall, Crazy Horse and others. He also told of the ancient migratory patterns from southwestern Minnesota to the Dakotas and speculated on Palen Golendar and his connection to the Lakota people. The Rings were mesmerized by his tales.

The day after their arrival, Johanna took him to Sachem Street across the green from the Norwich Free Academy, her old high school. Just a little down Sachem is an obelisk marking the burial site of Chief Uncas, the founder of the Mohegan tribe. Uncas had taken a disaffected group of followers and broke away from the Pequots. Ironically, James Fenimore Cooper borrowed Uncas' name as a central character in *The Last of the Mohicans*. Now Gordon could see where the first of the Mohicans was buried. On the corner of Sachem Street, just before the cemetery, is a small park built as a tribute to the Mohegans and Pequots. Its stone centerpiece is a calendar with the symbols the tribes used to designate the change of seasons and months of the year. Gordon was touched and felt the connection to his eastern brothers.

On their last night with Johanna's family, her father could not contain himself any longer. He bluntly asked Gordon to describe his confrontation with Seth Tilcotan. The room went silent for a moment as Gordon bent his head and fingered the talisman under his shirt. Johanna started to protest, but Gordon held up his hand to stay her words. As he paused, he thought of Johanna relating her uncle's story about confronting the devil in Africa, and realized that an oral tradition needed to be passed along to this wonderful family. Looking up, he told of their final encounter with evil in such a way that Johanna became the hero. Her memory of Fr. F X's ordeal in Tanganyka enabled her to inspire Gordon, Chuck, and Mr. Tolles. He modestly capped the story with his dispatch of Tilcotan, but the entire family was beaming at Johanna. For this, Gordon was greatly pleased. Johanna just blushed for the gift he had given her.

After a week with the Rings, their next trip was to the Tallbear family. They decided to go to the Denver Center to take care of some necessary business and drive north-north east to Pine Ridge. Johanna took the trip in stride and was eagerly anticipating meeting Gordon's family. When they arrived at the Tallbear home, Gordon burst out laughing when Johanna greeted his parents in the Lakota language. So that's what she's been doing every night for the past seven months. Teaching herself Lakota on the computer! What a woman!

It quickly became evident that Johanna's pen had been busier than Gordon had realized. Everyone in Gordon's family was fully aware of Gordon's heroic confrontation thanks to Johanna's letters. Now it was Gordon's turn to be embarrassed by the attention. He was treated as the second coming of Crazy Horse.

Gordon's parents were delighted with Johanna and they had a wonderful visit. Gordon even got her to take a sweat lodge. Johanna impressed the tribal members when she emerged from her fourth session in the sweat lodge. She looked him in the eye and said, "So what do you plan to do? Cook me and eat me?"

The next several days were spent horseback riding and seeing Gordon's father's mustang therapy program in action. Gordon seemed revitalized, though he still at times needed to squeeze the quartz stone to restore his strength. Upon their return to the Denver Center, they mapped out plans for their wedding the following spring. First would be the wedding in St. Patrick's Cathedral in Norwich, and then there would be a second Indian ceremony at Pine Ridge. When they got back to DC and announced their plans, Madison Tolles insisted on picking up the tab for the entire celebration.

Lakota Indians, Japanese Americans, African Americans, geeks of all stripes, and Irish by the truckload descended on Norwich to celebrate the occasion. Brendan, Damien, and Adrien Vanderwiel provided all the music. Joe Delaney regaled them with stories from Ireland. When it was over, Johanna's 90 year-old grandmother, Rose Malone, summed it up best: "Grand! It was just grand!"

. . .

Down in Antarctica (the United Nations was now debating renaming it Atlantis) the Denver Center teams planned the removal of the aircraft, the tools, and the gold plating. The decision, at least for now, was to leave the cavern complexes as they found them, complete with their computer systems in place. The entire Atlantean data base had been completely downloaded and stored at the Denver Center.

Following the joint National Geographic/Smithsonian announcement of these remarkable discoveries, there was uproar from the academic community world-wide. The orthodox Egyptologists (or Theologians, as they came to be derisively referred to) initially rebelled en masse at the announcement of these new discoveries. Gradually support for their cause dwindled, as did their grant funding.

The Egyptians were initially outraged that another culture prior to theirs was being given credit for their great architectural wonders. Madison Tolles fixed that with a series of well-publicized visits to Egypt accompanying the Secretary of State. In a statesmanship coup that coupled statecraft and marketing, they convinced the leadership of Egypt, and subsequently the population at large, that the Egyptians were simply an extension of the original Atlantean culture. Madison Tolles was passionate in communicating the idea that when Atlantis was doomed to slide into the Antarctic and the millions of Atlanteans who couldn't go into the temperature protected caverns were given permission to leave Atlantis, that many, if not most, settled in Egypt and evolved into the culture that has been well documented since 2900 BCE. He was most eloquent in his exposition that the Egyptians led the known world in science, architecture, and astronomy. So what if they had been given a nudge by a prior civilization. So had every other culture on the planet, but only the Egyptians had mastered the lessons.

Gradually the animosity turned to support, and the Egyptian government authorized the financing (with American dollars) of a new initiative to restore the Great Pyramid to its original state with the ultimate goal of returning it to its status as a functioning power plant.

The President of the United States, in a quiet, private ceremony, awarded Tolles the Presidential Medal of Freedom for singlehandedly averting a major international crisis.

The religious communities worldwide, after initial skepticism, generally embraced the discoveries as there was nothing specific in them that challenged any orthodoxy. The Vatican, as well as Jewish leadership, after exhaustive theological examination, found nothing, including the story of the great flood, to be in conflict with basic doctrine. The Vatican, in an extraordinary statement, endorsed the idea that God the Father was already working in mysterious ways by sending great people of peace to far flung regions of the world to bring education and healing to native populations long before the Son of God walked the earth.

When that statement came out, Johanna thought, "I'd always knew they would come through."

Moslem leadership worldwide concurred with both Christianity and Judaism, a real first for them, given that their religion originated from the Judeo-Christian foundation in the fifth century AD.

Buddhists and other eastern religions also examined the new discoveries in the context of the founding of their religions' beliefs and found nothing to counter any of their fundamental tenets.

Given that most of the major religions of the world had basic disagreements with each other on doctrine and theology, this general agreement was remarkable. The only exceptions were the extreme right wing fundamentalists based in the United States who desperately clung to the belief that the world was only five thousand or so years old, and that the dinosaurs were a work of fiction. They were increasingly marginalized and bitter. They promised that any building of a great Pyramid on American soil would be met with hundreds of thousands of demonstrators.

The major disputes came, not unexpectedly, from the oil, coal, and nuclear power communities. Following pre-arranged international plans to prevent panic at the potential loss in value of their stock, the President simply told them flat out, that their days as carbon based energy producers were numbered, and that all of the signatory nations to the new international energy agreement pledged unlimited funding for the retraining of workers in those industries. The industry leaders were not happy, and they lobbied Congress extensively to shut down this new initiative. But in the end, with even the most conservative congressmen buying into the new vision, they had to accept it. And as a practical matter, all the major oil companies over the past fifty years had bought up alternative energy technology patents anyway, so they essentially landed on their feet, just minus all the oil revenues. It would be a step back, but not a killer. As a sop to the power plants, the government allowed generous tax incentives for them to renovate their facilities to become energy collection stations. Also, all coal miners were given the incentive of government sponsored retraining in a wide range of technologies.

Within five years, almost all of the fossil fuel refining plants were shut down and dismantled. The cities where so many of these facilities existed were given federal incentives to convert the land to parks and ecological learning centers.

Arrangements were made with automobile manufacturers worldwide to complete the conversion of their vehicles to all electric systems. It turned into a boon for not only Detroit, but for the automobile manufacturing centers throughout the American heartland to be manufacturing completely green cars.

Aircraft manufacturers were similarly rewarded when they were given the technical design specifications to convert aircraft to the newly discovered electromagnetic power technology.

Even the OPEC nations got a fair deal out of the whole project. They were guaranteed to become principal players in the rapidly growing solar power industry.

Construction had begun on new collection stations throughout the Mid-East and southern Asia that would provide electricity to even the most remote regions of the planet.

NASA made plans to use the electromagnetic technology to launch space vehicles and their payloads cheaply and safely. They now also had the mag-lev technology to hover a microwave collection satellite in low earth orbit to receive the signal beamed from the new pyramid.

Excavation began at the pyramid site in the Black Hills. Crews cleared the soil above the granite bedrock and granite cutters leveled the rock platform using tools brought up from Atlantis. Just as Amon Goro did 12,500 years before, engineers built a temporary retaining pool around the area and flooded it with water. As the high spots of granite were cut down, more water was released from the 'pool.' Again, the high granite spots were cut and more water released until there was a completely flat surface – measuring as flat as the base of the Giza pyramid – upon which to lay the foundation blocks of limestone.

Various quarries around the country began the precision cutting of limestone blocks for the base level of the pyramid. A logistics plan was developed to create 'just-in-time' delivery of precision-cut limestone and granite blocks to the construction site. Crews were trained to master the hand-held devices so that as the aircraft brought the stones to the site, they could be guided into place with precision.

The work progressed according to plan, and the pyramid began to take shape.

Chapter 37

North America, 8,000 years ago

Soon after his talk with Eagle Claw, Palen and Morning Star were married in a tribal ceremony. The entire village celebrated the union of one of their own and this charming outsider. Within a few months, Morning Star and Palen conceived a child.

Palen's popularity with the tribe grew with each passing month. He continued to tell stories of the marvels he had seen, and of the giant island nation where his people lived. He sadly told of how the island was drifting to the coldest reaches of the planet, and how he feared that he would never see his people again. But he also told them that the Creator had blessed him by giving him a new home and a new family. The tribe shared his sorrow at the loss of his homeland, but also shared a common joy at his becoming a full-fledged member of their tribal family.

The time soon came for Morning Star to deliver her child, and in accordance with the tribal customs, the women of the tribe took over. Soon she delivered a baby boy who had beautiful green eyes like his father.

But Running Elk never got over his anger at this stranger having the privilege of marrying Morning Star. He waited and plotted. Soon he would have his revenge.

The autumn of the year was fast approaching, and the tribe was preparing to move a great distance to the south and west to a new location where the game was more plentiful for the winter hunts. As the camp was being broken down in preparation for the move, scouting parties were sent on ahead to see that the route was safe for the tribe to travel. Palen offered to join the scouts for two reasons. One, he wanted to do more to earn his keep with these good people. And, two, he wanted to take the opportunity of the scouting party to try to become friends with Running Elk.

Palen had spoken to Eagle Claw about this and the old man had agreed that it would be good for the harmony of the tribe. When he spoke to Morning Star about his plan, she was worried.

"I do not like this, Palen. Running Elk has a dark, evil heart, and I don't trust him. I fear that he will try to do you harm."

"Do not fear," said Palen. "He surely will realize that I mean him no ill will, and maybe I can convince him that it is better for us to be friends. We leave tomorrow, so it will be a few weeks before I see you again." With that, he kissed her and the baby, and held them in his arms until sleep came.

The next morning as the scouting party set out, Morning Star stood with the baby in her arms and waved to Palen as he and the group went off to the west and disappeared over the horizon. Tears trickled down her cheeks. She knew deep in her heart that she would never see him again.

There were only five in the group, which was considered sufficient as there had been a long peace with their neighbors, and there was nothing really to fear.

Running Elk showed visible anger that Palen was chosen to go on this journey, but Eagle Claw had told him that it was time to make peace with Palen, and the journey would be a good opportunity. Suddenly Running Elk became calm and said, "Yes, elder, maybe you are right in this."

The scouting party made its way west.

After they had been travelling for a few hours, Palen approached Running Elk and said, "I would like to become your friend."

Running Elk said, "Yes, stranger from the outside, maybe it is time that you and I get to know each other better."

As they walked, Running Elk taught Palen what to observe on the journey. He taught Palen about the various birds and forest creatures and their habits and habitats. He also taught Palen about the plants and which ones had edible berries and roots. They passed over many hills and valleys, and after several days of journey finally came to a vast area that was relatively flat with slow rolling hills, but fertile with many bushes bearing ripening berries. Broad, grassy, rolling plains extended as far as the eye could see. There was also a gently moving river to their south that flowed from west to east.

"Here is where the buffalo travel in great herds. Their meat will fill our stomachs for the winter and their coats will keep us warm in our lodges."

After they had travelled for many more days without incident, and with Palen entertaining them at the campfire at night with his seemingly endless tales of wonder, they chose a site for their winter camp. It was a beautiful sloping area with a fast rushing river running through it from north to south. They scouted out the area for many miles around to assure themselves that no other tribe had settled in the area.

Finally one morning, Running Elk told the other three scouts to head back to the main camp and tell them that the area was safe for the winter settlement. He said that he wanted to show Palen Golendar the country to the west where the buffalo hunts would take place. He said he hoped that Palen would get to see the great buffalo herds.

The three scouts headed east, and Running Elk and Palen headed west. They crossed the wide river at a shallow ford. The water ran fast with the melting winter runoff of the mountains to the west. Suddenly, Running Elk lost his footing and was swept off his feet by the rapid current. He quickly found himself in deep fast moving water and flailed about as he didn't know how to swim. Palen quickly stripped down and ran downstream to a point where the river made a sudden turn. Standing on the tip of a small piece of land, he dove in just as Running Elk's nearly exhausted body came by. Palen grabbed his hand and pulled him to the surface and worked their way to the western shore.

Running Elk was in bad shape. He had stopped breathing. Palen compressed Running Elk's chest several times and turned him on his side to force the water out of his lungs, but Running Elk had not responded.

Palen ran back to the crossing, quickly forded the river and grabbed his clothes and pack. Returning to Running Elk, he pulled the communications device out of his pack, pressed it to Running Elk's chest, and pushed on a series of indentations. Suddenly Running Elk's chest began to heave. He half sat up and turned to his side vomiting out copious amounts of water. Palen sat back and said a prayer of thanks to the Creator.

Later that evening Running Elk lay recovering at the campsite Palen had created. The fire and the broth Palen had prepared were restoring him. He said nothing, but struggled with deep conflicting emotions.

I should still hate him for stealing Morning Star, one side of his conscience told him. I should embrace him as a brother for saving my life, said the other. He lay back and spent the night in feverish dreams. He awoke to the smells of a breakfast of freshly cooked fish and berries that Palen had gathered, and ate ravenously.

"Are you ready to continue our journey?" asked Palen.

"Yes, White Hawk. I am ready for the next stage of our journey."

Palen was surprised that there were no words of gratitude from Running Elk, but that didn't deter his optimism.

At the end of the next day's journey, Running Elk told Palen, "Go on ahead to see what is over the next rise. You will be surprised." Just as Palen reached the crest of the hill, he felt a sharp pain in his shoulder. He stumbled and turned as a second arrow flew past his head. Running Elk shouted, "Thank you for saving my life, White Hawk, but that was a grave mistake. You have a price to pay for stealing Morning Star from me. Now you will know what it is to be hunted, you who fear going on the hunt yourself. I will give you a chance. Run, if you can, and I will follow and track you down."

Palen shed his innocence and naïve beliefs at that moment. He turned to face the west and started running down the slope. The arrow stuck in a bone in his shoulder and gave him great pain, but he had not lost much blood and still had his strength. He ran and ran, occasionally looking back. After he had gained about a quarter of a mile, he turned and saw Running Elk jogging down a slope at a modest pace.

As Palen tried to curve in one direction or another, he would look back to see Running Elk alter his course to intercept him. Palen knew that trying to go back and link up with the tribe would be impossible unless he could eliminate Running Elk as a threat. So he pressed onward, finding a comfortable jogging pace that would not exhaust him. He stopped at occasional streams to drink, eat some berries, replenish his energy, and then pressed on. He silently thanked Running Elk for teaching him what plants and roots were edible. Once he had gained enough distance from Running Elk, he pulled his device from its pouch and used it to burn off the shaft of the arrow and cauterize the wound. He was afraid to pull the arrowhead out as such an action might initiate major bleeding. He also knew that his device could be used as a weapon, but that action was forbidden by his people.

He pressed onward wondering at Running Elk's relentless hatred.

For five days, Palen kept the distance between them, but finally, without enough food to sustain him, and the wound throbbing in his shoulder, his pace slowed. He had crossed many streams that fed the major river to his rear, and occasionally he would seek the pools where fish could be found. He did find the occasional fish, which he ate raw, and that sustained him for a period.

Palen continued westward across the rolling hills and on occasion he would climb a butte and look back to see his pursuer. Running Elk could be seen a few miles back, moving forward on his relentless quest. Palen knew that in the long run it would be a losing battle.

Palen also knew that the device he carried in his pouch could end this nonsense very quickly, but he had been conditioned from birth, as had generations before him, to be non-violent. He was also well versed in the punishment for using it as a weapon. Atlantean law was uncompromising. To use it as a weapon meant that he had to forfeit his life. He was entrusted with the device to use it as a tool, not a weapon. He tried to brush aside any thoughts of harming Running Elk, but with increasing frequency these thoughts crept into his conscious mind.

Finally the rolling hills of the plains began to climb. He was working his way ever upward through the forested hills, with Running Elk always behind him. After endless days of weaving through valleys and draws, always westward, these beautiful hills gave way to a stark, barren landscape of spikey-spined rock formations and bleak terrain. Palen knew that the end would be coming soon, one way or another.

After resting himself against the soft clay base of a steeply climbing rock formation, he saw Running Elk approaching from a distance. It was now time to wait for the end.

Running Elk calmly walked toward Palen and slowly began to notch an arrow to his bow. As he raised the bow to shoot, Palen reached into his bag and withdrew the device.

"Are you going to have that thing sing to me?" asked Running Elk.

"Yes, Running Elk, it is about to sing your song," said Palen. He pointed it at Running Elk and pressed a sequence of indentations on its side.

Running Elk barely had time to register his surprise at the small hole in the center of his chest. He slowly dropped to his knees and toppled forward.

Palen Golendar wept. He came to the final realization that in spite of the conditioning of generations of his people, violence was a part of his nature. He knew that with such shame in his heart he could never return to the beautiful Morning Star and his precious child. He knew the punishment of death that awaited him in Atlantis should he ever return. He would be executed for using the translator device as a tool of violence. His violence, and his technology, must die with him.

He slowly stood up and turned to look at the stark, spiney peaks before him. Looking at the clay base of that formation he knew what he had to do. His device must never be found. Palen first sang a prayer to the Creator asking His forgiveness, then prayed for the understanding of his ancestors, and finally aimed the device at the bottom of the rock formation and began to cut a cave into its base. When it was more than deep enough for him to crawl into, he reached into his pack and pulled out a deerskin blanket, wrapped himself, and wedged in the hole as far as he could. He wrapped his face several times in the leather cape. Then he took his hand-held device, pushed a sequence of buttons, and dropped the device back into his pouch.

Suddenly, the ground began to shake. The hole he had dug vibrated and became wider and deeper, and then it swallowed Palen Golendar.

Chapter 38

Giza, 12,500 years ago

Amon Goro was pleased. The overwhelming bulk of the limestone blocks had been quarried and transported the short distance across the river to the building site without incident. Likewise the 55 percent quartz granite beams, 70 tons each, measuring up to twenty-seven feet in length had been precision-cut on both ends, both sides, and the bottom to an accuracy of 1/1000th of an inch.

Each beam would influence each other beam to vibrate at the same frequency. They were finely tuned to the earth's vibrational key by grinding and boring holes in their rough upper sides. Quartz is a terrific conductor of sound and is used to convert one kind of energy to another. The trick would be to make sure that each beam vibrated with the exact same frequency. Hence, before the beams were transported, the need to leave the upper surfaces rough and gouge out enough material so that the beam would vibrate in a frequency that was the exact match of each other beam. With a tuning fork and a chisel, this was easily accomplished by the music masters assigned to the task.

Once tuned, the beams were transported 500 miles to be precisely placed in the internal chambers and passageways as the external walls were being constructed.

Goro's pride in the design made him swagger about the construction site, drawing quiet snickers from the construction crew. The workers all liked him, but his cocky pride was something of a private joke among them.

Inside the pyramid Goro had created two major chambers and three passageways of granite. The small chamber sits low inside near the exact center of the pyramid. It has a gabled granite roof, the two halves of which meet to form a triangular peak. The roof angle transfers the pressure of the masonry above it to the outside walls.

305

At precision angles to that chamber he placed two shafts, one coming from the north and one from the south. Neither of these shafts ventilate to the outside, but rather stop 20 feet short of the external walls. From the small chamber, both of these shafts extend horizontally about six-feet, then angle upward, the northern shaft at 37° 28', and the southern shaft at an angle of 38°. The total length of the northern shaft is 240 feet and the total length of the southern shaft is 250 feet.

A horizontal passageway leading north from the small chamber connects to the lower end of the resonance gallery. This area is shaped as a rectangular parallelogram and angles upward to where it is connected to an antechamber leading to the large chamber sitting above the small chamber.

175 feet above the base of the pyramid, and positioned forward of center, to the south of the center line, was the large chamber. Above the large chamber are five superimposed layers of seventy-ton granite beams as a ceiling. Above that, just as in the small chamber, Goro placed another gabled granite roof to transfer pressure to the outside walls. There are nine granite beams above the large chamber, and a total of 43 of these beams throughout the chamber. The layers of beams above the large chamber are separated by enough space that an average sized person can crawl between them.

From an architectural and engineering standpoint, there is no need to have five levels of beams above the large chamber, and Goro wondered whether future discoverers would understand the significance of what he had done. He hoped that they would realize that these five layers were necessary to achieve the optimal resonance for the chemical reaction to be complete. Because of their quartz content, each was capable of resonant vibrations if the proper type and amount of energy was introduced.

In the large chamber the fine-tuned granite beams resonate in the same frequency of the earth, which resonates at 369.99 cycles per second. This has been tested and proven over the years. The entire King's Chamber, with one exception, resonates at that frequency.

The exception is the precision-cut granite coffer inside the large chamber. This coffer was once a solid block but was hollowed out with amazing accuracy that would only be closely matched in another 12,500 years. The coffer is unique in many ways, not the least of which is that when you hit the sides of the coffer, it resonates at 438 cycles per second. This is significant because that is the exact rate at which hydrogen is converted into energy. The precision cutting of the coffer was designed to produce sound at that particular resonance.

Goro had planned the design of this chamber to a very fine level of detail. The underside of the granite floor sat on a corrugated surface, much like an egg carton. The entire design of the room made it almost free-standing so that it resonated. Standing inside the completed room, he could hear the eerie ringing echoes. When he struck the side of the coffer, a deep bell-like sound resonated through the chamber.

A non-functional touch that Goro put on the design of the large chamber floor was the six rows of granite blocks. Superficially the individual floor blocks appear to have no particular arrangement as to size. From the far end to the near end, going from left to right, the first row has one large rectangular block, a slightly smaller rectangular block, and two much smaller rectangular blocks side-by-side at the far right. The next row has a narrow rectangular block at the left, followed by two larger rectangular blocks.

Each row is dramatically different from its neighbors. Goro knew that such random placement of blocks would beg the question from future discoverers as to why the builders simply didn't lay out a symmetrical floor plan. The common expectation would be that each row should have one beam.

Goro designed the floor so that the rows represented the planets - Mercury at the far end, followed by Venus, Earth, Mars, Jupiter, and Saturn – with each block representing an acoustical and mathematical representation of each planet and its orbit about the sun. He wondered whether this clue ever would be deciphered.

Goro knew that the parallelogram resonance gallery leading up to the large chamber was, and would be considered to be in the far future, an architectural marvel. It is angled upward at 26°17'37". It's height runs between 339.9 inches and 346.0 inches. The ceiling stones overlap each other 36 times over its length of 1,844.5 inches. These overlaps create a 12-inch tilt, and coupled with the vertical ends of the gallery, serve to continuously reflect sound upward to the large chamber. As no other ceiling in any other part of the pyramid has these characteristics, Goro knew that it could only be concluded that the ceiling in the Grand Gallery had an acoustical purpose.

The ledge along the walls running the entire length of the gallery was where the resonators were to be installed. The resonator converted vibrations to sound. In the gallery, the resonators maximized the transfer of energy from the source of the vibrations. In accordance with the design of the gallery, the sound was reflected and channeled into the large chamber. This channeling of sound triggered the oscillation of the granite beams. With this input of sound, the resonance would cause the entire granite complex to become a vibrating mass of energy.

Between the upper end of the resonance gallery and the large chamber sits an antechamber. Goro designed this chamber to filter the sounds that did not fit the frequency needed and only allow pure harmonic chords to enter the large chamber. Therefore, the antechamber was fitted with acoustic baffles to accomplish the task. Sound waves not coinciding with the desired frequency would be filtered out.

As any vibrating system can destroy itself through structural overload, there needed to be some controls, or methods to dampen the energy flow. Goro designed granite baffling plugs near the bottom of an ascending passageway well below the entrance to the resonance gallery to control the levels of vibration inside the upper chambers.

In the Great Pyramid, there would be a limit to what the granite could withstand as far as resonances were concerned, and therefore a dampening would be required. With the source of the energy being the vibrations of the earth, there was no way to turn off the source. That leaves only the controlling of the energy flow. First one can dampen it. Second is to counteract the flow of energy with an interference wave to cancel the vibration. Goro chose the dampening method because of its simplicity.

The attachment of vibration sensors to the bottom of these dampening plugs enabled the operators of this energy machine to monitor and control the flow of vibrations.

What a concept, Goro reflected proudly. By getting the interior of the power plant to vibrate in synchronicity with the earth's vibrations, a simple chemical reaction would generate a boundless supply of energy.

His original thinking was that it was theoretically possible to tap directly into the earth's energy and beam it out of the power plant. After listening to his colleagues, he redesigned his power plant concept, incorporating a small chamber that would first create the raw energy through the introduction of chemicals, a passageway to transmit the energy, an acoustical chamber to channel the energy at a certain frequency, a baffling chamber to allow only the proper note frequency to go through, and a receiving/transmitting chamber where the energy would be agitated and enhanced before transmission out of a south facing shaft. He also designed a drainage channel where excess chemical fluids would drain to a subterranean pit below the pyramid.

All that was needed was a storage chamber for the raw chemicals and two enclosed shafts by which to introduce them into the small reaction chamber.

From the bottom of a vertical shaft beyond the end of the southern shaft of the lower chamber, hydrated zinc chloride would be introduced into the lower chamber at a metered rate while a simultaneous introduction of hydrochloric acid solution was introduced from the northern shaft of the lower chamber.

A simple bronze grapnel hook attached to a piece of wood and placed in the southern shaft would float to the surface of the liquid being introduced. When the fluid filled the shaft nearly completely, the grapnel hook would make contact with two copper fittings and thereby shut off the flow of liquid chemicals. When the liquid level in the shaft dropped, the grapnel hook would break contact with the copper fittings signaling that more liquid should be introduced.

Therefore the unification of hydrogen - the fundamental element that fuels the sun – when coupled with the vibrations of the earth, would produce microwave energy.

The lower chamber produces the raw hydrogen gas that fills the interior passageways and chambers of the pyramid. Induced by vibrating pulses, the vibration of the pyramid gradually increases until it is in complete harmony with the earth's vibrations, in the key of F#, and propels the hydrogen energy along a horizontal shaft. At the end of the shaft, the hydrogen atoms are rechanneled through the resonance chamber through the baffling chamber to the upper chamber. Harmonically coupled to the earth's natural vibrations, the combined vibrations of the pyramid and the earth induce the resonators in the resonance gallery to produce sound which is focused up the passageway through the antechamber, where it is baffled to let only certain frequencies pass, and then is introduced into the large transmission chamber.

With the 55 percent silicon-quartz content of the granite beams in the transmission chamber, the room would resonate in harmony with the incoming acoustical energy. The quartz in the rock would be stressed and produce stimulated electrons. The combination of acoustic and electromagnetic energy covers a broad spectrum from the basic infrasonic frequencies of the earth to the higher ultrasonic electromagnetic microwave frequencies.

The hydrogen atoms, consisting of one proton and one electron each, would absorb this energy and the electrons would be "pumped" to a higher energy state. The northern shaft of the pyramid, has a metal lining, and would be the conduit by which a microwave signal is to be introduced into the transmission chamber. Microwave signals created by atomic hydrogen bombard the earth constantly. The microwave signal would be reflected off the gold plating at the top of the pyramid and then reflected down the transmission chamber northern shaft.

Passing through a crystal box amplifier located in its path, the input signal increases in power and interacts with the hydrogen atoms in the chamber. Hydrogen atoms would begin releasing energy as the process built exponentially in seconds. The stimulated hydrogen gas would convert into a beam of energy and be directed through the southern shaft to the outside of the pyramid.

Ah, thought Goro, life is wonderful. Tens of thousands of years from now, people will know that a greatly advanced civilization had once mastered the mysteries of the earth and the cosmos.

The gold plating of the upper third of the pyramid, as well as the white limestone cladding were now in place. Everything was ready for the chemical reaction to begin. Goro stood at some distance from the completed project in an honored position near the elder leaders of Atlantis. The silent carved lion stared mutely into the eastern sky. Goro nodded his head to initiate the reaction process.

Suddenly there was a great rumbling and signs of smoke pouring out of the northern and southern shafts of the pyramid.

Tezcar Tilcopan turned to Goro with a look that could turn him into a block of stone. "After expending our treasury on this five-year project, we get rumbling and smoke? You will fix this or it will be your burial site!"

Goro stammered out a hasty, "Yes, sir!" and fled to find the cause of the failure. Silently to himself he said, "Burial site? This is no burial site! This is the most incredible energy producing machine that has ever been built!" After conferring

311

with his engineering colleagues and conducting a complete analysis of any structural damage, he ordered repairs to be done immediately. The cause, it turned out, was an improperly placed baffle at the bottom of the ascending passageway. The problem had been caught early enough to prevent the pyramid from completely shaking apart.

Goro made his report to the elders and a new date was scheduled for the start-up.

This time it went flawlessly and the pyramid beamed a stream of energy out to a waiting collector in space where it was re-beamed to a collection site in Atlantis.

A few days later Goro received this message from Tezcar Tilcopan: "In a way I am sorry the experiment worked the second time. It would have amused me greatly to place you inside the structure and see you torn apart by the vibrations."

Goro did not leave his quarters for several weeks.

Do not stand at my grave and weep.
I am not there. I do not sleep.
I am a thousand winds that blow.
I am the diamond glints on the snow.
I am the sunlight on the ripened grain.
I am the gentle autumn's rain.
When you awaken in the morning hush,
I am the swift uplifting rush
of quiet birds in circled flight.
I am the soft stars that shine at night.
Do not stand at my grave and cry.
I am not there.
I did not die.

Hopi Prayer – author unknown

Chapter 39

The camera crews from all of the American and International news services were positioned on the hillsides overlooking the flat terrain below. The great pyramid looked so out of place on this remote South Dakota landscape, but there the pyramid stood, Its upper tiers clad in gold, its lower two-thirds clad in highly polished white limestone casing, holding center stage.

With the new Great Pyramid as a backdrop, well-coifed news anchors assumed the appropriate gravitas for the occasion, and informed their viewers of the significance of all that appeared on camera behind them.

Religious fundamentalists, never numbering more than fifteen people, had periodically protested the building of the pyramid over the past four plus years. A federal injunction kept them two miles from the site, and under the constant watch of US Marshalls. The injunction cited both safety and national security concerns.

Native Americans from every tribe in the country had converged on the Black Hills. From the Narragansetts in Rhode Island to the Navajo in Arizona; from the Inuit in Alaska to the Seminoles in Florida, vast groups of American Indians of all ages came to experience the wonder of the earth vibrating in harmony with the sky. A huge amphitheater had been constructed in front of the new 'Great Pyramid.' There for the past three days, every hour, on the hour, each family of tribes and tribal nations performed ritual dances in elaborate and beautiful traditional costumes.

The great highlight of the celebrations was the concert on the last night. Adrian Vanderwiel, Brendan Pell and Damien Cooper had composed a musical tribute to the people of Atlantis. Master guitarists, legends in their musical spheres, from every major musical genre, each had a spotlight solo during the performance. Classical, flamenco, rock, rocakabilly, blues, country, jazz, zydeco, and bluegrass solos highlighted the twenty-one minute *Atlantis Rhapsody*.

The following morning, just before sunrise on the summer solstice, all was ready.

Away from the media buzz, on a hill in a restricted area slightly northeast of the pyramid, a select group of people assembled. Chuck and Gretchen Kinoshi stood holding hands. Surrounding them were the entire crew from the Antarctic expedition. Standing front and center was Madison Tolles. In a few moments, Gordon and Johanna Tallbear arrived, along with large contingents from both Johanna's and Tallbear's families. Gordon, now greatly weakened and walking slowly, was leading Taboo, a wedding gift from Madison Tolles. Accompanying them were Joe Delaney and the American polo team and their families.

Once all were assembled, at a hand signal from Madison Tolles, the new Great Pyramid was activated. A musical chord co-directed by Damien Cooper, Brendan Pell, and Adrian Vanderwiel, was projected into the interior of the pyramid. The earth responded with its vibratory signature in F#, and the chemical reaction began. In a few moments, the sun came up over the horizon and reflected off the gold peak of the pyramid. The entire planet watched on TV and the internet as the energy beam sprung forth from the shaft leading from the King's Chamber. The beam was captured by a geostationary satellite and retransmitted across space to other satellites and ultimately down to earth collectors positioned at intervals across the planet.

Following the thunderous applause, and after the crowd down below dispersed and the television crews removed their equipment, Gordon turned to Johanna and said, "It's time, now, for me to fulfill my promise." She reached up and touched his face, gently running her fingers over the thin white scar that ran across his cheekbone. After kissing her passionately, Gordon turned to Chuck and said, "I am counting on you."

"What do you mean, cousin?"

"It is time for me to go."

"Not now, cousin. I mean I know you have to leave eventually, but we have a lot of work to do."

"Johanna will explain everything," answered Tallbear, who embraced his dear friend. He gave Gretchen a kiss on her cheek and said, "Take care of this character, will you?"

Chuck, looking devastated, just stood there aching at the loss of the man with whom he had shared such an adventure. He tried to remain stoic, but could not contain the flood of emotions. Tears began running down his cheeks. Gretchen held him closely.

Gordon shook hands all around and embraced Madison Tolles who cried with the pain of loss. With great effort, and as Johanna quietly wept, Gordon Tallbear, wounded Lakota warrior, slowly, painfully, and without assistance, mounted a patiently waiting Taboo and rode away. As they watched silently he

315

descended into the valley below. He crossed the open area of the amphitheater in front of the pyramid and paused for a moment to look at it. With a slight nudge from his moccasins, horse and rider ascended the hill to the west of the new Great Pyramid and vanished into the distant trees.

In her hand Johanna clutched an envelope. Madison Tolles and Chuck moved to her side as she struggled to gain control of her emotions. She asked everyone to wait.

When she composed herself, she opened the envelope.

"There is something that Gordon wanted to explain to you, but he didn't know how or when to do it. He privately shared this information with Mr. Tolles, Chuck and me some time ago. He asked me to share this with the rest of you today.

"Some of you know that he was once married and that his wife died tragically in a car accident. His grief was enormous, and for three years he wandered the world seeking answers. Eventually returning home, he went through the intensive spiritual and soul-cleansing ritual of a sweat lodge. After he emerged from his sweat lodge experience, he mounted his horse and disappeared into the wilderness for three days. On a hillside somewhere, he dismounted and lay on the ground. It was there that he had the intense spiritual experience of a full-blown vision. He wrote down what happened and sealed it in an envelope in anticipation of this moment. Now in his own words, I will read you his story."

Fighting the nausea she had been feeling for the past several mornings, she began to read.

After my three-day fast and extended immersion in the sweat lodge, I rode through the night, not even remotely aware of where I was going. At dawn, at the edge of a forest, near exhaustion, and with my mind totally blank, I slipped down off my mount and lay on a grassy slope. For the next several hours, I experienced an extraordinary vision.

In my vision, the sky turned dark grey. Hour by hour my breathing became increasingly more difficult. The temperature kept climbing until I thought I would melt. Intensive heat from forest fires pulled the breath from me. Then came the cold, a cold that not only penetrated my skin as the winter weather would, but a cold containing an evil chill that gripped the marrow of my soul. The sky turned to dark pewter and I could see black dust in the air. I became pained by hunger and thirst that could not be slaked.

An image surrounded by light shimmered in the distance. It was my only hope and I focused on it. Gradually, as the image came closer, the shimmering abated until I clearly saw a man on a horse moving toward me. My pain began to leave me. The approaching horse seemed to glide over the landscape. There was a black leather bridle but no saddle, just a cobalt blue blanket for the rider. The edges of the blanket fluttered in the breeze. The horse was ebony and had a snowy white star on its brow.

The man sat perfectly erect. As he approached, I could see that he was without age - neither old nor young. He appeared to be ... eternal. His visage was dark and serious, but I had no sense of fear. Long, dark hair flowed down his back. His piercing green eyes were accentuated by his full black beard. He was clothed in an immaculate white robe with full sleeves, and he wore sandals. His hands, weathered brown, appeared powerful and were deeply veined. He held the reins lightly. Behind his right ear the man had a small quartz stone braided into his long hair, and an eagle feather was fastened horizontally at the back of his head. He was otherwise unadorned. Light surrounded him, driving the darkness away. Peace fell upon me as he sang his words in a strange tongue. I somehow understood them.

"Be not afraid of your grief," the man sang. "Instead, embrace it and let it make you stronger.

"Share your strength with others. Keep your fears hidden.

"What you have seen so far is what will become of earth if nothing is done to change it.

"The earth itself provides the answer to the problems man has wrought.

"As you and your fathers have been true to your people, be true to yourself, and to the earth that is a gift from the Creator. In your travels, you have learned many things about the Eternal Spirit. Keep your mind, your heart and your body pure. Above all men, you have been chosen. You must lead the effort to find answers to the dilemma that chokes the earth, created by men of this age. You are to confront and destroy the evil that stands in your way.

"Know that dark spirited men plot against mankind to gain personal riches. Beware of their darkness and treachery, and especially of the evil one in their midst.

"Your quest will be full of both danger and opportunity. In the end you will come face-to-face with an evil that cannot be described. When you confront the man who serves the dark master, he will strike you almost mortally. But you cannot waver. You must destroy him or your quest will fail.

"The answers you seek will be found in long-secret caves far away.

"On the ground next to you is a small quartz stone. Carry this talisman with you always and you will have the strength you need to face any adversity.

"When you complete your quest and you can move forward no more, you must return here to this place and give your stone back to the earth.

318

"This you must promise."

And I swore to the man in my vision that I would fulfill my quest and return to this place no matter what stood in my way.

Johanna paused in her reading and wiped away some tears. "He wrote the following addendum just recently."

The time is near when we will see the fruits of our labors. The pyramid will be built and activated, and for now, at least, one of our biggest problems will have been solved. What I must do pains me deeply. I must leave my family, my friends, and my Johanna. This is my price. You have given me your love, and now I must leave you, perhaps forever. I love you all, especially you, my dear Johanna. And as I go away, I carry your love for me in my heart.

•   •   •

Acknowledgements

I'll do these in chronological order. These are the people I need to thank the most.

My first editor, Barbara Legg, for her evaluation, analysis, notes and communication. Thanks for showing me the art of descriptive writing. Still haven't gotten it completely, but I think I made a good stab at it.

My Guinness Book Club friend Jack Nolan for pointing out that less is more.

My dear friend, baseball, and golf buddy Kenny Sharpe who said Johanna and Tallbear are too perfect. Write your own book, Kenny.

My younger son Brendan whose unsparing comments regarding an early draft made me re-think a lot about character development.

My sister-in-law Joan for her invaluable advice about art.

My older son Matthew who did the major editing and taught me a lot about character development, story arcs, dramatic tension, ascending and descending action and lots more.

My final editor, my wife Kathy (is it really almost 45 years?), whose critical eye picked up the remaining flaws and gave the story added texture at critical points.